Praise for *The Improbable Life of Ricky Bird*

'A wise, tender but unflinching portrait of an ordinary family and the unordinary girl at its heart. Ricky – fragile, tough, endearing and funny – is a fabulous creation. She'll walk around in my world all year, and more.'
**Kristina Olsson, author of *Shell* and *Boy, Lost***

'Fierce and wonderful and utterly singular, Ricky embodies the sheer joy and transformative power of storytelling. This is a character you don't want to let go.'
**Kate Mildenhall, author of *The Mother Fault* and *Skylarking***

## Why readers love *The Improbable Life of Ricky Bird*

'The depiction of Ricky and Ollie's relationship is so special, peppered with hilarious and magic dialogue, and utterly authentic. I love the characters so much – I want to wrap them in hugs.'

'It's been a long time since words on a page have brought me so much joy – and heartbreak. Ricky's story made me laugh and cry and holler with rage for her, sometimes all at the same time.'

'This is a book that's dark and intense but on another level it reads as a lighthearted, playful book about a young girl who invents stories. It was totally heart wrenching. I'll be thinking about Ricky and her brother Ollie for a long time to come.'

'Bold, audacious and whip smart, Ricky is a born storyteller whose wild and whimsical imagination helps her and her little brother escape to magical places. Anyone who loves stories and words could not help but love her too – and want her to be the hero of her own story.'

'I was totally captivated by this story. I fell in love with Ricky and the other key characters – all of whom stayed with me long after I finished the book.'

'There are books in which stories become part of our own memories and others in which characters become part of our own families – and then there are beautiful books like this that miraculously manage to achieve both.'

## Why readers love *The Improbable Life of Ricky Bird*

'The most beautiful, raw, heartwarming and genuine story. I have never been more invested or attached to a character like I was with Ricky. The best thing I have read in many years – I want to read it again immediately.'

'A wonderful story of resilience, love and friendship forged in the most unexpected places. This story and the characters will stay with me forever.'

'What an incredible story. It's been a long time since I read a story with such unexpected force, with characters and situations that are so ordinary and yet blisteringly and unapologetically real. It almost hurt to read, and it certainly hurt to finish, and I will carry this story and Ricky with me for a very, very long time.'

'There were moments when I laughed out loud, moments I cried and moments I wanted to scream. I loved living in Ricky's world for a few days and I already can't wait to re-read this incredible novel.'

'Throughout Ricky's story, I was struck by the beautiful balance between darkness and humour. The ending left me in tears, but I also felt uplifted because, finally, Ricky felt seen. This is such a special book.'

'I find it incredible that a single author has such an understanding of people that they can create so many different, complex characters and bring them to life, without judgment or a need to censor away the discomfort.'

# THE IMPROBABLE LIFE OF RICKY BIRD

DIANE CONNELL

SIMON & SCHUSTER

London · New York · Sydney · Toronto · New Delhi

THE IMPROBABLE LIFE OF RICKY BIRD
First published in Australia in 2022 by
Simon & Schuster (Australia) Pty Limited
Suite 19A, Level 1, Building C, 450 Miller Street,
Cammeray, NSW 2062

10 9 8 7 6 5 4 3 2 1

Sydney New York London Toronto New Delhi
Visit our website at www.simonandschuster.com.au

A catalogue record for this book is available from the National Library of Australia

ISBN: 9781761101366

Cover design: Christabella Designs
Cover images: Shutterstock/Mironov Konstantin, Shutterstock/Ramcreative
Typeset by Midland Typesetters, Australia
Printed and bound in Australia by Griffin Press

The paper this book is printed on is certified against the Forest Stewardship Council® Standards. Griffin Press holds chain of custody certification SGSHK-COC-005088. FSC® promotes environmentally responsible, socially beneficial and economically viable management of the world's forests

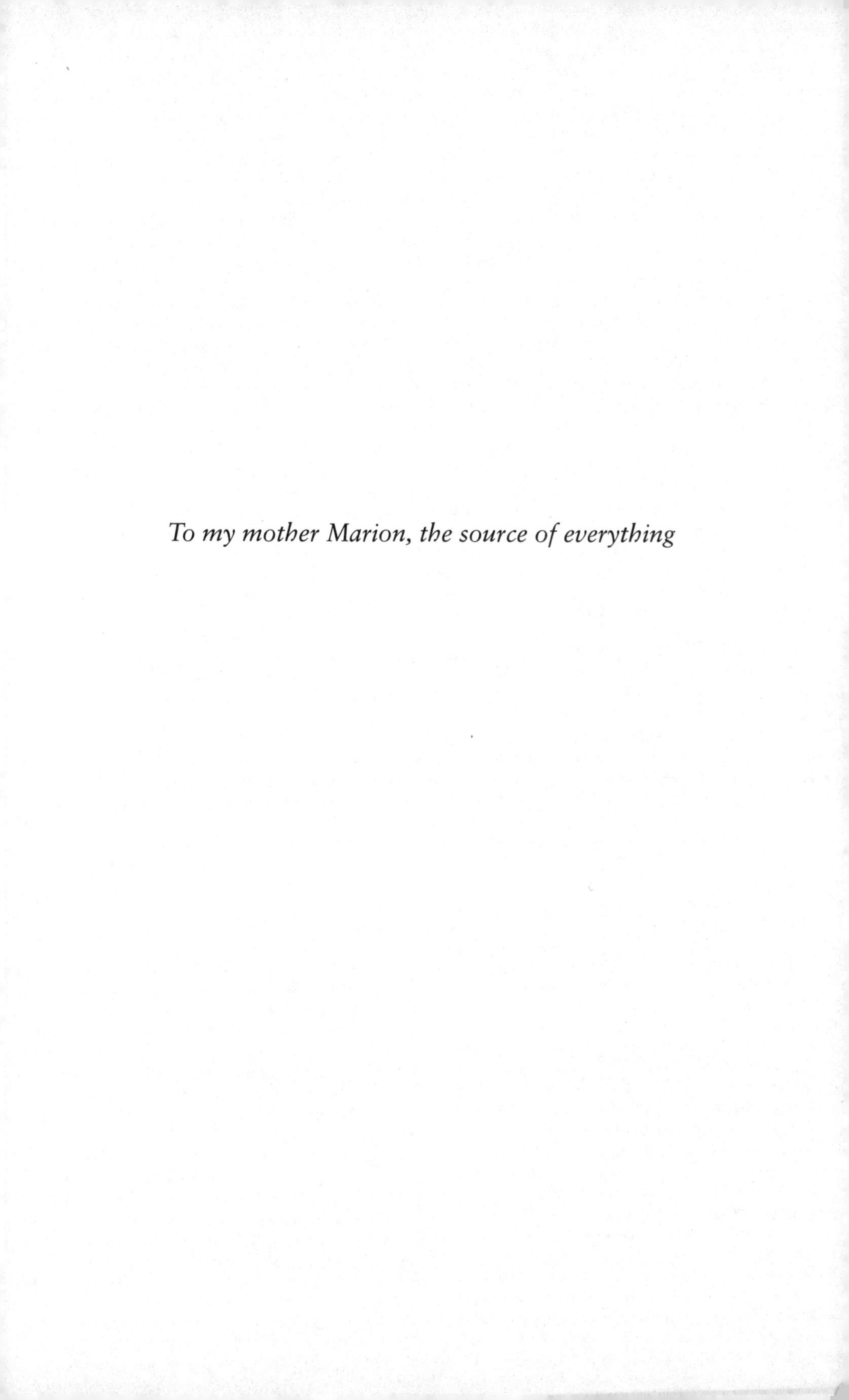

*To my mother Marion, the source of everything*

# 1

SHE BELIEVED THERE were two types of disaster. There were catastrophes like tidal waves and landslides that came crashing down on their victims with brutal and unavoidable force. Then there was the type of disaster that happened without fanfare, the terrible thing that crept up and slithered in. This thing was silent and relentless like decay but its accumulated effects were devastating. It not only destroyed your life but it also left you feeling impotent and guilty as if you should have noticed earlier and done more to prevent its advance.

Ricky's disaster had arrived with stealth. At first, the changes were minor and she had resisted in small ways. She'd worried but trouble had seemed like a distant possibility, so she didn't go all out to protect what she had. But things kept disintegrating and falling away until she realised it was too late to do anything. Now her father was packing things into boxes and she was powerless to stop him. She struggled to understand this change, to rearrange the way she thought and felt. But it wasn't any use. The undoing of her family and her life in Brixton was like the drip, drip, drip of water on stone, the wearing away of solid particles by soft persistence until finally there was a hole.

In the move to Camden, Ricky suffered a great loss. It was a yawning emptiness that terrified and disoriented her but what came in its place, the unspeakable slithery thing that inveigled itself, was far worse than any of her losses.

She heard Dan slam the back of the rental truck and leaned over the driver's seat to look in the wing mirror. It was a quick glance but he was already there, as if anticipating her. He raised his eyebrows and smiled at her reflection. She quickly sat up again.

He rapped his knuckles on the driver's window. 'Once I get the bike in the back we'll be ready to rock 'n' roll!'

Her mother laughed, which made Ricky want to scream because Dan was about as hilarious as an infection. She considered various diseases before settling on syphilis.

It was hot inside the truck's cab. The backs of Ricky's legs were sticking to the vinyl upholstery. Her ponytail was damp against her neck. She desperately wanted short hair, a boy's number three, but her mother said no. The ponytail was a compromise.

'How long is it going to take to get to King's Crescent?' Ricky asked for the sixth time.

'You know exactly how long it's going to take,' her mother replied. 'That must be the fifth time you've asked.'

'Sixth,' corrected Ollie.

Ricky elbowed her brother.

'Stop shoving him, Vicky.' Her mother reached over Ollie to put a hand on her knee.

She shook it off. 'The name's Ricky.'

'Actually, your name is Victoria. It was your grandmother's name.'

The previous day Ricky had decided her name had to go. 'If you insist on moving us to Camden, then I insist on a new name.'

'You know why we're moving.'

'Why we're leaving Dad, you mean.'

Ricky slid her hand into the pocket of her cargo shorts where her fingers curled around the container of junior multi-vitamins. They were a moving gift from her father. She needed to stay healthy and strong, he told her.

Her mother was looking at her. 'We'll still be in London.'

'The rubbish part of London.' Ricky imagined the King's Crescent Estate as a hostile wasteland populated by thugs and crooks. They would swear loudly and have homemade tattoos. Ricky wanted a tattoo about as much as she wanted head lice. They would have plenty of those on the estate, too.

'Don't make this more difficult than it already is.' Her mother sighed. 'We all need a change.'

'No, *you* want a change.'

'You know it wasn't working with your father. He wasn't working for a start. He hasn't had a proper job for a long time.' Her mother's voice was getting higher and higher. 'You know all this.'

'Dad works really hard on the allotment.'

'That's not work.'

'Dad's a gardener.'

'He's a gardener who doesn't work.'

'You're moving us to Camden so you can be closer to your new boyfriend.'

'Don't blame Dan. He's been really good to me. To all of us.'

'You hardly know the man. If it wasn't for him turning up you might have tried harder with Dad.'

'I did try hard. You know very well how hard I tried. You were there, Vicky.'

'Ricky.'

Her mother tilted her head. 'Okay, I'll call you Ricky if you make an effort with Dan.'

Ricky studied her mother through one eye. What was wrong with the woman? Couldn't she see what Dan was like? All that fake smiling and flashing of his strangely pointy teeth. Her mother said he had beautiful eyes but they were set too far apart. He may as well have been a bald eagle or a hammerhead shark. His other appearance crimes were a hipster beard and straggly, sandy hair that he sometimes wore in a man bun. *A man bun!* Had her mother gone mad?

The driver's door opened. Dan's sweaty man-smell filled the cab, a mixture of hot metal and dog breath. 'Camden, here we come!'

Ricky squeezed closer to her brother as Dan climbed inside, swinging himself up with the hand grip above the door to noisily settle himself in the driver's seat. As he dug in his pocket for the keys, his elbow bumped against the side of her chest. It was like a jolt of electricity, sending a rush of charged electrons surging through her body, aggressive and uninvited.

She jumped and let out a sound.

'Oops.' Dan raised his eyebrows comically. 'My bad.'

She felt her mother's hand on her knee. 'Stop being dramatic.'

Ricky stayed pressed against Ollie but sat up as the truck started moving. She had lived on the small council estate in Brixton all her life and loved every inch of it: the allotment, Brockwell Park with its crooked old oak, the overripe fruit smell of Electric Avenue, the way people were all different but everyone got along, mostly.

As the truck idled in traffic outside Brixton Station, she scanned the crowd gathered near the mouth of the Tube. Summer holidays had started in Lambeth, two days earlier than Camden. She pictured her friends meeting up in Brockwell Park, laughing and shouting. Summer in the park was magic. She thought of the Lambeth Country Show and felt her throat tighten painfully. Every year she visited the funfair in the park with her father. She couldn't remember a summer when they hadn't gone together. It was their special thing.

The engine shuddered. The truck started moving again.

Her brother gave her a small, nervous smile. At least the seating positions made it difficult for him to talk to Dan.

'How fast can this truck go?' asked Ollie.

The little swine was leaning forward. He was smiling at the enemy.

'It can go a million miles an hour.' Dan laughed. 'But I'll stick to fifty.'

Ricky added 'liar' and 'con artist' to Dan's crimes. She closed her eyes. If Ollie was going to stick a knife in her father's back, she was going to pretend he didn't exist.

Ricky was roused by loud beeping. They were in the middle of a large estate with a mixture of buildings, modern low-rise blocks of flats and mid-century, red-brick towers. The concrete of the pavement was a white glare under the bright midday sun. Weeds were growing between the paving stones. Nothing was moving, not even the leaves of the London plane trees on either side of the road. The place looked barren and uninhabited. Ricky could almost feel the air crackling with bad intentions.

At first glance, the long, pale-brick building didn't look terrible. Panels of white cladding had been recently added to freshen up its façade. Each of its three storeys had a communal balcony that fed into a central stairway. Ricky knew from the council plans that their flat was on the first floor.

Ollie was sleeping and began to whine that he was feeling sick as her mother undid his seatbelt. While Dan started unloading the truck, they followed their mother up the grubby steps to a scratched grey door with a spyhole. Ricky's mother was still fiddling with the keys when a pretty girl in a school uniform came up the steps behind them.

'Hello, what's your name and how old are you?' asked Ollie. 'Do you live here?'

'Yes,' said the girl, her eyes widening. They were brown and, unlike Dan's, they were located in normal positions on her face. 'My name's Samia. I'm twelve.'

'My name's Oliver Cromwell Bird. I am six years old and I'm going to start a new school in September.' Ollie was being very talkative for someone who was supposed to be sick.

'His real name is Oliver Edward Bird,' Ricky corrected. 'Oliver Cromwell' was their private joke, something she called him when he was being treacherous.

'If you can change your name, I can change mine.' He turned his back on Ricky but then said something that made her want to kiss him. 'This is my big sister. Her name is Ricky. It is not Victoria. She is twelve.'

'I'm more or less thirteen, a teenager.'

Samia nodded shyly before knocking on the door next to theirs. It opened and the face of a fierce-looking woman appeared. She frowned at Ricky before pulling Samia inside.

'Finally!' Her mother managed to push open the door. She gasped. 'Oh, god, no!'

The first thing Ricky noticed was the smell. It was sour milk, dirty nappies and old fish and chips. Sour, putrid and fatty. There was rubbish everywhere.

They were standing in the flat's kitchen and it was the messiest room Ricky had ever seen. Drawers and cupboards were hanging open. There were wrappers scattered over the countertops and half-empty takeaway containers piled in the sink. A tinfoil tray of tomato pasta was covered with long, green fibres of mould. Something white, a thick sauce of some kind, had been spilled or thrown over the cupboards and had dribbled to the floor.

Ricky followed as her mother moved trance-like through the living and dining room, and then down the hall to the bathroom before visiting each of the three bedrooms. The corner bedroom with windows on two sides was Ricky's. She knew it was hers because she'd chosen it from the floor plan. The room was bright but, like the others, its carpet was littered with paper and plastic. A ripped curtain was hanging off a broken rail. There was a collapsed pine bookshelf in the corner. Ricky ran her hand along its surface as she walked over to a window. Below their building was a playground. It was deserted and looked miserable, nothing like the massive adventure playground they'd left behind in Brixton.

'Don't cry, Mummy,' said Ollie, tugging her shorts.

'It's not that bad,' Ricky lied. 'I bet I can fix that bookshelf. I need a bigger one.'

Her mother didn't move or say anything. The tears had overflowed and were running down her cheeks.

'There's a playground.' Ricky pointed out the window. 'I could take Ollie down there for a while. It's got ducks.'

'Ducks!' Ollie said, excitedly.

Her mother moved to the window.

The playground was a narrow, fenced-off rectangle that stretched from the pavement to the back of the building. It was flanked on one side by a hedge and had a climbing frame, swings, a seesaw and two brightly coloured plastic ducks on springs. The ducks were dazzling red and blue and had strange long beaks that gave them a crocodile-like appearance. In one corner was a white plastic construction shaped like an igloo.

Ollie was frowning. 'Those ducks are definitely the wrong colour,' he said.

Ricky's brother knew a lot about birds and animals for a little boy. Whenever someone asked him what he wanted to be when he grew up, he would say 'David Attenborough' as if David Attenborough was a job like a policeman or dental technician.

'We could paint them,' said Ricky.

'They should be white.'

'I think we should muzzle them. They look like nippers.'

Ollie laughed.

Her mother sniffed. 'What kind of idiot puts plastic ducks and a fake igloo in a London playground? I doubt there's an Eskimo within a thousand miles.'

'Inuit.' Ricky couldn't help herself. 'You're not supposed to call them Eskimos.'

Her mother allowed herself a smile. 'How do you know these things?'

'Dad used to take me to the library, remember?'

Her mother's expression hardened. 'Stay in the playground. Don't let Ollie out of your sight and don't talk to any idiots.'

As they were going down the steps, Dan was coming up carrying two boxes. He smiled and started to ask where they were going, but before Ollie could respond, Ricky tugged him away. She'd been warned not to talk to idiots.

When Ollie pushed open the gate to the playground, Ricky glanced up and saw that her mother had come outside and was standing on the balcony with Dan. Her arms were wrapped around his neck and her cheek was pressed against his chest. She was crying again, her shoulders shaking. He was comforting her, his hand making circles between her shoulder blades.

Ricky watched the way his hand moved and sensed he'd done this before. There had been another woman, perhaps several other women, who had needed comforting. It was like witnessing a car accident or dog fight. Ricky had to close her eyes, scrunch them up until lights flashed behind her eyelids. She felt a tight pain in the centre of her chest and imagined herself fainting, sinking down until her head hit the pavement. She could almost hear the ugly crack of her skull against concrete. The thought of hurting herself and an image of her mother running toward her, shouting her name, steadied her. When she opened her eyes, she realised she wasn't the only one watching her mother and Dan. The neighbour had pushed open her kitchen window and was looking. The fierce woman noticed Ricky and shook her head before disappearing from view.

'I don't want to sit on a duck,' said Ollie. 'It might bite me and I could die.'

'If you sit on one of those stupid ducks the only thing you'll die of is embarrassment,' Ricky said.

'They're murder ducks.'

Ricky laughed. Ollie knew a lot of words for a child and liked to experiment with them, assembling sentences from overheard bits of conversation and television. He didn't care if his word soup made sense. It was one of the best things about him.

She gave him a squeeze as she lifted him onto a swing. He laughed, his silky hair catching the wind as she began to push.

Between shoves, Ricky looked around, desperate to find something, anything, that would take away the dread sitting in her abdomen like a clump of rotting leaves. The world as she knew it had ended and, apart from Ollie, she had nothing solid she could trust. She gave the swing another shove and stood on the tips of her toes.

There! It was a flash of something familiar in the distance.

She raised herself up again. Yes, she was sure. It was the top of a wigwam like the ones her father made out of bamboo. Somewhere near the tower blocks was a vegetable garden.

Ollie complained as she left him swinging to clamber up the climbing frame. The vegetable plot was located near a grove of trees and was bordered on one side by a ragged hedge. The lush, cultivated wedge of land looked out of place on the estate as if it had been photoshopped. It sat awkwardly between two tower blocks yet, despite its isolated setting, Ricky saw that it was south facing, a suntrap. It was neatly fenced and had a wooden shed in the corner by the gate. On one side of the shed was a frame with a climbing rose. It was a yellow rose, like the one her father had trained over the allotment fence.

'There's a nice garden over there,' she said, pointing.

'An allotment?' asked Ollie. He loved gardening as much as Ricky and had a particular soft spot for earthworms. 'Worms never argue or bite,' he was fond of saying.

'I'm not sure. It might be a community garden.'

'Does that mean we can go there?'

'Let's not get our hopes up.' But, of course, her hopes were already rocketing over the top of the towers. If they had access to a garden, summer in Camden wouldn't be a complete disaster.

Ricky swung down from the climbing frame and walked over to the igloo, kneeling down to sniff the entrance. Surprisingly, it didn't smell bad. In Brixton it might have reeked of urine or something worse.

'Dad once slept in an igloo,' she said, rocking back on her heels.

'No, he didn't.' Ollie was struggling not to look eager to believe her.

'He did. He went to Iceland with a team of huskies to collect alpine plants.'

'How many huskies?' Ollie was a dog man. Iceland and alpine plants were window dressing. It was all about the dogs for him.

'Sixteen.'

'Has Dan been to Iceland?'

'Don't be ridiculous.' She wanted to pinch Ollie on the back of his arm. 'Dan is forbidden to leave the country or go on an expedition because he has a criminal record. He was in prison for two years.'

'Why?'

Ricky had to invent a really bad crime or Ollie would continue to be nice to him. 'He stabbed a dog.'

His eyes widened.

'To death.' In her mind's eye, Dan was walking away from a small, lifeless form, a bloody dagger in his hand.

'What kind of dog?'

'A Cavalier King Charles spaniel.'

Ollie sighed in such a sad way that she almost told him the truth. She had to grit her teeth and force herself not to say anything. She needed her brother on her team.

The gate clanked.

A big, solid girl with sandy hair had entered the playground. She was tugging a reluctant dog on a lead, a fat black and white Staffie with an elaborate studded collar. The sign on the gate said dogs weren't allowed inside the playground but the girl didn't look like she bothered with rules. She had the flattened, pugnacious face of a fighter. Her hair was pulled back in a tight ponytail which sat high on the crown of her head. She was wearing high-waist skinny jeans and a pink t-shirt that matched her pink Nike trainers. She was older than Ricky and had small, defiant breasts.

'What's your dog's name?' asked Ollie, leaping off the swing.

'She's called Baby,' said the girl, pulling the lead. 'Don't touch her. She's dangerous.'

Before she or Ricky could stop him, Ollie was on the dog, rubbing it behind the ears. The girl tried to haul it away but Baby was too determined and, with a shake of the head, yanked the lead out of the girl's hand. Whining excitedly, the Staffie leaped on Ollie, knocking him over and making him shriek with laughter.

'My brother is a dog whisperer,' Ricky said. 'Dogs love him.'

'Baby doesn't love him,' said the girl. 'She's just pretending. Baby's a killer.'

Ollie was clearly in no danger. The dog was playfully snuffling and licking his neck. Ollie's laughter rang out over the playground as he ran into the igloo with the dog hot on his heels.

'My name's Ricky and that's my brother Ollie. We've just moved here.'

'From where?'

'Brixton.'

'Brixton?' The girl looked unimpressed. 'You'll need to toughen up if you're going to live in Camden.'

'Lambeth has more murders than Camden. I googled.'

'Ha! I bet you never had anyone murdered on your actual estate though, did you? A boy was actually killed right here. Dead as a doornail.'

'In this playground?'

'No, stupid. In one of the flats.' She lifted her chin. 'A paedo did it.'

'A paedophile?'

'That's what I said.'

'No, you didn't.'

'Shut up.'

The girl knocked angrily on the top of the igloo. When Ollie and Baby emerged, she pounced, grabbing the lead and dragging the dog toward the gate.

'My name's Caitlin Cloney. You better remember it.'

'Why?' asked Ollie.

Caitlin stopped. Her mouth hung open for a moment before she spoke. 'Because you should.'

'But why?' Ollie was an expert at asking questions. 'Are you going to be our friend?'

'No!'

'Can I be friends with your dog?'

'Piss off!'

'You shouldn't use that word.'

'Fuck off then!'

'Your dog doesn't like you.'

'Shut up!'

The gate clanged shut.

Ricky and Ollie looked at each other.

'That dog likes you.'

'Oh, I know that.' Ollie shrugged modestly. 'That girl is ridiculous.'

Caitlin Cloney was ridiculous but her hostility had made Ricky feel even more out of place and insecure. She scanned the grubby buildings and neglected gardens of the estate and ached for the familiar. She thought of the home they had left behind and imagined a new family moving in: bunk beds in her old bedroom, a new sofa in the living room, alphabet magnets on a different fridge in the kitchen.

She looked up at the windows of their new flat. Somewhere inside, Dan was with her mother, possibly touching or even kissing her. This thought sent a tremor of alarm through Ricky. He would visit more often now that they lived close. There would be no escaping him.

Ricky turned around to survey the miserable playground with its garish ducks and plastic igloo. There was nowhere safe here, nowhere to hide. It felt like the end of the world.

# 2

RICKY WAS SITTING next to her father. They were riding the ghost train together at the Lambeth Country Show, shrieking at the ghouls flying past. It was loud and hot inside the carriage. Her hands on the safety bar felt sticky. She looked down and saw that they were slippery with a dark liquid. Was it blood? When she looked up, her father was gone. She was still hurtling through the haunted house but was now alone with blood on her hands. The carriage entered a dark tunnel and slowed to a crawl. A high-pitched sound became audible. It was different to the other ghostly noises. It was a real sound, a whine. With horror, she realised that somewhere close someone was hurting a dog.

The first thing she felt on waking was relief. She didn't have to save an injured dog or search for her father inside a haunted house. But when she opened her eyes and saw the unfamiliar ceiling and walls, she remembered where she was and a feeling of dread wrapped around her heart.

She closed her eyes again, desperate to distract herself. If she could find something to look forward to, a foothold of hope, all would not be lost. She thought of her birthday and prodded around in her brain, looking for a sign of imminent celebration, some tinsel to take her mind off her troubles. Nothing. This had never happened before. There was always excitement leading up to a birthday. The anticipation was almost better than the actual event. Her mother had promised her a mobile phone but what use was a phone? She could hardly call her old friends in Brixton. She had nothing to tell them. The only thing Ricky wanted was a new BMX bike.

She got dressed, thinking about the bike she wanted, a shiny blue Cult Gateway with black wheel rims. She imagined the crunch of its wheels on a pebble path, the feeling of being weightless as she yanked the handlebars high and hoisted the bike in the air. Forget the stupid phone. A blue Cult Gateway was the thing.

Ricky's mother was in the kitchen. She was on her hands and knees with her head in the oven, scrubbing its dark interior and cursing to herself. She'd been cursing since the previous afternoon when the council had taken away the rubbish but refused to clean the flat at short notice. A tall, thin man had visited after the council had left. He was bald and had a gold ring in one of his ears. The ring had immediately put Ricky on guard. Earrings were affectations, like man buns, and according to her father, affectations were the slippery slope.

The bald man had greeted Ricky warmly with a friendly 'Hi'.

She'd frowned.

'You must be the daughter,' he said.

'You must be a friend of Dan's,' she replied, eyeing his earring. 'You've just missed him.'

'Dan who?'

Ricky didn't know Dan's other name. She was hoping he wouldn't be around long enough for it to be necessary. 'The Dan who's driving the rental truck back to Brixton Dan.'

He laughed. 'Is your mother home?'

The bald man was called Tim. He was the on-site manager of the estate. After listening to what Ricky's mother had to say, he inspected the mess in the flat, taking photos with his phone. There would be compensation, he promised. 'This should never have happened.' When her mother started crying again, he patted her shoulder in a familiar way. 'Don't worry, love. I'll make sure they look after you.'

Tim gave Ricky a wink on his way out and said he'd see her around.

'I doubt it,' she replied.

He laughed as if she'd said something funny and took the steps two at a time on his long legs.

She waited until he was off the premises before warning her mother.

'That man is creepy,' she said.

Her mother stopped trying to attach the hose to the vacuum cleaner. 'What do you mean?'

'Creepy, as in creepy creep.'

'Did he say something bad to you?'

'He winked at me.'

Her mother tilted her head to one side. 'And?'

'He had his hands all over you.'

'He was just being nice.'

'You hardly know him.'

Her mother gave her a look. 'How strange, you said the exact same thing about Dan. Do you think he's creepy, too?'

Ricky had a choice. She could tell her what she wanted to hear or tell the truth and face the consequences.

'The jury is out.'

'Here.' Her mother handed her the cleaner hose. 'While the jury's out, you can do the vacuuming. I've made up a bed for Ollie on the couch. He can rest while we tackle the worst of this filth. We've got to sleep in this place tonight.'

They had started with the bedrooms and spent the afternoon working their way up the hall and through the living and dining room to the kitchen. The final room to be blitzed was the bathroom, which had been sprayed last thing with something dangerous in a white bottle. The spray was supposed to kill fungus and bacteria and had to remain on the walls for several hours.

'No one's going to catch cholera on my watch,' her mother said as she emerged from the bathroom, eyes streaming. 'Hold your breath if you need to go tonight. Keep this door closed until tomorrow.'

But someone had gone to the bathroom in the middle of the night and left the door open because Ricky had woken with her nostrils tingling and her nervous system on high alert. But it wasn't the abrasive chemical that had disturbed her sleep. It was a terrifying dream that someone was standing over her while she slept. She could sense a man near her, a shadowy night visitor who was breathing rapidly through his nose as if he'd just climbed stairs. She'd woken abruptly with a prickling sense of danger. Her nose, burning from the chemicals, had picked up a smell, alien and unpleasant.

She'd sat up then, and in the light from her windows, checked to make sure she was alone before getting out of bed to close her bedroom door which had come open in the night. As she went over to the window that overlooked the playground, a man's voice became audible. He was shouting, 'Paula! Paula! Paula!' over and over at the top of his lungs.

Ricky looked down and could make out a figure leaning against the fence. The man spotted her and stumbled forward into the light of the street lamp, drunkenly, cupping his hands around his mouth.

'I'm going to kill you, you fucking bitch!' he shouted.

Ricky had slammed the window shut and jumped back into bed, her heart beating wildly as she pulled the covers up to her chin. She wanted to go to her mother but Dan had stayed the night and she could not bear to face him. The person Ricky needed right now was her father. He would have made her feel safe but he was on the other side of London. When she closed her eyes, she imagined the angry man scaling the side of the building and smashing his way inside to strangle her. The window frames had narrow ledges with metal railings, an easy climb for anyone with strong arms and agility.

'Mum, I need curtains for my room,' said Ricky. 'I couldn't sleep last night. There was a man outside my window.'

Her mother eased her head and shoulders out of the oven and threw a wad of slimy kitchen towel into the rubbish bin. Her expression was grim as she stripped off the blackened rubber gloves.

'How could there have been a man outside your window?' she asked. 'We're on the first floor.'

Ricky didn't like the look on her mother's face. 'He was below my window.'

'So, he wasn't outside your window.'

'No, but—'

'When you were in the playground yesterday, what did you say to your brother?'

'Normal nice things,' said Ricky.

'Did you tell him that Dan had stabbed a dog?'

Ricky shrugged.

'Why on earth would you tell a story like that, Vicky? It's a lie.'

'Ricky.'

'Answer me.'

'It was just a joke. It's been taken out of context.'

'It's not funny in any context. Dan would never hurt a fly. He's a very nice man.'

Ricky bit her tongue.

'It's also very unfair on Ollie. Your story scared him. You know how much he loves animals, especially dogs.'

Ricky didn't say anything.

'We all have to make an effort to get along. No more lies. Do you hear?'

'Where's Ollie?'

Her mother wiped her forehead with the back of her hand and left a dark smear above her eyebrows. 'He's in his bedroom. He's still not feeling well.'

Ollie was sitting up in bed, playing on the Netbook. He saw her and pulled the duvet over his head.

His room had been cleaned but nothing had been put away. He'd gone to bed early, before his clothes and toys could be sorted. Ricky started putting his t-shirts and underwear into the old, battered chest of drawers that Ollie had decorated with stickers from bananas and apples.

'Make sure you file them properly.' Ollie was peeping at her from under the duvet.

'I'm filing your underpants in the drawer for dangerous waste. They will be fumigated and burned,' she said. 'You hate them anyway.'

Ollie laughed and came out from under the duvet. He avoided wearing underwear whenever he could get away with it.

'I'm going to buy a flamethrower and burn them. They'll see the smoke in Brixton and send a chopper to rescue us.'

Ollie laughed harder. It was a fantastic thing his laugh, high-pitched and unpredictable, like a teaspoon running along the keys of a glockenspiel. Ricky pulled a pair of his tiny blue Y-fronts over her head and pushed her face through a leg hole to peer at him with a villainous expression. Ollie laughed again, louder and higher this time.

'I'm ready to rob a bank,' she said.

'We need a getaway car.' Forgetting he was supposed to be sick, Ollie pushed back the covers, ready for adventure.

'You can drive.' She held out his three-wheel scooter.

Ollie must have been itching to rob a bank because he was out of bed, and washed and dressed in record time. Ricky followed him to the kitchen where her mother was mopping the floor. Her face lit up when she saw him. He'd put on the top half of his Minions costume. The bulbous hood made him look top-heavy, a massive yellow head with string-like legs.

'Mum, we're going to rob a bank,' he said, casual as hell.

'You'll need some breakfast first. You can't go robbing on an empty stomach,' she replied.

She leaned the mop against the cupboards and pulled him to her, making a loud smooching sound as she kissed the padded hood. 'It will have to be toast because there's no milk for cereal.'

'Ollie and I can nick some yak milk when we go robbing,' Ricky offered. 'The bank will definitely have a yak in its vaults.'

Ollie squealed with delight.

'Ollie can milk it while I fill our bags with gold bars.'

'After breakfast, you can take your brother to the shops on King's Crescent. But listen carefully. I want you to follow the road and stick to the pavement. No detours until we know this estate better.' Her mother released Ollie. 'I'll give you some money so you don't have to bother a yak.'

Ricky had to bribe Ollie with the promise of an ice lolly to make him leave the scooter at home but he refused to take off the Minions hood.

It was market day on King's Crescent. People were setting up stalls, clanging and banging as they unloaded vans and laid out their wares on trestle tables. Ricky caught a whiff of spicy Caribbean barbecue and felt a stab of homesickness for Brixton market. She veered away from the stalls and propelled Ollie toward a large window decorated with a hand-painted sunflower.

'What is this place?' Ollie asked. The Minions hood had twisted around so that he was looking out of only one eyehole.

'It's a community centre.' Ricky was reading a notice taped to the inside of the window. 'They have summer activities.'

'Like what?'

She read out the description for the morning workshop. 'Storytelling with Katie, from real life to the page.'

'Is that it?'

'No, that's only for big shots like me.' She took a permission slip from a box taped to the window.

'What if you're little and cute?' Ollie tugged her t-shirt. 'Do they have buffalo rides?'

Ollie wanted a buffalo almost as much as he wanted a dog. The bigger the buffalo, the better. He already had plans for dung disposal. He was going to compost it and work miracles with the soil on their father's allotment. The worms would love it.

'No, surprisingly they don't.'

'It's a mistake.' He sighed dramatically.

'They have swimming outings to the lido.' She continued reading. 'But you have to be accompanied by a parent.'

'We've got a parent.'

'We've got two parents.'

'Not in Camden we don't.'

'Whose fault is that?' She frowned at Ollie's one visible eye. 'Dad will be missing us like hell by now. He's probably packing his bags. Hell, he could move to King's Crescent any day.'

'He'll never move here.'

'When did you become such a doubting Thomas?'

'My name is Oliver. I share the name with a great historical figure.'

The 'great historical figure' line was Ricky's. Ollie was a little plagiarist. 'What you don't want to become is a traitor.'

Ollie glared at her through the eyehole. 'I could say something.'

'What could you say?'

'Just something.'

'Just say it then.'

'What *you* don't want to become is a lady.'

'Ugh!' She shuddered. 'I will never become one of those!'

They continued walking through the market in silence. When Ricky decided he'd been punished enough for his disloyalty, they went into Costcutters where she bought him an ice lolly with the change from the groceries. Ollie was trying to work out how to eat it through the Minions hood as she led him away from the pavement and into the heart of the estate.

The garden she'd spotted the previous afternoon was an L-shaped plot that wrapped around the back of a six-storey tower block, extending into the wedge of land between the building and its neighbour. It was an odd, isolated setting for a garden, especially on a council estate. The only windows overlooking it were the tiny bathroom windows at the back of the towers.

While Ollie was busy with his ice lolly, Ricky reached over the fence and gently wound a tendril of sweet pea around her finger. It clung to her and through her fingertip she picked up the bud's moist intention. The sweet pea was reaching out to the world, pushing forth new leaves and tendrils. For as long as Ricky could remember, she'd been able to connect with growing things, to merge with the bustle and hum of their cells. She only had to still her mind and focus to connect with the wordless purpose of nature. It was like slipping, sinking and blending.

In recent months, however, life in the garden was becoming more resistant to her advances and she was getting clumsy, losing her way. She knew this had something to do with the changes that were happening to her body and it filled her with deep sadness.

She let go of the tendril and peered through the fence. Someone clearly loved the garden and had put a lot of effort into its upkeep. The plot was bisected by a neat flagstone path and had a mixture of raised and flat beds. In the middle was a bird-feeding platform set high on a metal pole, out of the reach of cats. On top of the platform was a small water bath and mounds of seeds and plump, water-soaked raisins, a favourite of thrushes and blackbirds.

Ricky noted the straight rows of carrot seedlings and garlic and thought of her father. He, too, was a fan of companion planting. Near the shed was a small bed of herbs and the climbing rose she'd spotted from the playground. The door to the shed was open and someone was moving around inside. She knelt down and reached through the fence to touch the delicate purple leaf of a young beetroot plant.

The shout knocked her back like a punch.

A large man had emerged from the shed. He was yelling and waving his arms.

Ollie tore the Minions hood off and, surging forward, grabbed the fence with his small fists.

'Don't shout at my sister!' he shouted.

The man stopped shouting. His hands dropped to his sides where they twitched with unfinished business. He said something incomprehensible as if he was speaking with a mouthful of mashed potato. His big, beefy face displayed a mixture of anger and confusion. He was tall and had wide shoulders. His large fingers were covered with the dark fibres of compost.

'We're not going to hurt your plants.' Ollie appeared to have understood the man. 'What's your name and how old are you?'

Any other adult would have told Ollie to get lost but the man dipped his head to listen carefully and appeared to take the questions seriously. It took a moment to understand the words he produced but the gist of it was that his name was Mr Snow or Snowy. He was seventy-six years old.

'That's a hell of an age,' said Ollie. 'Very, very old.'

Mr Snow nodded.

'Is this your garden?'

He shrugged, each shoulder working independently.

'So, it's sort of your garden but not really.'

He nodded.

'We know a lot about the gardening business. We're experts.'

'We have an allotment,' said Ricky, immediately remembering they no longer had any such thing. Her voice trailed off, choking with panic and loss.

Ollie took hold of her hand. 'Our father is a gardener and he taught us all about it. My sister handles the plant side of things. I know a lot about worms. I dig very good holes. We can help you.'

The whites of Snowy's tiny eyes flashed surprise. He shook his head and pointed to the padlock hanging from the gate. He patted the clump of keys on his belt.

'Please.' Ricky didn't mean to plead but a garden would be a refuge, a safe place where she could hide from the chaos of this alien new life. 'I'm really good at weeding and planting.'

Snowy shook his head again.

Ollie made a strange sound. He tugged her hand. 'Can we go back now?'

'Why?'

'I feel sick again.'

Ricky had to help her mother finish sorting out the flat while Ollie malingered in bed. They worked as a team, her mother scrubbing shelves and cupboards while she unpacked boxes and put things away. One of the first things she unpacked was a framed photograph of a family picnic in Brockwell Park. Ollie was still a baby in her mother's arms. Ricky was sitting next to her father, leaning in with his arm around her shoulder. Using the bottom of her t-shirt, she cleaned the glass before placing it on the shelf below the television. There, a nice reminder for her mother whenever she sat on the couch with Dan.

Ricky didn't understand her mother. What did she see in the man? The only thing he had going for him was his job. Dan was a roofer and often worked on dangerously tall buildings. In her mind's eye, she placed him on a church steeple, navigating his way around treacherous, moss-covered tiles. It was raining in this scenario, heavy pounding rain that had plastered his long hair over his face and eyes. Unable to see where he's going, Dan begins to slip. The slip becomes a slide. His life flashes before his eyes, all his mistakes and crimes. He sees himself stealing Ricky's mother and realises he's wrecked a happy family before hitting the pavement with a damp thud.

It was after three when her mother finally put down her scrubbing brush to make cheese and onion toasties. As a reward, she wrapped the toasties in paper towels so they could eat in the kitchen. Ricky loved eating on her feet. It made the experience more intense, as if at any moment someone might rush in and snatch the food from her hands. She glanced out the window as she chewed and saw teenagers in uniforms returning from their last day of school. They were laughing, making a racket as if summer was a red carpet being rolled out just for them.

'Vicky, why don't you take your brother down to the playground,' said her mother. 'He's been cooped up in that room all afternoon. He could do with some air.'

'I will if you call me Ricky,' she replied.

Her mother smiled affectionately. 'It's a struggle to call you something different after twelve years of Vicky.'

'Almost thirteen.'

'Ah, yes. Your special day is looming.'

Ricky's heart lifted at the mention of her birthday. 'Dad already calls me Ricky.'

Her mother's expression changed. 'All right, let's go back to our original agreement. I'll call you Ricky if you make more of an effort with Dan.'

'I am making an effort.'

'Be nicer. Talk to him when he talks to you and no more stories about stabbing dogs.'

Ricky imagined him sliding off the church roof again, the thud as he hit the pavement.

'Try not to hurt him. Dan's got feelings, too.'

'And you'll call me Ricky?'

'I'll try my best.' Her mother pulled her close. She kissed her. 'My girl, Ricky.'

'Don't call me that.'

'What? Now you don't want to be called Ricky?'

'Don't call me a girl. I'm not one of those.'

'Oh, honey.' Her mother kissed her again. 'It's not so bad being a girl.'

Ricky scrunched her eyes shut and buried her face in her mother's t-shirt.

*Yes, it was. Yes, it was. Yes, it was.*

It took a good fifteen minutes to get Ollie off the Netbook and out of bed. By the time they got to the playground, everyone had cleared off and they had the place to themselves.

'Want to join my boot camp?' asked Ricky.

Ollie shook his head. 'I'm too sick.'

'It's your funeral, Small Fry. You need to toughen up if you're going to survive on this estate.' Ricky had come up with an ingenious plan. For the next six weeks of summer holidays, she was going to do military-style exercises. If King's Crescent Estate was a battleground, she would become a soldier, one of the special forces who trained hard and did clever, dangerous things like rescuing people trapped inside submarines.

Ollie headed for the igloo. 'I'm going to hibernate.'

'Please yourself.'

Ricky had done over forty chin-ups on the climbing frame when Ollie called out to warn her that Caitlin's pink Nike trainers were approaching.

'I can't see her dog,' he said, sadly. 'There are two girls with her.'

Ricky swung down and leaped clear of the climbing frame like a gymnast. Her heart was thumping in a satisfying way.

Samia held the gate open for Caitlin and a tall, very pretty girl with long blonde hair. The new girl was wearing makeup and had proper breasts that pointed straight out like ice cream cones. She walked past Ricky without looking her way and sat on a swing. She took out her mobile and began scrolling.

'What are you doing?' asked Caitlin.

'I've been doing chin-ups,' Ricky replied.

'Doh!' She rolled her eyes for the benefit of the other girls. 'I mean what are you *doing*?'

It was some sort of trick question. Caitlin was smirking at no one in particular, waiting for Ricky to make a fool of herself.

'I'm training for the winter endurance trials on the Orkneys. I'm going there with my father in December and need to be fit enough to walk through snow carrying enough dry food for five days. I'm also brushing up on my Gaelic.'

Ricky heard Ollie giggle inside the igloo and struggled not to laugh.

Caitlin pulled a WTF face.

'Where are the Orkneys?' asked Samia, with genuine geographical interest.

Caitlin growled. Her troops were not supposed to fraternise with the enemy. 'How old are you anyway?

'Thirteen, more or less.'

'Ha, what a kid.' She shrugged for the benefit of the pretty girl on the swing. 'Abbie and I will be fourteen this year.'

Abbie glanced up but almost immediately went back to looking at her phone.

Caitlin narrowed her eyes and stared at Ricky's chest. 'I bet you don't even wear a bra.'

'I'll never wear one of those stupid things.' For the past couple of months, Ricky had been trying to ignore the small, burning lumps on her chest. They were not going to develop into anything. Nope. No way.

'Did you hear that?' Caitlin called out to Abbie. 'This twat says we're stupid.'

'No, she didn't,' said Ollie, emerging from the igloo.

'Abbie and I wear bras, so, according to her, we must be stupid.'

'You're twisting it around. Now *that* is stupid.' Ollie stood up and brushed grit off his knees. 'Where's your dog?'

Caitlin narrowed her eyes. 'She's resting.'

'Why? Didn't Baby want to come out with you?'

'Of course she wanted to come out with me, you stupid brat.'

'My brother's not stupid and not a brat.' Ricky's temper flared. 'He's a proper dog whisperer. He's been on TV and everything. Last month, the BBC filmed him whispering to a cocker spaniel.'

'Where?'

'In Brixton.'

Caitlin snorted. 'Bullshit.'

'It's true. Brixton is the dog capital of London. More dogs per head of population than any other borough.' This probably wasn't true but Caitlin didn't look like the fact-checking type.

'Look, there's Dan!' said Ollie.

Everyone turned to look at Dan who was striding up the path with a bunch of supermarket flowers. He saw them and raised his eyebrows in a friendly way.

Ricky cringed.

'Is that your father?' asked Caitlin.

'No! He's nobody.'

'He's fit,' said Abbie. She'd pushed herself off the swing and was watching Dan mount the steps with interest.

'No, he's not!' Ricky knew her voice was shrill but she couldn't help herself. 'He's really old, like forty or something.'

Ollie spluttered and covered his mouth with his hands.

He was halfway to the gate when he made a sound like a dog's bark. He must have been aiming for the grass outside the playground but missed it entirely.

Ricky watched in horror as his vomit sprayed over the legs of Caitlin, splattering the pink Nikes with a partly digested cheese and onion toastie.

# 3

OLLIE HAD BEEN sick again during the night and was running a fever. In her haste to get to a doctor, Ricky's mother signed the permission slip for the summer workshop without taking in a crucial detail. The workshop was not an all-day activity. It was held only in the morning. Ricky decided to keep this information to herself, at least for the time being.

She was surprised to find Caitlin's friend waiting outside the community centre. Abbie was leaning against the wall, pretending she had nothing to do with the noisy mob gathering outside. She looked awkward and out of place, too old and ladylike for a summer activity. She glanced up from her iPhone and rolled her eyes.

The door opened and a friendly woman in a red linen dress beckoned them inside. She was about the same age as Ricky's mother and had soft, hazel eyes. Her curly brown hair was anchored at the back of her head with a large plastic clip. She ushered them into a room which was furnished with a whiteboard and a long table. In the middle of the table was a stack of paper and a basket containing pens and pencils. Ricky waited for Abbie to sit down before taking the seat opposite her. Until she knew where things stood between them, she would follow the 'Keep your enemies close' rule.

'My name is Katie,' said the woman. 'I'm your facilitator for the summer creative workshop. A facilitator is like a teacher only nicer and a lot more fun.' She laughed. 'Now, let's get to know each other. First of all, who here likes to read?'

Ricky automatically put up her hand. When she looked around the table, she saw she was the only one.

'Good for you. It's easier to write if you know how to read.' Katie smiled. 'What's your name?'

'Ricky Bird.'

'Okay, Ricky, I'll go around the table but let's start with you. Please tell us something about yourself.'

'I am almost thirteen,' she said. 'We've just moved here from Brixton.'

Katie nodded. 'How are you finding Camden?'

Ricky allowed herself a smile. 'I've been warned to watch my back.'

Katie burst out laughing.

Encouraged, Ricky narrowed her eyes and looked across the table to Abbie. 'I'll also be watching my front.'

Abbie pulled a WTF face. 'Freak!'

The introductions were almost over when Samia burst through the door, hastily apologising for being late. She thrust the permission slip into Katie's hands and dived into the empty seat beside Ricky.

'I'm going to start by giving each of you a writing tool.' Katie was walking around with a basket, handing out notebooks. 'These are for you to take home.'

Ricky chose a simple black notebook. It was pocket-size and had unlined paper like a Moleskin.

'This workshop is not school.' Katie wrote on the whiteboard. 'It's creative play.'

There was no right or wrong, she explained. They were free to write whatever they liked but each day they had to produce something and that something had to be original.

'I'll start today's session by giving you a word. Think about what it means to you and then write or even draw something.'

Katie wrote 'Tea' on the whiteboard. 'You've got twenty minutes.'

Tea meant morning to Ricky. It meant her father sitting in his gardening clothes, drinking out of his green 'I DIG COMPOST' mug, teasing Ollie until he laughed so hard he spat out his cereal. Her father was a diehard Tetley's man. Cappuccinos were for hipsters, he insisted, bearded types and people from Paris, fools who wore leather shoes without socks. Cappuccino drinkers were superficial and known to bleach their teeth. Tea drinkers were earthy and honest. 'There's nothing wrong with brown teeth,' he told her. His teeth were not brown, at least not yet. 'I'm working my way up to it. Another ten thousand litres should do it.'

Ricky had written and crossed out at least fifty words before finally settling on a simple eight-word poem.

'Did you make that up?' asked Katie, her voice sharp.

She nodded, embarrassed.

Katie picked up the sheet of paper and told everyone to be quiet.

'A short poem by Ricky Bird,' she announced.

'Boil kettle
Make tea
Drink tea
Make pee.'

There was a moment of silence, a collective intake of breath, before the room erupted with laughter.

'It's wonderful, isn't it.' Katie was beaming, smiling at Ricky as if she was a genius. 'You're a genius.'

For the first time in days, Ricky allowed herself to relax. It felt wonderful to have Katie's approval. She loved the way everyone was laughing. It was like the old days in Brixton. Light and friendly. When she glanced across the table, however, she saw that Abbie was crumpling up her piece of paper and immediately felt sorry for her. Not everyone knew how to assemble words into a story. 'It's a gift,' her father told her. 'A handy gift to have if push comes to shove.'

When Ricky was Ollie's age, she'd been on the fringe of a conversation between her parents. A discussion about getting her a backpack for school had quickly turned into a massive argument over money. Her father didn't have any, he insisted, not a pfennig. Didn't his wife have a heart? He was still in shock after his bicycle tyre had exploded on the way home. 'Bang!' he said, clapping his hands. 'I thought I'd been shot. I was about to give myself CPR when I noticed my tyre. Flat as a pancake.' He'd spent the last of his money on a new tube and tyre. 'Rubber doesn't grow on trees, you know.' He'd stopped talking then and begun to laugh at himself, and despite her anger, her mother had started laughing, too.

Even as a small child, Ricky knew this was more of a story than a lie. Her father's storytelling was one of the things she loved about him and it was a talent he encouraged in her. 'If you can spin a good yarn, you'll get on in life,' he told her. 'A dog stealing a meat pie is a story. But it's a *good* story when an old dog steals a pie to give to a homeless man with one leg and three teeth. Now, if you want to up your game, make that a steak and kidney pie and give the dog a name like Mister Piddle Pants. The devil is in the detail.' Later that evening, after her father had showered and changed out of his gardening clothes, Ricky had gone through his pockets and transferred the twenty pounds she found there to her mother's purse.

The workshop had been the distraction Ricky needed. She forgot that the estate was rubbish and that she had no friends. Katie's praise had buoyed her. She walked home for lunch feeling like her old self, clever and popular. Her poem had found an audience. Another workshop like that and she'd be back in business.

She opened the door to the flat and her heart sank. Dan was standing next to the sideboard with a butter knife in his hand. He was making himself a sandwich, smiling as if he was King Tutankhamun and the kitchen was his personal pyramid.

'Hello, love!' he said, breezily.

'Hello,' she replied, coolly.

'Your mum's stuck at the hospital with Ollie. She asked me to pop in and look after you.'

She should have said 'thank you' but that would have been a bridge too far, a bridge as long as the Severn Bridge too far. Ricky fussed with her vitamins while she waited for him to finish with the bread and butter.

'What are those?' he asked.

'Vitamins. Dad gave them to me.' She squared her shoulders. 'They make me strong.'

'Why does a young lady like you want to be strong?'

'I might need to punch someone.'

He held up his hands in mock terror. 'I'd better watch myself then.'

Dan had made himself a ham sandwich so Ricky went for cheese. Cheese and pickle, one of her father's favourites. She'd just sat down at the table when Dan joined her.

'So, what did you do this morning?' His friendly tone implied she should overlook the fact that he was *persona non grata*.

'Poetry.' She took a bite of her sandwich to indicate conversation was over.

Dan nodded, expecting more. His eyes travelled from her face to the sandwich in her hands.

Ricky stopped chewing and positioned her arm in front of her chest.

'Is it poetry again this afternoon?'

She shrugged. It was not his business what she did. He needed to go back to work on a roof. The higher the roof, the better. She once again imagined him slipping and falling to a swift death.

'That's better. You're much prettier when you smile.'

She stopped smiling and put the sandwich down. She'd lost her appetite.

'Your mum won't be back till later. They're doing more tests on Ollie.'

'Why are they doing that?' Ricky had to ask. Only sick people had tests and Ollie wasn't sick. He was a faker, a Hollywood contender. Illness was a trick he pulled to get out of eating Brussels sprouts or putting away his Lego.

'They found something in his blood.' Dan raised his eyebrows cryptically as if he was privy to a sinister secret: her brother had iron filings in his blood and would have to stay away from magnets for the rest of his life.

Ricky studied her sandwich and tried to look uninterested. Knowledge was power and Dan was relishing it. She held her breath and counted to ten.

'What did they find?'

'Something that required tests.'

'You already said that.'

'Your mum said not to worry.'

Dan flashed a smile. It was an impression of a concerned smile and didn't fool Ricky for a minute. He was making sure she would worry away the entire afternoon.

Ricky whistled in a casual manner as she headed off in the direction of the community centre. Once out of view she doubled back and, sticking close to the hedge, followed the path under the trees to the back of the tower blocks. The gate to the garden was shut but not locked. She pushed it open and stepped inside.

Snowy was on his knees, transferring delicate lettuce seedlings to a furrow in the soil. His movements were stiff and awkward, his fingers too large and his hands clumsy.

'You're bruising them with your sausagey fingers,' she said.

Snowy stood up, surprised, shaking soil from his hands. He saw her looking at his fingers and hid them behind his back as if he'd been caught doing something wrong.

'I know how to prick out the seedlings without bruising them. Dad says I have the greenest fingers in Brixton.' She held up her hands and wiggled her fingers. 'Get a load of these babies.'

The old man frowned.

'I'll help you.' She moved boldly toward the tray of plants. 'You're going to ruin them if you keep pawing them.'

He seemed to consider his options for a few seconds before disappearing inside the shed. He reappeared with a pair of gloves. They were too big but it didn't matter. She was back in a garden and it felt brilliant.

Ricky was halfway through the tray of seedlings when she realised she was feeling less burdened and anxious. The soil was once again working its magic. What a strange business gardening was. It was work, like making a bed or doing dishes were work, but unlike either of these tedious activities, gardening never made Ricky tired. Rather, it invigorated her. Ollie, too. They always returned home happier and better behaved after a day at the allotment.

She nudged the tray forward with her foot and straddled the planting bed to make a fresh furrow with her finger. Her head was down and as she eased a seedling into the earth, she noticed Snowy's boots behind her. He was standing at the edge of the soil and was either watching her work or, the thought struck her, staring at her backside.

She stood up ready to challenge him but the old man had already turned away. A watering can was sitting on the spot where his boots had been. She went back to the lettuces, working quickly, keen to prove herself. Within less than ten minutes she'd planted all the seedlings in tidy rows. She picked up the watering can and, as she sprinkled the new plants, she noticed Snowy watching her again.

Ricky must have done well because Snowy got her to plant more seedlings before handing her a small garden fork and pointing to the overgrown herb garden. He didn't ask any questions or try to talk to her, but as she worked, she knew she was being observed.

After a couple of hours, she became aware that Snowy was making impatient noises. She took off the gloves and washed her hands, careful to remove all evidence of what she'd been doing, before collecting her backpack from the shed. He was waiting for her by the gate, padlock in hand. She wanted to tell him she would return the following afternoon but feared he would say no if she made her intentions known.

Snowy rummaged in his pocket and pulled out a bag of sweets, old-fashioned hard mints. She understood by the gesture that she had passed some kind of test. She took one to be polite and rolled it around in her mouth.

When she opened the gate, her limbs felt looser. Emotionally, she felt less scattered, more contained. Ricky was heading away from the garden when she heard someone approaching. She looked around for a hiding place, and dropping to her knees, squeezed through a gap in the ragged hedge.

A mobile phone sounded. The footsteps stopped.

She peered through the leaves and saw a teenage boy. He was short, more stocky than fat, and had a small head that sat awkwardly on a thick neck. His jeans hugged his thighs and were ripped at the knees. The sleeves of his oversized sweatshirt were pushed up above his elbows. The boy had dark blond hair, a shade lighter than the caterpillar of facial hair above his top lip. His chin bore the feathery hairs of a first beard.

'Stop fucking worrying. No one will see you,' he said, exhaling loudly into his phone. He looked down and kicked at the loose pebbles of the path with a blue Nike trainer. 'I'm telling you, I've checked it all out. There are no fucking cameras.'

Ricky held her breath. The boy only had to lift his head to see her. She was wearing khaki cargo shorts that rendered her invisible from the waist down but her red t-shirt was like a matador's cape, asking for trouble.

'He's not going to give us any grief. He's a halfwit. Just hurry the fuck up.' The boy put the phone away and took a Marlboro packet from his pocket. He lit a cigarette and coughed before spitting out of the corner of his mouth.

Without thinking, Ricky followed the arc of the projectile and immediately regretted it. Boys were disgusting. It didn't make sense that she wanted to be one but the deep throb of discomfort she felt within her developing body left her no choice. It was better to be a boy than whatever her body's treacherous hormones were trying to force on her.

She was wriggling out of the hedge when she realised someone else was approaching. There was no time to crawl back into her hiding place.

'Hello.'

She looked up.

'Fancy meeting you here.' The estate manager's head was cocked to one side.

He was examining her with interest, too much interest for Ricky's liking. She considered making a run for it but didn't fancy her chances, not with his long legs.

'Hello,' she replied, aware that Tim knew her mother and her mother didn't know where she was.

'I'm not going to ask what you're doing with that hedge.'

'Good.'

He laughed as if they were sharing a joke. His hands went to his belt where they hitched up his jeans, which had slipped low on his narrow hips.

Ricky kept her face expressionless. She wanted nothing to do with this over-friendly man.

'You didn't see anyone pass this way, did you?'

Was Tim asking if she'd seen someone or telling her that she shouldn't have seen anyone?

She shook her head.

Tim frowned as if he knew she was lying. He held her gaze for a moment before striding back the way he'd come.

Ricky dusted herself down and glanced at her watch. It was still too early to return home without arousing suspicion. Her mother had warned her not to wander around the estate but how was she supposed to get to know the place if she didn't do some exploring?

The tower blocks looked different from the front, desolate and imposing: three thick, red-brick spears surrounded by a barren expanse of concrete and tarmac. There were no trees or gardens on this side of the estate. The only green was a fenced-in rectangle of lawn. A second rectangle contained a small playground with a slide, swing and seesaw. Ricky saw no one as she crossed the forecourt. Feeling exposed and vulnerable, she hurried to the other side of the buildings where she spotted a narrow lane to take her back to her side of the estate. She paused as something familiar beside a bin caught her eye. It was a 'baggy' like the ones she often saw discarded around her old estate. The small plastic bags were what dealers used to package their drugs.

'Hey!'

She looked up and saw that she was not alone. Halfway down the lane were four teenage boys. They had seen her first and were already moving toward her, jostling in the way youths did with elbows and shoulders, out to prove something. One of the boys shouted again and they started running.

In an instant, Ricky was in flight. She was blood and adrenaline, an animal fleeing predators. She could hear the pounding of their trainers behind her as she sprinted back the way she'd come. The boys were yelping, voices high with excitement. They were no longer individuals with their own thoughts but a pack of dogs caught up in the chase, bound together by a single, dangerous purpose. Ricky's heart was drumming in her throat as she flew across the empty forecourt, past the tiny playground and rectangle of grass. She was almost at the path leading to her side of the estate when she heard the boys slowing behind her. They were shouting abuse now, calling her names and telling her what they were going to do to her. Bad things. They would show her.

Ricky didn't stop running until she was back on the relatively safe ground of familiar territory. Her lungs were burning and her legs felt like liquid as she followed the path behind the flats to a bench under some spindly birches. Once her breathing was under control and her hands had steadied, she opened her backpack and took out her new notebook.

Katie had explained at the end of the workshop that the notebooks were for recording feelings.

'Write or draw something every day and don't double think yourselves,' she advised. 'Just express exactly how you feel in the moment. It doesn't have to be positive or perfect. It doesn't have to make sense. This is only for you. Don't show it to anyone. That way you won't be tempted to censor or edit yourselves. Write what is real.'

To write something for herself was an alien concept for Ricky. She always made up stories for other people, if not for teachers then for her father or Ollie.

'Stay in the moment,' Katie had said. 'Catch your feelings and lay them down in words. This notebook will be a resource for the work we do this summer.'

Ricky pressed it open with the heel of her palm and, before she could reconsider, wrote the first thing that came into her head. When she'd finished, she looked at the words and experienced a moment of panic and then, strangely, a feeling of relief. Panic, because she had never, ever admitted such feelings to herself, and relief because it felt not completely awful to admit that she felt unsafe.

*I'm scared and lonely. He's watching me.*

Someone had attached a laminated poster to the gate of the playground. It was an advertisement for a summer funfair on Hampstead Heath and showed a montage of fairground scenes: riders emerging from a ghost train looking terrified, children laughing on a Ferris wheel and clowns juggling skittles.

She thought of the previous summer when she and her father had ridden the ghost train together at the fair in Brockwell Park. Later, they had gone to a shooting gallery where he'd won a pair of red earphones. The earphones were rubbish but the win had made them both giddy with excitement. At one point, he'd made her promise to never marry a clown. 'Those feet!' he'd laughed. 'You'd end up a slave to his bunions.'

'What are you doing?' Caitlin barked. She was alone, watching Ricky through the railings.

'I'm doing press-ups,' she said.

'During school holidays? What kind of freak are you?'

Ricky didn't reply. It wasn't something she could answer.

'Abbie said you wrote a dirty poem.'

She shrugged.

'Are you a lesbian?'

'No.'

Caitlin smiled. She now had something she could contradict. 'Yes, you are. You're a lesbian.'

Ricky swallowed.

'Go on, admit it.'

'Is that what you and Abbie are?'

'Shut up! I'm not a pervert.'

Ricky glanced at Caitlin's Nike trainers, expecting to see stains or evidence of scrubbing but her shoes were spotless. They were new, fresh out of the box. The white soles and pink uppers were pristine. The laces had fold marks. Why did Caitlin have two identical pairs of Nike trainers? Ricky was not about to ask. The less said about them, the better.

Ricky pointed to the funfair poster. 'Did you see this?'

'Funfairs are lame.'

'The one that comes to Brixton has an excellent ghost train. You get a hat and a map of the underworld.'

'Whatever!' Caitlin's eyes narrowed. 'You don't have to go to the stupid funfair to see a ghost train. My brother's got one that's a hundred times better.'

'Your brother has a ghost train?'

'I just said so, didn't I!'

'Where is it?'

'In our garage.'

'You've got a train in your garage?'

'You don't need an actual train, stupid.'

'A ghost train without a train? What do you use, a golf cart?'

'Shut up! It's more of a maze that you walk through but it's got a light show and everything. My brother works part-time as a DJ.'

As Caitlin described the exotic attractions of her brother's ghost maze, she became almost friendly. Against Ricky's better judgement, she began to feel flattered and found herself warming to the idea.

'So, are you coming tomorrow afternoon?'

'Where to?'

'To the ghost train.'

'In your garage?' Ricky could just imagine it. A bunch of rough, unfriendly kids dressed in white sheets, rattling chains. It would be rubbish.

'Abbie and Samia are coming.'

Ricky was still unsure of Abbie but Samia had been friendly or, at least, she hadn't been unfriendly.

'Well? Are you coming or not?'

'Okay.'

'It's not free. We need to cover expenses.'

'How much?'

'A tenner.'

'What?'

'Five quid.'

# 4

OLLIE WAS SITTING at the table eating ice cream and talking to Scotty, his soft toy dog. He was being precious and didn't bother to acknowledge Ricky as she sat down. His eyes were puffy as if he'd overslept but, otherwise, he was the picture of health. Ollie had shot up in the past year and had lost the chubby arms and legs of a toddler but he still had the creamy soft face of a baby. Ricky was secretly pleased. Kissing him was one of her favourite things, something she did only when it was clear she was doing it for his sake.

She watched him spoon ice cream into his mouth with slow, deliberate movements. His left arm was lying ostentatiously on the table, a cotton swab taped over the vein. It was an invitation to comment, one she pretended not to notice. She went to the kitchen where her mother was chopping vegetables with savage precision. She was a very efficient cook, a legacy of her years working in restaurants. She'd trained as a chef and planned to return to work once they were back at school.

'Can I have some ice cream?' Ricky asked.

'Dinner will be ready in two ticks,' her mother replied, throwing vegetable chunks into a spitting wok. 'Give me five minutes.'

'Ollie's got ice cream.'

'Ollie is not well.'

'Ollie's the picture of health.'

'Set the table.'

'He's milking it, Mum.'

Her mother stopped stirring the contents of the wok for a moment. Her expression was odd. She looked stunned, as if she'd just been asked to name the capital of Ghana. The next thing she said confused Ricky because it wasn't the telling off she was expecting.

'I hope so.'

Why would she hope Ollie was pretending to be sick? Ricky watched her mother carefully as she prodded the colourful medley of vegetables, trying to understand the thing that wasn't being said.

'But Ollie's all right, right?'

'I hope so.'

Ricky lowered her voice to a whisper. 'What do you mean?'

'He's to have more tests tomorrow.'

'So, he's probably fine.'

Her mother's gaze shifted to the far wall of the kitchen. She smiled weakly and nodded.

Ricky examined Ollie more carefully as she set the table. She was looking for evidence of pox or carbuncles but he looked perfectly fine, even finer than normal. His cheeks were pink and he clearly hadn't lost his appetite. His empty bowl had lick marks. When she'd had tonsillitis the previous winter, she hadn't been able to swallow anything for an entire day. Her mother had bought strawberries and blueberries and made her a smoothie with ice cream. It was so delicious that Ricky had pretended not to be able to swallow for another couple of days. On day three, her mother had made her eat toast. 'You're pushing your luck,' she said, after Ricky had ordered a mango smoothie with chocolate mint ice cream.

'What's wrong with you?' Ricky asked.

Ollie shrugged.

'There's nothing wrong with you, is there?'

He didn't say anything.

'You're faking it, aren't you?'

'I had proper tests.' He sniffed and pointed to the tape on his arm. 'They gave me medicine.'

'But if you were sick, you would be in hospital. They've sent you home so you must be fine and dandy.'

'But I feel sick.'

'If you were sick, you wouldn't be able to eat ice cream. This place makes me sick but I don't go around making everyone worry. You need to stop being ridiculous. You're not a baby anymore. You'll be going to a new school at the end of summer. You need to pull yourself together.'

Ollie's face brightened at the mention of school. 'I'm going to get a new uniform.'

She narrowed her eyes. 'You'll only get a new uniform if you're not sick.'

He smiled hesitantly. 'I'll probably feel better tomorrow.'

'Knew it.'

Dan arrived while Ricky was eating the stir-fry but remained in the kitchen talking in whispers with her mother. They stopped whispering when she took her plate to the sink. Dan gave her a wink.

'Hello, young lady,' he said.

Her mother smiled at Dan.

Ricky wanted to scream.

'Vicky, I'm going to call your father,' she said. 'You can have a word with him but you'll have to be quick. I need to top up my mobile.'

'Ricky,' she corrected.

Her mother sighed. 'Ricky.'

'When are we getting wifi?' She hated to ask in front of Dan but she wanted to video chat with her father. The thought of him gave her a tight ache in the centre of her chest.

'They were going to send an engineer out tomorrow lunchtime but I'll have to cancel. I need to go back to the hospital.'

'I could be here for the engineer.' Ricky tried to keep the eagerness out of her voice.

Her mother shook her head.

'But, Mum, we need wifi.'

'I could get jailed for leaving you on your own. You're only twelve.'

'More or less thirteen.'

'Even if you were thirteen, you'd still be a child and too young to be left on your own.'

'I can pop in again at lunchtime tomorrow and keep her company if you like,' said Dan. 'We're on a job nearby.'

Ricky stiffened. 'I'm fine on my own.'

'No, you are not fine on your own.' Her mother gave her one of her looks. 'The engineer is scheduled to come between twelve and two. Would that be a problem, Dan?'

'Happy to help out.' He smiled, all sweetness and light. 'I can throw a couple of sandwiches together.'

'As long as it doesn't cause you any trouble at work.' Her mother beamed. 'It would be a great help.'

Ricky tried to catch her eye. 'But I've been making sandwiches since I was seven.'

Her mother kept talking to Dan over her head. 'I didn't want to bother you again but I didn't know what to do about lunchtime. I thought I'd have to take them both to the hospital with me.'

Too late, Ricky realised her mistake. 'But I'd rather go to the hospital with you.'

'No, you can have lunch here with Dan. It will be easier for me to deal with your brother alone. He's having a scan and will have to keep absolutely calm and stay still. You'll only get him worked up.'

'No, I won't. Promise. I'll take a book.'

'That's enough now.' Her mother shook her head. 'Dan is going out of his way to help us. You want wifi. This way, you'll get wifi. End of story.'

'Don't worry, love. I'll keep my eye on the little lady.' Dan turned to Ricky and smiled. 'We're already getting along like a house on fire.'

'That's the best news I've heard all day.' Her mother took her mobile out of her bag. 'Here, please give your father a call now.'

Ricky felt the pain in her chest again. She hadn't spoken to him for three whole days. For a butterfly or a flying ant, three days was a lifetime. She realised she was trembling as she put the phone to her ear.

'Hello, Steph,' said her father.

'It's me, Dad,' she said, walking out of the kitchen.

'Even better. What's been happening, Sport?'

A vivid memory of the boys pursuing her from the tower blocks flashed through her mind. The thudding of their shoes and their shouts. The raw, animal terror of the experience. They would have hurt her.

'Nothing.'

'You must be doing something on your holibobs. Will they have a funfair in your neck of the woods?'

For some stupid reason, she felt an urge to cry. 'Yes.'

'Well, that's great. Are you missing me?'

It was stupid to cry. Stupid. She had to control herself. She was almost a teenager, virtually old enough to buy cigarettes and ride a motorcycle. 'I'm doing exercises and taking your vitamins.'

'That's the ticket.'

All the injustices and grief she'd been pushing down seemed to expand inside her like an inflating bouncy castle. She wanted to sob and roar, to sit on her father's lap and hide her face in his flannel shirt.

'I have to say goodbye now.' Her voice was breaking.

'Why so soon? Are you all right?'

'There's not enough money on the phone.'

Her father was still talking when she shoved the phone into Ollie's hands.

'Daddy!' he squealed.

Ricky had to force herself not to run. By focusing on her feet, one in front of the other, she made it to her bedroom without exploding. As she threw her back against the door, she burst into tears. She was crying for her father, for the allotment, for Brixton, for her disintegrating family. She was even crying for her old BMX bike. She'd still have the bike if they had used a proper removal company. The stupid rental truck had been Dan's idea. It had been too small. At the last minute, he'd dumped her precious bike next to the bins.

Ricky's chest was still heaving when Ollie knocked on her door. She knew it was him because the knock was at kidney level.

'Let me in!' he demanded.

'No.' She pushed her back hard against the door.

'I know you're crying.'

'No, I'm not.'

'If you don't let me in, I'll be sick.'

'Your fault for eating ice cream.'

'If you don't let me in, I'll tell them you're crying.'

The thought of Dan knowing about her tears made her want to start crying again. 'Don't come in until I say.'

'Okay but don't make me wait too long. I really do feel sick. It's touch and go.'

Ricky wiped her face with a tissue and patted some of her father's aftershave over her cheeks. It was proper aftershave from France that had come in a gold box. She'd taken it from the bathroom and hidden it from him as he was moving out. The smell was supposed to revive her but as the peppery fragrance filled her nostrils, it made her miss him all the more. She had to squeeze her eyes shut and count to ten.

Ollie must have been leaning against the door because he almost toppled over. After he'd righted himself and tucked his toy dog safely under his arm, he examined her in that peculiar knowing way of his.

'Dad said you didn't say goodbye,' he said.

'I did,' she replied. She stretched out on her bed, casually tucking her arms behind her head.

'Well, I certainly didn't hear you.'

'You should get your ears checked, Small Fry. You might have moths in them.'

Ollie sniffed, interested.

'Moths climb inside earholes at night and make themselves at home. They even order in tiny flatpacks from Ikea.'

Ollie giggled.

'It's no laughing matter.'

'It's a good thing I don't have moths in my ears.' Ollie gingerly sat on the edge of the bed. 'Do you want to see the hole they put in my arm?'

Of course Ricky wanted to see the hole in his arm. She wanted a hole in her own arm, several holes with plasters and a sling. She sighed dramatically. 'If you insist.'

The wound was more of a bruise than a hole and looked all wrong on Ollie's tiny arm. Taking blood from her small brother had to be up there with euthanising kittens.

Ollie was waiting for congratulations and sympathy.

'That must have hurt like hell,' she finally offered. 'What a bruise.'

'Nah, it didn't hurt,' he said, edging closer. 'Mum said I was very brave.'

'Were you as brave as Joan of Arc?'

'I was braver than Joan and her horse.' This was a game of theirs. The object was to name a famous person and respective animal. He leaned against her legs and patted the plaster back in place. 'Can we build a fort under your desk?'

No one loved forts more than Ricky. A fort was a place of safety and possibility. It shut out the world and enclosed her and Ollie within the privacy of any story she wanted to tell.

'It's probably not worth it.' She sighed. 'We'll have to go to bed soon.'

'I can build a two-minute fort.' He was already on his feet, dragging the crocheted rug from the end of the bed.

Ricky stayed where she was, trying not to look interested as he draped the rug over her desk. He worked with the energy of a healthy, motivated child. There was nothing weak or sickly about the way he manoeuvred the wooden chair over the carpet to create a tunnel. Ollie was panting with excitement as he furnished the interior with cushions before re-emerging to get Scotty and two of Ricky's toys.

Ollie knew her favourites, a worn elephant called Polly and a plastic Transformers toy called Reptilion. Without her ever admitting it, he also understood her dilemma: she loved toys but wasn't supposed to be playing with them anymore. No one her age did. Toys were for little kids but Ricky couldn't bear to give up Polly or Reptilion. They were like people to her. They came alive when she and Ollie played with them. Their world was rich and vivid, a wild place of unlimited possibility.

Ollie poked his head out from behind the crocheted fortress. 'Come into my parlour, said the quite nice spider to the big, hairy fly.'

Ricky removed her sandals and placed them tidily next to the chair. Before leaving Brixton, she'd watched a documentary about the Japanese tradition of leaving shoes at the door. They did this because of the distinction they made between inside and outside. Inside was for family and had to be kept clean and safe while the outside world was foreign and dirty. The Japanese removed their shoes at the door because they didn't want to contaminate the interior of their homes. They also had different slippers for the bathroom and toilet and even removed their shoes before throwing themselves from cliffs as if the afterlife was a home away from home.

This was what she was thinking as she crawled under the desk. She was leaving the dirt and troubles of Camden outside and entering somewhere safe and clean. She was back in Brixton. The table and chair were the same. The blanket was the same. The floor was different but Ollie had thoughtfully covered it with cushions. Sad feelings of the familiar and the lost welled up inside her.

Ollie gently placed his toy dog in her lap.

'Make Scotty tell a story,' he said. His voice was hushed and eager.

Within the crocheted walls of their fort, Ollie's toy dog was a storyteller, an old sea dog who had swum ashore after working as a pirate for seventy-five years off the Horn of Africa. Scotty spoke with a French accent from his days as a young poodle on the Riviera. But he was old and tired now and even had barnacles on his bottom, the mention of which always made Ollie laugh.

'Did I ever tell you about the time I was working on the good ship Brixton and caught a man-eating clam?' Ricky spoke in the voice of an old French poodle.

'No.' Ollie was already smiling.

'The clam was huge, the size of a garden shed. It had clamped onto the ship's anchor with its frilly lips and wouldn't let go.' She made Scotty scratch his head with his paw. 'We hauled that sea monster onto the deck but it immediately gobbled two of my best men and a barrel of salted anchovies. That clam was hungry and it was mean, the meanest clam the seven seas had ever seen.'

Ollie shrieked with delight. He loved a bit of impromptu rhyme.

'The clam had a long, long tongue which it wrapped around its victims like a lasso. *Slurp*. It pulled the poor sods between its shells and crushed them against football-sized pearls. *Crunch, slurp, slurp*.'

'Where were you, Scotty?' Ollie's eyes were wide. He knew his dog was going to be the hero of this story. Scotty always was.

'I was lying in my hammock when I heard the ship's horn parping out a code.'

'They have parps for clam?'

'Of course. Two long parps for clam. Three short parps for giant squid.'

Her brother nodded, satisfied.

'By the time I got to the deck, the clam had its tongue wrapped around old Captain Salty Whiskers and was squeezing him very tight. His eyes were popping out of his head like golf balls. He'd peed his pants with the pressure.'

Ollie was enjoying himself.

'The clam's tongue was so powerful, it made the captain parp, which was confusing because one parp of the ship's horn meant whale ahoy.'

Ollie was laughing with his mouth open, exposing his tiny milk teeth.

'The captain was on his last breath when I sank my canines into the tip of the clam's tongue. The clam screamed and spat out old Salty Whiskers. The beast struggled to wrench itself free from my teeth but I held tight, stretching its tongue across the deck like a rubber band. When I finally let go there was a *twang* and the monster was flung into the air like a pellet from a potato gun. It passed the clouds and kept going until it entered the stratosphere. That clam is still in orbit today and on fine nights you can see it pass overhead.'

'What about Captain Salty Whiskers?'

'He changed his name to Slim Whiskers. He was a lot taller after that squeeze job.'

As they dismantled the fort, Ricky became aware of a niggling feeling, a sense that something wasn't right, wasn't what it seemed. It had to do with the scene earlier in the kitchen. She'd been upset and distracted but there was something discordant she'd noticed but hadn't registered. Ricky put herself back in the kitchen. She was standing by the sink. Her mother was next to the sideboard looking over her head at Dan who was standing in the middle of the room. He had turned toward her and was looking at her, smiling.

Her scalp prickled. She felt heat envelop her neck and face and crossed her arms over her chest.

# 5

SAMIA WAS LIKE a nymph that had spent most of its life underground only to emerge into the world confused about the big yellow disc in the sky and the unfamiliar feel of wind beneath its damp wings. She was naïve, stubbornly so. Despite being raised on the King's Crescent Estate, she had the survival strategies of a hatchling.

Ricky and Samia had arrived early at the community centre and, without exchanging a word, had taken the same seats as the previous day. As others turned up and the room began filling with shouts and laughter, Samia took out the green notebook Katie had given her, pressing it open at the first page.

Ricky's eyes were immediately drawn to the words written in large, looping handwriting. These were Samia's private thoughts yet she didn't have the sense to hide them from prying eyes. It embarrassed Ricky to read what the girl had written. If Samia wanted a bra so badly, why didn't she simply ask her mother to buy her one?

Katie was telling everyone to pipe down when the door opened and Abbie floated into the workroom.

The room fell silent.

Abbie was dressed like a mannequin from a Primark window in a strapless coral pink top with a gauzy poncho over the shoulders. Her white shorts had frayed cuffs and her silver sandals had small heels. She pouted her shiny pink lips and, with a hand on her hip, twisted her body into an awkward selfie pose. She remained frozen like this for a surreal second or two before flopping into her chair with a bored 'Ha'. The previous day when asked who she most admired, Abbie had named Kim Kardashian. Ricky had asked her why.

'Poise and grace,' replied Abbie. Kardashian was a legend. She gave so much to the world. 'Too much.'

'A lot like Muhammad Ali then.'

Abbie made an *icky* face. 'I don't listen to rap.'

When it was Samia's turn to name an icon, she'd surprised everyone by choosing Serena Williams.

'She doesn't care what other people think,' Samia explained. 'No one messes with Serena.'

Ricky started paying her more attention after that. She was pleased Samia had chosen to sit next to her again.

'Today, we are going to work on something a bit more personal,' said Katie.

She was walking around the table, distributing large sheets of paper. It was unlined and had 'Something that Defines Me' printed at the top.

'It could be a poster on the wall of your bedroom or something you do every day like brushing your teeth,' she said. 'Think about it before you start writing or drawing. You can be serious or funny but whatever you choose, it has to be real.'

Ricky didn't need to think. For her, the best way to begin a story was to leap into the chaos of it. She began to write:

'Throughout history, people have built forts to keep themselves safe. Forts are usually made of stone and have high walls with narrow slits for arrows and funnels for boiling oil. When I build a fort, I use rugs and cushions but once I'm inside, I feel safe even though someone could easily stab me from outside.'

Samia's page was still blank.

'Have you ever visited another country?' Ricky prompted.

Samia nodded. 'Only Bangladesh.'

'Why not write about it?'

'It's not interesting.'

'To me it is.'

She looked surprised, disbelieving.

'Is it noisy?'

She nodded. 'There are people everywhere.'

'You could describe them. What they wear or eat. Do people in Bangladesh have pets?'

'They don't like dogs.'

'Poor dogs.'

'I like dogs but cats are my favourite.' Samia's face lit up. 'I want a kitten. A fluffy one would be best.'

'You could write about a fluffy kitten.'

'You think so?'

'Of course! You should write about something you care about.'

Samia picked up a pencil and after asking once again if kittens were a suitable topic, she began to write. Ricky went back to her story.

'I have been building forts for as long as I can remember. I built one under the table on the day my mother came home from the hospital with my brother Ollie. He was a tiny pink thing with no hair and I was very annoyed with him. He's six now and has improved a lot. If I had to choose between my brother and my Discovery Channel microscope, I would choose Ollie. That is saying a lot. I really like my microscope. I can see the bristles on insect legs. Insects are very, very bristly up close. Even their bottoms have bristles but I'll save that information for another story.'

The British Telecom engineer was in the kitchen when Ricky came home. Dan greeted her with exaggerated warmth and might have tried something ridiculous like ruffling her hair if she hadn't noticed him raising his hand and swiftly sidestepped him.

'Is this your daughter?' asked the BT man.

'No, we're just friends.' Dan laughed.

The BT man shot Ricky a look.

She shook her head.

The BT man frowned.

Dan laughed again, unaware that his stupid joke had fallen flat. 'I'm her new stepdad, more or less.'

She pulled a face.

The BT man gave Dan an impatient look. 'Show me where the wall socket is.'

Ricky was buttering bread when Dan returned to the kitchen. She could feel him looking at her, but kept her eyes on the sandwich she was putting together.

'Your mum called. She won't make it home until late afternoon,' he said. 'Will you be okay at the community centre?'

'I'll be fine until four o'clock,' Ricky replied. She wasn't lying. She would be fine and dandy until four.

'They need to give your brother another scan. A different kind.' He sucked air through his teeth in a self-important way. 'It's looking more serious.'

Ricky was aware that Dan was watching her carefully, waiting for a reaction so he could play the all-knowing, all-caring adult.

'Tell Mum I'm fine.'

'Are you sure you're fine, Princess?'

*Princess?* She wanted to scream. 'Of course.'

Of course, she wasn't. She felt sick. What was looking more serious and why did Dan know more about her brother's condition than she did?

Ricky took the sandwich through to the other room where the BT man was on his knees fiddling with wires poking out of a small hole in the wall. She put the plate on the carpet beside him.

'I made this for you,' she said. 'It's cheese and pickle. My mother made the pickle. She's a trained chef.'

'Thank you,' he said. 'That's kind of you.'

'She's very pretty.'

'Who's that, love?'

'Mum.'

He smiled.

'Please get the broadband working. I need to stay in touch with my father.'

The BT man looked concerned. 'Are your parents divorced?'

'It's just a temporary separation. Mum will come to her senses soon.'

'What about his nibs in the kitchen?'

'He won't be around very long.'

'Is that what your mum says?'

'No, he's got a very dangerous job. He's a roofer. I'm hoping for the best.'

It took the BT man a moment but she could hear him laughing as she walked down the hall. His laughter put a spring in her step. If she could generate enough bad feeling toward Dan it might have a cumulative effect. She imagined the accumulated feeling as the blast from a jet engine, powerful enough to blow him off the top of Westminster Cathedral.

She locked the bathroom door and leaned against the basin, basking in the glow of her small triumph. She allowed her gaze to wander over the toiletries on the shelf, taking comfort from the familiar shapes of her mother's creams and lotions. All the products were ordinary brands, bought in Boots on three for two deals. Her mother didn't need fancy stuff. She was a natural beauty. Far too good for the likes of Dan.

Ricky's eyes moved to the window ledge above the bath and came to an abrupt halt. The Lynx body spray was a new addition, a sinister and incongruous presence in the family bathroom. It was an intrusion, like a shark trying to mingle with a shoal of bluefin tuna. Dan was not part of the family. He did not live with them and had no right to leave his rubbish in the family bathroom.

Ricky wanted to barge into the kitchen and hurl the plastic bottle at Dan's head, drawing blood if necessary. She closed her eyes and started counting. What was happening to her, this yo-yoing between despair, rage, yearning and sadness?

When she opened her eyes, she realised she wasn't alone. A large house spider was elegantly climbing up the shower curtain. It was brown with a subtle pattern on its back, its segmented legs tapering to delicate points. Ricky was a friend to spiders. They ate aphids and, contrary to what stupid people believed, they didn't want to bite humans. On any other day, she would have scooped the creature into a glass and transported it outside to safety. But there were no glasses in the new bathroom and she couldn't pass through the kitchen without dealing with Dan and his attempts at friendship and intimacy.

She brought her face up close to the spider. It stopped moving and lifted its two front legs.

'Be careful,' she whispered. 'There's a maniac on the loose. He's got a man bun and smells like Lynx.'

Ricky imagined herself through the spider's eight eyes. She was a kaleidoscope of something enormous and menacing like the flying saucer in *Independence Day*.

'I'll come back later and put you outside.'

A ghost train was supposed to be a scary trip through an old, haunted mansion. But there was nothing remotely ghostly about the scene that greeted Ricky in front of the Cloneys' garage. The dirty white roller door was sitting in full sunlight. The sun was baking the driveway, its concrete slabs intensifying the heat and light, bleaching the colours out of everything.

Caitlin and Abbie had set up a trestle table in the only shade available under a scraggly tree. Ricky stood back for a moment to watch them unobserved. She felt drawn to and repelled by these girls. They were nothing like the friends she'd had in Brixton. Caitlin and Abbie were prickly and unreliable. They weren't even friends but at least they were available, more or less.

Baby was lying deflated under the table. The dog raised its head lazily and let out a half-hearted bark. Abbie put down her Coke Zero and elbowed Caitlin.

'Where's this great ghost maze then?' Ricky asked.

'It's in the garage. I already told you,' said Caitlin, all high and mighty. 'We're just waiting for my brother. He's the technician.'

'I thought he was a part-time DJ.'

Abbie rolled her eyes dramatically and made a 'Doh' sound. 'Pauly is a genius,' she said. 'He can do anything.'

Caitlin nodded modestly. 'A man for all seasons.'

'What do I get for five quid?' Ricky was rapidly going off the ghost maze idea. The girls had no idea of customer service. They could have at least pretended to be friendly.

'You get a ghostly experience with a world-class light show.' Caitlin raised one eyebrow, pleased with her advertising spiel. 'But I should warn you.' She dry-coughed for effect. 'Our garage has a genuine ghost.'

'Uh-huh.'

'It's the ghost of Caitlin's uncle.' Abbie couldn't help herself. 'He's a restless spirit.'

Ricky dug her fingernails into her palms to stop herself laughing. 'I take it he's dead then?'

Caitlin nodded gravely but not without pride. Not everyone had a dead uncle. 'He was murdered in cold blood. Stabbed through the heart and, er, in one of his legs.'

'*Mutilated*.' Abbie crushed the Coke can with her hands.

Caitlin flinched.

Ricky almost laughed again. 'Was your uncle some kind of gangster?'

'No, her uncle's actually a—'

Caitlin elbowed Abbie in the ribs.

'Ouch!' Abbie pouted. 'You shouldn't have told me if it's such a big, dirty secret.'

Ricky examined Caitlin carefully. Abbie had spoken of the uncle in the present tense. 'What's the big, dirty secret?'

'None of your business.' Caitlin narrowed her eyes.

'Is your uncle even dead?'

'Of course he's dead.' Caitlin shot Abbie a look. 'He looked extremely good for a dead person.'

'You saw your dead uncle?' Ricky had seen dead birds and a dead rat but never a dead human.

'They had an open coffin.'

'Did they put makeup on him?'

'Shut up! My uncle's not a faggot.'

There was that present tense again. 'But I read that they powder the dead.'

Abbie sniggered.

'I said, shut up! My uncle had a really huge funeral with horses and everything. The horses had big feathers, for your information.'

Ricky had once observed such a funeral procession move through Brixton. She'd been on her way to Tesco with her father when their route had been blocked by a long parade of rough-looking people in black clothing following a horse-drawn hearse. 'Look at those poor horses,' her father had said. 'They're embarrassed. Only crooks and royalty put plumage on an animal.'

'I don't get why your uncle wants to haunt your garage.'

Caitlin gave Ricky a warning look. She was asking too many questions. 'Because he fucking well wants to.'

With a mild *woof*, Baby announced Samia's arrival.

'Am I too late?' she asked, catching her breath.

'Yes,' said Abbie.

'Sorry.'

'But we might be able to squeeze you in.' A sly look came into Caitlin's eyes. 'Did you bring the money?'

Samia flashed a grateful smile and dumped a handful of coins on the table.

'Ha, ha! Did you rob a piggy bank?'

'I didn't rob it. It's mine.'

Caitlin snorted and counted the coins. Satisfied, she whispered something to Abbie.

They both laughed.

'What's funny?' asked Samia.

'Nah-thing,' said Abbie.

'No, what?'

Abbie smirked. 'Caitlin thinks your boobs haven't even started yet.'

'They have.'

Ricky winced.

'I'm getting a bra and everything.' Samia looked like she was about to cry.

'I'm not getting breasts,' said Ricky. 'I don't want them.'

The girls looked at Ricky as if she'd lost her mind. Their eyes fell on her chest, searching for signs of life but found nothing satisfying. Earlier that morning, Ricky had made a bandeau out of an old and very tight tank top. By cutting off the straps and doubling it over her chest, she'd flattened the small buds of her breasts into a satisfying plane. She'd pulled another tank top over this before putting on a baggy t-shirt.

'You're just saying that,' Abbie said, sliding her thumb inside the neck of her top and adjusting a pink strap. 'Everyone wants boobs.' Abbie let go of the bra strap. It pinged back in place. 'The bigger, the better.'

'Mum used to work with a woman who had a breast reduction. Her breasts were so big, they gave her blurred vision and headaches.'

'There's nothing wrong with my eyesight,' Abbie scoffed. 'My boobs don't give me headaches.'

'They would if they were too big. The bigger they are, the harder they fall. The really big ones sag and end up dangling in your drinks.'

The drinks comment seemed to have an effect. The girls were quiet for a moment as they considered the possibility of their breasts dangling in drinks.

Baby barked again, this time a proper dog bark.

Abbie sat up and pushed out her chest. She smiled daintily. 'Look, it's Pauly!'

By the way the girls had talked, Ricky was expecting a six-foot football player powering through the estate on a Segway. But Pauly Cloney was the teenage boy she'd spied from behind the hedge. Of course, he was Caitlin's brother. The chunky gene ran like a vein of gold through the Cloney line. He turned and said something to another boy, a wiry youth who was taking one step to every two of Pauly's.

An electrical feeling of alarm ran up Ricky's legs. The second boy was part of the pack that had chased her from the tower blocks. She moved aside as they sauntered past the small table. Without acknowledging the girls, Pauly lifted the roller door and they disappeared into the garage.

Ricky could hear them laughing behind the door and realised this was a setup, a cruel joke. She knew what teenage boys were like and didn't want to be trapped inside a hot, dark place with two particularly hostile ones. Caitlin was watching her, smiling, silently daring her to reveal herself as a coward. If Ricky backed out now, the two older girls would make her life hell.

The roller door opened a couple of feet. One of the boys whistled from inside.

Samia's eyes widened.

'Come on,' said Ricky, leading the girl to the gap in the door.

In front of Caitlin and Abbie, Ricky had remained calm but once the door was pulled down behind them, she was like a cat with its hackles raised, cautious and alert. It was humid and airless in the garage. Beside her, Samia was breathing heavily.

Ricky's eyes took a moment to adjust to Pauly's world-class light show, an orange lava lamp and single ribbon of Christmas lights. In the intermittent flash of the coloured lights, she assessed the situation. The garage was large, wide enough for two cars, but much of the space was taken up by boxes of merchandise stacked haphazardly against the walls. She recognised brand names on cartons: Sony, Philips, Toshiba, Samsung. There were also dozens of unmarked boxes, many of them overflowing with pans, crockery and other household items. Ricky counted seven boxes of Nike trainers.

In the middle of the garage, the boys had constructed a small citadel out of boxes. The entrance to this construction was a narrow tunnel inside a cardboard arch.

The lava lamp and Christmas lights were extinguished and the girls were plunged into darkness. The only light was coming from outside through narrow gaps around the roller door.

'Enter!'

The command had come from within the cardboard tunnel. A red light appeared, a flickering red glow, like a bicycle tail light.

Ricky felt Samia's fingers seek out her hand. She grasped them tightly and, hunching low, pulled her under the arch and into the tunnel.

The red light stopped flickering. Total darkness. Silence, apart from Samia's rapid breathing behind her.

*Bang, bang, bang.*

The noise was beside them and over them. The boys were pummelling the cardboard with their fists.

The drumming stopped. Someone started moaning.

'Woo. Woo.'

A ghostly head floated in front of them and then disappeared.

Samia squealed and crushed Ricky's hand.

When the floating head appeared again, Ricky recognised the boy from the tower block. He had a sheet over his face and a torch under his chin. She tugged Samia forward but when they got to the place where the head had been, the opening in the wall of boxes had been closed. Ricky held up her hand to a blade of light coming through a chink in the boxes. A sliver of visibility was better than total blindness. It gave her confidence.

They reached the end of the first tunnel and followed a bend to the left. They were moving away from the garage door and into total darkness when Ricky's knee hit a barrier. She stopped abruptly, causing Samia to bump into her.

Ricky could hear movement on either side of them.

Something brushed Ricky's face. It was fluffy like a feather duster. She raised her arm to push it away and, in doing so, exposed her torso. The assault was swift and brutal. A hand grabbed at her chest, squeezing and then twisting painfully before disappearing between the boxes.

Tears stung her eyes. It was the pain and shock of the violation followed by burning humiliation. Within seconds, her feelings had flipped to rage. Boiling hot, red rage. It was Caitlin's fault. It was Dan's fault. It was King's Crescent. It was her mother. It was the painful lumps on her chest. The shame of them.

Kicking away the barrier, Ricky tugged Samia forward, her free hand now a tight fist. The drumming began again, louder this time. It followed them as they came to yet another bend. So much for the maze. The boys had built a simple square of tunnels. By her calculations, they only had one more turn and they would be almost out of this hell.

'Wooooo!'

The ghostly moan was accompanied by a jet of warm air against her leg like a weak blast from a hand dryer. Ricky looked down and, straining her eyes, caught the reflection of something metallic. It was a tube about the width of an exhaust pipe. She lifted her leg, and with a mixture of rage and exaltation, kicked the end of the pipe, driving it back toward whoever was holding it.

'Argh!'

The cry was followed by the sound of something heavy falling on concrete. Then there was moaning, the genuine moans of someone in pain.

Samia whimpered.

'Don't worry,' Ricky whispered.

Samia whimpered again.

'Shhh.'

Ricky pulled her forward. As they turned the final bend, she could see light from below the garage door. They were on the home stretch.

'Ouch!' Samia bumped into her.

'What's wrong?'

'Someone pinched my bottom.'

Ricky saw the offending hand disappear through a narrow space between the boxes. She stopped moving and waited.

When it appeared again, she was ready. She swung her arm

down to karate chop the boy's wrist, hard and fast. The impact must have knocked him off balance because the arm fell to the ground. Without wasting a second, Ricky raised her foot and stamped down on the fingers with the heel of her trainer, twisting it around as if grinding out a cigarette. The crunching sound made Samia gasp but Ricky was already on the move, pulling her forward and out of the cardboard torture chamber.

Caitlin sniggered as they pushed up the roller door to emerge, blinking into the sunlight.

'You two look like you've seen a ghost. Did you shit your pants?'

Samia dropped Ricky's hand and announced weakly that she had to go home. Without saying goodbye, she rapidly started walking away.

'It was very scary,' said Ricky. Slowly, she began to create distance between herself and the source of the moaning that was coming from the garage.

'Lightweights!'

'It's a world-class operation,' Ricky edged further away. 'That uncle of yours couldn't keep his hands off us.'

'Ha, ha!' Caitlin stood up and squinted into the garage. She cupped her hands around her mouth. 'You can stop now. The suckers have left the building.'

The moaning continued.

Caitlin shoved the garage door further up. 'What the fuck?'

Pauly was lying on the ground with his back to them, moaning. He was writhing, his movements slow and deliberate. He rolled over.

Abbie screamed.

The boy opened his bloodied mouth and spat out something.

'Was that a tooth?' asked Abbie.

Ricky had made it to the footpath when the second boy stumbled out from behind the cardboard construction. He was cradling his hand. Tears were streaming over his cheeks.

She was running, wild and joyful, roaring with pent-up anger and excitement. She felt as if she'd swallowed a jar of bees. Her heart was pumping. Her bones were humming. Her feet were wings. She was flying across the estate like a swift. Nothing could catch her.

She burst through the garden gate with a *whoop* and dropped to a crouch, panting heavily until she regained her breath. When she looked up, she saw Snowy standing next to his roses, observing her with a pair of secateurs in his hand. He looked fearful, as if expecting trouble.

'Hello, Mr Snow,' she said. 'I've just been practising my sprint.'

She got to her feet and, after putting on the gloves she'd used the previous day, returned to the herb garden to resume weeding.

Within minutes, the smell of green things and the damp softness of the soil began to calm the craziness inside her. The Cloneys and their dark garage retreated from her thoughts. So did Dan and his sickening body spray. Very soon she was absorbed by the life of the garden. She was part of the earth and air. She was a plant putting down roots, reaching skyward to harness the gold of the sun and transform it into liquid green energy.

She had been working for half an hour when Snowy grunted in his strange language. He was holding out a big yellow rose, an old-fashioned, velvety thing.

'What a beauty,' she said.

When he grunted again, she took it from his outstretched hand. She pushed her nose into its soft, cool petals, breathing in deeply, her senses diving into the heart of the bloom.

When she looked up, filled with the rose, she found Snowy watching her, a look of suppressed excitement on his face.

# 6

HER MOTHER DIDN'T want to hear her side of the story. These days, she wasn't interested in anything Ricky said or did. When she wasn't at the hospital with Ollie, she was telling her daughter what she was not allowed to do or what she was doing wrong.

Ricky had been in Ollie's room, reading him a story, when her mother shrieked her name. A shout was never ideal but a shriek meant Code Red, batten down the hatches, man overboard!

She knew immediately that the person sitting at the dining table was Caitlin's mother. The unhappy woman had the same massive forehead and minuscule blue eyes as her daughter and son.

'There you are,' said her mother, as if she'd been hiding.

'Here I am,' Ricky replied.

'Don't be cheeky.' She pointed to the empty chair beside her. 'Sit down.'

Her mother's tone seemed to please Mrs Cloney. Her small mouth unpuckered a millimetre.

'This is Mrs Cloney.'

'I know.'

'Have you two already met?'

'No, I know her daughter, Caitlin.'

Her mother frowned, confused.

Ricky shrugged. 'They look almost identical.'

Mrs Cloney nodded with pride.

'Same big forehead.'

'That's enough!' Her mother's face was like thunder, booming thunder.

'My boy has no front teeth thanks to you!' hissed Mrs Cloney.

Ricky thought of her father and channelled his mantra: *Never apologise. Never explain.*

'Did you hurt Mrs Cloney's son?'

Ricky didn't say anything.

'Did you?'

'She did it all right and someone's got to pay to have his teeth fixed.' Mrs Cloney folded her arms. 'My son's not a liar.'

Her son was most probably a liar and definitely a creep. Ricky could have described how he'd grabbed at them in the dark but this would have prompted questions about why she was in the garage with two teenage boys when she was supposed to be at the community centre.

'Poor Pauly,' said Ricky, finally. She sighed dramatically.

Her mother frowned again.

'He goes to secondary school, doesn't he?'

Mrs Cloney nodded in a vague way. Pauly probably didn't attend school very often.

'He's a young man really.'

'That's enough.' Her mother was losing patience.

'But I want to apologise to Mrs Cloney. I'm very, very sorry about your son's teeth.' Ricky thought of how Pauly had cruelly twisted the flesh on her chest. It had been painful and humiliating. The boy deserved to lose every tooth in his stupid head.

Mrs Cloney pushed out her chin. 'Sorry is not enough. There's dental bills to pay.'

'I hope Pauly won't be embarrassed.'

'Why would my son be embarrassed? You're the one who hurt him.'

'He'll hate all his friends to know how he lost his teeth, won't he? Even though it was an accident.'

'It was no accident.'

'Is that what you want me to tell everyone, that I managed to knock the teeth out of such a big, strong boy on purpose?' She smiled sweetly. 'I'm only twelve and quite small for my age.'

'Shut up, you little bitch!' Mrs Cloney's chair hit the wall with a thud. She stood up and glared at Ricky before giving her mother the full force of her charm. 'My family has been living on this estate for over twenty years. We've got influence on the crescent. You need to control your daughter. She's a bloody menace.'

'I beg your pardon?' Now Ricky's mother was on her feet.

'You heard me. Sort her out or someone else will do it for you.'

'Is that a threat?'

'Call it what you like.'

'I don't care who you are or how long you've been here. No one comes into my home and tells me what to do with my daughter.' Her mother thumped the table. 'No one threatens my family!'

'You haven't heard the last of this.'

Ricky was on her feet and made it to the door before Mrs Cloney. 'I saw all the boxes in your garage,' she said.

Mrs Cloney shuffled her Nike trainers. Her face was the colour of a London double decker. 'Get out of my way.'

'How much is a new flat screen?'

'Shut up!'

'How much are the trainers?'

'Shut up, shut up!'

Ricky was smiling as she opened the door.

Mrs Cloney hissed through her teeth, too low for Ricky's mother to hear. 'Pauly will get you for this.'

With a loud curse, she burst out of the flat.

Ricky and her mother watched her stomp down the steps of the building, arms flailing.

'Why were you inside their garage?'

'I was walking home with a couple of girls from the community centre. We only popped in. I wasn't there for long.'

'You shouldn't have been there at all.'

'I'm sorry. I won't ever go there again.'

'Stay away from that boy. That family is bad news.' Her mother was about to say something else when her mobile rang. She gave Ricky a distracted nod before reaching into her bag.

Things would have gone very differently if they had still been living in Brixton. Ricky would have been properly grilled about the incident and punished for hurting the boy. She would have had her wings clipped and her pocket money cut.

None of these things happened. After the phone call, her mother had curled up on the couch and closed her eyes. She wasn't sleeping but it was clear she no longer wanted to talk.

As London began to bake and sizzle in the summer heat, Ricky's problems piled up like a shaky tower of Jenga. The most precarious piece, the piece that kept threatening to make everything fall apart was Ollie. She didn't understand what was going on with her little brother. He was now spending the bulk of his days at the hospital but no one would tell her why. When Ollie came home, he was quiet and distant. He needed more tests, her mother said, but how many tests did a six-year-old boy need? He was now sporting permanent plasters on both arms and had dark circles under his eyes. The hospital visits were also taking a toll on Ricky's mother. Her face was pale and her lips had lost their colour. Even her hair was dull. She'd become less talkative but more irritable, especially where Ricky was concerned.

She didn't say good morning when Ricky walked past the couch on her way to the kitchen.

Ricky stopped and retraced her steps.

'Are you and Ollie going to the hospital today?' she asked.

Her mother was looking at the blank television screen as if she was watching a programme. It took her a moment to register her daughter's presence.

'No, it's Saturday.'

'Can we go to the heath? It's got a lido.'

'No.'

'Why not?'

She frowned. 'We just can't.'

'But we never do anything anymore.'

'Don't whine.'

'I hate Camden. It's stupid.'

'Shut up!'

Ricky was shocked. Her mother never told her to shut up, ever. She blinked against the pressure of tears. 'Why are you so horrible?'

Her mother's eyes widened. 'What did you say?'

'I said you're horrible. Have you got your period?'

'Right! I'm calling your father. He can deal with you.'

'Good! He's a better parent than you anyway.' Ricky was boiling, boiling, boiling.

Her mother's mouth dropped open. Her eyes filled with tears. 'I can't believe you just said that.'

'You made us come to this stupid place because you wanted to be with your stupid boyfriend. Now Ollie is sick and it's all your fault. He was fine in Brixton.'

Ricky was Mount Etna. Her anger was molten rock, bursting out of her, rampaging over the town of Pompeii and destroying everything in its path: trees, old people, children, pet dogs. Nothing was safe. Life in the present was burning and the future was about to go up in flames.

A tear rolled down her mother's cheek. She wiped it away and took several breaths before looking at Ricky. Her expression hardened. 'Aren't you forgetting something?'

Ricky swallowed. It didn't feel right to make her mother cry but she couldn't back down now. 'No.'

'Your father has a girlfriend.'

'So?'

'So!' Her mother crossed her arms. 'So, it's not just me, is it? Sophie has been around for a lot longer than Dan.'

'She means nothing to Dad! NOTHING!'

Ricky ran to her bedroom and slammed the door. She snatched the crocheted rug off her bed and hurled it over the desk before crawling inside the makeshift fort. Wrapping her arms tightly around her knees, she closed her eyes and clenched her jaw. At any moment, her mother was going to burst in and read her the riot act.

Gradually, the pressure in her ears eased and the whirl of emotions subsided. As her mind stilled and cleared, self-doubt began to creep in. Her thoughts turned inward and accusing. She pictured her mother's tears and felt guilty. Her thoughts spiralled downward and she found herself regretting all her past mistakes. She remembered the spider she'd found in the bathroom. Why hadn't she picked it up and put it out the window? *Stupid.* She'd found the poor thing after returning from Snowy's garden. It was in the bath, crumpled after Dan had taken a shower, its elegant legs contracted in death.

The call of a blackbird flowed through her bedroom window, penetrating the woollen walls of her fort. She raised her head from her knees, eager to hear more of its song but the bird fell silent. Outside her window, leaves were rustling. Somewhere below, a child was crying. A man shouted. Something clanged, metal on metal. The man shouted again. A dog barked.

She pushed aside the rug and listened for noises inside the flat. Silence. No sound of her mother's footsteps. No one calling Ricky for breakfast. She poked her head out to look at her Wonder Woman clock but someone had turned it to face the window. She cursed Ollie for going through her things and crawled over to the clock.

It took her a moment to work out but she realised she'd been under her desk for only twenty minutes. Why did it feel like an hour?

'Can I come in?' Ollie's voice was small. It was the one he used when he'd had a bad dream and wanted to share her bed.

'If you must,' she said.

'I never thought I'd say this,' he said, sitting on the corner of the bed. He was wearing shorty pyjamas patterned with tiny robots. Scotty was under one of his arms. 'I'm bored with the Netbook.'

'Uh-huh.'

'Why are you on the floor?'

'I've been doing the exercises Dad taught me. I'm building my stamina.'

'I don't have any stamina.'

'Dad's coming over today.'

Ollie didn't say anything.

'I said, Dad's coming over today.'

He shrugged. 'Don't get your hopes up.'

'Not listening!'

Ricky closed her eyes and put her fingers in her ears. She was underwater, a Dover sole, invisible on the bottom of the English Channel. She pictured the sole's flat face with its odd, Picasso eyes and changed her mind. She was a killer whale with big teeth and an appetite for small boys who showed no loyalty. Ricky took her fingers out of her ears. She opened her eyes and glared at her brother.

'Mum said she was calling Dad.'

'Whatever.'

Ollie was like a carving knife. He could cut through her hopes with a word or sometimes just a look. It wasn't normal for a six-year-old to be so sharp.

Ricky glanced at the clock and immediately looked away. Ollie had been staring at his feet for at least a minute, waiting for her to say something. Sixty seconds had gone forever but this didn't seem to bother him at all. For Ricky, time was a massive, incomprehensible thing. Thinking about it was like swimming against an outgoing tide. If she fell into the trap of trying to figure out what it was, it pulled her under and made her feel as if she was drowning. She knew this feeling had something to do with her father, the way he broke promises and kept her waiting, but she couldn't bear to blame him. Blaming him was her mother's job. She was an expert at it.

She looked at the clock again. 'Have you been touching my things?'

'No, I have not.'

'Well, someone has been messing around in here and it's not the first time either.' Ricky had started noticing little changes in her room. Pens and pencils moved on her desk, a drawer opened and not shut properly, a pillow askew.

'It wasn't me.'

Ricky gave him a look.

'I've been at the hospital.'

She considered this.

'What's that?'

Ollie pointed to her notebook sitting on the small table next to the bed. Ricky had been writing in it before going to sleep and had forgotten to put it away. As Katie had predicted, it had become an outlet for things she couldn't share with anyone. She thought about what she'd written the previous evening: *There's no use saying anything. She won't believe me. She'll just get angry.*

Ollie sniffed, impatient.

'Katie gave it to me.'

'Do you write stories in it?'

'I've been writing stories at the workshop. Katie says I've got talent.'

'I could've told you that.' Ollie got off the bed and lay down beside her. 'Can I have a look inside your notebook?'

'It's private.'

'Just a peek.' He leaned his head against her shoulder. 'I am very private myself. Private, but a very good reader.'

The weight of his head and the touch of his downy hair on her neck made her feel like crying, not the crying she'd wanted to do after fighting with her mother but a soft, grateful release.

'It's private and personal.'

'Then the least you could do is tell me a story.' He sought out her hand. 'I'm not feeling well, you know.'

'I'll tell you a story if you tell me what's wrong with you.'

He closed his eyes. 'It's just sicky-ness.'

'Describe it.'

Ollie took a deep breath.

'I'm waiting.'

'I feel like I'm in a car on a twisty road.' He sniffed. 'Like I want to be sick. My head is sore. It feels like I'm wearing a very small hat.'

'What do the doctors say?'

'They only talk to Mum.'

'They think you're stupid but that's not all bad. It's better the enemy underestimates you.'

'I don't think they are the enemy. They're trying to fix me.'

'Don't nitpick.'

'I did hear one thing.' Ollie opened his eyes and looked at her.

'Well?'

'It was when I was having the first scan.'

'What did you hear?'

'The doctor was talking. She didn't know I'd taken out my earplugs. I heard her say something.'

'What?'

'She said, "It's got its own blood supply."'

Ricky felt a tremor travel up her spine. She took a deep breath and tried to bring her nervous system under control. She started counting to ten very slowly.

'That's hellishly interesting,' she said, finally.

'What?'

'Your condition. It's very rare.'

Ollie smiled. Rare was good. Very rare was excellent. 'What is it?'

'Promise you won't go telling people?'

Ollie snuggled closer. 'I won't. What is it?'

'You've got a very, very rare parasitic twin.'

'What's that?'

'It's like those wooden dolls of Mum's. You've got a miniature Ollie inside you, a copy.'

'Like a pet?'

'He's your twin brother so you should show respect.'

'What's his name?'

'He doesn't have one.'

'I'll call him Cromwell then.'

She put her lips close to his ear and lowered her voice to a whisper. 'Now, promise not to tell Mum you know about him.'

Ollie nodded and closed his eyes. After a few seconds, his breathing slowed and he began to sleep. Ricky closed her eyes and pushed her nose into the curve of his neck. She breathed in his little boy smell and felt herself relaxing and letting go.

The tap of something hitting the window roused her from sleep. At first she thought it was a bird but when she got up and looked outside, she discovered a ball of paper caught on the window ledge. Whoever had thrown it had disappeared. She flattened it out and found a handwritten message:

'You are personally invited to a séance. We are going to ask the spirits for guidance and need many hands. Meet us tonight at the playground at 11 pm. Come alone.'

Despite everything that had happened, all the recent trouble and misunderstandings, Ricky felt her spirits lift. Someone wanted her.

# 7

MOVING STEALTHILY LIKE a cat, Ricky climbed out of her bedroom window and, using the new strength in her arms, swung down from the narrow ledge to the top of the neighbour's fence. From there, she lowered herself to the path below the building.

As her feet touched down, she knew she was about to change her life forever. Never before had she done anything so absolutely wrong. Sneaking out of the flat in the middle of the night was foolhardy and dangerous. She stood completely still for a moment to savour her audacity and fill her lungs with the cool night air. Her heart was beating so hard, she could feel a vibration along the crowns of her teeth. It was dark and she was completely on her own in the middle of London. With a shiver, she thought of the drunk man who had shouted at her on their first night in Camden. Her mind, restless and alert, then latched on to the more urgent threat of Pauly Cloney. He could be hiding close by, waiting. If something happened to her now, there would be no witnesses and no one around to save her. She could be kidnapped, attacked, *murdered*.

As she began to move, she thought of Dan and avoided the pavement and glow of street lamps. Dan had started going out after dinner to the pub on King's Crescent and returning to the flat late at night. Ricky knew this because she'd been woken by the slamming of the front door. Her father would have been savaged for such behaviour but Dan could do no wrong in her mother's eyes.

Ricky followed the hedge until she was on the opposite side of the playground to the gate. As she peered through the fence, she saw two outlines. A mobile phone screen illuminated, throwing light over the faces of the girls. Ricky waited until she was sure they were alone before creeping up behind them.

'Evening!' she said.

Abbie and Caitlin jumped.

'Fuck sake,' said Caitlin.

'Where's the séance?'

'Follow us.'

'I'm not moving until you tell me where we're going.'

Caitlin shot Abbie a look. 'We're going to the haunted flat.'

'Is this another dead uncle?'

'Shut up.'

'It's a completely different dead person,' said Abbie.

'Who?'

'A boy. He was murdered inside the actual flat. It's been empty for ages but there have been sightings.'

'Of what?'

'Supernatural activity.'

Ricky didn't believe a word of it. 'How was he murdered?'

'Tortured and tortured until finally he . . . expired. Cigarette burns over his entire body. Bruises, slash marks. You name it.' Abbie dropped her voice to a whisper. '*Mutilated.*'

'How do you know this?'

'Common knowledge,' said Caitlin. 'The killer was on the sex offenders' list. Mum knows all about it.'

'Does your mother know you're out here?'

'Don't be stupid.'

'I left a note in my room just in case.' Ricky had left no such thing.

'Why?'

'If I go missing, Mum will know where to start searching for my corpse.'

'You're so fucking weird.'

The flat was a small end unit on the ground floor, its patio hidden behind a shabby, wood-panelled fence. Ricky put her eye to a gap in the panels and saw an upturned plastic chair and a mop leaning against a wall, nothing to indicate a crime scene. The curtains were closed and the lights were off.

Caitlin led them to the side of the patio and pointed to a sag in the fence. 'When you get up there, pop the window with this. It's not locked.' She held out an orange-handled screw-driver. 'Send out a signal when you've opened it.'

'Why should I go first?' Ricky asked.

Caitlin looked at Abbie. 'Told you.'

Abbie sniggered.

'You're scared, aren't you?'

Ricky didn't move. Of course she was scared and it wasn't because of ghosts. For all she knew, Pauly and his one-armed friend were waiting inside, eager to deal out some payback.

'Are you going to do it or just stand there looking stupid?'

Ricky snatched the screwdriver from Caitlin's hands. It was a large, heavy tool, the perfect weapon for smashing the teeth of an enemy, that was if the enemy had any teeth to smash.

'When you get inside, cup your hands around your mouth like this.' Caitlin formed a sound tunnel with her hands. 'Then call out, "Kakakoo".'

'Why?'

'Just shut up and do it.'

Ricky grabbed the top of the fence and swung herself up and over, landing quietly on the patio. The quicker she moved the better. The trick was to act, not think. She inserted the screwdriver into the aluminium window frame and wiggled. It popped and she tugged it open. She took a deep breath and climbed inside, landing softly on scratchy carpet.

Scrambling to her feet, she thrust the screwdriver in front of her like a sword. Fear was drumming in her ears. She pulled back one of the curtains to let in some light and saw that she was in the flat's living room. Her breathing was loud in the stillness of the empty space. She remained motionless for a moment, waiting for her heart to slow and the drumming in her ears to ease. The air was musty. The place had a dull, empty feel. With relief, she realised she was alone.

The sound of the girls' whispers drifted in through the open window, spurring her into action. She crossed the room and opened the door to peer into the kitchen. Streetlight was coming through a small window above the sink. Ricky could make out a pinewood table without chairs. Cupboards and drawers were open. The room was neglected and dismal but it didn't look like a murder scene. There were no bloodstains or chalk outlines. No smell of death.

Bolder now, she headed down the hall to the bedroom. She tried to imagine a murderer living in the flat but found it impossible. A stale, acrid odour pervaded the rooms. It was sad here, the sadness of an abandoned dwelling. She pushed open the bathroom door with the toe of her trainer and immediately regretted it. The smell was overwhelming. Hastily, she backtracked.

She stuck her head out of the open window and cupped her hands around her mouth. 'Kookakoo!'

'It's *kakakoo*, stupid.' Caitlin's head and then body appeared over the top of the fence. She landed heavily with an 'Oomph' before turning back to help Abbie.

Ricky stood to the side as the girls climbed through the window.

'We're alone,' she said. 'I've looked through the flat. It's empty.'

'I knew that,' said Caitlin.

'Don't go into the bathroom.'

'Why not?' asked Abbie, her voice quivery with fear.

'It stinks.'

'Of what?'

'Caca.' Ricky laughed. 'Caca-koo.'

'Shut up.' Caitlin plonked herself heavily on the floor and unzipped her backpack. She took out a cardboard sleeve and opened it on the carpet. There was haste to her movements but also a seriousness. Whatever she'd come here to do was important.

Ricky sat down opposite her. 'What's that?'

'It's a Ouija board, stupid.'

Abbie huddled close to Caitlin. 'It's for communicating.' She filled her lungs dramatically and looked around the room. '*With the actual dead.*'

The cardboard square looked like a board game. It had a double arch of letters in Gothic script and a row of numbers from zero to nine. In the space between the letters and the numbers was a skull with bloodshot eyes and no teeth. Caitlin placed a clear plastic cup upside down on top of the skull.

'Form a circle,' she commanded.

'But there are only three of us,' said Ricky. 'The best we can do is a triangle.'

'Shut up.'

'Why do you want to do this?'

'We have unanswered questions.'

'What questions?'

'You'll see. Before we can hold a séance, we have to establish a circle of trust. Each of us has to share a secret. It has to be something that no one else knows.' She looked at Ricky. 'You start.'

'Why me?'

'Shut up and just do it.'

Ricky thought of her secret. No way was she going to share it with these girls. The only person she trusted was Ollie and, even then, she couldn't reveal the full horror of it.

'Well?'

'I have one secret but you have to swear to never tell anyone. Cross your hearts and hope to die a truly diabolical death that involves having a hand chopped off. If you breathe a word of it, I'll put a curse on you both. Before bleeding to death, you'll get really bad acne.'

'Yuck!' Abbie did not want acne.

'Do you agree to keep the secret?' Ricky waited for the girls to agree. 'It's about my brother, the one your dog Baby likes.'

Caitlin spluttered. 'Baby doesn't like him.'

'Ollie has got a serious medical condition.'

Abbie and Caitlin exchanged excited glances.

'He's been spending a lot of time at the Royal Free.'

'The Royal Free Hospital?' said Abbie, her face lighting up. 'Has he got Ebola?'

'No.'

'Ebola makes you bleed out of your ears and nose.' Abbie could hardly keep the thrill out of her voice. 'And your bottom. That would be the worst bit.'

'He's got something worse than Ebola.' Ricky paused to give them time to consider something worse than bleeding to death through the backside.

'There's nothing worse than Ebola,' said Caitlin, finally.

'Breast cancer's worse.' Abbie grimaced. 'They cut them off.'

Caitlin pulled a face.

'It's really serious.' Ricky nodded dramatically. 'My brother has got something growing inside him, a kind of parasite.'

'Like a tapeworm?' Abbie sounded hopeful.

'No, it's called a parasitic twin and it's an actual human being but really small. It's like a crazy clump of cells. Mum should have had twin boys but her egg didn't split properly. The smaller bit got trapped inside the bigger bit, which turned out to be Ollie. It's been fine until now but it's started growing and is sucking the hell out of him.'

'I don't believe you,' said Caitlin.

But Ricky could tell she was impressed. A parasitic twin was so ridiculous that it was strangely possible. It was like having a Canadian beaver as a pet. The story needed another turn of the screw.

'It's got its own blood supply.'

'How do you know?'

'They did a scan. Ollie had to drink all this pink stuff. Then they slid him inside a machine like a big metal drum. He wasn't allowed to move.' She was blinding them with science, exaggerating the details Ollie had told her. 'The machine was really noisy. Ollie said it was like being inside a concrete mixer. He could hear banging through his earplugs. It's the magnets inside the scanner. Hellishly loud.'

'What-evah.'

'They found the parasitic twin behind his gall bladder.' Ricky pointed to the general area of the gall bladder. She'd run out of science and was now ad-libbing. 'It's brown and hairy. At first, they thought it was a hairball. Then it moved.'

'Yuck.' Abbie screwed up her face. 'Are they going to get rid of it?'

'They need to do more tests but an operation would be highly dangerous. It's very close to his vital organs.' She paused a moment for this to sink in before turning to Caitlin. 'Your turn.'

Caitlin nudged Abbie. 'You go first.'

Abbie's face became serious. 'You both have to promise not to tell anyone.'

Ricky nodded but she fully intended to share everything with Ollie. She knew the girls would be broadcasting whatever she'd told them.

'I've taught myself to purge on demand.'

'Like, vomit?' Caitlin looked intrigued.

'It's called *purging*. There's a whole purging community on the internet.' Abbie explained that she'd been doing it for several months. At first, the only way she could make herself sick was by sticking her fingers down her throat. 'There's a purge button at the back of your tongue. You press it with a finger and pop, up it all comes. If you keep doing it, you can train your throat muscles to spontaneously eject.'

Ricky had to ask the obvious question. 'Why do you want to make yourself sick?'

Abbie let out a small mocking laugh. 'Who wants to swallow food?'

'That's generally how the digestive system works.'

'That's why you'll end up fat,' Caitlin scoffed.

Ricky bridled. She hated comments about her body. 'I won't get fat.'

'Yes, you will. Ha, ha.'

'What about you, Caitlin? Why don't you tell me the big, dirty secret about your uncle?'

'Shut up!'

Abbie sniggered.

Caitlin was silent for a few seconds. 'My sister—'

Ricky stopped breathing, aware that something significant was about to be revealed.

'My sister had an abortion!'

'How old is your sister?'

Caitlin's eyes flashed. 'None of your business.'

'She just turned fifteen,' said Abbie.

'Shut—' Caitlin gasped. 'What the actual fuck?'

Everyone's eyes fell on the Ouija board. The plastic cup, which had been sitting upside down on the skull, now lay on its side.

Ricky became aware of how quiet it was. There were no voices outside. No cars driving past. No dogs barking.

'Why did you bring me here?'

'We had to,' Abbie's voice was barely audible. 'You need at least three people for a séance to work.'

'Let's get this fucking thing over with.' Caitlin righted the plastic cup and instructed everyone to touch it with a fingertip. Spirits would contact them and communicate through its movements. 'Keep your eyes on the cup and concentrate. Don't put any pressure on it. Just touch it.'

'I don't see—'

'Shhh!' Caitlin glared at Ricky. 'I'll do the talking. Spirits don't like noise. We don't want to upset him.'

'But—'

'Shut up.' Caitlin looked up at the ceiling. In a voice she must have practised in front of a mirror, she called out, 'We ask the spirit here to show himself.'

Nothing happened.

'I said, show yourself.'

Silence.

'We ask the spirit that haunts this flat to show himself.'

Ricky was on the brink of saying something when the cup started vibrating beneath her finger.

It moved a fraction.

Abbie let out a squeak.

Ricky glanced from Abbie to Caitlin, looking for signs of tampering but both girls seemed genuinely surprised, even frightened. She swallowed and tried not to show alarm as the cup began to travel away from the skull.

Caitlin murmured as it moved to the letter J.

'J,' she announced, unnecessarily.

As the cup travelled to the letter O, Ricky once again checked the faces of the girls. Both were now rigid with fear. The cup moved to the letter H and then N.

'John,' said Caitlin, her voice a shaky whisper. 'Welcome.'

There was silence.

She took a deep breath. 'Do you have a message for us?'

Beneath her finger, Ricky could feel the cup vibrate again.

It started moving, faster this time. Rapidly, it spelled out, 'B-A-D'.

Caitlin nervously glanced around the room. 'We come in peace.'

The cup moved to a single letter, 'K'.

'For god's sake. Just ask him so we can get out of here,' hissed Abbie. 'This place is creeping me out.'

Caitlin once again addressed the ceiling. 'John, we are looking for the paedo who used to live on this estate. You know who I mean?'

The cup vibrated violently. 'Y-E-S.'

'We need to find him.' Her voice was on the point of hysteria. 'Where is he?'

'C-L-O-S-E.'

As Caitlin opened her mouth to speak again a gust of wind caught one of the curtains, lifting it high and sending a flash of light into the room. The cup seemed to slither out from under the girls' fingers and hurl itself in the air. It hit the wall with a *ping*.

Caitlin was the first through the window, quickly followed by Abbie.

Ricky was waiting her turn when a noise behind her made her look back. It was a faint whisking sound as if someone was sweeping a wooden floor with a stiff-bristled broom. Her eyes travelled from the abandoned Ouija board to the doorway on the other side of the room. The door was now wide open and letting in a band of streetlight from the kitchen. Her eyes scanned the ceiling and the walls before returning to the Ouija board.

She caught her breath.

The cup had mysteriously made its way back to the board. It was spinning on its side as if someone was blowing on it or flicking it with an invisible finger. Ricky was transfixed, her eyes on the spinning cup, when a high-pitched noise penetrated the room.

Electrified by the car alarm, she threw herself out the window and over the fence, only allowing herself to breathe again once her feet were on the pavement. Her knees felt like rubber. Her heart was racing. She crouched next to the fence, trembling with fright. Something very strange had just happened.

Once her legs felt solid again, she stood up and looked around for the girls but the street was empty. Gone was her earlier bravado and exhilaration. It was the middle of the night and she was very much alone. She crossed the street and was hurrying past the playground when something heavy landed on her shoulder.

She gasped.

'What are you doing out here?'

Ricky's first reaction was one of relief. It wasn't a murderer. It wasn't even thuggish Pauly Cloney.

Dan's hand didn't move from her shoulder. 'Well?'

'I was looking for a cat.'

'At midnight?'

'I could hear it meowing. I thought it might be hurt.'

'Your mother would have a fit if she knew you were wandering around in the middle of the night.'

'Why are you wandering around out here?'

His expression changed. 'What I do is none of your business, Missy. I'm not twelve years old.'

'I'm almost thirteen.'

'So you keep saying.'

'You don't have to tell Mum.'

Dan nodded slowly. 'I think I do.'

'I'll never do it again.'

He shook his head and exhaled a gust of beery breath.

'Please.'

He tightened his grip on her shoulder. 'How do I know you won't sneak out again?'

'I just won't. Promise.' She made a cross over her heart. 'I've never done it before and I'll never do it again.'

'Is that so?' A tight, lopsided smile formed on his lips. 'All right then, let's make a deal.'

'What kind of deal?'

'I'll keep quiet about this on one condition. No, make that two conditions.'

His fingers were digging into her flesh painfully but she dared not move.

'First, you have to be nicer to me.'

She quickly nodded. 'Okay.'

'Second, you have to seal the deal.' He laughed and pointed to his cheek. 'With a kiss.'

She felt like screaming. The idea of kissing Dan was repulsive. She glanced at the place on his cheek where he'd pointed and thought of her mother. What choice did she have? She held her breath and counted to five.

As she pushed herself up on her toes, the weight of the hand on her shoulder threw her off balance. When her lips landed on Dan, they were half on his cheek and half on his mouth. His facial skin was rough but his lips were soft and moist.

She tore herself out of his grasp and wiped her mouth with her hand.

'See? That wasn't so hard was it?'

It was horrible. It made her feel sick.

He was smiling. 'Remember, young lady, we have a deal.'

# 8

RICKY CLUNG TO her father, enjoying the solid feel of him. He smelled potatoey like the earth and of the lavender oil he dabbed on himself.

'Had enough yet?' he said, laughing.

'No.' Her reply was muffled by his shirt.

He kissed the top of her head before disentangling himself with a laugh. It was the deep, special laugh he reserved for her. She could feel its vibration in her bones as he peeled her off him.

'Did you come by yourself?'

'We couldn't find anywhere to park so Sophie had to wait in the car.'

Ricky's throat tightened.

'Where's Ollie?' Her father was looking over her shoulder, trying to see into the flat from the doorway.

Couldn't he just focus on her for a minute?

'He's putting his shoes on. He's not very well.'

'Poor Ollie. I haven't stopped thinking about him.'

Her heart sank. 'He looks ridiculously good. Better than ever.'

'I suppose that's a good thing.' Her father moved back from the doorway to lean against the railing of the balcony.

He patted his pockets for his tobacco. 'Run inside and let your mum know I'm here, would you?'

What was she now, a messenger? 'You haven't asked how I am.'

'Sorry, Sport, we can have a catch-up over lunch.' He smiled. 'Go get your brother and we can get moving.'

Ollie was casually sitting at the dining table. He had socks on but no shoes. She glanced at his arm and her desire to bark at him immediately disappeared. The hospital had attached a plastic cannula to make it easier to take blood and administer medication. It was a horrible, alien thing that looked obscene on his small arm.

'Dad's waiting outside,' she said.

'I know.' Ollie's face showed not a flicker of excitement.

'Get your shoes on and go say hello. Chop, chop.'

'I'm not chopping.' Ollie got down from the chair. His movements were slow and deliberate. 'When was the last time Dad chop-chopped for us? He was supposed to come here last week.'

That was the thing with Ollie. He had the memory of an elephant.

'He's doing his best.'

'No, he's not.'

Ricky found her mother in the bathroom, brushing her hair. She had beautiful hair, thick and blonde with a cow's lick over her left eye. When she blow-dried it big and high, she looked like an American beauty queen, the type that waved from a pageant float. Ollie's hair would be the same once it got past its downy stage. Ricky's hair was fine and brown like her father's. It had a slight wave that her mother said was pretty. Ricky always made sure to bury this nonsense within her ponytail.

'Dad's here,' she said.

'Tell him I'll be a minute,' said her mother.

Ricky would tell him no such thing. They could all get themselves a courier pigeon if they wanted a go-between. She was tying Ollie's laces when she heard her parents whispering outside. She motioned for Ollie to stay put and went to the doorway to earwig.

'Don't have him out too long,' said her mother. 'I want him home before three.'

'He's my son too,' said her father.

'I hope he recognises you.'

'What is that supposed to mean?'

'You know exactly what it means.'

'Look, I'm doing my best.'

'No, you're not.'

Why did her mother have to bait him? If she'd been nicer, they wouldn't be living in Camden and the poor man wouldn't have to traipse across London to see his children.

The whispering stopped when Ollie appeared and threw himself into his father's arms.

'How's my baby boy?' he said, kissing Ollie loudly on the face and neck.

'I'm not a baby boy.' He laughed. 'I'm a mountain gorilla.'

'How do you make toast in the jungle?'

'I don't know.' Ollie wriggled with delight as his father snaked a hand inside his t-shirt and tickled him.

'You put it under a gorilla.'

'That's silly.'

'Shall we go to a jungle restaurant and get you a plate of lubba-dubba-dubba leaves to eat?'

Ollie giggled. 'Yes, please.'

Sophie didn't look happy to see them but she had one of those permafrost faces that gave nothing away. Her smiles were only ever brief abbreviations. She never showed her teeth or crinkled her eyes. Her father said she was shy but from what Ricky had seen, she was sadly lacking in the emotion department. Sophie was dull but life as a home-wrecker obviously suited her because she'd put on weight. Her face had lost its sharp, rat-like angles. There was softness and colour in her cheeks.

The place her father had chosen was not a jungle restaurant or even a restaurant. It was a small café located at the shabby end of Kentish Town next to a shop that had a table out front with plastic tubs of tired vegetables and small, viciously hot peppers, all selling for a pound. It was not until they had finished ordering and been served their drinks that he dared to ask Ollie how he was feeling.

'I'm okay,' he replied, noncommittal.

'That's quite a thing you've got on your arm,' her father said. 'Is that where they pump in the kryptonite?'

'Something like that.'

'Or do they attach a funnel and pour in your cup of tea with milk and one sugar?'

'I'm too little to drink tea.'

'Sprite then. Do the bubbles tickle when it goes in?'

Ollie shrugged.

Ricky watched her father struggling to get a reaction and couldn't bear it. Ollie was being a brat.

'I've been building my stamina, just like you taught me,' she said, curling her arm to demonstrate the healthy bulge. 'I can do over a hundred chin-ups without a break. Ask Ollie.'

Her father frowned. 'You're not making your brother do chin-ups, are you?'

'No.' Why didn't he see that she was trying to make *him* feel better?

'Ollie needs to take it easy.'

'He stays in the igloo while I do my body building.'

Her father glanced at Ollie. 'What's an igloo?'

'It's the home of the Inuit. I wrote a story about it at the summer workshop. It's made of ice and—'

'I asked your brother.' Her father gave her a look. 'Ollie? Are you going to talk to me?'

Ricky slumped in her chair and bit her lip. Her corneas were the Thames floodgates, holding back a king tide of salty water. She wasn't going to cry. No way.

Ollie was examining the cannula in his arm as if nothing important was happening. He spoke without looking up. 'Are you coming to live in Camden?'

Ricky held her breath and observed her father closely. When she'd first found out about the move to Camden, he'd told her not to fret. He would make sure they saw a lot of each other and if things got too lonely, he might even move north himself. Now, he shifted uneasily in his chair. His smile was strained.

'Two children's all-day breakfasts, no beans?' asked the waitress.

Sophie unhooked her handbag from the back of her chair and excused herself. She was rummaging inside the bag for cigarettes as she headed for the door. Her father clucked under his breath and followed her with his eyes, a look of concern creasing his features. He didn't return his attention to the table until the waitress brought over his and Sophie's meals.

'I've got some good news,' he said, picking up his knife and fork.

The waitress had placed a plate of toast in the middle of the table. It was giving off a tantalising buttery smell. Despite Ricky's recent policy of avoiding bread and butter, she took a piece and tore off a bite. It was delicious: salty, warm and fatty.

'Are you moving to Camden?' asked Ollie. He was like a terrier worrying a bone.

'Sophie and I have got something very important to tell you.'

Ricky's heart lifted. He *was* moving to Camden. He really was. It didn't matter that dull old Sophie would be tagging along. The important thing was that their father would be living near them and they would almost be a family again.

'What's the news?' asked Ollie.

'We're going to have a baby.'

The toast turned to polystyrene in Ricky's mouth. There was no flavour, no moisture, no joy. She couldn't chew. She swallowed and had to will the lump to descend her reluctant throat.

'When?' Ollie was a pragmatist.

'In about four months.' Her father had his head down, scooping beans onto his fork, avoiding her eyes.

Ricky's head was whirring. A pregnancy was nine months. Her father had known about the baby before their move to Camden.

'You've known for ages.' Her voice was unstable. 'Before we moved.'

Her father nodded in slow motion. His attention was on his food. He was chewing slowly, using every muscle and scrap of connective tissue in his lean cheeks.

'What is it?' She had to know. Was the baby replacing Ollie or her? 'A girl or a boy?'

Her father looked up, vexed. 'It's not an it. It's a she. You're going to have a baby sister.'

If Ollie hadn't put his hand on her knee at that precise moment, Ricky didn't know what she would have done. His small palm was hot. The heat radiated up her thigh, travelling to her chest where it found her heart and wrapped it in warmth.

She glanced at her brother and saw that he, too, was sad. She understood that part of his sadness was about her. Ollie knew how much she needed her father, how she needed him to love her. A new sister would dilute his need for her. She wouldn't be special anymore. She would be second in line, possibly even third in line.

Ricky's mother looked relieved when they returned home early. Ollie had fallen asleep in the car and had to be carried inside. Her father put him on the couch and covered him with a rug before swiftly retreating to the balcony, eager to get away. He'd parked in a driveway and Sophie was waiting in a hot car for him. The hug he gave Ricky was brief. She closed her eyes and buried her nose in his flannel shirt, searching for lavender and the earthy smell of the allotment but all that had been obliterated by the spliff he'd smoked on the drive back. He'd opened the car windows to let the smoke out but the smell of cannabis was dense and cloying. It stuck to him like the stench of failure and disappointment.

Ricky was curled up on her bed, facing the wall, when her mother came in and sat next to her.

'It might be nice to have a sister,' she said.

Ricky didn't answer.

'You'll have to build a bigger fort.'

'I don't want a stupid sister. I already have a stupid brother.'

'You don't mean that.'

'But Ollie is hardly ever here and when he is, he's always sick.'

Ricky felt her mother put her arms around her and didn't move. It was a lopsided hug because she was curled so tight on her side. She made as if to shrug off the embrace but didn't try very hard. She loved being held by her mother, especially today.

'Thank you, honey.'

The vibration of her mother's voice so close to her ear tickled her pleasantly.

'What for?'

'For being nicer to Dan. I appreciate it. It really helps.'

Ricky remembered the feel of Dan's skin and the moistness of his lips. She shuddered.

'Why don't you go outside and get some fresh air before tea? I see your friends are in the playground.'

'They're not my friends.'

'They could be if you tried being friendly.'

Her mother would never have encouraged her if she'd known the big girl was a Cloney. Ricky was not about to tell her.

Caitlin and Abbie were sitting on the swings with an open bag of Doritos on the ground between them. Baby was lying to the side of the swings, as far from Caitlin as her lead would allow. The girls glanced up from their phones but Ricky was too low on the food chain to warrant a 'Hello'.

Ricky leaned against the igloo. 'A strange thing happened after you ran off the other night,' she said.

Caitlin rolled her eyes at Abbie. 'We never ran off,' she said.

'Sure you didn't.' Ricky snorted. 'I just thought you might be interested to know what happened.'

The girls were quiet, waiting for her to continue.

'I saw something.' She filled her lungs and lowered her voice. 'Something *paranormal*.'

'Did you see a ghost?' Abbie couldn't help herself.

Ricky hesitated for dramatic effect. 'I'm not sure. But before I tell you what happened, I want to ask you both something. Were either of you pushing that cup around the Ouija board?'

She studied Caitlin and Abbie carefully for evidence of lying but both of them looked genuinely nervous as if they, too, had been surprised by the events of the séance.

'So, what did you see?' asked Caitlin. Her voice was harsh but her expression was uncertain.

Ricky smiled to herself. Caitlin was afraid.

'Well?' Caitlin was glaring.

'At first I heard a noise, a whining sound.'

'And?'

'The temperature suddenly dropped. It became icy cold in the flat. I could hear someone crying in one of the rooms. Then a strange light appeared. It was like the dot of a laser pointer but it was blue.' She took a deep breath and shook her head slowly. 'The light wasn't coming from the window. It was in the room with me, hovering.'

'Hovering.' Abbie was spellbound.

'Then it started moving. Dancing.'

'Like an angel?'

Ricky nodded. 'Or a lost soul.'

Nobody said anything for a moment. Caitlin was scuffing the ground with the heel of her trainer.

'You're such a liar,' she said.

'If I'm a liar, I dare you to go back there tonight, by yourself.'

'Shut up!'

'Coward!'

Caitlin dropped the dog's lead and leaped off the swing, flying in an arc to land inches from Ricky.

'I'm not a fucking coward!'

Ricky could feel Caitlin's breath on her face but didn't move. *Go on*, she thought, *just try it*. She was younger and smaller but today she was burning with anger, and anger made her invincible.

After a few seconds, Caitlin sat back down.

The gate clanged.

'Brilliant,' Caitlin said. 'Just the person I was waiting for.'

'Who, me?' Samia asked.

'Doh.' Caitlin gave Abbie a look. 'We're going to the funfair tomorrow. Want to come?'

Samia's eyes widened. She glanced at Ricky and quickly looked away. 'When are you going?'

'In the morning.' Caitlin knew everyone attended the workshop in the morning.

'But I have to go to the community centre.'

'I knew you'd try to weasel out of it. I told you, didn't I, Abbie?'

Abbie nodded.

'We can go to the funfair, Samia,' said Ricky. 'I'll write a note to say my father is taking us. I can do his signature with my eyes closed.'

'But you don't have a father,' said Caitlin. 'Ha, ha.'

'Of course I have a father.' Ricky felt an almost uncontrollable urge to shove the girl to the ground and pummel her miserable face. 'He just dropped me and my brother off. We had lunch in Camden Town.'

Abbie snorted.

'Sure you did.' Caitlin was smirking. 'What did you eat?'

'Full English. No beans. Ice cream for dessert.' Ricky hadn't been able to eat a thing after her father had announced the pregnancy. The betrayal had crushed her. 'Dad's been in America. He's always travelling with his job. He had jetlag.'

'What does your father do?' asked Samia.

'He works for TV. They're doing a big documentary on the Arizona cactus. Dad wanted to bring us back a prickly pear but he wasn't allowed.'

This was too much information for Caitlin. She stood up and grabbed Baby's lead. 'So, are you coming to the funfair tomorrow or what?'

Ricky caught Samia's eye. 'Yes, we are.'

She waited until the girls had drifted off before following the path to the garden. Her chest was aching and she was longing for the comfort of the soil and the green. She needed to connect with something bigger than her rage and sorrow.

Snowy was kneeling, hand-raking around some mature cabbages. One of his knees must have been bothering him because he was wearing a flesh-coloured elastic bandage. He heard her and turned, shyly dipping his chin in greeting.

'I saw my father today,' she announced.

Snowy's eyes were on her. He was listening.

'His girlfriend is going to have a baby. It's a girl.' She didn't know why she was telling him this.

The old man cocked his head, interested.

'He's making a big mistake. He doesn't need another daughter.'

He frowned.

'One daughter is enough.' Her eyes had filled with tears. She fell silent.

Snowy uttered a strange, strangled sound.

Ricky became aware that he was watching her carefully and stiffened under the animal-like intensity of his gaze. His eyes were avoiding hers but he was completely focused on her. Ricky no longer felt angry and invincible. She was raw and vulnerable, and Snowy knew it.

The old man mumbled something and pushed himself up off his knees. Gesturing for her to follow, he led her to the far corner of the garden, a hidden place she'd never noticed. Between the fence and a lattice of beans was a narrow cavity. At first, she didn't see what he was trying to show her. It looked like a mound of the hay Snowy scattered over the beds to keep weeds down. She waited for him to step back before squatting down to get a closer look. Gently, she brushed aside some of the dried grass to reveal a black plastic sheet. It was draped over a wooden box that was lying on its side. Snowy grunted and pointed. She could hear him breathing heavily behind her as she lowered herself to all fours and peered through a gap in the plastic.

Something hissed in warning. She could see eyes staring back at her. After a moment, she could make out a small lumpen thing in the corner of the box. It was a cat and there were two tiny shapes nestled in the fur of its belly.

She looked up at Snowy. 'Are those kittens?'

He held up two fingers.

She peered once again into the box. One was black. The other was a grey tabby like its mother. They were very small.

She stood up, wiping her knees. 'They've just been born.'

Snowy nodded.

'Can I help look after them?'

The old man shrugged.

'Please.'

'I'd like to keep one when they're old enough,' she continued. 'Maybe we can have the mother, too.' Her imagination was galloping ahead. 'I know another girl who wants a kitten.'

Snowy took out a sachet of cat food from his pocket and squeezed the contents onto a chipped floral saucer. He put the saucer next to a bowl of water near the opening. He then rearranged the plastic sheet to create an opening before scattering fresh hay over the box.

Ricky felt completely different as she walked away from the garden. She imagined Ollie's joy when she brought the cat and a kitten home, the squeal he would make. They would look after them together, teach them tricks. It would be like having their own family, one they could love and keep safe. She would call the tabby mother 'Lola'. It might take some work to tame her but Ricky was up for it. The cat would be a project, something to focus on, like her exercises.

She was so deep in thought that it took her a moment to realise someone was calling out to her.

She stopped. A spiky tremor travelled up her legs.

Pauly Cloney was sitting lazily on the bench under the birches, his thick legs open. One arm was stretched along the back of the seat, the other lying at the top of his thigh near his groin. His face looked normal but when he opened his mouth, Ricky saw a plastic mouthguard where his top teeth should have been.

'You love letting that old pervert touch you up, don't you?' he said.

Anger flared inside her like a blowtorch.

'I've been watching you.'

'Shut up.'

'I know what he does to you.'

'I said, shut up.'

'Enjoy your teeth while you still have them.' The boy leaned back on the seat and laughed. 'I'm going to smash your face in when you least expect it, bitch.'

# 9

RICKY HAD IMAGINED a souped-up, posher version of Brockwell Park but Hampstead Heath was completely different. It was bigger, wilder, hillier and much, much more beautiful. When they reached the top of Parliament Hill, the green wonder of it all unfurled before them. It was a park like no other she'd visited. The midsummer grass was almost waist high. Its seed heads were fat and heavy, their smell dense and musky.

'I'm glad I'm wearing a bra,' said Abbie with a false TV-person laugh. 'It makes walking so much easier.'

'I'm wearing a sports bra. I'm not taking any chances with the pair I've got,' said Caitlin. Her eyes sought out Samia. 'Have you even got a bra yet?'

Samia nodded in a noncommittal way and kept walking.

'What colour is it?'

Abbie snorted.

'Why are you both so obsessed with a couple of chest glands?' asked Ricky.

The girls stopped walking. They were in an avenue of large trees. It was like a cathedral with a leafy, green ceiling. Somewhere in the distance, a woodpecker was giving a tree trunk hell. Ricky had absorbed all this within a second but the others seemed oblivious to these marvels. They were staring at her with a mixture of confusion and outrage.

'That's disgusting,' said Abbie.

'It's science. They're just milk glands surrounded by tissue and fat.'

'Mine are not surrounded by fat.'

Ricky shrugged. 'Breasts are for making milk, like a cow's udder.'

'They are not chest glands and they are not like cow udders!' Abbie's face was bright pink. 'You're sick!'

Caitlin laughed, loud and high. It was a vicious sound that contained the threat of senseless cruelty. Ricky was bracing herself for what was about to come next when a deafening noise was suddenly over and around them.

*Thud, thud, thud.*

They all instinctively crouched low as a helicopter seemed to swoop down from outer space. The wind generated by its rotors set branches clacking and leaves rattling as it hovered above the trees before disappearing over the crest of the hill.

Ricky recognised the helicopter from a story written by one of the boys in the workshop. He'd described how the playing fields below Parliament Hill were sometimes used by air medical services requiring rapid access to the Royal Free Hospital.

'I bet that's an air ambulance,' said Ricky. 'It might be carrying a heart or a lung. They pack the organs in ice.'

Samia let out a whimper. She'd been present when the boy had described organ transplants. He'd been going into gory detail when Katie noticed Samia's reaction and stopped him.

'Someone is probably turning blue right now at the Royal Free.'

The girls were silent for a moment as they contemplated an actual blue human being.

'We're prime donor material.' Ricky was getting into her stride. 'Young kidneys are worth a fortune on the black market.'

'No one's getting mine,' said Abbie.

'What if your kidney could save the life of someone you loved?' Ricky thought of Ollie. She would give him a kidney, a lobe of lung or any bone marrow she had going. Hell, he could have her stem cells, too. Ollie could take his pick. 'What if the person was a boyfriend and he was going to die if you didn't give him your kidney?'

Abbie's face twitched.

Caitlin elbowed her.

Abbie sighed and reluctantly agreed that her boyfriend could have a kidney as long as the surgery didn't leave a scar.

'What if you had to give him a kidney and a foot?'

'Gross.'

'Let's get out of here.' Caitlin started walking again. 'We haven't got time for your weirdness.'

They could hear the funfair as they emerged from the trees, the metallic *ting-ting* of fairground music and the mechanical whirring of the rides. The fair looked garish and out of place on the heath, an island of bright colours and machinery, caravans and trucks, surrounded by grass and trees.

Ricky hung back to savour the noisy chaos, buoyed by memories of past fairs with her father. The others had linked arms and were walking three abreast like showgirls. Caitlin was in the middle, pulling everyone forward, always in the lead and in a hurry.

Ricky caught up with them at the dodgem circuit. It was incredibly noisy next to the track, loud rock music and machinery punctuated by the clank and thump of cars crashing into each other. The girls weren't looking at the dodgems. Their eyes were on the operator, a thin girl with her hair pulled back tightly off her face. Despite the warmth of the morning, she was dressed in skinny jeans and boots with a tight leather jacket zipped up to the collar. She looked about fourteen but had to be older. Chained to the side of the ticket booth was a shiny, old-style perambulator. A chubby baby boy was sitting up, eating something that had coloured the lower half of his face red.

'She could be your sister,' said Abbie, who had to shout to be heard over the roar and clunk of the dodgems.

'No, she couldn't!' shouted Caitlin.

'She's about the same age. If she'd kept the baby—'

'Shut up!' Caitlin shoved Abbie against the guardrail.

The dodgems stopped with a bang.

'No fighting near the track!' the girl operating the dodgems shouted. 'Take it to the shooting gallery if you want to kill each other.'

As they walked away, Ricky could tell Caitlin was struggling. She couldn't afford to fall out with the prettiest girl on the estate. Abbie was a trophy. She raised the status of whoever she was with.

The girls were passing the Ferris wheel when Caitlin casually asked Abbie for the time.

Abbie dutifully took her iPhone out of her bag. Her reply was stiff but not hostile. 'It's just after eleven.'

'Let's go to the ghost train,' said Caitlin.

'I thought you said it was rubbish,' said Ricky.

Caitlin's face flashed anger, the anger she'd been suppressing since the clash with Abbie. Her mouth opened and then closed again. A sly look came into her eyes. 'I think you should be the judge of that. I dare you to ride it by yourself.'

The dare seemed to cheer up Abbie. With a girlie laugh, she linked arms with Caitlin.

The façade of the haunted house was decorated with coffins and gravestones and had three-dimensional bats with red eyes suspended over the entrance. Ricky noticed the paint had faded in places and some of the wooden panels had chunks missing. A dented carriage with a bench seat for two was sitting stationary on the small track. There was howling coming from behind the metal doors of the house.

Ricky could have refused the dare but a yearning for connection to past summers had welled up inside her. The ghost train was her favourite ride, the one she took with her father.

'Why don't your friends want to ride with you?' asked the youth in charge of the ghost train. He was thin and had a bloom of acne over his nose and cheeks. His name was Bevan, according to his name badge. 'Have you got nits?'

'No, have you got pubic lice?' she replied, reaching out to take her ticket.

He laughed and playfully held on to the ticket. She had to give it a tug to remove it from his hand.

'You seem to know a lot for a little girl.'

Ricky could smell cannabis as he reached over her to click the safety bar in place. His knuckles dug into her hip. She jumped.

He laughed again and banged the side of the carriage with the flat of his hand.

Ricky waited for excitement to take hold as the car nosed its way through the doors of the haunted house with a clatter and a bang. It was noisy and dark after the brightness of the sunny morning. As the carriage entered a grotto with steaming vents and flashing orange lights, something tickled the top of her head. She ducked as a ghost loomed out of the darkness, howling in her ear. The car rumbled past a legion of skeletons dancing on gravestones. Another ghost and three old hags stirring an airborne cauldron flew past. Normally, Ricky would be shrieking and laughing, and squeezing close to her father. There were bats and demons, black cats and red-eyed ghouls but none of these things thrilled her. Something scraped across her arm as she passed through a dungeon and the next moment the carriage was bashing open the exit doors and she was blinded by sunlight.

Blinking, she looked around for familiar faces. She put her hand over her eyes and scanned the people milling around the rides. As the truth dawned on her, she had to swallow several times and force back tears. The girls were probably hiding somewhere close, watching as she climbed out of the carriage, waiting for her to cry.

Bevan was smirking. 'I see your friends dumped you.'

'They're not my friends.'

'The fat one definitely isn't. As soon as you were inside, she ran off with the pretty one. They thought it was a great joke.'

'And the other girl?'

'The Pakistani?'

'She's British, as British as you.'

'No need to get all prissy, Bessie No Mates.'

'Where is she?'

'The fat one came back and dragged her away.'

At least Samia had not willingly abandoned her. If Ricky could just focus on that, she wouldn't burst into tears. The trick was to act as if she didn't care. Hell, if she put her mind to it, she could probably convince herself it was true.

She'd been walking for several minutes, not paying attention to her surroundings, when she realised the sounds of the rides were behind her and she'd reached the outer edge of the fair. In front of her, sitting under a tree, was a large, green wooden barrel on wheels. The gypsy wagon had tiny windows with red and white polka dot curtains and a crooked metal chimney. Its ornate door was open.

Next to the door was a sandwich board describing Madame Tina, the All-Seeing Eye, as a finder of lost things, a shepherdess of lost souls and a mender of broken hearts. Tina was a 'full-blood Romani' whose ancestors first came to Britain on a pirate ship. Like her mother and grandmother before her, she was blessed with the gift of sight. Palmistry and tarot card readings were five pounds.

'You look lonely,' said a voice from within the wagon.

Ricky stepped back as a woman stuck her head out of the doorway. Her face was large and crisscrossed with the fine wrinkles of a smoker. She was wearing heavy eyeliner and had a paisley scarf tied around her head. A pair of reading glasses was pushed up high on her forehead. She had several gold chains around her neck, the longest of which bore a large Egyptian symbol. Ricky recognised the Eye of Horus, the all-seeing eye and symbol of protection. The fortune teller had rings on every finger including her thumbs. Some fingers had two rings. Most of them were jewelled but Ricky's eyes were drawn to the large gold ring on her wedding finger. It was a scarab beetle with small, ruby eyes. Ricky had a reference book on Egyptology and knew that the scarab was a symbol of rebirth.

'I'm alone,' Ricky said. 'That's different from being lonely.'

The woman raised her eyebrows, amused.

Ricky waited for her to reveal whether this was a good or bad thing.

'Well?' Madame Tina smiled. 'Are you coming in or not?'

'I've only got four pounds.'

'I've heard that before.'

It was cosy inside the wagon, like one of Ricky's forts but bigger and better furnished. When the fortune teller closed the door, the interior became dim without being dark. Several flickering tealights were casting a warm glow over everything.

The fortune teller sat down and pointed to a chair on the other side of a small, high-legged table. 'Cards or palm?'

Ricky had never had her fortune told. 'Whatever you think is best, Madame Tina.'

'Forget the Madame. Call me Tina. Show me your paws.'

Tina scooped up Ricky's hands and turned them over to study the palms, gently pinching the fingers as if to check their thickness. The fortune teller's own hands were large and long. Her fingers were bony with big knuckles that anchored her many rings in place. Ricky's attention was once again drawn to the scarab beetle. The tiny jewels of its eyes winked in the candlelight.

Tina dropped Ricky's left hand and, flicking her reading glasses down, lifted the right hand close to her face.

'I see secrets.'

Ricky shivered.

'There's loss or grief.' Tina pulled on her fingers to flatten the palm. 'Some sort of trouble.'

Ricky shook her head but her eyes must have betrayed her because Tina gently placed her other hand on top of hers. Her touch was like electricity and light. It snaked up Ricky's arm.

'Now, let's have another look.'

When Tina lifted her hand, Ricky saw that her palm had turned pink, as if illuminated by a bulb under the skin.

'Let's look at the positives, shall we?' Tina smiled. 'You're resilient and you have strength, quite a boyish or masculine strength. If you had been born in another age, you might have become a warrior.'

'Like Joan of Arc?'

She pursed her lips. 'Do you know what happened to Joan of Arc?'

'Yes.'

'Well, then.' She applied herself to the palm again. 'You're carrying something, a burden or burdens. You feel shame and there's fear. Fear of something or perhaps someone.'

When Ricky didn't respond, Tina continued. 'Right now, you don't have much in the way of defences. You're exposed.'

The fortune teller squeezed Ricky's hand. 'I want you to listen carefully.'

As Ricky concentrated on Tina's face, she became aware of the flickering of the tealights on the periphery of her field of vision. The small candles seemed to be multiplying, their flames elongating into flares. She had to blink a couple of times to dispel the illusion.

'Be very careful who you trust. There are individuals around you who do not wish you well.'

She thought of Pauly Cloney, his thick thighs and sneering promise of revenge.

'A person or people will not be as they appear. Be wary of promises of friendship. Their intentions are otherwise. They can hurt you.' Tina caught her eye. 'They're not already hurting you, are they?'

Ricky bit the inside of her lip and shook her head.

'When things get really difficult, someone will come into your life. He or she is like a gift.'

'How will I know who this person is?'

'You will have a lot in common. You might even share a birthday.'

'When will this happen?'

'Soon.'

Tina got up and opened the door.

'Now, remember what I said. Be careful who you trust.' The fortune teller looked over at the fairground and frowned. 'You shouldn't be wandering around a place like this on your own. It's not safe for a young girl.'

The fair looked different after the cosiness of the wagon. The neglect she'd noticed at the haunted house was now evident everywhere. She paused at a glass booth half filled with soft toys and noticed that one of the panels was cracked. The metal grabber hand had dropped down and was buried in the toys as if exhausted. The colourful prizes in the fishing alley looked cheap, the boxes were dusty and dog-eared. At the shooting gallery, a man holding one of the air rifles was arguing with his girlfriend. He was shouting and waving the gun while the operator watched, a lazy smile on his face. The heat of the midday sun seemed to magnify the garish colours and metallic noise of rides. It was loud and alien. The funfair now felt unsafe.

Ricky was making her way through a narrow opening between two long caravans when someone caught hold of her forearm, pulling her up short.

'What's the hurry, darling?' The man was in his fifties, wiry and unshaven. He was sitting in the doorway of a caravan. He smelled of sweat and the previous evening's alcohol.

Ricky tried to move away but the man held her tight. She shook her head. 'Let me go.'

'Where's a pretty little thing like you going on a day like this?'

'Let me go.'

'I'm only being friendly.' He stood up. 'Why don't you come inside? You might like it.'

Something about the man's smile flicked a switch inside Ricky's head. The smile was almost a sneer and it implied she was powerless. Adrenaline surged through her body. She didn't realise she'd bitten his fingers until he dropped her arm.

He cried out and lunged at her, but Ricky was already running. With a blast of energy, she vaulted over a metal barrier and out of the fairground. She was still running when she reached the summit of Parliament Hill. She stopped, hands on knees, to catch her breath. A laugh bubbled up her throat. It was wild and breathless, more like a sneeze than a laugh.

She stood up and let the warm breeze dry her sweat. London was rolled out below her like a prickly carpet. She could make out the Shard and the Gherkin. The dome of St Paul's Cathedral was almost buried by the buildings of the City. Ricky couldn't see Brixton but she knew where it was. If things got really bad, if they became unbearable, she could walk there. It would only take half a day.

As she began to descend the hill, Ricky realised the fortune teller had not asked for payment. It was a small thing, a tiny kindness, but it buoyed her. She became aware of the smell of summer grass. Somewhere not far away, a crow was making a racket.

# 10

Mister-Monsieur Oliver Cromwell couldn't understand it. He kept losing weight despite eating huge meals. His hips stuck out like shoulder blades. His shoulder blades stuck out like wings. The only part of his body that wasn't shrinking was his stomach. It was getting bigger and rounder.

One day Mister-Monsieur woke to a loud 'Pop'. He lifted his pyjama top and saw that his belly button had popped inside out. It opened and a tiny hand emerged. Then another. A head appeared.

He gasped. The likeness was unmistakable. The small person had his face. Same close-set eyes. Same round dollop of a nose. He couldn't tell if the small man had his teeth because he wasn't smiling.

'Hello,' said the small man. 'I am your twin.'

'I don't have a twin,' said Mister-Monsieur.

'Yes, you do. I live behind your liver. Some people call me a parasitic twin but I'm more like a fellow passenger. Imagine your body is a bus. We are both travelling on the same bus but I'm seated in the VIP area.'

'Are you going to leave now?'

'I will vacate when I am good and ready, thank you very much.' The small man gave him a nasty look. 'You must eat more chocolate finger biscuits.'

Before Mister-Monsieur could ask him why, the small man disappeared inside again.

Mister-Monsieur was frightened. He did not want trouble with this fellow passenger. He had several vital organs inside his body and did not want anyone meddling with them.

He followed the small man's instructions yet despite doubling and then tripling his intake of chocolate fingers, his body continued to shrivel and his bones began to soften and shrink. Meanwhile, his stomach swelled and swelled.

By the third week, Mister-Monsieur had to quit his job to stay in bed to eat biscuits. He became weaker and weaker.

By the fifth week, he was so poorly he could no longer lift his hand to his mouth. He was lying on his back looking at his enormous stomach when his belly button popped open again. Out climbed his parasitic twin, leaving Mister-Monsieur's body flattened on the bed like a banana peel. His bones had completely dissolved and all that was left of him was empty skin.

While Mister-Monsieur watched helplessly, the parasitic twin dressed himself in clothes from his wardrobe and, using his comb, tidied his hair in the mirror.

'You are a handsome devil,' the parasitic twin told his reflection.

He leaned over Mister-Monsieur and began blowing into his belly button, inflating him like a balloon until his body began to float above the bed. The twin then opened the window and pushed the floating balloon outside.

There was a breeze and, before long, the balloon that used to be Mister-Monsieur was floating over the houses of the town, heading higher toward the clouds. The last thing Mister-Monsieur saw before heading off toward Germany was his twin making a rude sign with his finger from the window.

'What is this?' asked Katie, shaking her head.

'Just a story,' said Ricky. Her face was hot from reading it aloud. She wanted to disappear, like the balloon of Mister-Monsieur.

'Did you make it up?'

'Yes.'

The story had taken days to write. Ricky had laboured over every word, writing and rewriting. In the first telling, she'd made everything over-descriptive. The parasitic twin had a Hungarian accent and smoked long, dark cigarettes. She'd gone back over it and stripped the story bare but, in doing so, had also robbed it of its charm. When she went over it again, she added description but with a lighter hand. The devil was in the detail, as her father said, and she was careful to choose the right details. She'd been delighted with the final draft and, blinded by pride, had readily volunteered to read it out at the workshop. Now she regretted her eagerness. No one had laughed or said anything. The room was quiet, a stunned silence.

'It's, well, very strange and very dark.' Katie frowned as if searching for words.

Ricky swallowed.

'But it's also original and remarkably sophisticated. I think you might just be a writer, a very good writer.'

Ricky allowed herself a small smile.

'Why a parasitic twin?'

Ricky glanced at Abbie. The girl's head was down. She was looking at her phone and probably hadn't even listened to the story.

'I have a personal interest.'

Katie laughed. 'Have you ever been to the Hunterian Museum?'

She shook her head.

'Perhaps I should organise a field trip there. They have specimens of parasitic twins and lots of other fascinating things preserved in jars.' Katie addressed the room. 'Who would like to take a hugely educational field trip to a museum?'

Ricky was the only one to put up a hand. The words 'educational' and 'museum' were not music to the ears of Camden's youth.

'Do we have to pay?' It was Samia, her voice hushed with embarrassment.

'I'll sort all that. You'll just need a travel card for the bus.' Katie nodded encouragingly.

Samia glanced at Ricky and quickly looked away. 'I'll have to check with Mum.'

Katie was asking for other volunteers to read their stories when there was a knock at the door.

The door opened and Ricky hunched down in her chair as if to make herself smaller.

'You must be Katie,' said Dan. He was smiling, Mr Congeniality.

'How can I help you?' Katie replied, her tone brisk and teacher-like.

'It's about that little ragamuffin over there.' He pointed to Ricky.

'You're Ricky's father?'

'I'm her mother's, well, partner I suppose. My name's Dan.' He gave her another of his smiles. 'Ricky didn't tell me her teacher was so pretty.'

'I'm a facilitator.'

On hearing the word 'pretty', Abbie stopped texting. She sat up and pushed out her chest.

Sensing the girl's interest, Dan turned and smiled.

Abbie beamed.

'What is this about?' Katie's voice was icy.

Dan handed her a note. 'I'm afraid Ricky can't come back this afternoon. Her mum is stuck at the hospital. I'm supposed to drop her off there.'

Katie raised her eyebrows. 'Ricky is not attending a workshop in the afternoon.'

Ricky held her breath. This was it. The game was up.

Dan frowned, confused.

She waited for everything to unravel.

'Right,' he said, finally. 'We'd better get going.'

Ricky kept glancing at Dan out of the corner of her eye, waiting for him to say something. As they drove to the hospital, she took care to be courteous and friendly. She thanked him for picking her up and then again for the sandwich he bought at the WH Smith kiosk. She even let him guide her through the hospital with his hand on her back.

Ollie looked tiny and vulnerable in the big hospital bed with his toy dog tucked in beside him. His face was pale apart from reddish circles under his eyes. It was one thing to have her brother ill at home but to see him in a strange, public place looking so unwell made her want to kick off the bed's brake and wheel him to freedom.

Ollie's eyes were closed but she could tell he was aware of her presence. Ricky could never sneak up on him. He always knew when she was close.

Her mother was sitting next to the bed on a blue vinyl armchair. She barred her lips with a finger as Ricky sidled up to her, wrapping an arm around her daughter's waist and pulling her onto her lap. The smell of her mother was delicious, like the musky grass of the heath. Ricky pressed her nose against her neck, breathing in her motherliness. Over the top of her head, her mother thanked Dan and said goodbye. Ricky waited to hear his retreating footsteps before completely relaxing.

'I wanted to see you now because I'll be spending the night here,' her mother whispered.

Ricky lifted her head from her mother's shoulder. 'Why?'

'They want Ollie to stay in for observation. They've given him some medication and need him to spend the night here.'

'I'll stay, too.' Ricky noticed a flicker of interest in Ollie's face and knew he was listening. 'We can take turns watching over him.'

'That's not possible.'

'I'll sit really quietly and read my book.' The previous day, Katie had given her a book of short stories by Alice Munro. 'These are sophisticated stories about ordinary people,' she'd explained. 'But you have a sophisticated reading level and if you're going to be a writer, you should start at the top.'

'The hospital won't allow you to stay.'

'Can I stay with Dad then?'

'He's got nowhere for you to sleep, honey. You know that. Sophie's only got a one-bedroom flat.'

'I can sleep on the floor. It would be like camping.'

'You can camp here with me until Dan finishes work. He'll stay at home with you tonight. Depending on how things go, he might have to stay a few nights.'

'I don't want that, Mum.'

'We have no choice.'

'Please, please, please.'

'Don't be silly now.'

Ricky's jaw stiffened. She felt like throwing up but there was no food in her stomach. She hadn't eaten the sandwich from the kiosk.

'You're getting so big and bony.' Her mother kissed the top of her head and gently nudged her off her lap. She stood up and straightened her rumpled clothes. 'Would you sit with Ollie? I need to eat something and pee. I also need to call your father.'

Ricky waited until her mother was out of the room before tickling Ollie's ear. 'You can stop pretending now.'

He smiled and opened his eyes.

'You've ruined everything, you know.'

'What?' His voice was hoarse.

'I was going to visit some kittens.'

Ollie opened his eyes fully. 'What kittens?'

'Mr Snow has got two of them hidden in his garden. He's been feeding the mother.'

'Can we have one?'

'We should have two, the mother and a kitten. Animals are better in pairs. Ask Noah.'

Ollie laughed, which made Ricky worry that he might have a fever because her joke wasn't particularly funny. She was capable of saying much funnier things.

She slipped her hand under the covers and felt around until she found his hot little fingers. She squeezed them.

'What's been going on?'

'They gave me a big injection this morning. Then they hooked me up to that bag of juice.' He held up his arm with the cannula. 'They said I have to stay here.'

'You do realise you're going to be famous, don't you? You're the only person with a parasitic twin in the whole of the British Isles and Ireland. Your twin is money in the bank.'

'I don't care about money or being famous.' His voice was small. 'I want to go home.' Ollie's eyelids were getting heavy. His hand softened inside hers. 'I'm a little tired now to tell you the truth.'

Ricky's throat hurt. She didn't want him to be tired or ill or under observation. His place was at home with her, wherever home was these days.

'Can you tell me a story?'

She waited for Ollie's eyes to close before beginning. 'Once upon a time there was a small dog. A tiny dog. A crumb of a dog with two heads.'

Ollie laughed sleepily.

Ricky lowered her voice to a whisper. Each of the dog's heads had a personality. One head liked to lick and nip while the other liked to sink his teeth in and chew. This made things difficult because they shared the same body.

Ollie murmured as she described how the dog's two heads argued over a tennis ball.

'The heads swore at each other and punched holes in each other's ears with needle-sharp teeth.'

She stopped to listen.

Ollie's breathing had slowed and become deeper.

When she was sure he was asleep, she began another story.

'When Mum was pregnant for the first time, something very strange happened.'

Ricky checked again to make sure Ollie was still sleeping.

'She was supposed to have a boy. That's what should have happened. But somehow the chromosomes and hormones got mixed up into a kind of casserole and the baby came out all wrong. It was a boy but it was born with the wrong carcass.' Ricky realised she was sweating. A prickly halo of moisture had encircled her scalp. She had to get this out, get it over and done with. 'Things have started happening to the carcass. Disgusting things. Things that horrible men notice. They want—'

Ollie opened one of his eyes and startled her.

'You're just going through puberty,' he said, shutting his eye again.

'You little faker. I should pinch you,' she said. 'How do you know that word?'

'You're not allowed to pinch me because I'm ridiculously sick.' He kept his eyes closed.

'Tell me how you know that word.'

'What word?'

'The word starting with P.'

'Mum said it.'

Ricky didn't want to know but she had to ask. 'Who did she say it to?'

When Ollie didn't respond, she pinched him on the back of the arm. It was a soft pinch, more of a threat than the actual thing.

'Ouch!' Ollie opened both his eyes. 'It doesn't matter.'

'Of course it matters.' She raised her voice. 'Out with it.'

'She was just talking to someone.'

'Someone who?' But she already knew and it made her feel sick.

'Dan.'

Ricky pulled her legs up and sank down in the chair to hide her face behind her knees. She wanted to disappear, to run away and die in a dramatic and terribly painful way. She imagined hurling herself off a high cliff like the Japanese in the documentary, her shoeless body bouncing against rocks on its way down before splashing into an angry ocean, never to be seen again. How could her mother have done this? It was bad enough that she'd noticed the changes despite all Ricky's precautions and layers of clothing but it was utterly horrifying to think of her sharing these insights with Dan.

Ollie was sleeping when her mother returned. She'd put on lipstick and tied her hair back. She looked almost normal.

'I've called Dan,' she said. 'He's going to pick you up here after work.'

'Please don't make me go home with him. It's not—'

'What? It's not what?'

'It's—' Once again, she imagined throwing herself off the cliff. The awful thud as her body hit the rocks and the splash as she fell into the sea. 'I just don't want to.'

'I've got no choice.'

Ricky was finding it difficult to breathe. 'I want to stay here with you and Ollie.'

'Let's not start this again, please. Don't make things more difficult for me than they already are. You have no idea how exhausted I am.' There were tears in her mother's eyes. 'How about I get Dan to buy kebabs on the way home? You love kebabs.'

'I'm not hungry.'

'You will be in a couple of hours.'

'No, I won't.' Kebabs were what she ate with her father. It was too much. She wanted it all to stop. 'What's really wrong with Ollie, Mum? When is he going to get better?'

Her mother's gaze drifted to the bed. Her face tightened. Ricky could tell she was struggling not to cry.

'They still don't have all the information.'

'About what?'

'About what's making him so ill.'

'He's going to get better, right?'

'He's in the best place right now and has a very good medical team.'

It was not until Ricky was in Dan's van heading home that she realised her mother hadn't answered her question. She had not said, 'Yes, Ollie is going to get better.'

# 11

HER MOTHER CAME home in the morning to wash and change her clothes before Ricky left for the workshop. She looked exhausted. Her lips were pale and her voice was raw. She flopped on the couch and took a deep breath before making an announcement. She had some good news: Ollie was coming home later in the day. He'd slept through the night and the doctors were pleased.

'Have you been good for Dan?' she asked.

Ricky nodded.

'What did you do last night?'

'I read in my room.'

'I hope Dan wasn't too bored.' She sighed. 'We've thrown the poor man in at the deep end. It's so good of him to take care of you.'

'What time are you bringing Ollie home?'

'Later on today. I don't know exactly when so it's probably easier if you skip the community centre this afternoon. I'll ask Dan to pick you up at lunchtime and bring you to the hospital.'

Ricky gritted her teeth. When Dan had picked her up the previous evening, all she could think about was that her mother had discussed her body with him. It was a hideous betrayal, one that made her burn with shame. She couldn't touch the kebabs he'd bought on the way home. She was pushing chips around her plate when he'd started talking, his voice chatty and neutral.

'So, what do you get up to in the afternoon if you're not at the community centre?' he asked.

She watched him open a second can of Heineken and felt her throat tighten.

'You're not the good girl you pretend to be, are you?'

She braced herself.

'Do you have a boyfriend?'

'Of course not!'

'Whoa!' He laughed and held up a hand. 'Sounds like you're hiding something.'

'It's not like that.'

'Then why doesn't your mum know what you get up to?'

'It's nothing. I'm just working in a garden.'

'What garden?'

'There's a garden near those big tower blocks.' She gestured vaguely in the direction of the buildings. 'We've just harvested the last of the broad beans.'

'Who's "we"?'

Ricky didn't want to tell him about Snowy but there was no way to avoid it. 'Mr Snow. He's a gardener, like Dad.'

Dan stopped smiling. 'Are you spending time alone with a strange man?'

'I'm alone with you, aren't I?'

'We're not strangers, Missy. I'm more or less family.'

'Mr Snow is not a stranger.'

'Then why not tell your mother about him?'

'She's never asked.' Ricky was trying hard to keep a poker face but she was aware that Dan was holding all the aces.

'Sounds like you don't want her to know.'

'Please don't tell her!'

Dan put down his kebab. He narrowed his eyes. 'That wouldn't be right, would it?'

'I really need the garden. I really, really need it.'

'But it's not right. If your mum finds out, she'll be very upset. Not just with you but also with me. I'd be like an accomplice or something.'

'She'll never find out. She's too busy with Ollie. She doesn't care what I do.'

'Hey, that's not nice.'

'It's true.'

Dan gave her a sympathetic smile. 'Look, I'm not blind. I can see your mother doesn't have time for you at the moment but I'm here for you in the meantime.'

Ricky had to blink back tears. 'What if I show you the garden?'

'I don't know.' He sucked air through his teeth. 'This could get me in all sorts of hot water.'

'Please, just meet Mr Snow. He might still be in the garden. You'll see.'

Dan put down his beer and leaned back in his chair. 'If I go along with this, you'll owe me. Big time.'

'I'll do the dishes and the washing. I'll keep the flat clean.'

He was looking at her, smiling. 'That would be a start.'

Snowy was putting his tools away when they arrived. He saw Dan and stood perfectly still. His big face turned bright pink. A hoe dropped from his hand.

'Hello, Mr Snow,' Ricky said.

His eyes tracked from Dan to her.

'Don't worry. Everything's okay.'

He made one of his noises.

'This is Dan. He just wants to see where I'm spending my afternoons.'

Dan made as if to shake Snowy's hand but stopped himself when he realised no hand was being raised to meet his.

'Hello,' he said simply. 'Nice garden you have here.'

Cautiously, Snowy nodded.

'So, the little one has been helping you in the afternoons?'

Snowy glanced at Ricky, flashing the whites of his eyes.

'Do you mind if I have a look around?' Dan was already moving into the garden, following the neat path between the planting beds, walking with his hands behind his back as if he was inspecting the Queen's Guard.

Ricky stayed by the gate, her eyes on Mr Snow, who was making nervous huffing noises. She needed to convince him there was no problem. Nothing had to change. They could carry on just the same, the two of them. They had to. The garden was the only place where she could drop the burden of her disintegrating life and connect with the bustle and hum of all that grew there.

Dan was returning from the back of the garden. It was now or never.

'You're not in any trouble. Dan just wanted to see the garden.'

When Snowy didn't reply, she felt compelled to fill the silence, to remind him they had a tacit agreement, that Dan's appearance changed nothing between them.

'Do you remember my brother Ollie?'

He gave her a cautious nod.

'He's in hospital at the moment.'

Snowy made a noise, a whimper.

'But Ollie will get better soon and then he'll visit the garden with me.'

He glanced away, his eyes settling on the hoe lying at his feet.

'It looks like you know what you're doing,' said Dan. 'Very neat and tidy.'

Mr Snow was watching him out of the corners of his eyes as if expecting a blow. When it didn't come, he picked up the hoe and started walking away.

'I'll see you tomorrow, Mr Snow,' Ricky called out before following Dan through the gate.

'He's not all there, is he?' said Dan.

'He's got some sort of disability. He can't speak very well,' said Ricky.

'He looks harmless enough, I suppose.'

'It's good of him to let me work in the garden.'

'And all you do is gardening?'

'What do you mean?'

He laughed. 'Never mind.'

But she did mind. She thought of what Pauly Cloney had said and worried.

That evening, Ricky had gone to bed in a heightened state of anxiety and passed a restless night of hyper-coloured dreams. She was chased by a shadow, choked by an assailant and trapped in a windowless room with a ceiling so low that she could not fully stand up. Just prior to waking, she'd found herself in a garden where huge spiders had spun webs that hung like fishermen's nets. Flattening herself on the ground, she'd spied a narrow tunnel and by crawling on her belly had made her way out of the garden to a forest of strange leafy trees. But when she looked closer, she saw that the long, bright-coloured leaves were snakes. They were dangling from branches, their small heads probing the air, seeking her out.

The dreams had been relentless and surreal, one folding into another, seamlessly defying logic and giving her no rest. She was hiding, running and thrashing her way out of dark, cluttered lanes and tight, windowless rooms. Just before dawn as the birds began singing outside her window, she'd started to windmill her arms in the thickening air. It was Ricky's first attempt at flight and she was clumsy and unsure. Her feet lifted. Her body began to float. As she rose to consciousness, she managed to bump along a few inches off the ground.

She'd woken in a state of wonder. The feeling of being suspended, of being unshackled from gravity, remained alive within her like a tiny flicker of hope.

Dan waited at the entrance to the hospital to let an old lady through and then again to help a teenage boy in a wheelchair.

'That was nice,' said Ricky. It cost her to pay him a compliment but they were playing by new rules now, Dan's rules.

He smiled. 'My good deeds for the day.'

When they got to Ollie's ward, a nurse led them to a large room partitioned with blue concertina curtains. Ollie was at the very end, near the window. He was sleeping in a narrow bed with his arm on a pillow next to his body. A bag of cloudy liquid was feeding into his arm.

Her mother got up from the armchair next to the bed. She looked about a hundred years old. Her clothes were wrinkled and her hair was messy. Ricky was making her way across the room when she realised her mother was not looking in her direction. Her eyes were on Dan.

'You're an angel,' she said, wrapping her arms around him. She pressed her face into his shoulder, thanking him profusely.

Stunned, Ricky backed away. By the time they had separated, she was on the other side of Ollie's bed.

Her mother glanced over and must have seen the hurt in her eyes. 'I'll just say goodbye to Dan and then we can have a catch-up,' she said, hastily steering him out of the room.

But it was awkward when she returned. They'd missed their moment and, despite her mother insisting on a hug, a proper connection didn't happen.

'Why is Ollie in this big room?' Ricky asked.

'He's only here while they give him some special medicine,' said her mother.

'But he had medicine yesterday.'

'They're trying something different.' She undid Ricky's ponytail and ran her fingers through her hair, untucking it from behind her ears, rearranging it to frame her face in a more feminine way. 'You're pale.'

'I'm fine.' Despite her own bruised feelings, Ricky recognised her mother's exhaustion.

'Are you eating properly?'

'Can I have a kitten, Mum?' Ricky didn't mean to ask but the words had burst out of her as she rushed to avoid her mother's question.

'A kitten needs a lot of attention, honey. We can't give it that right now.'

'Ollie would like one, too.'

'Ollie wants a dog.'

'He'd settle for a kitten. I've already checked.'

'How did you check?'

'I asked him.'

Her mother glanced at Ollie.

'It would be good for his health. People with pets live longer and happier lives. That's a fact.'

Her mother winced. 'When did you ask Ollie?'

'I asked him yesterday.'

Her mother frowned.

'There's a cat on the estate with two kittens. You wouldn't have to spend money on my birthday. It would be the perfect present.'

Her mother was still looking at Ollie. 'It's not all about you right now.'

Why did she have to say that? Of course it wasn't all about her.

'Are you crying?'

'No.'

'Oh, honey.' Her mother's expression softened. 'Let's see how Ollie's treatment goes before we make any decisions about kittens.'

When the bag of liquid had been emptied into Ollie's small body, he was wheeled back to the same room as the previous day. He now had a roommate, a bald boy with dry, scabbed lips. According to the whiteboard above his bed, the boy was called Aaron. Whatever disease Aaron had was not a good one. The boy was very thin. His skin was pale yellow. Ricky waited for her mother to take a toilet break before investigating. She was reading his chart when he opened his eyes.

'What disease have you got?' she asked. Her mother would have killed her for asking this but there was no time to beat around the bush. She only had a few minutes.

'I have leukaemia,' said Aaron.

'Uh-huh.' Ricky wished she hadn't asked. Leukaemia was a type of cancer and she didn't like to think of Aaron's chances. She'd read his chart and knew he was only seven years old. The thought that he could die any minute made her agonise over what to say next.

'What's that boy's name?' Aaron lifted his bony arm and pointed to Ollie.

'His name is Oliver Cromwell Bird. He's my brother.'

'What kind of cancer has he got?'

'Don't be ridiculous!' Her voice was unnecessarily loud.

Aaron's eyes widened. He looked as if he was going to cry. 'Where's my mummy?'

'I'm sorry. I didn't mean to upset you.' She didn't want Aaron to cry. He looked so ill and pitiful.

His bottom lip was quivering.

'Your mother called while you were sleeping and said she would be here soon. She advised me to talk to you in the meantime. She said you are a very good boy.'

A hesitant smile appeared on Aaron's chapped lips. 'I am a very good boy. You can ask the nurses.'

'I already have. They gave you five stars. Gold stars with glitter.'

Aaron's smile widened to expose new front teeth. One was still only half grown, a jagged stump. 'Are you sure your brother doesn't have cancer?'

She had to control herself. By the look of things, Aaron would not live to see his tooth finish growing. 'It's not cancer.'

'But I thought—'

'If you have to know, Ollie has a very rare condition.'

'What's that?'

'He has a parasitic twin. It's like a human being stuck inside a human being. The inside twin is attached to his lung and is sucking the life juice out of him. That's why he's so weak.'

Aaron considered this for a moment. 'Will Ollie die?'

'Of course not.' Ricky thought of Aaron's half-formed tooth and forced a smile. 'Neither will you.'

'That's good news.' Aaron looked pleased. 'Are you sure your brother is not going to die? He looks quite sick.'

What was this boy's problem? She felt like pinching him. 'My brother is too famous to die. If you bothered to watch the news you'd already know that.'

Aaron looked unconvinced. 'He's very white.'

'That's because he's wearing TV makeup. He was interviewed by the BBC this morning.'

'Wait.' Aaron held up his bony arm again. 'Ollie is a TV star?'

'Ollie and his twin. It's a double act.'

'I've never met a TV star before. They sometimes visit the children's wards but you have to be sick at Christmas to get the good ones. Amanda Holden visited a while ago but that was during *Britain's Got Talent*.'

'Ollie's coming home today.'

'I wouldn't be so sure.'

'I am sure.'

'Are you annoying this boy?' Her mother had returned and was standing at the foot of Aaron's bed.

'I was just telling Aaron that Ollie's coming home.'

Her mother smiled at the boy. 'I hope we haven't disturbed you.'

'I'm going to ask Mum to bring in her laptop.'

Ricky's mother nodded.

'We're going to watch Ollie on TV.'

'Oh, that's nice.' Ricky's mother always said 'that's nice' when she thought someone was talking rubbish.

'I missed Amanda Holden but one of the nurses said Simon Cowell might come next time.'

'From *Britain's Got Talent*?'

'He's got a lot of hair. It comes out of his shirt.'

'Yes, he has.'

Aaron sighed. 'I need to sleep now.'

'We'll try to keep it down.'

Her mother raised her eyebrows as they headed back to Ollie's side of the room. 'Poor kid,' she mouthed.

'He's got leukaemia,' Ricky whispered.

Her mother made a sad face. 'The medication must be affecting his brain.' She retrieved her handbag from the floor next to Ollie's bed and took out ten pounds. She told Ricky to go downstairs and buy some sandwiches and drinks.

Everyone else must have had the same idea because there was a massive queue at the hospital cafeteria. Ricky wandered over to the WH Smith kiosk to examine the grim assortment of boxed sandwiches. As she reached into the refrigerated display for an egg sandwich, the lights flickered. She put the sandwich back and the lights stopped flickering. She picked it up and they started flickering again.

Behind her someone laughed. She turned and saw a boy about her age. When she looked at the display again, the lights had stopped flickering.

'You must carry a charge like an electric eel,' said the boy.

She laughed. It was the sort of cheeky thing she might say.

He waited as she paid and then followed her out. 'Are you visiting someone, too?'

'My brother. He's sharing a room with a boy called Aaron who's seven years old. Aaron's got cancer.'

The boy pushed the button for the lift. 'My mother's got cancer.'

'What kind?'

He tapped his head. 'Brain.'

'Does it make her head swell?' Ricky imagined brain cancer growing like a cauliflower, ballooning inside the skull and making the bones expand.

'She looks perfectly normal. She's just really sleepy.'

'My brother is sleepy, too, but he doesn't have cancer.'

'Okay.'

'My name's Ricky.'

'Jack.'

'Do you live nearby?'

'King's Crescent.'

Ricky smiled. 'Me, too.'

The lift arrived and they both stepped inside. She only needed to go to the sixth floor but she rode with him all the way to the eleventh. By the time the lift finished its ascent she knew that Jack not only lived on the same estate but he'd also moved to Camden recently. His mother had fallen ill almost immediately. She'd fainted while they were unpacking.

Ricky got out of the lift, eager to prolong their time together.

'Camden seems to make people sick,' she said.

'You're not sick though.'

'No, but there's a lot about my life that makes me sick.'

He laughed. 'Would some chocolate make you feel better?' He dug in his pocket and pulled out a Crunchie.

'Thank you.' She was delighted by the gift. 'But what about you?'

'I took two.'

'You *took* two?'

'You didn't see me pay for them, did you?' He was smirking. 'Now you've received stolen goods, so you're a criminal too.'

Ricky surprised herself by laughing. She'd never received anything stolen in her life.

'How old are you, Jack?'

'Almost thirteen.'

A thrill went through Ricky.

Her mother was standing in the corridor talking to a nurse when she returned to the ward. She saw Ricky and followed her into Ollie's room.

'They're going to keep Ollie in,' she said. 'I'll be staying with him again.'

'Please let me stay, too,' said Ricky.

'It's not up to me. They won't let you.'

'I can hide under the bed. I'll be as quiet as an ant. You won't even hear my antennae move.'

'Sorry, honey. I've already called Dan.'

'Please, please, please.' Panic was rising in her chest. 'I don't want to go home without you.'

'Come on. You're a big girl now.'

'I really don't want to.'

'It's just for tonight.' Her mother clucked sympathetically. 'Where's our lunch?'

As Ricky reached into the plastic bag, she experienced a brief moment of dizziness. It was like the flicking off and on of a light switch. She steadied herself against the bed before handing the boxed sandwich to her mother.

'Thanks. Where's yours?'

'I already ate it.'

This was the first outright lie she'd ever told her mother. Until that moment, the most dishonest thing she'd done was not tell her things and this she'd only started doing since arriving in Camden. Ricky had never kept secrets in Brixton, even when it would have been better not to say anything. That's what her father explained after she'd told her mother about the cannabis plants he grew at the allotment. 'Honesty is generally the best policy,' he told her. 'But you don't have to tell a fat person he's fat or a short person he's short. They know these things. Just like your mother knows I have the odd puff. I would never encourage you to lie because that would be wrong. But let's agree that what goes on at the allotment, stays at the allotment.'

Ricky thought of the Crunchie in her pocket. It was wrong but wrong in an exciting way, like driving a car faster than the speed limit. The chocolate bar was precious, something to mark her new friendship. Before they'd parted, she'd discovered they shared the same birthday. Jack was the new friend Tina had mentioned. He was the gift.

She watched her mother opening the egg sandwich and felt queasy. Despite not eating since the previous day, she wasn't the least bit hungry.

# 12

THE FLAT DIDN'T feel like home without her mother or Ollie. Her brother's absence was more like a presence because it was large and grey, a fearful darkness that billowed out of his empty bedroom. Ricky made sure to keep her own door closed and her window open but the smell of Lynx body spray permeated the flat and infiltrated her bedroom, a constant reminder that Dan was never far away.

Ollie's stay in hospital was extended by a day and then another day. A whole week had passed and there was still no talk of him coming home. They were doing tests. He was sedated. They were trying different medications. Blah, blah, blah. Ricky had stopped asking what was wrong with her little brother because she was always given the same non-answers.

When her mother did come home, it was to wash and check that there was milk in the fridge and bread on the sideboard. She was harried and distracted, more concerned about clean clothes and groceries than about her daughter's wellbeing. When she talked to Ricky, it was brief, her eyes tracking to the top of her head as if she had a to-do list and was already thinking about the next thing. She didn't ask questions and didn't seem interested in what Ricky was doing. This would have been bearable if her father had been around but he'd become elusive since breaking the news of Sophie's pregnancy. He still called but a new, serious tone had crept into his conversation. Being serious was totally out of character for him. Her father had always been a joker and a storyteller. Humour was their thing, a reference point that defined their relationship. Without it, Ricky felt lost and out of step.

Unable to find her way back to their former safe place of trust and intimacy, Ricky withdrew. She started restricting the information she shared, offering concise replies to his repetitive and uninspired questions. She was all right, she insisted. Everything was fine. Yes, Dan was very kind. They were lucky to have him. Camden was great. The summer workshop was fun. Katie had given her a new book of short stories by William Trevor. He was ace. Katie was organising a field trip to the Hunterian Museum.

Ricky kept returning to the last afternoon she'd spent with her father at the allotment. It was a bittersweet memory of planting seedlings that would mature in late summer; basil and bell peppers she would never taste. It had been just the two of them. Ollie had stayed at home to help their mother pack. The day had been beautiful, a high and wide blue sky filled with birdsong and the rustle and whizz of insects. Ricky had thrown herself into the garden, channelling the tornado of fear and self-doubt whirling inside her. When they stopped for lunch, her father had given her the multivitamins and a lecture about the importance of exercise. King's Crescent was a tough place, he'd warned. She would need to stay healthy and be strong.

'When I was your age, I'd already swum the Channel,' he'd said. 'This was all in a dream, mind you, but it was a very realistic dream so it counts for something. Your grandmother found me in the garden in the middle of the night. I was swimming in my sleep and had almost reached the neighbour's wall. If their dog hadn't started barking, I might have made it to France.'

Ricky had laughed despite herself.

He'd chuckled, pleased to have lifted her mood. 'Your nan never got the grass stains out of my pyjamas.'

'I don't want to leave, Dad.'

'I don't want you to go either, Sport.' He'd put his arm around her and kissed the side of her head. 'But I'll always be here for you and I'll come and visit. You never know, one day I might even move to Camden.'

This conversation now felt more like a movie she'd watched than an actual memory. It was hard to believe that only a few weeks earlier they had been eating biscuits together on the garden bench. Ricky ached for his contact and affection but underneath the loneliness and longing, she blamed herself for his new coolness. As if to torture herself, she replayed the scene in the café over and over. With each replay, her behaviour became more unreasonable. She'd been awful, repulsive. Why had she driven him away like that? It had been the shock of his announcement. She hadn't anticipated a new sister. If only she could have that afternoon again, she would do it differently. Why did she only get one chance? Why wasn't life like a video game you could experience over and over again, getting better with each play?

Even Mr Snow had become cold and unfriendly. Since Dan's visit, he now greeted Ricky with a simple nod and showed her what to do by pointing. She'd broken an unspoken agreement by bringing a stranger to his garden. He no longer trusted her.

Ricky knew he was constantly observing her but, whenever she looked at him, his eyes were always focused on a point over her shoulder.

She doggedly kept returning because the garden was the only place where she could forget about the mess she was making of everything. Here, she could let it go and become part of something bigger, the relentless cycle of growth, fruition and decay.

With the arrival of the cat and kittens, her visits to the garden had become even more precious. Her heart beat faster at the thought of them. The kittens' eyes had now opened. They had fattened up and were moving more. With some of the money her mother left for groceries, she bought cat food, luxury stuff in gold tins. Lola had been suspicious at first but after several food deliveries, she'd stopped hissing. Ricky knew it was stupid, but she needed the cat to accept her. If she could convince Lola to like her, it would prove she wasn't completely unlovable. Ricky needed someone or something to want, or at least need, her.

'Have you seen a blue handbag?'

Ricky stood up in time to see Snowy disappear behind the lattice of runner beans. An old woman was standing by the fence waving an orange plastic Sainsbury's bag. In her other hand was a cigarette.

'I think I left it under one of your marrows,' said the woman. She took a drag on her cigarette.

'They're courgettes,' Ricky replied. 'Your handbag isn't here.'

'They are marrows, dear.' The woman nodded, insistent.

Ricky didn't contradict her again. The old lady's hair was sticking up as if she'd just got out of bed. She had a wild look in her eyes.

Crouching next to the courgette plant, Ricky pretended to search for a handbag. 'I'm sorry but it's definitely not here.'

'I must have left it in Edinburgh.' The woman sighed heavily.

Ricky picked her way across the garden. When she got to the fence, she noticed the old lady was wearing slippers. They were the soft, padded kind without a rubber sole. She wasn't properly dressed for outdoors. Her top was actually a nightie tucked inside a blue pleated skirt. The nightie was made of a light synthetic fabric with pink flowers. It was buttoned up wrong and made her bosoms look lopsided.

'Can I take you home?' Ricky asked.

'Not until I find my handbag. It's full of valuables. Bulging.' Her gaze dropped to the courgettes again.

'If you tell me your name and address, I'll contact the authorities.'

The woman frowned. 'I must have left it on the train. Eggs always give me a headache. Nasty things. Nothing like the chicken which is a very nice creature.'

'Please wait there. I'll come around to where you are.'

Ricky hastily washed her hands. Aware of Snowy's eyes following her, she threw on her backpack and hurried out of the garden.

When she linked arms with the old lady, she could feel bones under loose flesh. The woman seemed shrunken and defenceless. She became passive, allowing Ricky to lead her forward like a dance partner. Lifting her chin, the old woman began walking in a graceful manner.

'Can you tell me your address, please?'

'Address?' The woman shook her head, confused.

'Yes, where you live.'

'It's here somewhere.'

'Do you think you will recognise it?'

'Of course I will. I'm not mad.'

The estate had at least six identical buildings. Ricky began at the flats nearest the garden, pointing out furniture and belongings on the balconies in the hope that the old lady would recognise her home. The woman chattered in a frantic, disconnected way as they followed the path behind the buildings. Boats made her seasick, she said. But they had cleaned up Camden Lock. People used to throw their rubbish into it. Dead fish. A terrible stink. It was sad about the boy though. He'd been too young to die like that.

'What boy?' Ricky asked, slowing her pace. 'The boy from the empty flat?'

'You can't leave a flat empty.' The woman tugged Ricky's arm to keep moving. 'People smash windows and dump rubbish. Rats. I see them all the time. The size of them. As big as cats.'

'You mentioned a boy.'

'No, I didn't.'

'Yes, you di—' Ricky stopped walking, alerted by a familiar smell.

'Why have we stopped?'

'Shhh.'

Ricky could hear the loud, dangerous laughter of teenage boys. The smell of cannabis was heavy in the air. Despite her awareness of possible danger, an image of her father came into her head. He was sitting in the doorway of his garden shed, smoking a spliff after a day at the allotment.

'What's going on?' The old woman tried to disentangle herself but Ricky clamped her elbow tightly over her arm. She barred her lips with a finger and pulled her behind the wall of a flat.

Ricky was trying to peek around the wall when the old woman let out an impatient 'Well!' and, with her shoulder, shunted them out of their hiding place.

Two youths were sitting on the grass under the shade of a tree. They were about sixteen and didn't look like they belonged to the estate. Their clothes were too new and they both had fashionable haircuts. They gave her an unfriendly look but their hostility wasn't rough or raw like Pauly Cloney's. It was more show. Ricky wasn't sure if this made them more or less of a threat than the local youths. Posh boys, particularly stoned posh boys, might do something reckless to prove they were hard. Her first impulse was to run but she couldn't leave the old woman. The teenagers had been drinking. A half-empty bottle of Strongbow cider was sitting upright on the grass between them.

The bigger of the boys pushed himself to his feet, stumbling drunkenly.

'What the fuck are you looking at?' he sneered.

'Nothing,' Ricky replied.

'You calling us nothing?'

Ricky shook her head and attempted to pull the old woman away but her slipper caught. She tripped and stumbled. Ricky heard the boys laugh but she held the woman close to prevent her falling and continued leading her away. Despite the danger and the difficulty of guiding the old woman across the uneven terrain, it felt good to be helping someone more vulnerable than herself. The woman's weakness gave her strength.

Old age was like youth, thought Ricky, but at opposite ends of a bell curve. The centre of the arc was where all the power and control were concentrated. Those at the low points had little or no authority to make decisions about their lives. Someone like Dan didn't merit the power he held over her.

His only qualification was his age and that was not something he'd earned. The system was unfair. It took away her freedom and her voice.

The old woman didn't pay attention long enough to recognise any of the flats but the walking seemed to have a calming effect. After a few minutes, she stopped talking nonsense and started making sense. She took a cigarette out of the plastic bag and sparked a lighter against its tip, breathing the smoke deep into her lungs.

Her name was Beatrice, she said, exhaling with gusto. People called her Bea, 'Like a busy bee. I never sit still.' Bea was a Londoner, Camden born and bred. There was no better place to live than King's Crescent. She shared a flat on the estate with her son. It was small but cosy. She had her comforts: Thorntons, a reclining chair and a flat-screen TV, Korean apparently. Her son had bought it on the cheap from another resident, a woman with a foul temper. Bea smoked but it was one of life's pleasures and no one was going to make her stop.

'Do you recognise where we are?' Ricky asked.

'It's not easy for the girl,' Bea said. 'I blame the mother.'

'Which girl? What's her name?'

'That woman drank the whole way through her pregnancy. I thought she'd give birth to one of those frog babies.' Bea took another drag and coughed before continuing. 'Surprise, surprise, the girl came out normal. Well, as normal as someone could be with a bitch like that for a mother. The very day she came home with the baby, she stole my rings and took all my money. Cleaned me out, she did. Never seen her since.'

The old woman had become more and more agitated as she told this story. Her face had flushed and there was sweat on her upper lip.

'My son doesn't care if I live or die. He's an idiot. I only stay alive for the girl. God knows what would happen to her if I wasn't here.'

Bea started crying. At first it was just a sniffle but, as Ricky led her to a bench near the playground, she started sobbing like a child, her shoulders shaking, the noise loud and uncontrolled.

'There, there,' said Ricky. These were the words her mother used to soothe her when she was upset. Just saying them made her want to cry, too.

'I worry about the girl. She has such stupid ideas. Her father doesn't care about her, or me for that matter.'

'I know how you feel.'

Bea's sobbing slowed. She looked at Ricky, her red-rimmed eyes full of tears. 'What do you mean?'

'Nothing.'

'It's not nothing. Spit it out.'

'My brother is in hospital and my mother is always up there with him. My father is in Brixton. He's going to have another baby and has no time for me anymore. I hate it here but I have nowhere else to go. It's like prison. I don't have any friends. Everyone thinks my mother's boyfriend is great but he—'

Her voice broke.

Ricky took a deep breath and tried again. 'He—'

Bea nodded, encouraging, but Ricky couldn't get it out. She had to swallow several times before she could talk again.

'Everyone is angry with me except Katie but she's only a facilitator so she doesn't count. I hate myself and I hate the feeling of worms wriggling inside me all the time.' She lifted her hands to her chest. 'Everything is changing. I hate it. I have to stop it.'

Beatrice was completely still. Her eyes hadn't left Ricky, who had been speaking wildly without censoring herself.

When she stopped to catch her breath, the old lady took hold of her hand. She squeezed it.

'It feels like everything is wrong,' said Bea.

Ricky nodded, fearful of blurting out more secrets.

'Just do your best and keep going.' Bea patted her hand.

Ricky was blowing her nose with one of Bea's tissues when she felt something wet touch her calf. As she reached down to rub behind the dog's ear, she saw Caitlin's pink trainers.

'I found her!' Caitlin shouted. 'Over here.'

Abbie was breathless. 'Granny, where have you been? I've been so worried about you.'

Beatrice let go of Ricky's hand. She reached out to Abbie, who pulled her gently to her feet.

'What a time we've had,' Bea said. 'They gave us oysters gratin.'

'Oh, Granny. No more of this going off on your own.' Abbie put her arm around her grandmother.

'But I wasn't on my own. I was with a friend.'

Abbie shot Ricky a look over her shoulder. It was brief but contained no malice.

Caitlin lingered after Abbie and her grandmother left. She was fussing over her dog but Ricky could tell she was at a loss. Girls like Caitlin needed to have people around them. She needed troops to feel powerful. Ricky didn't want to be a foot soldier but neither did she want to be on her own.

'My brother is going to be interviewed on Sky TV,' she said. It was highly unlikely the Cloneys paid for Sky.

'Sky is rubbish. Everyone knows that,' Caitlin replied.

'He was interviewed by Amanda Holden.'

'She's rubbish.'

'It's a programme about people with strange medical conditions. My brother's condition is one of the rarest apart from that man in Birmingham with six fingers. Ollie might even get flown to America. Business class.'

'Ha! At my school there's a boy with one leg. He said he was born like that but everyone knows he got it chopped off by a Muslim.'

'Why would a Muslim chop off his leg?'

'Because they're evil.'

'Samia is Muslim.'

'Shut up!' Conversation with Caitlin was a minefield. 'The ones you've really got to watch are the perverts. This place is crawling with them.'

'Uh-huh.'

Caitlin tugged Baby's lead. 'I'm going to the Crescent. Are you coming or not?'

The invitation was a command. Caitlin wanted Ricky to go with her but had to make it sound like a favour.

Market day was coming to an end on King's Crescent. People were packing away their wares and taking down the canopies and metal structures of the stalls. The vendors took no notice as the girls wandered past. They had been sitting in the hot sun for the good part of the day and wanted to go home.

Baby veered toward a Caribbean food stall, straining at the lead. The stall was partly dismantled but there was meat sitting on the grill. It was charred and glistening with fat. Ricky started walking faster as saliva surged into her mouth and acid rose in her throat. She was struggling to control the urge to vomit when Caitlin and Baby caught up with her outside Costcutters.

'I always do a double knot here,' said Caitlin, making an elaborate show of tying Baby to the lamppost outside the supermarket. 'Dog thieves.'

Ricky couldn't imagine anyone wanting to steal the fat old Staffie. 'What would they want her for?'

'Gypsies take them for dog fights.'

'Baby doesn't look like a fighter.'

'You're right. She's too valuable. They'd ask for a ransom.'

'How would they know who to contact?' There was no disc on Baby's collar.

'Do you know how fucking boring you are?' Caitlin patted her mouth as if yawning.

Ricky followed the girl into Costcutters. It was a small supermarket with four narrow aisles. The place smelled vaguely of chemical air freshener and had a low, tiled ceiling with fluorescent tube lighting. One of these lights was flickering over the liquor aisle. The rapid blink-blink of the fluorescent bulb made Ricky feel nervous and electrical. She hurried through the aisles, eager to leave. The supermarket had one cashier and a man on the door, a security guard. The two men looked like brothers.

She was at the counter paying for cat food when someone started shouting and swearing loudly. Caitlin emerged from the back of the shop, pushed from behind by the wiry security guard.

'Get out!' he shouted. 'Don't come in here stealing!'

'I wasn't stealing!' shouted Caitlin as she was bustled outside to the pavement. 'This shop is rubbish. Your prices are too high and you're thieving Paki bastards!'

This seemed to enrage the man behind the counter. He pointed a finger at Ricky.

'You get out, too!' he shouted. 'You're banned.'

'I didn't do anything,' she protested, but the security guard had returned and was already pushing her toward the door.

With a shove, Ricky was ousted from the shop. She tripped over Caitlin who was squatting next to Baby, untying the dog's lead.

Caitlin stuck her elbow out to protect the dog. 'Watch out, you stupid cow!'

The guard was shouting from the doorway but Ricky could no longer hear his words. Her ears were ringing with shock and embarrassment, her attention caught by a familiar figure standing outside the pub on the other side of the road.

'Hey, leave those girls alone!' shouted Dan as he sprinted across the road. 'If you touch either of them again, I'll have you up for assault.'

'They are thieves,' said the security guard. 'They tried to steal alcohol.'

This was news to Ricky. She began to stutter but Dan was quicker off the mark.

'Bullshit.' He placed a hand on her shoulder. 'I know both of these young ladies and they would never steal.'

'They are thieves and bitches. They are banned from this shop for life!'

'Watch your language, mate! These girls are minors.'

'They can fuck off!'

'One more word and I'll deck you.'

The security guard opened his mouth but didn't say anything. He was younger and a lot smaller than Dan.

'Let's get out of here.' Dan waited for Caitlin to finish untying the dog. With a hand on each of their shoulders, he steered them away.

'We didn't steal anything,' Ricky said. Her mouth was so dry, she almost couldn't get the words out. 'We really didn't.'

Dan gave her a sceptical look.

'It's them who are the thieving bastards,' said Caitlin. 'Mum says their prices are daylight robbery.'

'Is that so?' Dan snorted. 'Mums tend to know what they're talking about.'

'Your name's Dan, isn't it?'

He nodded.

'We've seen you around.'

'Who's we?'

'My friend Abbie and me. Abbie fancies you, chronic.'

Dan laughed. 'She's probably a bit young for me.'

'She thinks you look like Poldark.'

'You're making me blush.' Dan laughed again.

As they neared the estate, Caitlin caught Ricky's eye. She winked and pointed to the pocket of Ricky's cargo shorts.

Ricky was confused at first but then became aware of something bumping against her leg.

It wasn't very big but its liquid contents gave it weight. Discreetly, without attracting Dan's attention, she reached down and folded the flap of her pocket over the miniature bottle of vodka.

# 13

RICKY HAD EXPECTED her mother to grill her about the trip to the museum but she'd signed the consent form without reading it. These days, she didn't seem to care about herself let alone about her daughter. She'd been sleeping in the armchair next to Ollie's bed for over two weeks and was looking worse for it. Her hair was lank and uncombed. She wore no makeup and only occasionally changed her clothes. Her face was different, too, frozen somehow, washed of emotion. When she looked at Ricky, it was without any emotional charge. She spoke in a flat monotone.

Ricky couldn't bear to think too much about her mother or their disintegrating relationship. It was too complicated and painful. Nothing between them was solid anymore. The ground kept shifting. She had to push down her feelings because when she tried to make sense of where she and her mother were, she felt engulfed by emptiness. How could her life have changed so much in such a short time? Her old family life was distant and alien. Memories of that time were getting mixed up with the strange, vivid dreams she was now experiencing on a nightly basis.

She'd stopped going to her mother for affection because she no longer held her properly. Her hugs were loose and disengaged. When they were at the hospital together, her mother's eyes were always on Ollie yet his eyes were almost always closed. When he did open them, he was drowsy and quiet. Ricky could tell he was always listening but he was either too sick or too exhausted to respond. Her brother was like a woodlouse, silently curled in on himself, waiting for the right moment to unfurl.

A week or so after their first meeting, Ricky had bumped into Jack again at the hospital cafeteria. He was sitting at a table on his own, eating salt and vinegar crisps.

He greeted her warmly and held out the bag to her. 'Have a crisp,' he said.

'I've just eaten, thank you.'

'I doubt it.' He laughed. 'You've got skinny.'

Ricky was stunned. No one else had noticed she wasn't eating, not even Dan and they shared the same dining table. Dan never questioned her tiny portions or her excuses about having already eaten. He never checked what she did with the grocery money. As long as there was something for him to eat and beer in the fridge, he was happy.

'How's your mother?'

Jack shrugged. 'Not so good.'

'My brother isn't very well either.'

'Mum isn't talking anymore. She just stares without looking.' He put the crisp bag to his lips and shook the crumbs into his mouth.

'What would happen to you if—'

'If?' He scoffed. 'You mean, *when*.'

'Sorry.'

'I tell you one thing that will happen.' Jack lifted his t-shirt. Below one arm was a long, triangular bruise. It was recent, blue in the centre with a lighter purple edge. 'I'm going to kill my stepfather.'

'Your stepfather did that to you?'

'I didn't do it to myself.' He let his t-shirt drop.

Ricky was shocked. 'Shouldn't you go to the police?'

'No.'

'But you've got bruises. That's proof.'

'What if the police believe me? They'll take me away and I won't be able to see Mum.'

'You're just going to take it?'

'The way things are going it won't be for much longer.'

Ricky understood what this meant and didn't say anything.

'When the time comes, I'll make the bastard pay.'

'How?'

'I might set him on fire while he's sleeping.'

'You can't do that.'

'Can't I?'

The next time they met it was at the outdoor kiosk next to the hospital entrance. Jack waved her over, a big smile on his face. He wiped the mouth of his orange juice bottle and held it out to her as she sat beside him. Every time Ricky was in his company, she found herself relaxing and dropping her guard. Jack was generous and open, unafraid to show his rawness and vulnerability. His troubles made them equals and because they were equals, she could be herself.

She told him about Bea and the missing handbag, and the train to Edinburgh with oysters gratin. Jack laughed but not unkindly.

'I'll end up like her one day,' he said. 'They'll find me wandering around in my nightie, looking for my handbag.'

He performed a pantomime of walking with a handbag over his arm. He moved like a woman, with exaggerated delicacy and grace, not caring that people could see him. His boldness thrilled Ricky. He did what he liked and didn't care what others thought. She wanted to be like him. She didn't want to care or feel. She wanted to laugh at herself despite all her problems. At the very least, she didn't want to cry.

She wished Jack had been able to go with them to the Hunterian Museum. He would have distracted her with his wildness and humour and she wouldn't have made such a fool of herself. He would have done something to make everything seem like a joke.

It was the tiny kitten that was her undoing. She couldn't stop looking at it. The formaldehyde had bleached it, making it translucent white like a wax sculpture. Katie and Samia had moved along the display cases to check out other pickled animals but Ricky couldn't stop looking at the small feline face and body. There were claws on its miniature paws. Every feature was perfect. The entire kitten was perfect or at least it had been once. Ricky studied the tiny umbilical cord attached to its abdomen. The poor thing hadn't been given a chance. The kitten had never tasted milk or filled its tiny lungs with air. It had been taken out of its mother's womb before it was born. How could someone do that to such a small, perfect creature?

Until the kitten, she'd been fine. Better than fine. The Hunterian Museum was fantastic, even better than the Imperial War Museum near Brixton. The exhibits were all real things, skeletons and creatures bobbing inside jars. The only audio-visual bit was a screen showing videos of real operations on real people. Samia had turned a funny colour and quickly moved on but Ricky had stayed to watch, fascinated, as doctors removed a tumour from inside a man's head. The surgeons were surprisingly rough, jostling the brain with their metal instruments as they snipped and sucked, before removing a large white blob.

Samia had revived when they got to the giant man. Charles Byrne was seven and a half feet tall, impressive even for a skeleton.

'I would love to be that big,' she said.

'You would have to eat ten fish fingers to everybody else's one,' said Ricky.

'I don't eat fish fingers.'

'You wouldn't be able to ride a bike.'

'I don't ride a bike. Neither do you.'

'I do.'

Samia frowned. 'I've never seen you.'

'I had a BMX but I had to leave it behind when we moved.' Ricky pictured her old beloved bicycle dumped beside the bins and felt her throat tighten. 'I'm probably getting a new one for my birthday.'

She probably wasn't getting any such thing. She wasn't even sure her mother remembered that she was about to turn thirteen.

'Look over here. These two were the original Siamese twins,' said Katie. 'They're called conjoined twins these days.'

The photo showed two men with long ponytails. They were posed together, arms around each other, as if they were good friends enjoying fun times. Ricky already knew about conjoined twins and examined all the photos in the display. The men were posed the same way in every photo.

'These brothers were a bit like your parasitic twins, Ricky. They were identical twins from a single egg that failed to separate fully.'

Ricky tried to figure out where the twins were joined.

Katie noticed her interest. 'They were joined at the hip.'

'How did they get their trousers on?'

To Ricky's surprise, Samia started laughing, a proper guffaw that brought tears to her eyes. Ricky had never seen her laugh but recognised the high-pitched sound she often heard coming through the shared wall of the flats. The outburst contained joy and freedom.

Only Ricky and Samia had turned up for the Hunterian field trip. Katie had invited everyone but visiting a museum was not a high priority for the youth of the estate. Neither was a creative workshop. Attendance had dropped since the beginning of summer. Abbie was often absent.

Ricky had been enjoying herself until the pickled kitten. It was the unfairness of it that prompted her tears. She imagined the tiny thing being ripped out of its mother's womb. The shock of cold air. Eyes shut, paws paddling against a grotesque power. She'd felt a pulling and falling sensation. The room seemed to dim before brightening again. With a wrench, she became one with the kitten, her senses screaming as its body was plunged into the cold solution, liquid filling its nostrils and poisoning its lungs. She was drowning, being drowned.

'What on earth's the matter, Ricky?' asked Katie, who had rushed back when she heard her gasping for breath.

Ricky couldn't say anything or explain. Everyone was looking at her. She was choking and crying.

Katie put her arm around her shoulders and guided her into the ladies. It was a big washroom with three cubicles and a long marble bench. Ricky felt herself being lifted, and then she was sitting on the bench next to a basin. Katie's arms were around her and she was sobbing into her shoulder.

They were convulsive sobs. All the tears she'd been holding back were jolted out of her with great contractions of her diaphragm. When she finally lifted her head from Katie's shoulder, she saw that Samia had followed them inside. The girl's back was against the washroom door as if to block intrusion. She was staring at Ricky, her eyes wide with concern.

Katie took wet wipes out of her bag. She ran one under the cold tap before wiping Ricky's face.

'Can you tell me what's wrong?' she asked. 'Is there a problem at home?'

Ricky looked into Katie's eyes and recognised a readiness to understand and help.

'You know you can tell me.'

She felt the ache in her chest travel up to her throat. She just had to say it, get it out. Katie was listening.

Ricky opened her mouth to speak. 'It's—'

'What? You can trust me, Ricky.'

She could trust her. She knew she could. But when she glanced over Katie's shoulder, she saw Samia. The girl seemed to be holding her breath, waiting.

'It's, it's nothing,' said Ricky, her voice thick with emotion.

'It didn't sound like nothing.' Katie squeezed her shoulder.

'I saw the kitten in the jar.' She hiccupped and almost started crying again. 'It's so small. Someone killed it before it was born.'

'It was the kitten that made you so upset?'

Samia mumbled something.

Katie turned to her. 'What is it, Samia?'

'There's blood,' she said, pointing.

Ricky looked down and saw a red, coin-sized spot on the inner seam of her shorts, between her legs. She covered it with her hand and closed her eyes, ashamed and confused.

'Oh, sweetie,' said Katie, giving her another hug. 'It's just your period.'

'No, it's not!' Ricky burst into tears again. How could she express what was happening to her? She felt overwhelmed and disgusted with herself.

'This will be why you're not feeling yourself.'

She shook her head. 'No.'

'There's nothing wrong.'

'You don't understand. Everything's wrong.' Ricky could feel her face burning with shame as she pulled away from Katie. She closed her legs to hide the blood and covered her face with her hands. 'I hate what's happening. I hate myself.'

'Well, we don't hate you, do we, Samia?'

Ricky opened her fingers a crack and saw Samia shake her head.

'Let's clean you up.' Katie rooted around in her bag and removed a small white plastic packet. Inside was one of the pads Ricky had been shown in Sexual Health. Katie put it in her hand and explained how to remove the adhesive strip and stick it to her underpants. 'Go into a cubicle and take off your pants and shorts. Throw them under the door. I'll quickly wash and dry them.'

Avoiding their eyes, Ricky got off the bench and locked herself inside a cubicle. Shame had turned her into a robot. As she cleaned herself with the wet wipes, she could hear the tap running and then the hand dryer. A few minutes later, her underpants were passed back under the door, magically clean and dry. Next came her shorts.

When she finally emerged, Katie put her arms around her again. Ricky went limp with shame and gratitude. She almost started crying again.

'Now, we're going to make a pact.' Katie made them all hold hands and waited for them to nod in agreement. 'Ricky, you will have to tell your mother about this but otherwise, none of us will talk about what has happened here with anyone else.'

'Can I tell my mother?' Samia looked awkward. 'I'm not allowed to keep secrets from Mum.'

Katie looked at Ricky. 'Would you mind?'

Ricky shrugged. It didn't matter about Mrs Mitra. It was Caitlin and Abbie who mattered.

'Apart from your mothers, this will be our secret. You know the good thing about secrets?' Katie squeezed their hands. 'They bind us together. We are now a secret club.'

Katie's words had a soothing effect on Ricky. It was the thought that she wasn't completely alone. There were people she could trust, even if the trust was limited to this tiny moment in time. Solidarity offered safety and comfort, two things she desperately craved in this new life.

'I think we've seen enough dead things in jars.' Katie ushered them out of the washroom and led them down the stairs toward the exit. 'Let's get some ice cream. My treat.'

Opposite the museum was an old-fashioned park with London plane trees, massive ones that must have been planted when the streets were unpaved and smelled of horse dung. Ricky breathed in deeply and looked up at the light filtering through the leaves, some of which were as large as dinner plates. She closed her eyes and enjoyed the big, still energy of the trees as it travelled up her legs and through her bones like warm oil. It was a feeling of wellbeing, an age-old, gigantic silence radiated by mature trees. The bigger and older the tree, the more powerful its force field. She opened her eyes and noticed Samia was standing beside her. A hesitant smile on her lips.

They crossed the park to a small hut selling brightly coloured gelato and ice cream. The girl serving had a strange, floppy cloth cap and bad teeth which she displayed when Katie encouraged them to order huge ice creams.

'Make them mega cones,' she said. 'We deserve them.'

Ricky hadn't eaten anything for at least a day but, inexplicably, she now wanted an ice cream, a big one like Katie had described.

'Can I have chocolate?' said Samia. 'In a candy cone.'

'Have three flavours. Push the boat out,' said Katie. 'Look, there's mint chocolate chip and cherry.'

But Samia wasn't greedy or ambitious. She simply wanted a single scoop of chocolate. 'I like chocolate.'

'I'll have mint chocolate chip and cherry, and salted caramel,' Ricky said. 'Please.'

It was a mega ice cream, a big waffle cone with three different blobs which she had to immediately start licking. They found seats under one of the massive trees and devoured their ice creams in silence. Ricky began to feel sick before she'd finished but it was a happy sick, the happiest she'd felt for weeks.

While Samia was washing her hands under the tap next to the drinking fountain, Katie asked Ricky if she was feeling better.

'Yes, thank you,' Ricky replied.

'You know, it's a real pleasure having you in the workshop.'

The compliment took Ricky by surprise. 'I like it. I mean, I like writing. And reading, of course.'

'How are you enjoying the Americans?' Earlier in the week, Katie had given her a book of classic American short stories.

'I'm over halfway through.'

'Who do you like best so far?'

'Carson McCullers.'

'Wonderful writer. And how about you? Are you keeping up with your notebooks?' There was something in Katie's tone, a suppressed interest.

'Yes.'

She nodded, wanting more. 'Are you recording your dreams?' The previous week, Katie had given them all a second notebook and introduced a new exercise. Each morning, as soon as they woke up, they were to write down their dreams before they were forgotten.

'I do it every morning, like you said.' It had become a ritual, something Ricky did first thing without thinking. She never edited and virtually never re-read what she had written. By recording her increasingly bizarre dreams, she found she was able to remove the worst of them from her conscious mind. It was like emptying a vessel of dirty water down a drain. What remained of the nightmares were outlines, mere ghosts of the vessel's foul contents.

'Are you also finding it helpful to write down your inner thoughts?'

Ricky nodded. 'Do you write down your thoughts?' She had never asked Katie anything about herself.

'Yes, I do. I think of it as catching butterflies. Your ideas are the butterflies and your notebook is a net. If you don't catch these wonderful things, they dance off to another flower. By writing them down, they become yours to keep. It's a very good daily practice. When you start writing seriously, which I hope you will do, this practice will help give your writing energy and authenticity.' Katie gave Ricky a serious look. 'You must know by now that you have a very special talent for telling stories.'

Ricky felt her face turn red. These days her mother often accused her of telling stories.

'I don't tell lies.' Of course she told lies, whoppers. Mega lies.

'No, no.' Katie placed a hand on her arm. 'What I mean is that you can write, really write. Your grammar is a bit all over the place but these things are unimportant. It's the ability to create a story out of thin air that's important. You have the most inventive imagination I've ever seen in someone your age.'

Ricky could hear what Katie was saying but her head was filling with a strange noise that prevented her from believing the words. No, she wasn't special. She was rubbish. If she was special why did her mother look through her these days? Why had her father turned his back on her? Why had they abandoned her to someone like Dan? It was as if they wanted to punish her, as if she deserved punishment.

'That story you wrote about the spaceship, for example. Lots of people write about spaceships but you described the hazards of being marooned on another planet with remarkable depth and feeling. I totally engaged with the girl and felt her loneliness and fear.'

Unable to say anything, Ricky simply nodded. The thought of her being good at anything now seemed impossible, a lie. She was a liar and a troublemaker.

The ice cream in her stomach had brought back the wriggling feeling. All the earlier optimism had turned to acid in her mouth. She felt sick. She wasn't what Katie thought she was. She wasn't a good girl. Dan knew what she was. He was always telling her.

# 14

RICKY TRIED TO control herself but her legs had a mind of their own. One minute she was reading in her bedroom and the next she was galloping up the hall, flinging open the door and throwing herself at her father, wrapping her arms around his waist like sticky octopus tentacles. She could hear Dan's footsteps behind her but she kept clinging to her father, breathing him in, her heart thumping, thumping, thumping.

'Someone's pleased to see you,' Dan said with a chuckle. 'Must be nice to be appreciated.'

Her father disentangled himself and, reaching over his daughter's head, shook Dan's hand. 'I appreciate everything you're doing,' he said.

'Just doing my bit.'

'Thanks for taking care of her,' he replied.

*Her?* Ricky felt as if she'd been punched in the solar plexus. She imagined the blow shattering her sternum, sending jagged splinters into her heart and lungs.

'She's been no trouble. Well, not too much anyway.' Dan chuckled again. 'In times of crisis, we do what we have to do.'

'As I said, I appreciate it, mate.' Her father looked at her. 'You good to go, Sport?'

'Dad, I've been good to go for weeks!'

She tugged her father's hand, eager to be out of there and alone with him. Delighted by the rough feel of his gardener's hand and thrilled to be holding it again, she turned, giddy with joy, and saw the look on Dan's face. She had to grip her father's hand tightly to make the terrible feeling go.

'I won't hold you two up then.' Dan laughed but it was an empty sound.

They had to walk to the hospital, her father explained, because the car needed a new battery and he didn't have fifty quid to spare. He'd come from Brixton by bus.

'Are you enjoying the holidays?' he asked.

Ricky had two choices. She could tell the truth or she could say a load of rubbish to make him feel better.

'Yes,' she replied.

'Are you settling into the new estate?'

'Yes.'

'Made new friends?'

An image of Caitlin popped into her head and she almost laughed. That psychopath would never be a friend. Samia wasn't quite a friend either but at least she wasn't an enemy. Jack! Now there was a friend. She hoped they would bump into him at the hospital and she could introduce him to her father. Her dad would tell Jack one of his stories and they would all laugh together. Jack would love him. He would love Jack.

'How are you spending your days?'

The less Ricky said about what she was doing, the better. 'I'm going to the community centre.'

'Uh-huh.'

But she couldn't help herself. She was craving affirmation and wanted him to see her, to say something nice. 'Katie says I'm talented. She says that writing is my game.'

'Who's Katie again?'

Her heart sank. He had completely ignored the 'talented' bit. 'She's the facilitator.'

When they got to the Royal Free, Ricky had to show her father the way because he'd never visited Ollie in hospital. She scanned the tables as they walked past the cafeteria but there was no sign of Jack.

Ollie's room looked different, bigger somehow. The curtains were open and the hot afternoon sun was blasting through the window, bleaching the floor and walls sodium white. Her mother was hunched in the armchair next to the bed. She didn't get up or greet her father as he pulled a chair over to the opposite side of the bed.

In silence, they gazed at Ollie. He was asleep. His arms lying neatly along his sides like a soldier. The covers were pulled up to his armpits.

It was her father who finally broke the silence. 'How are you?'

Her mother looked terrible. The skin of her face was clinging to the bones as if shrink wrapped. There were swollen, dark bags under her eyes, which seemed to have moved back into her skull. Her greasy hair was pulled off her face in a scruffy ponytail.

She gave him an exasperated look. 'How do you think I am?'

'I think you must be tired.'

'No shit, Sherlock.' She rolled her eyes and glanced in Ricky's direction. Her gaze was empty. She looked forlorn, lost.

Ricky wanted to comfort her but couldn't move from the end of the bed. She felt awkward and was fearful of rejection. A thing as simple as giving her mother a hug had become an expedition over a wasteland littered with traps and obstacles. It might have been possible if they had been alone but her father's presence created a divide. Her mother knew how much she loved him and Ricky's awareness of this immobilised her. Times had changed. Camps had formed. Ricky didn't belong in either camp but this was probably not how her mother perceived it.

'How is he?' Her father spoke quietly.

'It's hard to tell.' Her mother shrugged. 'They're keeping him sedated.'

'When will we know?'

Her eyes flicked to Ricky. She shrugged again.

What they weren't saying to each other was expanding between them like a heavy, noxious plume of smoke. Unable to bear the weight of it, Ricky turned away. She was halfway across the room when she realised why it looked different. Aaron wasn't in his bed. It had been stripped, the pillows tossed in an untidy heap at the foot of the bed. Her eyes darted to the small wheeled unit next to the bed. With relief, she recognised several of his belongings and a bottle of Lucozade. She sat on the chair next to the unit and pulled up her feet. She pressed her forehead to her knees and tried to quiet the thunderous sound of her heart in the silent room.

Once again, her father was the first to speak. 'Does he sleep like this all the time?'

'More or less.' There was bitterness in her mother's voice, the old resentment plus a new, hotter anger. 'They medicate him after the treatment to stop him becoming agitated. He sleeps most afternoons. It's very hard on him.'

'He doesn't look in any state to be going home.'

'They've done all they can for the moment.' Her mother's voice broke. She had to take several breaths before continuing. 'They need to wait to see how the treatment goes.'

Her father whispered something.

'But I've already told you all this.'

'I didn't expect him to look so—'

'—so what, so ill?' Her voice was an angry roar.

'There's no need to be—'

'What? If you weren't so self-obsessed, you would have been here. You would have seen his decline.'

'I didn't come here to argue.'

'What did you come here for then?'

'My son.'

Ricky felt herself disappear. One moment, she was flesh and bones and the next she was weightless, no longer anchored to the room or her parents. She was a transparent balloon filled with helium, floating upward.

'Fuck you!'

Her mother's shout snapped Ricky back into her body.

'For god's sake, Steph. Calm down.'

'Don't tell me to calm down!' Her mother was leaning out of her chair, her face red and swollen with anger, the tendons of her neck taut. 'I pity your girlfriend and I pity the child she is going to bring into this world. You will disappoint them and let them down. You are poison.'

Ollie's eyes opened. They tracked around the room until they found Ricky. He winced and closed his eyes again.

'Stop it!' Ricky shouted. 'You've woken him up!'

Her parents fell silent, their attention galvanised by the little boy lying between them. Her father reached out, confused at first by the drip line before finding Ollie's hand. He squeezed it but got no response. He swivelled around in his seat and gave Ricky a confused look. Her mother was also looking at her. She was frowning.

It was a relief to get away from them. Ricky took the stairs two at a time all the way down to the cafeteria. She was shaking and felt undone by what had just happened. It was all wrong.

In Brixton, she'd once watched a boy slice open an old golf ball he'd found in his grandfather's shed. Inside the knobbly skin was layer upon layer of rubber band. When the boy bounced the ball, the band began to unwind. She had watched, fascinated, as it unravelled in a volatile, chaotic way, getting smaller and smaller with each bounce. Now she was the one unravelling, sloughing off layer after layer of herself – her history, her identity, her family, her friends – all the things that had once given her life meaning.

Ricky had been desperate to see her father, eager for a chance to put things right and make it up to him after the mess she'd made of their last reunion. She'd been determined to prove to him that she was over her earlier jealousy, that she accepted Sophie. The new baby would be her sister after all. One day she would tell her stories and make her laugh. Ricky's head had been full of these things when her father had arrived at the flat. But the scene at the door, the way he'd pulled out of her embrace and talked over her head had shaken her. Then there was the look she'd seen on Dan's face. She'd lost her footing and, in hesitating, had lost her moment. Hurt and fearful, she'd closed down.

The cafeteria was hot and full of people. Ricky bought a Diet Coke and was drinking it through a flattened straw to make it last when Jack tapped her on the shoulder.

'Would you like one?' he asked, sliding a bag of wine gums across the table.

'No, thank you,' she said.

'Go on. They were free.'

'You shouldn't do that.'

'I'm a minor. They're hardly going to throw me in the slammer, not with this baby face.' He fluttered his eyelashes. 'Anyway, I'm celebrating.'

Ricky took a green wine gum, her favourite. She pushed it to the side of her cheek for later. 'What is there to celebrate?'

'Mum's coming home.' Carefully, he resealed the bag of sweets and put them in the pocket of his cargo shorts. 'Once they've organised carers and nurses, they're going to send her home in an ambulance.'

'Does that mean we can meet up on the estate?'

'Of course.'

When Ricky returned to Ollie's room, she was feeling less blown apart. Aaron was back in his bed and both he and Ollie were sleeping.

Her father stood up. 'You ready to go?'

She nodded and glanced at her mother.

'Do you want me to come tomorrow?' she asked.

'I might be coming home tomorrow,' her mother replied. She spoke quietly without emotion or excitement.

'Ollie, too?'

She nodded but her expression seemed to be saying something else.

'That's good news, right?'

She smiled weakly. 'Yes, it is.'

Her father was subdued as they left the hospital. He walked quickly, pulling her along. Ricky found she almost had to run to keep up. She wanted to reconnect with him and was trying to think of something funny to say when he tightened his grip on her hand.

'I hear you've started menstruating,' he said, slowing his pace.

Ricky's face became hot. 'It wasn't a period. It—'

'It's a tricky time, what with your hormones raging. I can see you're finding it difficult to control yourself.'

Her scalp prickled. 'What do you mean?'

'Your outburst back there.'

She wanted to point out that they had been the ones arguing. Her protest had nothing to do with her hormones. She was not going through puberty. It was not menstrual blood on her shorts. Even the lumps on her chest had stopped growing, she was sure of it. Her body was returning to the way it was before everything went haywire. She needed to speak up but talking about her body was impossible.

'You woke Ollie up.'

'Ollie did not wake up.'

'I saw him open his eyes.'

'Don't talk rubbish.'

'It's not rubbish. You missed it because you were shouting at each other.'

'We were not shouting. For god's sake, this is about *you* shouting.'

'But—'

'It's your behaviour we're worried about.'

She started crying then, large soundless tears. He wasn't even trying to listen. How could she tell him anything if he no longer heard her, if he no longer believed what she said?

'I hope you're behaving yourself for Dan.'

She felt like she was going to suffocate, to faint.

'Your mother and I owe him a great deal. It's very good of him to take care of you all this time. By the sound of things, you haven't exactly made it easy for him.'

If she hadn't been crying, she would have asked what he meant but it was impossible now.

'You need to pull your socks up.' Her father wasn't looking at her. He was walking fast, eager to get her home and be rid of her.

She felt something inside her collapse and allowed herself to be pulled along. There was no use saying anything. He'd already made up his mind.

Ricky was putting her key in the door when her father brushed her hand away. He knocked loudly and waited.

'Hello, mate,' said Dan. He gave her father a friendly smile. 'I hope it wasn't too hard on you seeing the little fellow like that.'

Ricky watched her father work his throat. It was something he did when he was uncomfortable.

'No, it wasn't easy,' he said. He placed his hand between Ricky's shoulder blades and propelled her toward the open door.

'Welcome back, Princess.' Dan chuckled.

Ricky turned and saw that her father was already moving away.

'Dad, wait! Please, don't go!'

He shook his head and took another step. 'I can't stay.'

'But—'

'What?'

'You haven't given me a hug.'

'Ah, you're right,' he said. Smiling now, he scooped her up in his arms. 'You take care of yourself, darling.'

It was the word 'darling' that made her burst into tears again. She clung to him, sobbing into his neck until he put her down and pulled her arms from around his neck.

He laughed gently. 'You're as light as a feather.'

She hiccupped and shook her head. She wanted to tell him about the body building exercises and vitamins. She was being good, following his advice. She wanted to convince him to take her with him but she was hiccupping and couldn't stop sobbing.

When she finally calmed down, she found herself sitting at the dining table with half a glass of water and a box of tissues. She couldn't remember how she'd got there. Dan was observing her from the other side of the table.

'Feeling better?' he asked. 'It was like you had a fit. I thought you would never stop bawling.'

She examined the water. There were small bubbles caught on the inside of the glass. The water looked still but was really alive, a glass of agitated particles crashing and bashing against each other. It was how she felt.

'It's hard on you, isn't it?'

She glanced at Dan.

'Not having your father around and everything.'

Ricky didn't say anything. She was struggling to control the chaos of emotions.

'Pity you can't stay with him.'

She looked at Dan properly then, grief and fury exploding out of her. 'He wants me to stay with him! He just can't have me at the moment!'

Dan's expression changed. 'You need to tone it down.'

'You don't know anything about him!'

'Cut the attitude, Missy.'

'You don't understand anything.'

'What did you say?'

'I said, you don't understand.'

'No, *you* don't understand.' His voice was steely. 'I didn't sign up for this shit show. It's not my fault you've got a deadbeat dad.'

'He's not a deadbeat!'

'Where is he then?' Dan snorted. 'Open your eyes, kid. I'm the only one here. The only one helping you out.'

'You don't need to help me.'

'Don't I?'

'No, you don't!'

Dan leaned back in his chair.

'I'm fine.'

'Really?'

'Yes!'

'Well, Princess, from what I've gathered, you're anything but fine. You're all over the place, telling lies left, right and centre. You're skiving off in the afternoons doing god knows what with that old man and now you've been banned from a supermarket for shoplifting.'

Ricky felt pressure building inside her ears. 'I didn't steal anything.'

'That's not what it looked like to me.'

'I didn't.'

'Listen, the only reason I've kept my mouth shut is because I feel sorry for you, and let's face it, I'm the only who's got any time for you these days.' He crossed his arms. 'No one believes anything you say. Your parents think you're trouble. Right now, I'm the best friend you've got.'

She clenched her jaw against the pressure in her ears. There was a roaring sound inside her head.

Dan seemed to notice her distress. His expression softened. 'Look, I'm just trying to do what I can to make things easier until . . . you know.'

'What?'

'The inevitable.'

She shook her head.

'Your brother—'

A strange spasm rumbled up Ricky's throat. She was aware of a sound coming out of her mouth but she couldn't hear anything. There was too much pressure and noise. She understood that Dan was saying something terrible but she couldn't hear his words. The roaring in her ears was like the sound of a hurricane battering a coastal town, hurling cars in the air, ripping metal roofs off houses, bending coconut palms in half and smashing windows.

Dan's mouth was moving, mouthing soundless words.

Ricky knew he was patting her hand but she couldn't feel anything. It was as if the layer of skin cells between her hand and its immediate surroundings had blurred. Instead of a defining membrane, there was a cushion of air or energy. It was spongy and resistant.

She was dissolving upward, away from him and from herself, up and out into a place of complete calm. She was part of the air, untouchable. Up there, she felt an overwhelming sense of ease and safety.

# 15

HER BRAIN, GROGGY on waking, refused to kick into gear. She walked toward the garden feeling disconnected from her surroundings, the path beneath her feet and the cloudless sky overhead, as if an invisible barrier had been erected around her. She could see the world but did not feel part of it. A blackbird raised the alarm with its *chink, chink, chink* and she stopped as the call broke through the fog of her thoughts. She was searching for the bird at the top of the tower blocks when she became aware of voices. Someone was in the garden with Snowy. She recognised the voice of the estate manager.

'Stop worrying,' Tim said. 'It's a storm in a teacup.'

Snowy protested.

'I told you I'd look after you.'

Again, Snowy said something in protest.

'They've got nothing on you. Nothing.' Tim coughed. 'I think you're forgetting that I'm the one in charge here.'

There was silence. Ricky imagined Snowy's soppy face, his big hands hanging by his sides.

'Stop fretting. Just carry on as if you've done nothing wrong. You'll only make things worse if you say anything.'

Snowy remained silent.

'I'll come back in a couple of days but if there's any trouble, you know where to find me.'

Boots crunched on the pebble path. Tim had walked several paces before he noticed Ricky huddled beside the gate. His face clouded.

'Do you get a kick out of spying on people?' he asked.

'I wasn't spying,' she replied.

'Why are you always wandering around the estate on your own?'

'I'm not wandering and I'm not on my own.'

'Oh, excuse me. I don't see your army.'

'I'm on my way to meet a friend.'

'What kind of friend?'

'The friendly kind of friend.'

'You're a cheeky little thing, aren't you?' He laughed. 'Where's your mum?'

'She's at the hospital. She's bringing my brother home today.'

Tim thought about this for a moment. 'Well, that sounds like good news. Wish her all the best from me.'

Mr Snow shoved a piece of paper into her hands as she opened the gate. It took Ricky a moment to understand its significance. The flyer had the address of the RSPCA in Archway.

'No!' she said. 'You can't do that.'

Snowy nodded. Yes, he could do that.

'But Lola is feral. No one will want her and they don't keep cats like her. They will take her kittens away and put her down.'

Mr Snow shook his head. He flapped his arms. The cats couldn't stay. It was a garden not a zoo.

'But I can look after them. I've been feeding them every day.'

He shook his head again.

She was getting desperate. 'But I've already found homes for them.'

He frowned.

'Mum says we can keep the cat and one of the kittens. My friend wants the other kitten. I just have to wait until my brother is better. He's coming home from the hospital today. Please, let them stay here a bit longer. Please, please, please.'

Mr Snow shuffled his big feet.

'If you let them stay, I'll do anything for you. *Anything*.'

Snowy exhaled so slowly that Ricky could hear the air whistling through the hair in his nose. The old man was looking at her in his intense, animal way, avoiding her eyes but taking in every bit of her. He was perfectly still. His hands were dangling by his thighs, waiting to be given instructions. He cleared this throat and opened his mouth. Ricky waited for him to say something but nothing came out. He closed his mouth again and made a noise as if struggling to talk through a muzzle. After flapping his hands hopelessly against his sides, he nodded. Ricky turned and made her way to the back of the garden.

At the sound of a tin being opened, Lola's nose appeared. She remained half hidden in the box, hovering just out of arm's reach, eager but cautious. Ricky nudged the cat food closer and waited for the cat to start eating. From inside she could hear snuffling and movement. She relaxed. The kittens were safe and she would make sure they stayed that way.

Ricky filled the water bowl and threw away the empty tin before putting on gardening gloves and getting down to the chickweed that was starting to choke the young lettuces. Once her hands were in the soil, she began to relax. The tight knot inside her began to loosen. Her mind began to drift.

The previous evening something extraordinary had happened. She'd either fainted or had a seizure. It felt like a time slip. One moment she'd been at the table with Dan and the next she was gone. She couldn't remember their conversation or what had happened. The memory of the evening was unclear, as if smudged.

She rewound the events of the previous day in her mind, recalling the hospital visit and her distress at the conflict with her parents. The anguish she'd felt after her father dropped her home had made her feel ill and lightheaded. Had she fainted? She'd hardly eaten for weeks. Hunger had been replaced by erratic bursts of energy and bouts of dizziness. Her perception of light and dark had also begun to change. She often saw shadows on the periphery of her field of vision or patches of light, hovering close, flickering. More recently, she'd started to lose moments, fractions of seconds, as if she was standing still while the world turned on its axis.

Ricky was tidying the freshly weeded soil with a rake when she heard shouting. She dropped to her knees and peered through the wigwam of sweet pea. Paul Cloney was standing on the other side of the garden gate with two youths. She recognised the one with a blue cast covering his arm and hand.

'You can't stop us coming here, old man,' said Pauly. 'We can go wherever we like. This is our estate.'

Snowy was standing near the shed, a pair of secateurs and a ball of string in his hands.

'You don't own this garden. It's public land. It belongs to the council. In other words, it belongs to us.' Pauly turned to say something to his friends. They laughed.

Snowy's fingers twitched on the ball of string.

Pauly moved closer until his soft abdomen was pressing against the gate. 'You hear me or are you deaf as well as dumb?'

Snowy tried to say something but it came out as splutter and a growl.

'Is that all you've got to say for yourself, you old retard?'

Again, his friends laughed.

Snowy held up the hand with the secateurs and gently waved them at the boys.

'Are you threatening me with those, you old prick?' Pauly's face reddened. 'I know what you are. I've seen you with that girl. You make her do things, don't you? Filthy stuff.'

Snowy dropped his arm. His body stiffened.

'You're a fucking old pervert.'

The boys were all laughing now, big open-mouthed, machine-gun laughter. The youth with the cast raised his good arm. Something flew in the air. A can of Monster energy drink bounced against Snowy's leg, sending an arc of spray across the soil. Pauly swore and rattled the gate against its posts. He kicked the fence a few times and spat in Snowy's direction before swaggering off. His friends trailed him, laughing the way boys laughed in gangs, hard and humourless.

Snowy was standing on the same spot, the string and secateurs still in his hands, when Ricky emerged from behind the sweet pea.

'Are you okay, Mr Snow?' she asked, stooping to pick up the can. 'Pauly Cloney is a moron.'

Snowy was silent but the piece of string dangling from his hand was alive. The old man was shaking.

'Just ignore them.'

He turned to face her and held her gaze for a few seconds before looking down at his feet. He filled his lungs and indicated that she should go.

'But I didn't do anything.'

He shook his head. She had to go.

'But I can come back, right?'

When he didn't look up from his feet, a dark, ugly feeling took hold of her. She didn't know what she would do if she lost the garden. It was the thing that held her together, the one place where she felt safe and whole.

Without saying goodbye, Ricky swiftly retrieved her backpack and left. She was numb. Her head was full of noise.

In the glare of the afternoon sun, the playground looked more like a place of punishment than play. She swung herself up the climbing frame and, closing her eyes against the fierce light, began methodically doing chin-ups in blocks of thirty. It was a battle she waged against herself. Each time she reached thirty, she began counting again, pushing against pain and exhaustion to complete another and yet another thirty.

When she finally stopped and opened her eyes, she became aware of a flashing light, the blue flashing light of an ambulance.

Ricky scrambled off the climbing frame and reached the vehicle as a familiar figure was getting out. Smiling weakly, her mother pulled her into a clumsy embrace, making way for the paramedics who were manoeuvring a gurney out of the back of the ambulance.

The gurney's wheels bumped as they touched down. Ollie's eyes opened and blinked against the harsh sunlight but in the moment before he closed them again he smiled at Ricky. She followed the paramedics up the path, her mother running on ahead to open the door of the flat. Ollie looked shrunken and vulnerable out in the open. Ricky could sense people watching from their windows and stayed close, daring anyone to come near, ready to spring into action and fight to the death to protect her baby brother.

The ambulance team carried on through to Ollie's bedroom, brisk and efficient but also careful not to bump or jostle. They checked his pulse and blood pressure and set up a drip stand next to the bed.

As her mother was seeing them out, Ricky knelt down next to his bed.

'Welcome back, Small Fry,' she said.

Ollie opened his eyes. They were watery and far away. 'Hello, Big Fry,' he whispered.

'It's about time you got home. The BBC needs you, pronto. They want to put you in a show with a talking monkey. His name is Pickle and he has a vocabulary of thirty words. Twenty-five of them are swear words. The BBC has to use a bleeper when he talks.'

Ollie laughed in a small, wheezy way.

'They've never had anyone with a parasitic twin before. It will be a first for Great Britain, probably the world. You'll be famous.'

He smiled weakly.

'I told Aaron you're famous.'

'Aaron's gone.'

'Where?'

Ollie shrugged his small shoulders.

'Did he go home?'

'I don't think so.'

'Where did he go?'

'I think he died.'

Her mother caught the tail end of the conversation as she came into the room. 'What were you saying about Aaron?'

'It was Ollie. Not me.'

'What do you mean?'

Ricky didn't want to mention the boy's death. 'Nothing.'

'Ollie's had a big day and needs to rest. Follow me. I want you to do something.'

Her mother led her into the kitchen. 'Here's the thing about Ollie. They've taken him off a lot of his meds but he's still on very strong sedatives. They make him sleep all the time. Do you understand?'

'Does that mean he's finished his treatment?'

'More or less.' Her mother inhaled deeply. 'Let's have a proper talk about this later.'

She gave Ricky twenty pounds and a list. 'I want you to go to Costcutters and get some groceries. We're out of the basics.'

'I don't like Costcutters.'

'It doesn't matter if you like Costcutters or not. They've got the freshest eggs.'

'Other places have got good eggs.'

'For god's sake. Why are you always so difficult these days? Just do as you're told.'

Ricky sat down on the steps of the building and closed her eyes. Why hadn't she kept her mouth shut? Now her mother would check the receipt.

'Are you all right?'

She opened her eyes.

Samia was standing in front of her, frowning. 'You were talking to yourself.'

'No, I wasn't.'

Samia didn't say anything.

'I need your help.'

'What kind of help?'

'I need someone to buy groceries. Mum wants me to go to Costcutters but I'm not allowed in there. It's a long story and it's all Caitlin's fault. If you help me, I'll buy you an ice cream, a chocolate one.'

'I don't need an ice cream. I'll help you anyway.'

'But it would be fair.' Ricky got up from the step and showed Samia the list. They started walking. 'I also need some cat food.'

Samia's eyes widened. 'Do you have a cat?'

'Yes, but it's a secret and you have to promise not to tell anyone.'

'Promise.'

'I'm looking after a stray cat with two kittens.'

'Kittens!' Samia squealed. 'Can I see them?'

'Yes, but not yet. I have to wait until they're a bit bigger. They're in someone's garden. I'm the only one allowed in there at the moment.'

Samia made her promise to show her the kittens, cross her heart and hope to die, before continuing with her to King's Crescent.

They were outside the supermarket sorting out the change from the groceries when Ricky spotted Caitlin and her mother approaching.

Mrs Cloney's face tightened. She stopped and held out her arm to stop her daughter.

Caitlin pulled a face.

'I have a good mind to talk to your mother again,' said Mrs Cloney. 'You're lucky your brother is sick.'

Anger surged through Ricky. She was not lucky and her brother was none of this woman's business.

'I also have a good mind to tell her about your shoplifting.' Mrs Cloney wagged a finger. 'You had no right dragging my girl in it.'

'You don't have a good mind if you think I am a shop-lifter.' Ricky glared at Caitlin. 'Tell your mother what really happened.'

'I *did* tell her,' said Caitlin. 'You stole a bottle of booze. It was in your pocket!'

'I didn't steal it. You must have put it there.'

'You fucking liar!'

'Don't argue with the thieving little bitch.' Mrs Cloney took hold of her daughter's elbow.

Caitlin narrowed her eyes and scowled at Samia. 'You should know better than to hang out with thieves.'

Mrs Cloney gave Samia a pointed look before turning to her daughter. 'Don't waste your time on scum like this.'

Samia waited until they were out of earshot. 'Did you steal alcohol?'

'No.'

'Why did Caitlin say you did?'

'She's scared of her mother.'

'But why was it inside your pocket?'

'I don't know.'

# 16

'YOU'VE WORKED VERY hard today,' said Katie. She was walking around the table, handing out new notebooks. 'You all deserve a reward.'

Ricky turned the smooth, dark blue notebook over in her hands. It was the perfect size for the pocket of her shorts and had an elastic band like a Moleskin. Samia had chosen one with a purple metallic cover. Every notebook was different.

'You'll notice these are nicer than the last lot.' Katie laughed. 'We've had a few dropouts so I decided to use the extra funds on upgrades. Don't be put off by how nice they are. Crack them open and start writing. They're quality note-books because your thoughts are worth it. Now go out and enjoy the rest of this beautiful, hot summer's day.'

Katie cornered Ricky as she was putting the notebook in her pocket. 'How are you?'

'Okay,' Ricky replied.

'Not sad anymore?'

Ricky thought of her father. 'I'm okay.'

'You can talk to me, you know. It helps to talk about problems.'

'I don't have any problems and I'm not sad.' She avoided Katie's eyes. 'Everything is fine and dandy.'

'Well that's good news because I know what it's like to be sad and I wouldn't wish it on anyone.'

'You get sad?'

'Yes, of course I do. Sadness doesn't have to be about tears. It can simply be about feeling lost. Sadness can make you feel smaller and smaller until you feel so tiny, you think you don't have a voice anymore.'

As Katie spoke, Ricky felt pressure rising inside her. It was like steam accumulating under the lid of a saucepan on a hotplate. It was swirling and building. The desire to vent was overpowering but Ricky had to keep a lid on it. If Katie knew what she was really like, she wouldn't want anything to do with her.

'Don't lose your voice, Ricky.'

'Okay.'

'And don't forget to put your notebooks somewhere safe. That way you won't be afraid of someone reading them, and you'll feel free to write whatever you need to write.'

'I have a good hiding place.'

'Good.' Katie laughed.

Ricky didn't need to be reminded to hide the notebooks, especially the one for her thoughts. It had become a vault of secrets, a container for the private observations and feelings that tumbled out when she wrote without thinking. Her second notebook, the one in which she recorded her dreams, worked in a completely different way. It was like an anchor. It helped keep her grounded and in the present. By keeping a daily record, Ricky was better able to stave off the nightmares that were increasingly seeping into her conscious mind, colouring how she felt and thought, confusing and reducing her.

Ricky's mind, dulled and wary during the day, burst to life when she fell asleep. Elaborate scenarios played out against a backdrop of vivid detail: the frayed end of a shoelace, the texture on the skin of a python, discoloured teeth, broken eggshells, mould on a windowsill, ragged fingernails, muddy footprints, peeling paint, a ticking clock, the smell of Lynx, rust on the bars of a birdcage. Her dreaming mind was a busy place of dark rooms and cul-de-sacs. If she wasn't trying to escape from something, she was looking for a place to hide, her feet moving without gaining traction. There was little rest and no safety when she fell asleep.

In one recurring dream Ricky had to navigate her way out of a tiny room that fed into a labyrinth of narrow passages with doors leading into other tiny rooms and hallways, a relentless maze without windows or escape. Another repetitive theme was spiders. These lurking predators should have been frightening but, even in her dreams, she wasn't scared of them. It was their webs that caused her problems. They were tangled, sticky things. They held her down or kept her trapped.

The previous evening, with her mother sleeping in the next room, Ricky had experienced her first real flying dream. She had not flown very high but, by circling her arms like a swimmer, she was able to remain several feet off the ground and travel over the sleeping estate. As she hovered like a drone above Snowy's garden, she noticed a small flare of light near the gate. She swooped lower and saw that it was Pauly Cloney. He was standing next to the hedge as if waiting for someone. He finished the cigarette he was smoking and tossed the butt into the garden before lighting another.

The feeling of flight came back to Ricky as she walked home from the community centre. It felt real, as if it had actually happened, as if flying was just a leap and a flapping of arms. What a relief it was to have her mother and brother home. It didn't matter that Ollie was in bed. Just having her family near her again, particularly at night, made all the difference.

Ollie opened his eyes as she entered his room. He looked brighter, more like his old self.

'Come closer,' he said, patting the bedcovers. 'I won't bite but I might nip.'

Ricky moved the plastic tubing aside and sat on his bed.

'You've lost weight.'

'I've got lots more muscles.' She flexed her bicep to demonstrate her superpowers. 'I can do fifty press-ups and over two hundred chin-ups without stopping.'

Ollie considered this for a moment. 'Why do you want to do two hundred chin-ups?'

'I've got to stay strong. Certain individuals would like to mash potato me.'

'Pauly Cloney?'

'Public enemy number one.'

'Mum says brains beat brawn. You've got quite a big head.'

'You've got quite a small head. It's like an onion.'

Ollie smiled. 'Have you made any friends while I've been away?'

'I think so.'

'Samia?'

'She's friendly to me but she's also friendly with Caitlin. Jack is a proper friend.'

'Is he cute, like me?'

Ricky tried to describe Jack but apart from being short and thin he didn't have any outstanding features. 'He looks ordinary. Ordinary people are hard to describe.'

'What colour is his hair?' Ollie was a details man.

'It's kind of brown, light brown or maybe it's dark blond. When you stop all this being sick rigmarole you can meet him. He'll like you.'

'How do you know he'll like me?'

'I just know. If you ask any more questions, I'll have to beat you pink and purple.'

Ollie laughed. It wasn't his regular high-pitched squeal but it was the best she'd heard from him in a while. She was considering how to make him laugh again when her mother called from the kitchen. Ollie touched her hand as she got up.

'I know something's wrong.'

She wanted to contradict him.

'You're not eating. I can tell.'

Her mother was standing next to the hob, stirring something in a frying pan. She looked rested, more like her old self. Her hair was brushed and tied back, and she was wearing a clean t-shirt and jeans. She pointed to the dining table which was set for two, and then followed Ricky in with the pan of scrambled eggs. There was parsley in the eggs, just how she liked it. Ricky immediately began to eat, not in the pretend way she did in front of Dan, but with proper mouthfuls. She was buttering a piece of toast when her mother began to speak.

'We need to have a serious talk,' she said. 'About Ollie.'

Ricky stopped buttering. It took her several attempts before she could swallow her mouthful of eggs.

'I wanted to do this while we're alone.' Her mother put down her cutlery.

'Dan already had a big talk with me.' The words galloped out fast and loud. Ricky had to stop her mother before she ruined everything.

'Dan talked to you about Ollie?'

'Yes, so you don't have to say anything.' The roaring in her ears had started.

'But it wasn't his place.'

'I think he was trying to be kind. I was upset because—' She had to steer her mother away from the terrible thing.

Her mother nodded, waiting.

'—because Dad made me cry.'

'What?'

Ricky now had her mother's full attention. She never criticised her father, ever.

'How did he make you cry? What did he do?'

'It was after we left the hospital. He told me off for shouting at him. I tried to explain that it was because he'd been arguing with you but he wouldn't listen.' Ricky was feeling progressively sicker but there was no going back now. She had to sink the knife in, sacrifice her father to save what was left. 'I was crying when I came home. Dan said everyone was under pressure. He was just trying to explain.'

Ricky's lies were like a tsunami, gathering mass and momentum, rolling over breakwaters, its black water engulfing towns, houses, cars, people. The tidal wave had just claimed its first victim.

Her mother frowned. 'I should be happy that you and Dan are getting along but I want to be angry.'

'Please don't be angry with him.'

Her mother shrugged. 'I did tell you he was nice, didn't I?'

Ricky nodded.

'He's been incredibly kind.'

Ricky couldn't bear it. She had to change the subject. 'Mum, can we get that kitten we talked about?'

'What?'

'The kitten. And the cat. You said you'd think about it when Ollie was home.'

'I don't think Ollie—' Her mother's eyes filled. She took a deep breath and picked up her mug of tea. Her hand shook as she put it to her lips.

'But a kitten would make Ollie happy.'

'I don't think—'

'It would make me happy. And when I'm happy, everyone's happy.' This was something her father used to say. It was a family joke, something that made everyone laugh because it was so ridiculously selfish.

'It's not as simple as that.'

'I was only joking.'

'I know this is a big ask but right now you need to put your wants aside and think of others.'

'But—' Ricky thought of others all the time. Couldn't her mother see this?

'We're all struggling. I need you to show some maturity. You're not a little girl anymore. You're almost a young woman. Your body . . .'

Ricky let the roaring sound block out what her mother was saying. Her body's changes were a mistake, a biological hiccup. She just had to keep up her training and everything would return to what it was before.

Her mother was giving her one of her 'understanding' smiles. 'We'll have to get you a bra soon.'

Ricky stood up. It was an abrupt, involuntary reaction like a spasm. 'Thank you for lunch.'

'But you haven't finished.'

'I had two bananas in my backpack. I ate them before coming home.'

'What a shame.'

'Sorry, Mum.'

She was in the bathroom cleaning her teeth when she heard Ollie call out. She dropped her toothbrush and hurried to his room.

'What's wrong?' she asked.

'Nothing. I just want you to tell me a story.' He sniffed. 'Have you been sick?'

'No.'

'Well, someone has been sick and it wasn't me.' Ollie bit his lip and looked at her through one eye. 'Hmm.'

'Hmm, yourself.'

'It was awfully dull in the hospital. Tell me a nice story. One of your special ones.'

Ricky made him budge over so she could lie beside him.

'This is a story about a very nice cat called Lola,' she began. 'She was black and white and was often mistaken for a penguin.'

Ollie was a fan of penguins.

'Lola wanted a nice home with nice people and a nice supply of fish terrine.'

'Lola liked it nice.'

'Zip it.' Ricky poked her elbow into his ribs. 'She lived in a garden owned by a horrible man called Mr Pigsworth. No one knew he was cruel to Lola because he always wore a smile when he left the garden. This smile was kept in a rusty box which was hidden in the garden shed. When people saw Pigsworth outside the garden they all said, "There goes that nice smiley man Mr Pig-something." What they didn't know was that when he took off his smile, he was a swine.'

'I don't think I like this story.' Ollie closed his eyes.

'Hold our ponies. It gets better.'

'Make it get better fast.'

'One night, Pigsworth came home late from the pub. He'd been drinking pigtails and was drunk. He saw Lola and tried to kick her but he missed and lost his balance. As he fell, his head hit the floor and the smile fell off. Pigsworth was knocked unconscious. He'd also crushed his nose and for the rest of his life it would resemble the snout of a pig.'

'Oink, oink.' Ollie provided sound effects.

'Lola nudged the smile with her paw. It didn't move. It was playing dead which is what mice do when nudged by a cat. Lola licked it. Still nothing. She brushed her tickly whiskers against it. It laughed. Lola picked it up with her tiny paws and put it on her face. Her tail stiffened with excitement. She lifted her nose and sniffed something wonderful. It was called freedom and it smelled sweet and delicious. With her tail held high, the small and very smiley cat called Lola walked out of Pigsworth's life.'

'Did she get fish terrine and meet nice people?'

'Yes, she did. Terrine from a gold tin, served on a velvet cushion.'

'Pigsworth was nasty to her,' Ollie said, 'so, even though it ends well, I still feel sorry for her.'

There was no pleasing some people.

'I also feel sorry for you.'

'Don't worry about me. I'm fine and dandy. You're the one with the parasite.'

'But you're the one who's getting sadder and sadder.'

# 17

WHEN RICKY WOKE at six o'clock there was nothing on the end of her bed and nothing on the kitchen table. By rights she should have cried but since the awful afternoon with her father, a trench had opened between her thoughts and her feelings. It was like a moat around a castle. From the castle tower, she could see the things that should upset her but nothing could get close enough to hurt her, or at least not with any real intensity.

Ollie was propped up on his pillows, waiting for her.

'Happy birthday,' he said.

'You can forget the happy bit. Mum's forgotten,' she said.

A nurse had visited the previous evening and moved the drip stand to the other side of the bed. A comfy chair had been brought in for visitors. It was a simple change but it made the room friendlier, less of a sick room and more like a bedroom where a sultan might entertain his viziers from the comfort of his pillows.

'Everyone keeps worrying about me and forgetting to do all the normal things like being nice to you or shopping for groceries. We're out of toothpaste.'

Ricky glanced at the drip stand and wondered how Ollie could have known what was going on in the flat. He was right about the toothpaste. She was brushing her teeth at least five times a day, ten on a bad day.

'You need to get better. Then things will go back to normal.'

'I'm doing my best but I get terribly fatigued.'

She smiled at her little brother's fancy word. 'That's your bloody parasite.'

Ollie raised his eyebrows. 'You said "bloody".'

'Cromwell is a bloody freeloading bastard and a bum.'

'Bummy, bum, bum.' Ollie laughed.

'You can't swear on the bloody BBC so you bloody well need to get it out of your bloody buggery system before you go on bloody air. Or you will get bleeped like bloody mad.'

'Bloody buggery bollocks and a bleep.' He laughed, louder this time.

'If you keep it up, I'll have to sell your bloody interview to those silly bastards at ITV. They would love a bloody parasitic twin.'

Ollie squealed with delight.

'What's all this noise?' Dan was standing in the doorway in his underwear, rubbing his eyes.

'Sorry.'

'It's just gone six o'clock.'

'I'm sorry.'

Dan frowned as if expecting more, an explanation or further apology. When none was forthcoming, he shuffled back to her mother's bedroom.

Ollie gave her a look. 'Why are you acting so funny?'

'I'm not acting funny.'

'Why did you keep saying sorry?'

She got up. 'Would you like a cup of hot chocolate?'

Ollie always wanted a cup of hot chocolate. 'If you insist.'

Ricky was spooning sugar into Ollie's hot chocolate when her mother came into the kitchen. She was wearing her old Japanese-style cotton wrap. Her feet were bare. They were pretty feet, narrow and bony. Her toenails still bore traces of the blue nail polish she'd painted on before leaving Brixton.

'How much sugar have you put in there?' she asked. 'Hot chocolate is already sweet.'

'One level teaspoon,' Ricky replied, stirring in at least four heaped ones. 'I'm sorry for waking Dan.'

Her mother frowned. 'It's not like you to apologise.'

'I'm turning over a new leaf.'

'Have you broken something?'

'When are you going to wish me happy birthday?'

Her mother's face flashed surprise and then embarrassment. She grabbed Ricky and gave her a hug.

'Happy birthday, love.'

Ricky swallowed. Her mother hadn't called her 'love' for weeks. How had she become so unlovable?

'You feel smaller. Have you lost weight?'

She pulled out of her mother's embrace. She was still in her pyjamas without the bulk of layers. 'Stop talking about my body all the time.'

'Okay, okay.' She held up her hands. 'I'm going to come clean. I haven't bought you any birthday presents.'

Ricky winced.

'I've spent too much time at the hospital and I've been so busy since Ollie came home. Paperwork, phone calls, nurses.' She sighed. 'I've not had a moment to get you anything. I hope you understand.'

She understood all right.

'I'll make it up to you. I promise. I've been putting money aside for that BMX bike you like.'

'Please keep your money for something important. I'd be happy with the kitten. It's going free. So is its mother.'

'We've already talked about that. Drink your hot chocolate while I make you a special birthday breakfast.'

'I already ate a sandwich. I was up early and got hungry.'

Her mother scanned the bench for evidence of sandwich making.

'I cleaned up after myself. I learned a thing or two while you were away.'

'Well, I'm glad something good has come out of all this.'

Ricky carried the hot chocolate to Ollie's room.

He took a sip and pulled a face. 'It makes my teeth hurt. It's very sweet.'

'I can tip it down the sink if you like.'

'They hurt in a good way.'

'They're only baby teeth. I should do you a favour and pull them out.'

Ollie shook his head. 'Has Dad called yet?'

'It's early days.'

'Did you get any presents?'

'Not yet but I'm working on Mum about the cats.'

'I've got a present for you but you have to close your eyes and hold out your hand.'

Ricky felt something very small and light placed on her palm.

'Keep your eyes closed and make a wish.'

Just one? She wanted so many things. Most of all she wanted everything to go back to the way it was before.

She gritted her teeth. *Please make Ollie better,* she wished. *Please, please, please.*

She opened her eyes and saw a tiny, white origami bird on her palm. It was a Japanese crane, the symbol of peace.

'Pull its wings open.'

Inside the folded wings, Ollie had written two tiny words. 'Love' and 'You'. The paper bird was much better than a new bicycle. It was probably even better than a kitten.

'I made it myself.'

She kissed him on the top of his head. 'Thank you. It's perfect.'

'What did you wish for?'

'I can't tell you or it won't come true.'

'A new bike?'

'My lips are sealed with superglue.'

'You're silly.'

She kissed him again.

When her father hadn't called by nine o'clock, Ricky reluctantly set out for the community centre. She was late but her disappointment outweighed any fears about not being on time. She was now a teenager, she reminded herself. It didn't matter what her parents did or didn't do. If they didn't care, she wouldn't care. If they kept it up, she would tell them all to go to hell. Not Ollie, though. She'd never tell him to go to hell. The tiny paper bird, safely flattened inside her notebook, was a talisman. Ollie was going to get better. She would have her brother back before the end of summer.

'Ricky!'

She blinked, confused.

It took her a moment to get her bearings. What had happened? As she looked around her, she realised she was standing under a tree in front of the haunted flat. How had she got there? She had no recollection of walking through the estate. It was another time slip. A longer one this time, minutes rather than seconds.

'Ricky!'

Jack ran up to her. He was looking scruffy and less substantial, as if he hadn't been washing or eating. One of his hands was bandaged.

'Happy birthday!'

Of course, it was also Jack's birthday. 'Happy birthday to you, too!'

'Let's celebrate.'

'I have to go to the community centre.' The workshop would have already started. Katie would be wondering where she was.

'But it's our birthday. Let's go on an adventure.'

'Where?'

'To the heath.'

'What happened to your hand?'

'You don't want to know.'

'I do want to know.'

'I'll tell you if you come with me.' He waved his bandaged hand for her to follow and started walking away.

Ricky hesitated. Skiving off from the workshop without giving Katie a note was like sneaking out of her window at night. She watched Jack disappear into the small grove of birches and hurried to catch up.

They were walking in single file behind the flats when Ricky spotted Beatrice. It was her bright orange lipstick she noticed first. It had been applied haphazardly over and around her lips but it matched the Sainsbury's bag on her lap. Bea was sitting on a white plastic chair on a patio cluttered with mismatched garden furniture. She was wearing a pink dressing gown and, apart from the lipstick, she looked perfectly normal. Her hair was combed and her bosoms were covered. She was smoking a cigarette.

'Hello, Bea,' said Ricky. She signalled for Jack to wait.

'Hello yourself,' she replied.

'Where's Abbie these days?' Ricky hadn't seen the girl for a couple of weeks.

'She's probably with her boyfriend.'

'She's got a boyfriend?'

'That's what I said.' Bea lit another cigarette, drawing the smoke deep into her lungs.

'How do you know?'

'I read her diary, of course.'

Ricky had to run to catch up with Jack, who was on the move again. They skirted the playground and took the narrow path through the tower blocks, only slowing down once they were out of the estate. As they entered the heath, the heavy musk of summer grass rose up to greet them. It was the smell of summers with her father and Ollie, of the allotment and Brockwell Park picnics with her family. It filled her with yearning and an empty nostalgia that was so sad she almost turned back.

'Come on!' Jack took her by the arm and pulled her forward.

Next thing, they had left the path and were running through long grass, up, up, up toward Parliament Hill.

Ricky's lungs were burning by the time they reached the summit. She could taste metal as they paused to catch their breath and gaze out over early morning London. The sun was still low but already there was a heat haze over the city. There was no wind and not a single cloud. Today was going to be a hot one.

Then they were off again. Downhill this time with Ricky in the lead. Her feet pounded the hardened earth as she raced through the cathedral of trees, retracing the route she'd taken with the girls earlier in the summer. Running was like flying, it lifted her up and out, softening her at the edges, blurring her body, making her one with the air. When she ran, she could forget everything that was wrong with her life. Running was freedom, burning lungs, thumping heart and a blank mind. She thundered though the trees and down toward the ponds.

At the bridge, she slowed and glanced back at her friend. The sun had just breached the tops of the trees and for a fiery moment it illuminated Jack in a golden halo of light. The flash of sunlight lasted mere seconds but the vision made Ricky's heart soar. Jack looked otherworldly, radiant like an angel.

They walked side by side from the bridge to the crest of the hill. The fairground area now looked sad and abandoned. There was nothing to show that this had recently been the site of a small village of lorries, caravans and sideshows. Ricky looked around, mentally reconstructing the layout of the fair, before leading Jack along the wooden fence to the place where the gypsy wagon had been sitting. It was at the outer edge of the grounds, next to a large tree. There, she found deep grooves in the pebbled surface, wheel ruts where the wagon had been parked. She remembered the small door, the tea candles and the comfort she'd experienced in Tina's company. With the toe of her trainer, she nudged the pebbles, dislodging something small and shiny. She stooped to pick it up. After rubbing it on her t-shirt, the red eyes of the scarab ring twinkled in the sunlight.

'That must be worth a mint,' said Jack.

'I know who owns this.' Ricky was in shock. How could Tina have lost something so precious? 'I need to take it to the police.'

'You can't.'

'It belongs to the fortune teller.'

'How are you going to explain where you found it without getting yourself into trouble?' Jack laughed.

'But I need to get it back to Tina.'

'It's your birthday. Think of it as a present.'

Ricky put the ring in the pocket of her shorts but immediately took it out again. It wasn't safe there. She put it on her middle finger, turning the heavy beetle inward and clenching her fist to make sure she didn't lose it.

The scarab ring should have made her happy but, instead, Ricky found her mood sliding into grey feelings of doubt and anxiety. The ring was too valuable to keep but Jack was right, she couldn't show her mother or the police. It was like a curse. It would bring her no good, she was sure.

Her legs felt heavy as they made their way back over the heath. The earlier carefree joy of her birthday had vanished. She and Jack walked in silence, parting at the edge of the estate.

'What happened to your hand?' she asked.

'It's a burn.'

'How did you do it?'

'Someone did it for me.'

'Your stepfather?'

'Not for much longer.' He took a cigarette lighter out of his pocket and flicked it a couple of times until it sparked into flame.

*

Ricky was hiding the ring in her underpants drawer when her mother came into the bedroom.

'What are you up to?' she asked.

'Just tidying my things,' Ricky replied.

'Come into the dining room.'

'In a minute.'

'Now!'

Alarmed by the tone of her mother's voice, Ricky slammed the drawer shut and followed her down the hall to the dining room expecting to find a policeman with a gun and a warrant for her arrest. She stopped in the doorway. On the table was a birthday cake. Ricky could tell it was a banana cake, one of her mother's special ones with nuts and pumpkin seeds. She counted thirteen candles. All of them alight.

'Well, hurry up,' her mother urged. 'Make a wish.'

Ricky closed her eyes.

It was the same wish as before but with something extra. *Please make Ollie better,* she wished. *And please, please make Dan die. Please make it happen soon.*

# 18

RICKY HAD GONE to the garden after lunch but when she tried to open the gate, she'd found it was locked. She was rattling it when Mr Snow came out of the shed.

'Why can't I come in?' she asked, fear gelling the lower half of her body. In the week following Pauly Cloney's visit to the garden, she'd worked like a whirlwind to prove herself. She'd forked compost through all the empty beds and removed virtually every weed from the garden. Surely, Mr Snow knew what she'd contributed to the place.

Snowy was standing with his legs apart, as if braced for an onslaught. She could tell by his face that he was not going to let her enter.

'Let me in.' Ricky tried not to plead but it was impossible to keep the rising panic out of her voice. 'Please.'

He shook his head.

'I won't be any trouble.'

Snowy didn't move.

'I'm a good worker, the best you'll ever have. I've done all those fiddly things you can't do. I've planted and weeded. What about the garlic spray?' Ricky had given him her father's secret insecticide recipe. She'd done it because she felt the garden also belonged to her, that she had earned a place in it.

His face twitched.

'Please.' She was whining now. 'You don't know what it's like for me. I need the garden. I really, really need it.'

He shook his head again, slowly and deliberately. His mind was made up.

'But who will feed Lola?'

He mumbled something.

'What?' The inside of Ricky's head flashed bright. It was a flare of heat, the flame tip of a Bunsen burner.

Snowy mumbled and raised his hands. He didn't want to argue.

'No!' Her voice was louder this time, menacing. She was finding it difficult to control herself. 'Don't you dare call the RSPCA!'

Snowy dropped his hands.

They stood in rigid silence on opposite sides of the gate. One, two, three seconds. She had to rein herself in, find a way through, salvage something. The cats, at least.

'Move the cat box next to the fence. I'll feed them through it.'

Snowy filled his lungs slowly, moaning slightly as he exhaled. He was scared. It was obvious in the way he was standing and the small noises he was making.

'Just do it!'

Shocked by her own anger, part of Ricky's mind broke away to observe and try to make sense of what was going on. It wasn't like her to speak so harshly, especially not to someone like Snowy. She could see that he was trapped and frightened. She'd forced him to let her work in the garden and it had brought him only trouble, first Dan and now Pauly Cloney.

Perhaps there were others. She thought of the conversation she'd overheard between him and Tim.

Snowy hadn't moved.

'Look, I won't cause you any trouble. I'll be very careful. I'll make sure no one sees me come and go.'

With a long, noisy exhale, Snowy turned away. Walking slowly, he headed to the back of the garden.

Ricky glanced at the bed of soil she'd prepared earlier in the week. It was rich and loamy from all the compost. In a fortnight or so it would need weeding again but she wouldn't be there to do it. The lettuces she'd planted when she'd first arrived were almost ready to harvest. So were the bell peppers, aubergines and tomatoes she'd been tending. Her eyes travelled to the herb garden near the gate and back to the wigwam of sweet pea. She stopped and returned her attention to the herb garden. Something was caught in the tiny branches of the lemon thyme. She narrowed her eyes. It was a cigarette butt, small but ominous. How was this possible?

The previous evening she'd had another strange and frightening dream. She wasn't even sure it was a dream. She'd been asleep when she became aware of a terrific pressure, a ringing in her ears that had increased to a deafening pitch before giving way to another sensation. Something had started walking around her body, a small creature like a cat. She could hear the sound of its paws rustling the bed covers as it moved around her. Something heavy sat on her chest. It was bigger than a cat this time, a medium-sized dog or badger. When she tried to move, she found that her limbs would not respond. It was as if her body belonged to someone else, as if she was trapped between sleep and waking. She concentrated all her energy and tried to move her arm. When that didn't work, a hand. A finger. Nothing. Cold fear took hold of her. She could do nothing, neither fend for herself nor run away, when the weight moved off her chest and a large shadow appeared over her bed. It was moving around her as a surgeon might move around a body during an operation. She felt as if she was falling. She'd woken in a state of utter terror and remained awake for several hours, too afraid to close her eyes, and only slipping back into a fitful sleep near dawn.

Lola followed several paces behind Snowy, meowing loudly as he carried the wooden box to the far edge of the garden. He placed it against the fence as Ricky had instructed and stepped back clumsily. The cat hissed and darted inside the gap in the plastic covering.

Ricky waited for Snowy to scatter hay over the box and retreat before flattening herself on the ground. There was mewling and scratching coming from inside the box. When the kittens quieted down, she opened a tin of salmon terrine and, after emptying it into the saucer, slipped it under the fence. A nose appeared. Lola poked her head out and, after giving her a quick glance, began eating. Ricky filled the water bowl and opened a second tin.

The cat's head was down. She was eating hungrily when Ricky wriggled her hand through the wire mesh and, reaching out, gently touched the top of her head. Lola stiffened, her yellow eyes dilating. Gently, Ricky began stroking her head with the tip of her finger. The cat remained unmoving, the fur on her spine raised, expecting an attack. When it didn't come, she put her head down and resumed eating.

It was a small thing, a tiny victory, but the cat's acceptance of this intimacy made Ricky feel remarkably grateful. She'd lost the garden but at least she still had the cats, and if Lola could be tamed, she might be able to convince her mother to take them in. All was not lost.

Ricky was walking quickly, her head full of plans, when she heard a shout. She wouldn't have noticed Caitlin if she hadn't called out. The girl was sitting alone in the playground, wedged into a swing, her hand looped through Baby's lead. The dog was sitting away from her, straining at the leash. Ricky pushed open the gate and walked over to the igloo. Caitlin had put on weight over summer. Her backside had ballooned and she'd developed a spongy layer around her middle. This roll of fat hung unhappily over the band of her trackpants.

'Why are you smiling like that?' she asked. 'You look like a halfwit.'

Ricky leaned against the igloo. Caitlin couldn't hurt her. Not today. Even if she kicked her, she would feel no pain.

Sensing a subtle shift in power, Caitlin's expression became friendlier. 'Someone set fire to a wheelie bin last night.'

'Where?'

'Out the back of our place. We might have been burned alive if the fire brigade hadn't turned up. The bastards had pushed the bin against the building outside Pauly's bedroom.'

'Who would do that?' Ricky had shown Jack where the Cloneys lived.

Caitlin narrowed her eyes. 'Someone who doesn't like my brother, obviously.'

'Uh-huh.'

'The police have been. They're saying it's vandalism of the highest order. Endangerment of life. They've taken fingerprints.'

'Of what?'

'The bins.'

'Why did you tell your mother I was a shoplifter?'

Caitlin snorted. She kicked the rubberised ground with the heel of her trainer. 'Because you nicked that vodka. That's why.'

'No, I didn't.'

'How did it get inside your pocket then?' Caitlin tried to jump off the swing but her hips caught and she had to sit down again to avoid embarrassing herself. 'You're so weird.'

'We can't all be ordinary.'

'Ordinary is better than weird.'

'Why?'

Caitlin frowned. She wasn't used to having her meaningless statements questioned.

'Why is it better to be ordinary?'

'Shut up.'

'You always say that.'

'Well, you should shut up. You're so fucking weird. That's why you've got no friends.'

Caitlin's words were like a slap. Ricky closed her eyes against the sting and pictured herself running through the musky grass with Jack. When she opened them again, she saw Caitlin was smiling, pleased she'd had an effect.

'Why does Baby hate you?'

'Fuck off!'

Caitlin angrily jerked the lead in her hand. Startled, Baby growled and lunged at the girl. The dog's jaws opened and snapped shut, missing Caitlin's knee by half an inch. She screamed and dropped the lead, yanking her legs up and away from the dog.

'No!' Ricky rushed at the dog and grabbed it by the collar.

Baby froze, flashing the whites of her eyes.

With her free hand, Ricky found the end of the lead and pulled the dog away. 'Come with me.'

She led Baby over to the gate. 'Now, sit.'

The old Staffie obeyed, her head at a submissive angle, awaiting command or punishment.

'Good girl.' Ricky stroked the dog and felt her relax under her hand.

Caitlin lowered her legs but didn't move from the swing.

For the first time since they had met, Caitlin was completely disarmed. The girl was exposed and humiliated. Now was Ricky's moment to completely destroy her opponent. She had to seize it and crush her once and for all. But something – a deep feeling of discomfort – held her back. What was it? Pity? Mercy?

In the silence that followed Caitlin began to collect herself.

'I don't know why you think you're better than everyone.'

'I don't think that.' If Caitlin only knew.

'Don't lie. You act like you're special but really, you're just . . . disgusting.'

Ricky swallowed. 'Disgusting' was the word she struggled with every day. It was the reason she didn't look in the mirror anymore, why she avoided being naked and showering, why she wore the makeshift bandeau beneath layers of clothing, why she had more or less stopped eating.

Caitlin smiled. 'We all know what you get up to in the garden with that filthy old pervert.'

'I don't do anything.'

'Yes, you do. It's disgusting.'

There was that word again. It was like the flashing light on the roof of a police car. Ricky had to run from it, create as much distance between herself and the crime of her body. She had to prove she wasn't disgusting.

'I don't even go to the garden anymore.'

'Yeah, right!'

'I don't!'

'You love that old pervert.'

'I don't.' Ricky knew she should be defending Snowy. She should be denying that he was a pervert but she was angry with him for banishing her. 'I hate him.'

'Rubbish.'

'I do. I hate him.'

'Why do you give him blow jobs then?'

'I don't.'

'Pauly has seen you. He says you love it.'

'He's a liar.'

Caitlin stiffened. Her face darkened. 'Don't call my brother a liar. If anyone's a liar, it's you.'

Ricky shook her head.

'Mum's got a list of all the perverts on the estate. I'll tell her to add your name to it.'

'I'm not a pervert.'

Caitlin struggled out of the swing and snatched the dog's lead from Ricky's hand. She tugged Baby through the gate.

'You're a big liar and a disgusting perv. And your brother doesn't have a stupid parasite.'

'Yes, he does.'

'I know what's really wrong with him.'

Ricky's head began to fill with pressure. 'Don't.'

But Caitlin was laughing, triumphant. 'We all know what's going to happen to him.'

Ricky stood in the doorway of Ollie's room, watching her brother sleep. His cheeks were a healthy pink. His breathing was regular. Everything was shipshape.

Ollie opened his eyes.

'How did you know I was here?' she asked.

'I get a feeling,' he said. 'It's like standing next to the toaster when it's about to pop.'

'I saw Baby just now.' She sat on the chair next to the bed.

'She's a nice dog.'

'She hates Caitlin.'

'Poor Caitlin.'

'She's not poor.'

'Hmm. I think she is actually.'

'You're getting better.' Ricky was telling him, not asking him.

Ollie was silent for a moment. 'I certainly feel better since I came home.'

'It's a very good thing they gave you treatment over summer. That way you won't lose any school days. You'll be fine and dandy by the start of the school year. You must be looking forward to mathematics and spelling.'

'Did they get rid of Cromwell?'

'No, but they managed to shrink the little bastard.'

Ollie smiled at the swear word. 'Now what?'

Ricky explained that the medication had reduced his twin to the size of a green olive. Cromwell would keep shrinking until he was small enough to find his way out of Ollie's ear.

'You'll hear a lot of crackling as he squeezes through all that curly tubing.'

Ricky's mother poked her head in the doorway. 'I want to talk to you,' she said. 'Come with me.'

The top drawer of Ricky's tallboy was open. Her mother held up the gold scarab ring.

'What's this?' Her voice was icy.

'A ring.'

'Don't be smart.'

Ricky swallowed. Her father said that the best lies were close to the truth.

'This is an expensive ring. Where did it come from? You didn't steal it, did you?'

'No. I found it.'

'Where and when, and why were you hiding it?'

'I wanted to tell you but I didn't want you to be mad with me.'

'Why would I be mad with you if you found it?'

'Because I wasn't where I was supposed to be.'

'What do you mean?'

'The day Dad took me to the hospital and you two had that fight—'

'It wasn't a fight.' Her mother sighed. 'It was a disagreement.'

'Whatever.' Ricky brushed her off, Caitlin style. She had to claw back some power if she was going to survive this. 'I was upset. So, when you sent me downstairs to get a sandwich I didn't go to the cafeteria.'

'Where the hell did you go?'

'I left the hospital and walked down to that little traffic island in the middle of the road. There's a war monument. The ring was just sitting there, on the step. I wanted to tell you but then I would've had to admit that I was somewhere I wasn't supposed to be.'

'Anything could have happened to you. For god's sake. You're only twelve.'

'I'm thirteen.'

'You're still a kid. You can't go wandering the streets by yourself.'

'But I was upset. You and Dad were angry and Ollie was so sick.'

'That's no excuse for not telling the truth.' Her mother rubbed her eyes. She looked frazzled. 'You have to stop being like this. I've got so much on my plate right now.'

'It was only because I was upset. I won't do it again.'

'I need to be able to trust you. I'm struggling here.'

*No, I'm struggling.*

# 19

'IF YOU COULD change one thing about your life right now, what would it be?' asked Katie.

'Can it be anything?' asked Samia.

'Doh!' said Abbie.

Samia blushed and hunched lower in her chair.

Katie smiled kindly. 'Great to have you back, Abbie. We've missed you.'

Abbie leaned back to adjust the V of her t-shirt and draw everyone's attention to her décolleté. She'd either gone up a bra size while she was away or was now padding with chicken fillets.

'So, tell us, Samia, what would you like to change?'

Samia glanced from Katie to Ricky. She took a deep breath. 'I'd like to change Mum's mind and get a kitten.'

'Just a kitten?'

Samia nodded.

'Good for you.' She looked at Ricky. 'What about you?'

Ricky couldn't say what she really wanted to change because that would cancel out her birthday wish. 'No offence, but I'd like to be back living in Brixton,' she said.

'No offence taken.' Katie laughed. 'Abbie?'

'I would like to change my lips.'

'But your lips are perfect as they are.'

Abbie's face brightened before immediately closing down again. 'No, they're not.'

'Oh, *yes* they are.' Katie looked around the table. 'Who thinks Abbie's lips are perfect?'

Ricky was the first to put up her hand. Everyone followed, even Katie.

'Now, who thinks Abbie is pretty?'

Again, everyone raised a hand. Abbie was the prettiest girl on the estate. She was the prettiest girl Ricky had seen in Camden. Why would someone like Abbie doubt her looks? It didn't make sense.

'Do you believe us now?'

Abbie shook her head but she was trying not to smile.

'Now, imagine that you've got what you want. How would your life be diff—'

Katie was interrupted by a knock at the door.

Samia stood up when she saw her mother but Mrs Mitra motioned for her to sit down again. She whispered something to Katie who glanced at Ricky.

'You need to go with Samia's Mum.'

Ollie had been taken by ambulance to the hospital, Mrs Mitra explained. The small woman's manner was brisk and matter of fact. She told Ricky not to worry, her mother was with Ollie. But Ricky was already shaking, her imagination flying ahead. Her brother was a tiny cadaver being wheeled into the hospital mortuary where he would be put into a refrigerated drawer, a small one specially designed for children and dwarves. She cursed herself. She should have stayed home with him instead of going to the stupid workshop. Things had been ridiculously good these past few days. Having Ollie and her mother at home had helped dull the pain of losing the garden. They were almost functioning as a family, just the three of them. Dan had visited once but otherwise had been staying away. It was Dan who now opened the door to the flat.

'Hello there,' he said. He gave Mrs Mitra his charm offensive smile.

Mrs Mitra nodded.

'Thanks for fetching the urchin.' Dan was the perfect gentleman. Everyone said so, even Ricky's father.

Mrs Mitra didn't move. Her face was impassive.

He held up his keys. 'We're off to the hospital in a couple of ticks.'

Again, his words were met with cool silence.

'Well, thank you.' Dan looked rattled.

Mrs Mitra turned to Ricky. 'You take care.'

Dan raised his eyebrows after she left. 'What's that old bint's problem?'

Ricky waited until they were in the van, on their way to the hospital, before asking about Ollie. The image of him lying in a chiller had become fixed in her mind. This scene now seemed more real than the immediate surroundings of Dan's van. The scuff marks on the door, the cardboard triangle of Tesco sandwiches on the dashboard, the rubber bands around the sun visor; all of these details had the feel of a film set. Unreal and temporary.

'He had some kind of fit,' said Dan. 'That's all I know. Your mother will tell you more.'

Dan was eager to get back to work. His boss had noticed him leaving the site and given him a warning. He'd been taking too much time off, skiving off work to look after her. His fingers drummed on the steering wheel. 'I hope you appreciate all the sacrifices, little lady.'

Ricky knew he was looking at her, waiting for acknowledgement.

'Did you miss me while I was away?'

Of course, she hadn't missed him. She could hardly bear to be in the same vehicle with him.

'I hear you had a cake for your birthday.'

She nodded.

'Thirteen, eh? You're a proper young lady now. The boys will be queuing up. All the neighbourhood tomcats will come sniffing.'

Ricky clenched her fists.

'Have you gone all shy on me? Cat got your tongue?' He chuckled at his joke. 'I tell you who's pleased we're getting along. Your mother.'

She nodded. It was true.

'She showed me that ring you found. Solid gold by the looks.'

Ricky shrugged.

'You didn't nick it, did you?'

'Of course not!'

'Oi!' Dan flashed her a look. 'No need to be like that.'

'But I found it!'

'Hey, Princess. Remember, I saw you get nailed for shoplifting.'

She just had to stay calm and keep her tone neutral, not provoke him. 'I didn't steal anything from Costcutters.'

'That's not what the shopkeeper said.' Dan put his indicator on and began backing the van into a car park.

Ricky steeled herself as he reached his arm over the back of her seat. The thought of his bare skin so close to her neck was unbearable.

The engine died. Dan turned to her.

'Look, I know why you're going off the rails. Your parents aren't exactly doing their jobs, are they?' He smiled and shook his head. 'I can see you're lonely. And I know all about your lady hormones.'

Heat surged up her neck, flooding her face. She felt warmth in her fingertips as she undid her seatbelt.

'Mind if I give you a word of advice?'

She wanted to scream. Of course she minded. She minded the very sound of his voice, his footsteps, the way his mouth changed when he drank beer, the sound of his coughing in the morning. The metallic fattiness of his sweat. The stench of his body spray. She reached for the door handle, poised for escape, aware that at any moment his mood could turn and he could make life very difficult for her.

'You're at that age now, and with all that's going on, your mum probably hasn't had time to sit you down and give you a proper talk. So, here's some advice from someone who knows a bit about the birds and bees.'

Ricky held her breath and began counting.

'You're probably starting to look at boys. Boy meets girl and all that.'

*Four, five, six. . .*

'They'll tell you nice things and promise you the world but don't give them the time of day. Boys your age are only after one thing. Know what I mean?'

*Twelve, thirteen. . .*

'Your parents aren't much use to you these days.' He took the keys from the ignition. 'But old Dan here is looking out for you. We're special friends, you and me.'

Ricky leaped out of the van and walked quickly to avoid having an unwanted hand on her back. She was now so desperate to get away from him that she was hyperventilating.

Ollie had been placed on a different ward. It was smaller and quieter and looked a lot more serious than the previous one. He was in a room by himself with a large window. Ricky's mother was huddled in a chair next to his bed, looking small and deflated. She stood up when she saw them and, without greeting Ricky, walked with Dan to the corridor, closing the door behind them.

Ollie opened his eyes and smiled weakly.

'Hello, Big Fry,' he said.

'Are you a frog now? Your voice is a croak.'

'I'm a tadpole with a very long tail.' He rubbed his eyes. 'Why am I here?'

'It's nothing serious. You fainted, which was not a very manly thing to do.'

'I'm not a man. I told you, I'm a tadpole.'

'That parasite has made it to your ear and is messing with your balance.' She reached under the covers and felt around for his armpit, wriggling her finger inside to tickle him.

'I want to go home.'

Ricky could tell by the machines around his bed that this wasn't going to happen. 'They want to keep you here for observation. You're a scientific wonder. Everyone wants a piece of the action.'

Her mother stuck her head in the doorway. 'Will you be okay here with your brother while I have a chat with the doctor?'

Ricky waited for the door to close before resuming their conversation. She didn't want to talk about Ollie's illness because talking about it was tempting fate.

'Do you remember Abbie?'

Ollie frowned. 'The pretty girl?'

'She wants plastic surgery, a new nose and teeth veneers. And a boob job.'

'Why?'

'She doesn't like the way she looks.'

'But she's so pretty.'

Ricky explained that when Abbie looked in the mirror, she saw something huge and lumpen. 'Like a silverback gorilla crossed with a hippopotamus but with warts the size of tangerines and hairs like kebab skewers.'

'She's too skinny for a hippo. She's more like a flamingo.'

'She's trained herself to vomit without using her fingers. It's a skill.'

'Is that what you're doing now?'

'No. Not really.'

Ricky didn't vomit *all* the time like Abbie. She only did it when she couldn't avoid eating and the weight in her stomach made her feel disgusting. Food dulled her while emptiness gave her energy. When she did her exercises on an empty stomach, she felt like part of the air. The thinner she became, the less visible and vulnerable she felt. Food had become the enemy.

'You're getting like a skeleton.' Ollie narrowed his eyes. 'I can tell you're wearing two pairs of shorts.'

She was never able to hide anything from her little brother. Even when he didn't say anything, she knew he knew things.

'There's a good reason.'

'Hmm.'

'The thing is—' She took a deep breath. 'I'm really a boy.'

Ollie's eyes tracked to her chest.

She crossed her arms. 'It's true.'

He didn't say anything but his expression was doubtful.

'I was born in the wrong body. I've had proper tests done to prove it.'

'Where did you have the tests?'

'Remember when I visited the museum?'

He nodded, cautiously.

'They had a little machine near the giant man. You had to prick your finger and put a drop of blood on a piece of glass.'

Ollie flinched.

'It didn't hurt.'

He relaxed.

'After I did my test, a scientist came out and took me to another room which had a lot of computers. He put a plastic cap on my head. It had wires that were connected to a big computer. He asked me a lot of questions. Some of my answers made his laptop beep.'

'What was the name of the scientist?'

'Dr Alfred Donglebottom.'

Ollie laughed. 'Why didn't you tell me this before?'

'I worried that if Amanda Holden got hold of this information she would pass you up.'

'I wouldn't mind.'

'The thing is, Donglebottom put me on a special diet. I am only allowed to eat ten per cent of what I normally eat. He's specifically told me not to eat coconuts or earwigs.'

Ollie started to laugh again but his eyelids were getting heavy. His fingers on top of the covers twitched.

He was asleep by the time Ricky's mother returned. She wrapped her arms around her daughter's shoulders and kissed the crown of her head. Ricky leaned back into the embrace and together they watched Ollie sleep. His hair, which hadn't been cut since leaving Brixton, was spread out on the pillow as if he'd been electrified. His cheeks had lost their pinkness and his skin had taken on a milky, translucent quality. The veins on his temples and eyelids were visible. He looked exquisitely fragile, more like a perfect doll than a small human being.

Ricky felt her mother tighten her arms around her shoulders and knew she was thinking the same thing. Despite Ollie's illness, despite her absent father, despite the fact that they were in a hospital and not at home, this moment of being together with Ollie next to them was perfect. Neither of them wanted it to end.

When it was time to go, Dan called and got Ricky to go down to the street where he was waiting in his van on a double yellow line. He looked tired and started the engine as she was climbing inside.

At the corner of King's Crescent, Dan had to stop the van for a pedestrian on the crossing. He grumbled as a woman pushing a baby buggy crossed in front of them. He was revving the engine impatiently when Mrs Mitra stepped onto the crossing pulling a shopping trolley. Ricky could tell by the way she was walking that the trolley was heavy.

'Hurry up, you old bag,' Dan grumbled. 'I've had a shit day and need a beer.'

Mrs Mitra couldn't have heard him but some instinct made her look up. She saw Dan and slowed her pace. Her expression was fierce.

Dan gave her a finger wave from the steering wheel. 'I think she fancies me.'

'That's Mrs Mitra.'

'I know. I've met her. Remember?' He glared at Ricky as if she'd spoken out of turn.

She felt the glare's menace and looked down. She was following Dan up the path to the flat when he abruptly stopped walking. He raised his hand and pointed.

'Hey!' he shouted. 'What the fuck do you think you're doing?'

A teenage boy was hanging from the window ledge outside Ricky's bedroom. His feet touched down on the downstairs neighbour's fence and he let go with his hands. He leaped backward to land on the grass with a thud.

Dan took off after him but the boy had a head start. He was already on the other side of the playground before Dan had reached the building.

Ricky realised she was shaking and sat down on the steps. She pulled her legs into her chest and put her forehead on her knees. She was tiny, she told herself, a very small colourless knot of cells. If she squeezed hard enough, she could fade into the grey of the concrete steps. She was still hunched in a tight ball when Dan returned a couple of minutes later, red in the face and out of breath.

'That little bastard was trying to break in.'

She didn't say anything.

Dan looked up and squinted. 'You left your window open.'

'Sorry,' she said. She hadn't left the window open.

'I can't trust you, can I?' He shook his head. 'If we hadn't turned up, that little prick might have burgled the place. My laptop's in there.'

Ricky followed several paces behind as Dan climbed the steps.

'Did you recognise him?'

'No.'

'You sure you don't know him?'

'I'm sure.'

'You'd better be telling the truth. I don't want yobs hanging around you.'

'They don't.'

He was shaking his head as he opened the door. 'I'd never know with you. Always the quiet ones.'

Dan's laptop was sitting on the table. The television was still attached to the wall and her mother's silver trinket box was on the shelf under the mirror. Nothing had been taken or moved in the main rooms but the moment she pushed open her bedroom door, she knew he'd been in there.

The room had an oily, boy smell. Things on her desk had been moved. The pillow from her bed was on the floor. The wardrobe door was ajar and the drawers of her tallboy were hanging open. She imagined his filthy hands touching things and felt invaded and vulnerable. Her bedroom had been contaminated.

She didn't find the note until she was changing her sheets: 'We know who started the fire. Tell your friend he's dead already. Just like you, bitch.'

Paul Cloney had used her green Sharpie and a sheet of her A4 paper. His letters were tightly bunched and slanted to the left. It was the handwriting of a serial killer.

Ricky threw the note and her green pen into a rubbish bag and continued cleaning her room.

She needed to warn Jack.

# 20

'WHAT IN GOD'S name have you done to your hair?' asked her mother. She was angry, red-faced angry. Even the tips of her ears were pink. 'I couldn't believe it when Dan called. You've really upset him this time.'

'Sorry,' Ricky replied.

'Sorry? Is that all you can say?' Her mother let out a howl-like sob and turned her back on Ricky. Her shoulders sagged. She sighed deeply. 'Why did you do this to yourself?'

'I don't know.' She noticed her mother's shoulders shaking and felt sick.

Ricky had been doing the breakfast dishes when her mother burst into the flat looking frantic and half mad. Her eyes were bloodshot. The skin around them was purple and swollen. She'd spent yet another night at the hospital and was looking rough and grubby, like one of the women they gave money to on the street.

Ricky hadn't done it to upset her. It was as if something had possessed her, a wildness. She'd woken in the middle of the night from chaotic dreams with her heart thumping. Her mind had been like a tornado, whirling and whirling, sucking up thoughts, sounds, colours and memories, and mixing them up, making everything loud and ugly, and electrified with danger. It was like being trapped in a roomful of barking dogs, each one wanting her attention and eager to bite.

Unable to focus or think her way out of the noise, she'd got out of bed and opened her window. The moon was almost full, a big glowing ball hanging in the sky. The following night, there would be a full moon, a supermoon, but it was already like a spotlight, lighting up the estate, giving everything a strange glow like a photographic negative. The metal fittings of the playground swings looked like they'd been buffed with polish. Silver light was bouncing off the railings and concrete paving stones.

A cat had run out from inside the igloo and leaped over the fence. A figure had emerged from behind the hedge. It was a boy, dressed in black with a hoodie hiding his face. Ricky had recognised Jack by his wild walking style, the way he swung his arms. He looked up and waved but didn't stop moving. He was in a hurry, his movements quick and determined. He was gone before she could raise her hand to wave back.

Dan's snores were coming from the open door of her mother's bedroom as she tiptoed down the hall to the kitchen. She opened the cutlery drawer and ran her fingers over the blade of the largest of her mother's knives. It was a Wüsthof, a razor-sharp chef's tool made from the best German steel. The scissors were in the same drawer, tucked down the side. They were hairdressing scissors, long and pointed, ideal for stabbing someone through the heart. They felt dangerous in her hand.

Ricky retraced her steps with mechanical precision as if she was a robot controlled by an invisible operator. Taking care not to make any noise, she locked herself in the bathroom and pushed a towel against the gap at the bottom of the door before turning on the small fluorescent light over the mirror.

As it flickered to life, she stripped off her pyjamas and t-shirt and struggled out of the bandeau. She caught a whiff as she pulled it over her head. The old tank top had not been off her body for weeks. Every one of those weeks had been hot and she'd been exercising. The cotton smelled dank and sour.

Before she could have a change of heart, Ricky filled her lungs and turned to face the mirror. It was the first time she'd dared look at herself since the vile changes had started occurring. As she lifted her arms, a deep cave formed under the arch of her diaphragm. Her ribs were like the batons of a fence, each one distinct and neatly spaced. There were small tufts of hair in the deep hollows of her armpits. At the place where her legs joined, there was another dark outcrop. It wasn't dense like her mother's but it was still evidence of her body's treachery. Most surprising were her breasts. The two painful buds on her chest had indeed stopped growing. At least she'd succeeded at something. With her fingertips, she prodded one of the tender lumps and felt a thrill at the thought of getting rid of them completely.

Excited now, she picked up the scissors and stepped into the bath. First to go was the hair under her arms. She worked quickly, careful not to nick herself as she snipped with the pointed scissor tips. She held up her arms and checked in the mirror to make sure it was all gone before sitting down with her feet inside the bath. She parted her legs and, working more slowly this time, removed all trace of the hair that had grown there.

As she cleaned the hair out of the bath, Ricky felt freer and cleaner, less disgusting. She leaned over the sink and pulled the hair away from her face. She held it high, stretching it taut before picking up the scissors again.

The sound of the metal scissor arms slicing through her hair was electrifying. She lifted another hank from the crown of her head. *Chop*.

Ricky hadn't intended to cut it so short but once she'd started, a madness had taken hold. The feel of the scissors slicing through her hair had driven her into a frenzy. She was panting by the time she stopped cutting. It was only when she stepped back that she realised what she'd done. Her hair was a hacked mess of different lengths. She'd filled the basin with it. Ricky looked at herself again and, although she knew what she'd done would get her into trouble, she thrilled at the image before her. There was no trace of girl in the face staring back at her. It was all angles. All boy.

'You'll have to go to a hairdresser.' Her mother tore a tissue out of the box on top of the microwave and dabbed her eyes.

Ricky nodded.

'I don't have time for this.'

'I'm sorry,' said Ricky. She was sorry for upsetting her mother but she was not sorry about cutting her hair. The uneven stubble felt a million times better than having hair around her neck or in a ponytail. She would never grow it long again, ever.

'Are you really?' Her mother searched her face.

She nodded.

'Why did you do it?'

'I don't know.'

'I can't believe you've done this when your little brother is lying sick in a hospital bed. Ollie needs me. He needs his mother. This attention-seeking behaviour of yours is so unfair.'

How could Ricky explain that she'd been trying to do the very opposite? She was trying to make herself disappear, to strip away anything remotely feminine and whittle herself down to something small and unnoticeable. Ricky didn't want to be soft or sweet or pretty. She didn't want the attention of men or boys. She wanted out from the hell of her body, to cut and smash her way out if necessary. It had taken enormous self-control for her not to stick the points of the scissors into her skin and tear gouges in her flesh. The haircut was nothing compared to the damage she wanted to inflict on herself.

'We'll have to sort out that mess on your head.' Her mother looked around for her bag. 'Put some shoes on. We'll see if anything is open. I have to get back to the hospital.'

Someone had been busy on the estate. Every second lamppost now had a photocopied notice taped at eye level, adult eye level. Despite her foul mood and haste, Ricky's mother paused to read one of the flyers.

'What on earth?' she said, frowning. 'I hate this kind of thing. It's mob rule.'

The flyer was an announcement of a meeting to be held in the small square in the middle of the estate. A committee calling itself 'Residents for a Safe Neighbourhood' was asking locals to join them to discuss the eviction of criminals from the estate. The meeting was to be held in two days' time.

'God help us! The idiots will be forming a lynch mob next.' Her mother started walking again.

'Caitlin says there are sex offenders living here.'

'Is that the girl with the toothless brother and idiotic mother?'

She nodded.

Ricky's mother stopped walking. 'Think for a minute. How would that lot know anything about the personal histories of the residents of this estate?'

'But her mother says—'

'You met her mother. She's a small-minded, nasty piece of work.' She waved her hand at one of the notices. 'This so-called committee is dangerous. They're vigilantes. They'll end up accusing innocent people. Someone will get hurt.'

The only hairdresser open on King's Crescent was a barbershop offering men's cuts for eight pounds. The barber looked at Ricky and raised his eyebrows. He muttered something in a foreign language before announcing that the only way to tidy it up was to cut more off. The hair was of various lengths. He would need to use clippers to get an even look.

'I will have to give your boy a number one around the sides,' he said.

Ricky smiled.

Her mother sighed. 'She's a girl and try to leave as much on her head as possible.'

The clippers gave Ricky a uniform prickly stubble. She couldn't stop running her hand over it as they walked home. They were walking fast, her mother eager to get back to Ollie. They slowed down as they neared the playground, where a group of people was gathered next to the gate. Tim was inside the playground talking to two policemen. A council worker was sweeping up broken glass outside the igloo.

Mrs Cloney saw them and pushed her way out of the small knot of people. Her hand was raised. She was pointing and was about to say something when Ricky was pulled away by her mother. She looked back as she climbed the steps and saw what Mrs Cloney had been pointing at. The red duck had been doused in white paint. A Dulux tin was lying on its side in a pool of paint near the base of the duck's metal spring.

Before leaving for the community centre, Ricky put on her father's old gardening cap. She'd taken it from the shed on her last visit to the allotment. It was army green and had to be adjusted to fit her head.

'Can you do something for me?' her mother asked.

Ricky nodded.

'Can you try to be good?' She flattened her lips into a hard line. 'Dan is at his wit's end and I'm not sure I can deal with another shock like today.'

'I'm sorry.'

'So you keep saying. I'm having trouble holding things together right now. I'm so tired, I can hardly think straight.' Her mother raked her fingers through her hair. She was talking more to herself than to Ricky. 'I hardly know who I am anymore.'

'I really am sorry, Mum.' Ricky was, too. She didn't want to hurt her mother.

'Will you promise to be good?'

'Yes.' She would try.

Her mother kissed her before adjusting the peak of the cap over her forehead. 'I suppose it will grow back. At least this ugly old cap will keep the sun out of your eyes.'

Katie gave the cap a lingering look but didn't say anything or tell her to take it off.

'Why are you wearing that stupid thing?' asked Abbie.

'My father brought it back from California,' replied Ricky.

'It's ugly.'

Ricky shrugged.

'It makes you look retarded.'

'Well, you look fat.'

Abbie's eyes filled with tears.

Ricky immediately regretted what she'd said.

'Bitch!'

'Is there a problem?' asked Katie.

'She, she called me fat.' Abbie had started crying.

'Ricky?' Katie looked at her for an explanation.

'I'm sorry. I didn't mean it.'

'It's not like you to be mean.' Katie was examining her. 'What's going on?'

'Nothing.'

'Is everything all right at home?'

'Tip top.' Ricky pulled the peak of the cap lower to hide her face. She thought of the red duck and wished someone would tip white paint over her. She wanted to be blanked out, obliterated.

Katie returned to the whiteboard but Ricky could feel her eyes on her during the workshop. As soon as Katie announced lunchtime, Ricky was out the door. But when she saw Dan's van parked outside the flat, she kept walking. The thought of sitting at the table with him, pretending to eat, made her feel sick. He would start by asking questions about the haircut, questions she couldn't answer. Then he would get angry again. She couldn't face it.

Snowy was in his shed and didn't see her arrive or crouch down next to the garden fence. She opened a tin of cat food next to the cat box and waited. Lola appeared after a few seconds and started eating. Once again, the cat allowed Ricky to stroke her and for a brief moment even purred.

Dan's van had gone when Ricky returned from the garden. The striped tape had been removed from the playground and Caitlin and Abbie were sitting on the swings looking at their mobiles as if nothing had happened. They glanced up as Ricky entered, following her with their eyes as she went over to inspect the duck. Either the paint had been on too long or the council worker had been lazy. The plastic surface of the duck was smeared with white paint. Some of the white blobs were still sticky.

Ricky leaned against the igloo, pulling up a knee to stand on one leg.

'You must have heard the noise last night,' said Caitlin.

Ricky shook her head.

'But you live up there.' She pointed to the flats.

Ricky nodded.

'You must have heard *something*. The cops reckon at least ten bottles were smashed here.'

'I didn't hear anything,' she said. 'I'm a very deep sleeper. Like a corpse.'

Caitlin gave Abbie a look. She narrowed her eyes. 'You're such a liar.'

'Why would I lie?'

'To protect someone.'

Ricky watched Caitlin trade smiles with Abbie and waited for it.

'Mum says last night's vandalism was a warning. The perpetrator chose this playground for a reason.' Caitlin eased herself off the swing and picked up a shard of glass that had been missed by the cleaner. 'They want us to stop our campaign or they'll start hurting children.'

'I never see children in this playground.'

'Shut up.' Caitlin walked over to Ricky. 'Your flat overlooks the playground yet you say you didn't hear anything.'

Ricky didn't move as the shard of glass was waved in front of her face. 'Correct.'

'You're lying.'

'What about you? Your flat overlooks those bins that were set on fire? Didn't you hear anything?'

Caitlin stopped waving the glass. 'Fire doesn't make any noise. You can't smash bottles without making a racket.'

'What if the bottles were smashed somewhere else and then dumped afterward? The ground here is rubber. It would almost be silent.'

'You seem to know a lot about it.' Caitlin gave Abbie another look. 'You're protecting that dirty old man, aren't you?'

Before Ricky could react, Caitlin lunged at her, grabbing the cap by its peak and whipping it off her head. The girl's eyes widened. With a shriek, she burst out laughing. She was pointing, waving the cap as Ricky danced around her, trying to reclaim it.

'She must have nits,' said Abbie, leaping off the swing and swiftly moving to the gate.

'I don't have nits,' Ricky said.

'Why the skinhead then?' Caitlin dropped the cap with a snigger, kicking it away from her.

'I did it for charity.' Ricky retrieved the cap and pulled it back over her head.

Caitlin scoffed. 'Who would want your poxy hair?'

'It's not about donating hair. It's about shaving your head in support of cancer patients.'

Caitlin smirked. 'Ha, you'd know all about that.'

Ricky swallowed. 'It's for breast cancer.'

'Eww.' Abbie grimaced.

'You still look stupid.' Caitlin was smirking. 'At least you'll be safe from nonces now.'

Abbie didn't look so sure. 'Not if the nonce is a homo.'

# 21

'THANK YOU FOR everything you've done,' said Ricky's father.

'Least I can do, mate,' Dan replied.

'Is she ready?' he asked.

'She was here a minute ago. She was giving the place a bit of a tidy up before their return.'

'Good to know she's keeping out of trouble.'

'I wouldn't go that far. Ha, ha.' Dan's laugh was a dry, unpleasant sound like a dog scratching behind its ear.

'We'd better get our skates on.' Her father sounded impatient. It was very early in the morning for him. They had to get to the hospital before eight to meet with Ollie's consultant.

'I'd better get my skates on, too. I can't afford to be late again. The boss isn't happy about all the time I've been taking off to babysit.'

Her father mumbled something in an apologetic tone.

'It will be hell on the roof today. They reckon it's going to be the hottest day of the year and I'll be sitting out in it, replacing tiles. A factor fifty day, I reckon.'

Her father cleared his throat. 'I appreciate everything you're doing, mate.'

'It's what you do, isn't it?' Dan was extracting every particle of gratitude while he had her father trapped at the door.

'Not everyone would be so—'

'—accommodating? Least I can do, mate.'

Ricky's father must have run out of patience because he finally called out.

'Come on, Sport, get a move on!'

Ricky got off the couch where she'd been listening and came into the kitchen.

'Where have you been?' Her father raised his eyebrows, clearly relieved but also puzzled she hadn't thrown herself into his arms.

She glanced at Dan before replying. 'I was just tidying up for Ollie.'

'Let's hope he can come home today.' Her father gestured for her to hurry.

She didn't move. 'I've vacuumed and dusted and done all the washing.'

He nodded. 'Come on then. We're going to be late.'

'Good girl.' Dan patted her on the back. 'I'll see you later, Princess.'

Her father kept glancing at her as they descended the steps but she kept her eyes on her feet. He was still watching her as they followed the path to the pavement. In the past, she would have been chattering by now, telling him a story, something clever to impress him or something to make him laugh.

He saw one of the flyers on a lamppost and stopped. His eyes narrowed and his cheek twitched. He started walking again.

'Is there any truth to that?' he asked.

'Mum says the people who are doing it are dangerous,' she said.

'Which people?'

'The people who put the notices up.'

'And who are these people exactly?'

'It's mainly Mrs Cloney, I think, and a few others she can boss around. She's telling everyone the estate is a dumping ground for paedophiles.'

'Do you even know what a paedophile is?'

'Of course.'

Her father frowned.

'A boy here was killed by one. The flat where he lived is still empty. People say it's haunted.'

'Who told you that?'

'Caitlin. Her mother is Mrs Cloney.'

'Is that true?'

Ricky shrugged. 'Mum says Mrs Cloney is a piece of work.'

'Your mother usually knows best.'

'Usually?'

'Well, she makes mistakes sometimes.' He laughed. 'She married me, didn't she?'

'Yes, she did.'

Her father looked stunned. Ricky wasn't supposed to agree with his self-deprecating jokes. When he spoke again, there was an edge to his voice. 'What about you? Are you behaving yourself?'

'I'm fine and dandy.'

'Have you made any friends yet?'

'One.'

'Only one? You used to have so many.'

'That was in Brixton.'

His expression softened. 'You'll make new friends once you go to school.'

Ricky doubted it. She'd become marked in a way that put people off. At her old school, there had been a boy called Marcus Wagstaff with a large red port wine stain on one side of his face. Marcus looked completely normal on his non-birthmark side but he only had to turn his head to appear damaged, as if someone had pressed a hot iron against his cheek until the skin had burned and bubbled. Everyone knew it was a birthmark but they still called him Big Bacteria and treated him like he had the plague. Ricky felt sorry for Marcus but her friendship wouldn't have done him any favours. At her school, girls didn't mix with boys after the age of ten.

Ollie's eyes were closed and he appeared stiff, as if his limbs had been arranged for viewing like the body of Vladimir Lenin.

She waited for her parents to leave the room to meet the doctor before gently poking him.

'Ouch,' he said. His eyes opened. 'You look funny with that hat.'

'You look like Comrade Lenin,' she said.

'Mum said you cut your hair off.'

'Boys look ridiculous with long hair. Just look at Dan.'

'You said boys?'

'Yes, I did.'

He examined her. 'Did you eat lunch?'

'I ate a tennis ball.'

Ollie smiled weakly. 'No, you didn't eat a tennis ball.'

'You're right. I ate two tennis balls.'

He smiled again.

'I worked up an appetite cleaning the flat. I gave your room a spit and a polish. I spat on all your toys and then polished the hell out of them with one of my dirty socks. I even changed your sheets. I changed them for some old sheets of newspaper.'

Ricky had dusted, scrubbed and polished every room of the flat apart from one. She'd intended to tidy her mother's bedroom but when she got to the door, she couldn't bring herself to enter. She'd hovered at the threshold, wanting to make things nice for her mother but unable to cross the invisible border. The bed was unmade and there was dust over the things on the nightstand. She'd looked at Dan's clothes spilling out of the black Adidas sports bag on the floor and been overcome by nausea.

'Am I going home today?'

'That's the plan, so you better look sharp.'

'I feel a million times better.'

'You should do. They've spent at least a million pounds on you.'

'I want to go home.'

'You're coming home. They are sick and tired of you here.'

'I've been quite sick and tired myself.' He yawned.

'Get as much sleep as you can now because we have to stay up tonight to see the supermoon.'

'What's that?'

'The moon is going to be really big.'

'How big is big?'

'Bigger than your huge white bottom, which is saying something.'

'My bottom is tiny and cute.'

'It's a superbum.'

'No, it's . . .' Ollie ran out of oomph before he could finish his sentence. Within seconds, he was asleep.

When Ricky's parents returned they were with a small, bright-eyed woman. Her shiny dark hair was pulled off her face and fastened at the back with a green scrunchy. The scrunchy made her seem young but when she smiled, deep wrinkles appeared around her eyes. She was Doctor Shah, she said, Ollie's consultant.

'I'd be happier if he stayed one more night to make sure he's stable,' she said.

Her mother glanced at the armchair on the other side of the bed. Her big cardigan was draped over its back. There were pillows wedged either side of the seat. It was like a nest.

'I'll stay here with him!' Ricky blurted out.

They all looked at her.

The skin around the doctor's eyes wrinkled again. 'That's a kind offer but the hospital doesn't permit children to stay overnight.'

'I'm a teenager.'

'Still too young, I'm afraid.'

Ricky looked to her father. 'Can I come back to Brixton with you? Please, please, please.'

He laughed awkwardly. 'You know that's not possible.'

'Don't make me go back to the flat, please.'

He frowned and shook his head. 'Come on now. Don't be like that.'

'Who is looking after you?' asked the doctor, bypassing Ricky's father to ask her directly.

'I don't need looking after. I can—' Ricky saw the look on her mother's face and stopped talking.

'But surely you're not on your own?'

'No, of course not,' said Ricky's mother. 'Someone is staying with her at home.'

'An adult?'

'Yes, of course.' Her smile was strained. 'My partner.'

Ricky knew she'd said the wrong thing because no one spoke to her after the doctor left.

Her father said they had to go.

Ricky trailed him in silence as they took a shortcut through the heath, keeping to the treeline to avoid the glare of the sun. The large concrete paddling pool and playground were already crowded with children who were shouting and laughing. The previous summer she and Ollie had been playing at the Brockwell Lido just like them. Her father had called them seal pups because they loved the water so much. They had climbed all over him and jumped from his slippery shoulders.

His silence now was like an enormous weight. She pictured it as a slab of granite lashed to her back. It was pressing down on her, making her smaller and smaller. The air was getting squeezed out of her lungs. Her throat was flattening. Her breathing was laboured.

He was striding on ahead, oblivious. She was struggling to keep up with him.

'Dad!' she said, louder than intended.

He stopped abruptly as if shot with a dart.

Ricky hadn't planned what to say next. She'd just wanted to make him look at her, see her.

They had stopped next to the outdoor gym circuit, a small obstacle course consisting of wooden poles and metal bars. A tall, wiry youth was doing chin-ups on one of the bars. He'd taken off his shirt. The dark skin of his V-shaped back was shining with sweat.

'I can do over three hundred chin-ups now,' she said.

Her father shook his head. 'For goodness sake. Stop exaggerating.'

Stung, tears filled her eyes. She had to swallow before she could speak again, her voice rising dangerously, threatening to break. 'It's true. I can show you but I'll need to warm up first.'

'I don't have time to play games.'

'I'm not playing games.'

'Look, you've got to stop all this.'

'All this what?'

'All the tall stories and the tantrums. You're driving Dan mad.'

Ricky felt as if she'd been stabbed in the chest. 'What do you mean?'

'You know what I mean. We're lucky he's been so patient.'

'But he—'

'Your mother and I had a talk today about your behaviour.'

Ricky's hurt gave way to frustration. 'That makes a change.'

'What do you mean?'

'That you two are talking.'

He made a sound with his tongue, a cluck. 'You've got to stop this.'

'Stop what?'

'The negativity. You're too aggro.'

Ricky blinked back tears.

He started walking again.

Ricky's heart felt like an old-fashioned metal bomb, heavy and dangerous. The fuse was alight and slowly fizzing.

'We've all got to pull together and get on with it while your brother is poorly. Your mother is exhausted. Dan is doing his best. He's been amazing, considering what he's had to deal with. Can you just put your head down and try not to cause any more trouble?'

Ricky realised there was no way to make it right with her father. She'd lost all credibility. Anything she said would be twisted and used against her. She clenched her fists and kept her head down until the desire to cry passed.

They continued in silence to the community centre where he abruptly deposited her outside the doors with a brief hug and the words, 'Be good.' Ricky followed him with her eyes as he walked away. If he turned to wave, everything would be all right. He hadn't meant what he said. It was a misunderstanding. She watched him walk past Costcutters and cross the road. *Now, he would turn.* She held her breath as he slowed outside the pub at the end of the street. *Now.* He paused to take the phone out of his pocket and, without looking back, he turned the corner and disappeared.

She could see the top of Snowy's head as she followed the hedge to the back of the garden. It was bobbing up and down as if he was raking or hoeing. She moved swiftly to avoid being seen and crouched down next to the fence.

Something was wrong.

She lay flat on her stomach and put her hand under the fence, feeling around. Nothing. The box with the cat and kittens was gone.

Snowy looked up as she pushed open the gate. His face showed surprise and then alarm. He held up a hand, warning her not to come any closer.

'Where have the cat and kittens gone?' asked Ricky. She was shaking. Her legs felt hot and electrical.

Snowy said something and shook his head.

'What happened to them?'

He repeated what he'd said.

'But I told you not to give them to the RSPCA!'

He shook his head.

'I told you!' Her voice was loud. She was shouting. 'I was looking after them. They were mine!'

Snowy was shaking his head, making strange noises.

'You fucking old pervert!'

Ricky's eyes were stinging with tears. She could hardly see but somehow her hand found the trowel in the bucket near the shed. Its handle was encrusted with soil and felt gritty in her palm.

The metal edge made an ugly sound as it hit Snowy's head. Through the mist of her tears she could see his mouth open. He blinked, confused, as blood began to spurt out of the cut on his forehead.

Then she was running. The bomb inside her chest was fizzing, fizzing, fizzing.

She made it to the rubbish bay behind the flats and slid down the grubby wall next to a wheelie bin. Closing her eyes, she imagined herself leaping from a high white cliff, her body bouncing down jagged rocks to an angry ocean. When she plunged into the dark sea, she let go and felt herself being pulled under.

# 22

RICKY WOKE WITH a jolt, surprised that she'd fallen asleep in the rubbish bay in the middle of the day. Somewhere overhead a lone blackbird was singing, filling the sky with its big, beautiful sound, lifting her heart with yearning.

She closed her eyes and tried to reconnect with her dream. She'd been flying, suspended above the ground, chop, chop, chopping her arms through a friendly soup of gases. It had been wondrous, realer than real, but as she'd been jolted from sleep to waking, something had slipped away from her. It was like a secret handshake or a manoeuvre that allowed her to fly. She could sense it lurking somewhere in the folds of her brain. If she could just find it and nudge it into her conscious mind, she could pump her arms and float up to where the thicker air molecules would hold her. She could rise above the bins and all the troubles brewing on the estate, flying higher and higher until she was safe, hovering way above Camden.

She opened her eyes and noticed a flash of colour, bright red against something soft and black. She stood up and saw that it was a black velvet cape with red satin lining. It was draped over the side of a wheelie bin as if its owner regretted throwing it away and wanted someone to find it. She studied the cape for a minute or so, trying to decide what to do. It was brand new with fold marks from the packaging. If she didn't rescue it, someone would throw it in the bin and it would be buried beneath bags of stink: fish bones, tea leaves, old utility bills, cat litter, wet paper towels. She couldn't let something so beautiful get ruined.

She slipped it over her shoulders, tied the ribbon around her neck and began making plans. It was big, a cape for a proper magician like the Great Lafayette. It enveloped her like a tent and made her feel safe but it was too hot for a summer afternoon thick with heat. From under the peak of her cap, Ricky could feel the dull white ache of the sky, pressing heat and humidity down like a steam iron. What an ugly summer it had been, dense and suffocating. The sun's relentless glare seemed to follow her everywhere, bouncing off the concrete paths and walls of the estate. She could feel the heat collecting in the bricks and mortar, the aluminium joinery and metal downpipes. It felt as if the world was going to melt, collapse inward and dissolve into its fiery, molten core.

Caitlin was sitting alone on a swing, looking at her mobile. She glanced up at the sound of Ricky opening the playground gate.

Ricky parted the sides of the cape and fanned air inside. She wanted to take it off but had noticed a spark of interest in Caitlin's eyes.

'There's going to be a supermoon tonight,' she said.

Caitlin snorted. 'What?'

'It's a full moon but it looks much bigger and brighter because it's closer to the earth.'

'Why are you wearing that stupid thing?'

'You mean my professional magician's cape?' Ricky held it out like bat wings to showcase the red satin lining.

'You look stupid.'

'Dad brought it back from New York.' She twirled around so Caitlin could see the hood. 'He went to a famous shop for professional magicians and hypnotists. He bought it for me specially.'

'I don't believe you.' Caitlin bounced the heel of her trainer on the ground under the swing.

'It came with a book.'

'Where's the stupid book then?'

'Mum said it's too good to take outside but I've already memorised the good bits. I can saw a person in half without losing any organs. I also know how to hypnotise people.' Ricky was overheated and feeling reckless. 'I'd offer to practise on your dog but I see Baby didn't want to come out with you again.'

'Shut up! Shut up!' Caitlin's eyes flashed.

Ricky flapped the two sides of the cape. It was like a tandoori oven inside the velvet.

Caitlin's gaze shifted. She smiled. 'Oh, look. A guinea pig.'

Samia greeted Caitlin shyly before sitting on the swing next to her.

'Bird has got a nice surprise for you.' Caitlin's eyes were shining with mischief. 'She's going to hypnotise you.'

Samia let out a squeak. She shook her head.

Ricky had to think of something, anything, to put hypnotism out of the picture.

'It's too dangerous in this heat.'

'Ha!' Caitlin sniggered, triumphant. 'Knew you were lying.'

'I don't want to be hypnotised anyway,' said Samia, weakly.

'It's true. In this heat hypnotism could *kill.*' Ricky gave Samia a meaningful look.

'What-evah!' Caitlin wanted blood. 'Samia, are you ready?'

Samia's huge eyes widened. Clearly hypnotism was not something she wanted to happen.

'A hypnotist needs a willing subject.' Sweat escaped from under Ricky's cap and trickled down her neck. 'You can't hypnotise a subject against her will unless the subject is a chicken or possibly a duck. Chickens are very suggestible. If you had a bantam hen I could demonstrate my techniques. Roosters would obviously be more of a challenge.'

'Shut up. Samia doesn't mind having a go, do you?' Caitlin was grinning.

Samia's eyes were now too large for her face. She looked at Ricky, pleadingly. 'You wouldn't make me do anything bad, would you?'

'Of course she wouldn't!' Caitlin wriggled out of the swing with an unusual burst of energy.

'I don't want to take off my clothes. Don't make me take off my clothes. I want nothing off, top or bottom.'

Samia was sidling toward the gate when Caitlin grabbed her.

'Bird!'

Ricky cringed.

'Hurry up and hypnotise her!' Caitlin's expression was wild.

Samia held up her hands in weak protest. She looked as if she was about to explode with fear.

Ricky was hot and lightheaded, prickling with nerves and weighed down by the heavy cape. She felt like throwing up despite having nothing in her stomach. She glanced from Caitlin to Samia.

'Don't worry,' she said, finally. 'I won't make you take off your clothes.'

'Promise?' Samia was on the verge of tears. Her bottom lip was quivering. 'I really, really don't want to take them off.'

'Promise, but you have to sit down.'

Despite the sauna of the cape and the pressure of having Caitlin breathing down her neck, Ricky had to stop herself from laughing as Samia gingerly climbed onto the blue duck. The girl moved in slow motion as if already under a spell. Once aboard, she had to sit stiffly to prevent the duck rocking on its spring.

Ricky crouched so that she was level with the duck's beak.

'Now, I'm going to ask you to look into my eyes.' She made her voice calm and no-nonsense.

For the first time since they met, Samia looked directly into her eyes. It must have been uncomfortable because she immediately blinked and looked to Caitlin for reassurance. When she turned back to Ricky, she was fighting tears.

'You will do as I say.'

Samia wiped a tear from her cheek and nodded.

Ricky squatted lower so that Caitlin couldn't see her face. She placed her hands on Samia's head and mouthed, 'Don't worry.'

Samia frowned. 'What?'

'What?' Caitlin repeated behind her.

Ricky dug her fingers into Samia's scalp. The girl whimpered and tried to pull away but Ricky's hands were clamped to her head. She was going to have to do this the hard way with some improvisation and the threat of violence. Tipping Samia's head back slightly, she forced her to maintain eye contact.

'You are in my power. You will do whatever I ask because I am your master.'

Samia blinked. Her scalp seemed to soften beneath Ricky's fingertips.

'I am in control of your mind. You cannot escape the Great Ricardo.' She heard Caitlin snigger but maintained focus. 'You cannot resist me. I repeat, you are in my power. On the count of ten, nine, eight . . .'

Samia blinked and let out a soft sigh between her teeth. Her head became heavy in Ricky's hands. She sighed again and if Ricky hadn't been holding her head, she might have fallen off the duck. When she slumped forward, Ricky grabbed her by the shoulders so that her head came to rest against her chest.

'What's happening?' Caitlin stood up, her expression a mixture of enthusiasm and suspicion.

'I think she's in a trance.' Ricky pushed Samia upright. She had to struggle because hypnosis had made Samia incredibly heavy. Her head was dangling off her shoulders as if her neck was broken. 'Help me get her off this thing.'

To Ricky's surprise, Caitlin rushed over, eager to be of assistance. Holding Samia under the arms, they managed to drag her limp body off the duck and lay her on the ground, face upward. Samia's eyes were open like a dead person's. Her body was completely still. Ricky put her ear to her chest and, despite the loud, anxious drumming of her own heart, she was relieved to hear vague thudding coming from below.

'Is she dead?' Caitlin looked thrilled by the possibility.

'No.'

'Are you sure? She looks just like our first dog.' Caitlin smiled hopefully. 'But he died of natural causes.'

'She's not dead.' Ricky undid the cape and threw it over the duck. She waved her hand in front of Samia's face. Nothing. 'She's in a trance.'

'She doesn't look much different.' Caitlin laughed. 'Lights on, nobody home.'

'We've got to do something.' Ricky thought of the wound she'd inflicted on Snowy's head. She didn't want 'murder' added to the list of her recent crimes.

'Let's take off her clothes.' There was excitement in Caitlin's voice.

'No.' Ricky remembered the fear in Samia's eyes. The girl didn't wear a hijab or scarf but neither did she wear shorts or sleeveless tops.

'It will cool her down.' Caitlin was already trying to unbutton Samia's blouse. It had long sleeves and was done up all the way to the collar.

'Don't do that.' Ricky imagined herself in Samia's place and shuddered at the thought of Caitlin undressing her in a public playground.

Caitlin was cursing to herself. The small buttons on Samia's top were slowing her down.

'She said she didn't want us to take off her clothes.'

'Shut up.'

'It's not right.'

Caitlin let out a frustrated howl and taking either side of the blouse in her hands, tore it in two. The soft fabric ripped, buttons popped and flew off. Samia's features contorted for a moment. She blinked. Ricky waited for her to wake up but, after a grimace, her face resumed its vacant expression. Samia was deep in a trance, evidently unaware that she was lying in the middle of the estate with her bare chest exposed.

'Look!' Caitlin stood up. She was laughing. 'I knew she had no tits.'

Ricky was trying to pull the two sides of the blouse together when someone screamed, loud and high. The gate clanged. Ricky was shoved aside.

'You've killed my little girl!' wailed Mrs Mitra, splaying her hands over her daughter's chest. She glared at Ricky, her eyes bulging. 'What have you done?'

'She's not dead.' Ricky plucked the cape off the duck and handed it to Samia's mother. 'She's just in a trance.'

Mrs Mitra hastily arranged the cape over her daughter, covering her completely apart from her head. Samia's eyes were still open, staring vacantly at the sky. She now looked properly dead, laid out in velvet finery like a dead duke.

'I'm sorry about this, Mrs Mitra,' said Caitlin, her voice taking on an uncharacteristically sweet tone. 'Bird hypnotised your daughter. I warned her not to do it.'

Mrs Mitra gave Ricky a ferocious look as if she wanted to eat her. 'You did this?'

'I only hypnotised her. I didn't—'

'I told her not to do it, Mrs Mitra. I warned her.'

'That's not—' *True, fair, kind.* None of these words was powerful enough to describe what Caitlin wasn't.

'Un-hypnotise her!' Mrs Mitra grasped Ricky's arm, twisting it painfully so that she was forced to kneel beside Samia. 'Now!'

Ricky waved her hand over Samia's unblinking eyes.

The girl didn't move. Her face remained expressionless.

'You could try pinching her,' said Caitlin, helpfully.

'Don't you lay a finger on my daughter!' warned Mrs Mitra.

'I was only trying to help.' Caitlin gave Ricky a sour look. 'You heard her. Do something.'

Ricky cupped her hands around her mouth and put them to Samia's ear. 'You are under my power. You are under the power of the Great Ricardo and will do as I say.'

Mrs Mitra growled menacingly.

Ricky lowered her voice so that only Samia could hear. 'When I clap my hands three times, you will wake up and remember everything that has happened here.'

'Hurry up!' Mrs Mitra was getting impatient.

Ricky's lips were touching Samia's ear. 'I repeat: you will remember everything that has happened here.' She looked up and saw that Caitlin was laughing. She put her lips to Samia's ear again. 'Tell Caitlin to go fuck herself.'

She clapped three times.

Samia let out a long sigh. She blinked and, as she sat up, the cape fell away. She looked down and let out a high-pitched wail, quickly pulling up the cape to hide her chest.

'Ha, ha. Too late. We already saw them.' Caitlin was enjoying herself. 'You're as flat as a pan—'

'Go fuck yourself, Caitlin!'

Everyone stopped breathing. Even the blackbird fell silent. Someone in the building above opened a window. Samia's eyes flashed panic. She glanced at Caitlin and then at her mother. She frowned, confused.

'Sorry, I don't know why I said that. I've never used that word before.'

Mrs Mitra hissed something in Bengali and yanked Samia to her feet. Her daughter started crying loudly as her mother tied the cape around her neck. She jabbed a finger at Ricky. 'You're coming with me. I want to talk to your mother.'

'My mother's not home.' Ricky didn't move.

'Come with me!'

Caitlin was now laughing openly and loudly.

'It's true. Mum isn't home.' Ricky had started to feel sick; a big, shaky, painful sick as if a bloated man-of-war jellyfish had taken over her abdomen and was reaching its stinging tentacles out to all her fingers and toes.

Mrs Mitra caught the sleeve of Ricky's t-shirt and pulled. She was like the engine of a train, shunting Samia through the gate and pulling the criminal behind her.

'Please, I don't want to go ho—' Ricky's voice petered out as she was towed out of the playground.

Mrs Mitra pulled her along the path and up the steps to the flats. Ricky couldn't talk because the jellyfish had reached into her head and was squeezing her brain with its stingers. Her ears were ringing as if a swarm of insects had now arrived and surrounded her head. There was acid in her mouth. She had to lock her jaw shut because she wanted to throw up.

Mrs Mitra stopped outside the door of the flat and, nudging Samia aside, pulled Ricky in front of her like a human shield. She rang the doorbell and then knocked impatiently.

Dan opened the door and glanced at Ricky. He noticed Mrs Mitra and put down his can of Heineken.

'Hello,' he said cheerfully. He smiled widely, his Mr Conviviality smile. 'I see you've brought the wanderer home.'

Mrs Mitra thrust Ricky from behind.

Dan had to step aside to avoid a collision as she was propelled through the doorway.

'Who are you exactly?' asked Mrs Mitra.

Dan bridled. 'Excuse me?'

'You are not the girl's father.'

'No.'

'Where is her mother?'

'She's at the hospital. How can I help you? It's Mrs Mitra, isn't it?'

'Tell this girl's mother that she has to stay away from my daughter.'

'Why? What's the scamp been up to?'

'She hypnotised my daughter. That's what she did.'

Dan glanced at Samia and raised his eyebrows. The girl was wrapped in the cape, crying loudly, her shoulders shaking miserably.

He smirked. 'I take it the hypnotism wasn't a good experience.'

'It is not funny. You can't go around hypnotising people and then removing their clothes.'

Dan turned to Ricky. 'Oh, so you've been removing clothes as well?'

'That's what I said.' Mrs Mitra was glaring at Dan.

'I'll make sure her mother hears about it.' His voice had become serious. 'I'm very sorry about what happened to your daughter.'

Mrs Mitra hesitated a moment, her eyes narrow and fierce. She let out a loud hiss. With an angry shake of the head, she turned away, pushing her daughter along the balcony.

Dan closed the door. 'That was awkward.'

Ricky shrugged.

'So, you're a hypnotist now?'

'I hypnotised her but I didn't—

'—take her clothes off?'

'That's not what happened.'

'Well?'

'I'm sorry.' Her legs felt hollow and weak, as if they had been stripped of their bones.

'It's easy to say sorry now but you shouldn't have hypnotised that girl in the first place. What is it with you? First you hack your hair off, then you disappear on me at lunchtime and now this. Why do you keep doing these things?' From the expression on Dan's face, it was clear his question didn't require an answer. He leaned against the door. 'That nosy cow next door expects me to tell your mother.'

Ricky edged backward until she was pressed against the sideboard.

'And if I don't tell your mother and she finds out, I'll be right in the shit.'

Dan picked up the can of beer and drank several mouthfuls. He belched and wiped his mouth with his hand.

'You need to learn that actions have consequences. You don't know how lucky you are that I've been so understanding. How many times have I saved your arse now?'

Ricky could feel the handle of the cutlery drawer behind her. She ran her fingers over its metal edges. Inside were her mother's knives.

'I'm the only one looking out for you here, Princess. I'm the one cleaning up the mess you're making of everything. You don't make it easy for me with that attitude of yours.'

Dan took another gulp of beer.

'I don't know why I bother. That bloody father of yours doesn't give a toss. Your mother is falling apart.'

In her mind's eye, Ricky was opening the drawer behind her. She was taking out the long German knife, the one with a razor-sharp edge.

'So, are you going to behave and do as I say?'

'What do you mean?'

Dan was moving toward her. 'You know what I mean.'

# 23

SHE WOKE WITH the light of the full moon shining in her eyes. Its big face was at the window, throwing silver over everything. The glass of water on her bedside table looked alive, as if it contained hundreds of bioluminescent creatures. Ricky tapped the glass and the illusion vanished. She sat up and, as she pressed her knuckles into her eyes, she was transported back to her dream.

She'd been standing in the middle of Snowy's garden. It was dark and the garden was crackling and rustling with activity. Something moved over her foot. It felt long and cool, like a damp strip of rope. It slithered. She looked down and saw that the ground around her feet was moving. It was a tangle of brightly coloured ribbons. The ribbons had pointy heads and tiny bright eyes. She lifted one foot and then the other, realising that the dense layer of air held her up, poised above the danger below. As long as she stayed in the air, she was safe from the snakes.

The sensations of danger and weightlessness were tingling in her fingers as she pushed back the covers. She saw the cape on the end of her bed and began to recall the events of the previous day. The blood gushing from Snowy's head. The bins and Samia flopping forward over the playground duck. Caitlin ripping open the girl's blouse. The ping of buttons. Mrs Mitra's shriek. She remembered the reluctance of her limbs and the feeling of numb horror as the woman pulled her back to the flat. Dan opening the door. The beer in his hand. But what had happened after Mrs Mitra left? How had she retrieved the cape from Samia? Had she fainted again? Ricky had no recollection of going to bed. There was no memory of it at all. Nothing, only numbness. She didn't even have feelings about what she didn't remember, good or bad. It was all vague and dreamlike as if it had happened to someone else.

She swung her legs out of bed and realised she was only wearing the top half of her pyjamas. Either she'd gone to bed without putting on her bottoms or had kicked them off in the heat of the night. She glanced at the chair. Her shorts and t-shirt were neatly folded over its back. She stood up and found herself staggering, almost falling. She held on to her chair until the dizziness passed. Without turning on the light, she put on the clothes of the previous day. Before climbing out of her window, she tied the cape around her neck.

Her feet hit the ground below the flats with a dull thud. She remained crouched in the shadows for a minute to get her breath and allow her heart to slow. The full moon was like a white-blue sun. It was so bright she could see the tiny bathroom windows of the tower blocks in the distance. There was complete silence on the estate. Not even the crickets were stirring.

Avoiding the moon's white glare, she kept to the shadows. Her feet felt light, as if at any moment she could jump, bounce and begin to fly. As she neared the empty flat, she heard someone sniffing and knew immediately that it was Jack. He was crouched next to the wooden fence, his chin on his knees. His eyes were large and moist in the moonlight as if he'd been crying.

'What are you doing here?' he whispered.

'I couldn't sleep,' replied Ricky.

She wrapped the velvet cape around her body and sat down next to him. One of his cheeks looked odd, misshapen. The bruise under his eye was dark and fresh. The corner of his mouth was also swollen. There was a smear of blood under his nose.

'You've been hurt.'

He shrugged.

'It wasn't Pauly Cloney was it?'

He shook his head.

'Your stepfather?'

He narrowed his eyes. 'I'm going to kill him. Stab him right through the heart. I've already got the knife.'

'But you'll get into trouble.'

'So?'

'You need to tell someone about what he's doing.'

'Not yet.' Jack wiped his eyes. 'I have to wait for Mum.'

'But you need to do something now.'

He shook his head.

'Really. The sooner the better.'

'All right.' He stood up. 'Let's go do something.'

'I mean, you should go to the police.'

Jack laughed dangerously. He took a lighter out of his pocket, flicking it to make it spark. 'I have a better idea.'

'I doubt it's a better idea.'

'Come on!' Jack was already walking away.

Ricky hurried to catch up. She had to stop him before he did something bad. He was walking swiftly in a determined way, ignoring her as she tried to talk him out of using the lighter. He stopped in front of a garage door.

'This is the Cloneys' place,' she whispered. 'You know about Pauly. It's dangerous for you here. We need to leave before they see us.'

Ignoring her, Jack took a thick marker pen out of his pocket. Ricky had seen boys in Brixton use the same markers to tag buildings with swirling, illegible signatures. Jack pulled the top off with his teeth and, as she watched, frightened yet also fascinated, he began writing on the metal roller door. His message was not an illegible squiggle like the Brixton tags. Jack's capital letters were perfect, at least a foot high. His message was impossible to miss.

Ricky heard voices and whispered a warning but Jack kept writing as if he didn't care about being caught. She flattened herself against the building as three men approached. They were talking loudly and laughing, jostling each other drunkenly, play fighting. They slowed as they neared the Cloneys' garage. Ricky held her breath and waited for them to notice her friend silhouetted against the white of the garage door. One of the men stumbled. His friends rushed forward to help him regain his footing. They were almost close enough to touch Jack but, by some miracle, they never turned or looked his way.

Jack laughed but his recklessness was making Ricky nervous. He was acting as if he wanted to be caught, as if he didn't care if he got hurt.

She tugged his elbow. 'I don't want you to get into trouble.'

He laughed again. 'You mean *you* don't want to get into trouble.'

'That, too.'

'What do you want to do then?'

She shrugged.

'Shall we visit your kittens?'

She bit her lip. 'We can't.'

'Why not?'

'Mr Snow got rid of them.'

'What?'

She took a deep breath. 'I told him not to but he did it anyway.'

'Let's teach that old bastard a lesson.' Jack was already on the move.

'No!' She thought of the cut she'd inflicted on Snowy. It had been deep, spurting blood. 'We don't have to teach him anything.'

The early morning call of a blackbird pierced the silence of the sleeping estate. Ricky looked up and saw that the sky was beginning to change colour. The silvery light of the moon was giving way to the faint gold of morning light.

She grasped Jack's elbow again but he shook her off. He was no bigger than her but he may as well have been made of steel. He was wound up, in a heightened state. Ricky realised she couldn't stop him. Wrapping the cape around herself, as if for protection, she followed, her heart banging along her collarbone.

She tried several more times to talk to him as they hurried along the path to the tower blocks but Jack was beyond reach. His breathing was ragged with excitement. He sounded like a dog chasing a ball.

She pleaded with him. 'Please, I don't want any trouble.'

His face was hard and emotionless. His pupils were dilated, his teeth clenched. He raced ahead, scrambling over the garden gate like a small monkey. He dropped to the ground and disappeared behind the shed.

She heard the clang of metal. The head of a rake appeared. It disappeared only to appear again. Jack was hacking at the garden, destroying the vegetable beds, smashing his way through all the things she'd planted and tended. She saw the wigwam topple over and watched in stunned silence as the stalks of corn were flattened. A lattice fell. Jack was like a typhoon, turning and turning, destroying everything in his path.

The rake clanged against the metal bird feeder. A light went on in one of the small windows overlooking the garden. She hissed at Jack, but he was too far from her to hear.

She had to get to him and make him stop or they would both be in serious trouble. She pulled herself up on the wire mesh of the fence.

'Jack,' she whispered. 'You've got to get out of there. You've woken people up.'

He looked at her but his eyes were blank, his face white and damp. His hand disappeared into his pocket. It emerged with the lighter. His movements were mechanical, like a cyborg programmed for destruction.

'No!'

But he was already on his knees, holding the flame against the hay stacked next to the shed.

'Please, don't!'

The dry grass smouldered at first. Then it caught. With a *woof* it burst into flames.

A window opened above the garden. Someone shouted.

Jack scurried toward her and threw himself over the gate. Behind him, the flames were crackling and growing, hungry for the dry hay.

Ricky jumped down but the cape snagged on the fence. Frantically, she tried to undo the ribbon around her neck but she'd double knotted it and couldn't get it undone. She tugged the cape, flapping it, trying to rip it off her neck.

There were voices above her now, more than one. Lights were going on. More windows were opening.

Desperate, she leaned back on her heels and with both hands tried to pull the cape off the fence. It ripped and gave a little. She pulled again. She was panting, panicking.

'Come on,' called Jack.

He was standing next to the hedge, white and frail like a phantom. His eyes were no longer blank. They were large and luminous.

She waved her arm. 'Run!'

He didn't move.

She waved him away again. 'Go!'

He shook his head.

'I said, go!'

He gave her a lingering look before spinning away. He began to run.

The hay was now ablaze. Flames were reaching upward like the snakes of her dream, feeling their way over the wooden sides of the shed, flickering up to its roof. Tendrils of orange and yellow had discovered the hay she and Snowy had spread over the soil beds. The flames licked the dry grass tenderly as if savouring its taste before travelling over the earth with terrific hunger.

Ricky applied her teeth to the knot under her chin, locating a loose fold of ribbon. She tugged with her teeth clenched. The satin of the ribbon softened. The knot opened. The cape fell away.

She was free to go, to run, but instead she hesitated, her mind seizing on a memory of the previous year when a rabbit had found its way into the allotment and spent the night eating all the delicious young plants. Her father had cornered the small creature the next morning but instead of trying to flee in the face of danger, the rabbit had frozen, its large eyes dull with resignation. It had gone limp in his hands as he scooped it up but had revived the moment he released it, instantly dashing off into the undergrowth and to freedom.

Someone gripped Ricky's arm. She cried out and went rigid with terror.

'Sorry, I didn't mean to scare you.'

In the distance, Ricky could hear the siren of a fire engine.

'Are you okay?' Tim's voice was gentle. He looked as if he'd come straight from his bed. He was wearing tracksuit bottoms and a t-shirt. His long feet were bare.

She managed to nod, aware that a small crowd was gathering, attracted by the blaze.

'Let's get you home.'

# 24

HER MOTHER'S LIPS were trembling. They were pale, the same colour as her face. She kept rubbing her eyes and raking her fingers through her hair.

They were sitting at the table, waiting for the police to arrive.

'I can't bear this,' she said finally.

Ricky avoided her eyes.

'This is the last thing I need.'

'Sorry.'

'Sorry?' A small whimper escaped her mother's lips. 'Is that all you can say?'

'I am sorry.'

'Do you realise what you've done?'

Ricky shook her head. She hadn't done anything.

'You're in serious trouble. We all are. The police could accuse me of child neglect.'

'I'll tell them you're not neglecting me.'

'It doesn't matter what you say. They'll see it as child abandonment.'

'But I wasn't abandoned.'

'They'll think I left you in the care of a man you hardly know.'

'But I've known Dan for at least two months.'

'God, don't tell them that!' She let out a small moan. 'I'm terrified. The whole thing is terrifying.'

Ricky felt nothing, not even tired, which was strange because she hadn't slept since being taken home, hours before.

Tim had been kind to her despite the fire and despite the fact that she'd been caught at the scene. He'd not asked her any questions or used any force. He'd simply said she had to get home. 'The fewer people who see you at this stage, the better.'

They had made it as far as the playground when Mrs Cloney had come flying along the path, flapping her arms. She was dressed only in a nightie and slippers and didn't seem to care that Tim or anyone else saw her.

'Someone's written a load of filth over our garage door,' she shrieked.

'It wasn't me,' said Tim.

'You're the estate manager. It's your job to sort it out.' Mrs Cloney glanced at Ricky, her eyes widening with recognition. 'What is she doing up at this hour?'

Ricky thought of Jack and was seized by a wild feeling. 'I've been jogging,' she said.

Tim let out a snort.

'You little liar!' Mrs Cloney put her hands on her hips.

'I'm training for a triathlon. It's for charity.' Ricky was light-headed, gripped by hysteria and on the verge of uncontrollable laughter. 'The charity helps people who've lost their teeth.'

'Shut up, you little bitch!' She glared at Tim. 'I bet she had something to do with the destruction of my property.'

'Your garage door is council property, and on this estate we don't call children that word.' Tim stepped forward, blocking Ricky from saying anything more. 'I have no idea who defaced your garage door. It could have been any number of people.'

'What do you mean by that?'

He held up his hands. 'Let's just say you're well known to many.'

'You are supposed to be protecting us!'

'No, that's the job of the police.'

Mrs Cloney pointed to Ricky. 'That girl broke my Pauly's teeth. She's been caught shoplifting. She tried to pin it on our Caitlin. I had to step in and clear our name.'

'Quite a crime spree for someone so young.'

Mrs Cloney let out a yelp of frustration. 'Are you taking the piss?'

'Possibly.' Tim started walking away, nodding for Ricky to follow.

'You haven't heard the last of me.'

'I would have to be listening to hear anything more.'

As they walked up the path to the flat, the sun breached the horizon in a burst of dazzling yellow light. Everything that had been silver an hour earlier was now bathed in gold. The playground, illuminated by this fiery blast, looked like a shining theatre stage. The swings, igloo and climbing frame could have been the props of a glittery pantomime. Ricky imagined the ducks coming to life, bouncing on their springs and flinging themselves over the fence to freedom. Her fingers tingled with a desire to fly.

Tim knocked politely but when he got no response, he pounded on the door with his fist.

'What the hell?' asked Dan. He was dressed only in underpants and was blinking at the bright, yellow light.

'Can we come in?' asked Tim.

Dan glanced at Ricky and his expression switched from anger to confusion. He looked at Tim again and pulled up the waistband of his boxer shorts.

Tim put a hand on Ricky's shoulder and asked her to make a cup of tea while he and Dan had a chat in the other room. Their voices were low but over the sound of the boiling kettle she could make out questions about her parents. Tim stopped what he was saying to thank her when she brought in the mugs of tea.

'Ricky, I will now explain what we're going to do so there won't be any surprises,' he said. His manner was kind but firm.

She nodded cautiously.

'I'm going to call your mother and then I will call the police.'

The mention of 'police' should have alarmed her but she was feeling numb and detached. Tim's calm manner seemed to take the worry out of the situation.

'They will have to investigate what's just happened at the garden. It's best you give your side of the story first before things get out of hand.' He smiled. 'Do you agree?'

She nodded 'yes' but when she glanced at Dan, she saw something unexpected in his face.

Tim followed her gaze. 'This must be awkward for you.'

'Yes,' Dan said.

'It can't be easy.'

'We've got to rally in times like . . .' His voice petered out.

Tim nodded.

'The Dunkirk Spirit and all that.' Dan sniffed. 'I try my best but obviously it's not easy.'

'Of course.'

'I've had to pull her out of a few scrapes. A bit of trouble.'

'Trouble?'

Ricky held her breath and waited for it.

Dan glanced at her. It was brief but contained a warning. 'Just a bit of monkey business.'

'What kind of monkey business?'

He smiled at Tim and shook his head. 'Nothing serious. Kids' stuff.'

Tim held his gaze. 'I'm going to make those calls now. I suggest you put some clothes on.'

Dan disappeared while Tim was on the phone. Within minutes he was back, dressed in work clothes, saying he had to get going.

Tim waited for him to leave before addressing Ricky. 'By the look on your face, I take it Dan's no father figure?'

She shook her head.

Tim raised his eyebrows.

Ricky's mother must have run all the way from the hospital. She burst through the door, gasping for breath. Tim sent Ricky to the kitchen again to make more tea while he explained what had happened. When she returned bearing two mugs, her mother was looking less frantic. She took the tea without acknowledging her daughter and bit her lip as Tim explained what was going to happen.

'I have to leave now,' he said. 'I need to put on some shoes and get back to the garden. Try not to worry.'

The policewoman's round cheeks were mottled with rosacea. She was tall and, in the chunky stab vest of her uniform, she seemed to take up the space of two people. Ricky's mother led her through to the couch which she dominated with her bulk. Her name was Officer Ryan. 'But you can call me Trish,' she said, plucking at the knees of her trousers to create space in the synthetic material. She was gathering information, she explained, while her colleague investigated the vandalism and fire in the garden. She spoke slowly as if every word was important.

'Was it you who destroyed the garden?' she asked.

Ricky shook her head.

'Did you set the fire?'

Again, she shook her head.

'I have a problem.' She paused to let this sink in. 'Several people say they saw you do it.'

'It wasn't me.'

'But you don't deny you were there?'

'No.'

'So, there was someone else with you?'

Ricky didn't say anything.

'Who was it?'

'I can't say.'

'Here's the thing.' The policewoman leaned forward, resting her elbows on her wide knees. 'Starting a fire on a council estate is a very serious offence. If you don't tell me who did it, you might be blamed.'

'That's not fair,' her mother protested.

The policewoman held up a hand. 'Mrs Bird, there are witnesses who say your daughter was seen inside the garden. It will be her word against theirs unless we have another name.'

'But my daughter would never do such a thing.'

'Does she often go out at night?'

'She never goes out at night.'

'But you haven't been at home much lately, have you?'

'As the estate manager explained, I've got another child in hospital. But I always make sure Ricky has adult supervision.' Her mother was looking desperate and defensive.

'Who is the adult?'

'My partner.'

'He's not Ricky's father?'

'Dan has been extremely kind. It's been very difficult. My son, Ollie, he's very—'

Trish held up her hand again. She turned to Ricky.

'Is Dan looking after you well?'

Ricky looked at her mother and noted the desperation in her eyes. She nodded.

'He's been very good.' Her mother couldn't help herself.

The policewoman wrote something down. 'I'm going to send someone around, a case worker. I'd like an assessment.'

'Assessment? There's nothing wrong with my daughter.'

The policewoman gave her mother a meaningful look. 'It will be an assessment of the home situation. You, your daughter and your partner.'

'Surely that's an overreaction.'

'Mrs Bird, your daughter has been wandering around at night unsupervised and appears to have damaged property and started a fire.' The policewoman stood up. 'We are not overreacting.'

'But I've got a very sick child in hospital.'

'I'm sorry about your son. I'll try to get someone to you today, hopefully soon.'

'What am I supposed to do?'

'I'm afraid you will have to stay here and wait. I won't be far away. My colleague and I will be talking to your neighbours.'

'I hardly know the neighbours. We haven't been here long.'

'You'll be surprised how much they know about you.' Trish gave Ricky a look.

An icy silence descended after the policewoman left. Her mother retreated to her bedroom and, within a few minutes, the sound of light snoring could be heard through her half open door.

Ricky should have been anxious or afraid but she felt detached from all feeling. It was as if she was sitting above her body, controlling her limbs with very long wires like a puppeteer. She curled up on the couch and closed her eyes.

The scrape of the front door disturbed her. She glanced at the clock. She'd been asleep for over an hour; a heavy, dreamless sleep.

Dan called out 'Hello' but when no one answered he began to make himself lunch. The kettle was filled. The sandwich bread was removed from its plastic bag. As he opened the fridge, she imagined him reaching for the butter and cheese, a greedy look on his face. She was listening to the sound of the bread knife sawing the sandwich in half against the chopping board when someone knocked on the door.

'Hello,' said Dan, cheerily. 'You've caught me eating lunch.'

'Pardon the interruption.'

Ricky sat up. What was Mrs Cloney doing here?

'No problem. I'm sure you're worth the interruption.' Dan chuckled.

Mrs Cloney laughed, daintily. 'My name is Cath, Cath Cloney.'

'Dan. How can I help you?'

'I'm here on behalf of a community group. You might have seen our notices.'

'Afraid not.'

'You may not be aware that there are convicted sex offenders living on this estate.'

Dan was silent for a moment. 'Sorry?'

'Perverts. The government has been rehousing them on this estate. We want to know that our children are safe when they go out to play. You'll have heard about the playground. Booby trapped with broken glass. Now there's been another fire.'

'I don't understand.'

'They're trying to intimidate us, to make us stop our campaign.' Mrs Cloney let out a loud sigh. 'Last night it got personal.'

'Someone attacked you?'

'They attacked my garage door. They've accused me of something. Me, of all people.'

'Have you been to the police?'

'They don't want to know. They're more concerned about the fire in the garden.' She cleared her throat. 'I saw the cops here this morning. A very bad business all this. Highly suspicious.'

'What do you mean?' There was an edge to Dan's voice.

'What business does a young girl have being out alone in the middle of the night? You know, my Pauly has seen her with that old man.'

'What old man?'

'That Mr Snow. He's got no business mixing with a child.'

'Really? I had no idea.'

'I tried to talk to the estate manager but the man laughed in my face.' She sighed again. 'Mark my words, there's more to this than meets the eye.'

'What do you mean?'

'The estate manager and that old man are as thick as thieves.'

'Is that so?'

'As I said, it's highly suspicious.'

Ricky realised she'd been holding her breath and exhaled silently. Something very wrong was happening but she had no power to stop it or put things right.

# 25

RICKY STAYED IN her bedroom to avoid her mother while they waited for the case worker. She was too tired to do anything and too wound up to read or sleep. From her window, she couldn't see the garden but she had a good view of the playground and the path to the tower blocks. Anyone looking up would have seen her at the window but her neighbours were only interested in life at eye level.

Over the next couple of hours, Caitlin and Abbie came and went from the playground, Samia and her mother set off and returned with a shopping trolley, and Tim crisscrossed the estate several times on his long legs. Even Bea walked under her window. The one person Ricky didn't see was Jack.

The case worker didn't turn up until the end of the day. Her name was Naomi and she looked more like an older, dishevelled version of Katie than the monster Ricky had been expecting. Naomi waited until they were seated around the table before explaining that they were going to have a discussion and that Ricky was an important part of it.

'I'd like to make it clear that no one is on trial here,' she said. 'My job is to help you.'

Ricky's mother seemed to relax.

'The police are still talking to people and have not finished their investigations.' Naomi looked at Ricky. 'You have to understand that wrecking a garden is one thing but setting a fire in such close proximity to public housing is dangerous. Someone could have been hurt. The police are taking it very, very seriously.'

'My daughter didn't set the fire,' said her mother. 'She's already explained that there was someone else.'

Naomi did not take her eyes off Ricky. 'The police have talked to witnesses who say you were alone. There's no CCTV camera over the actual garden. It's a bit of a blind spot. But they've viewed footage from other cameras around the estate and found no evidence of anyone else with you. Can you explain that?'

Ricky shrugged. Any explanation was going to get Jack into trouble.

'Is everything all right, Ricky?'

She nodded but Naomi kept looking at her until she was forced to say 'Yes'.

'What sort of question is that?' Ricky's mother was trying to stay calm but there was panic in her voice.

'Please.' Naomi held up her hands. She wasn't implying anything, she explained. It was a standard question and it was her job to ask it and get an answer. She was here to help, she repeated. Anything they told her would be used for that purpose.

'Perhaps it's better if I start with you, Mrs Bird.' She opened a spiral notebook and glanced at some handwritten notes. 'Why was your daughter spending her afternoons without adult supervision?'

'She wasn't unsupervised. She was at the community centre.'

'She's not been attending afternoon workshops.'

'That's not true.'

Ricky could feel her mother's eyes on her. She ran her tongue around the inside of her mouth, looking for moisture. 'It's not Mum's fault. She didn't know. I sort of tricked her.'

Her mother gasped.

'The police spoke with your neighbours. Were you aware that Ricky was caught shoplifting in one of the local shops?'

'What?'

'She stole some alcohol, apparently, a miniature bottle.'

Her mother let out a moan.

'Mrs Bird, your partner was there. He intervened.'

'That can't be true. He would have told me.'

'It did happen, I can assure you.' Naomi turned the page of her notebook. 'Ricky has also been out wandering at night. She and a couple of girls broke into an empty flat.'

'I know nothing about this.'

'It seems there is quite a lot you don't know.'

Ricky glanced at her mother. She looked more bewildered than angry.

Naomi continued reading from her notes. 'Your neighbour also alleges that Ricky knocked some teeth out of her son's mouth.'

'It was an accident. The kids were mucking around inside a dark garage.'

'That's not what the boy's mother told the police.'

'Oh, please don't listen to anything that woman says.' Her mother sighed. 'She's a troublemaker.'

'The police also spoke to the girls who were there at the time. They said Ricky lashed out with a weapon. She broke another boy's fingers.'

*Girls?* Ricky hoped Samia hadn't betrayed her.

Her mother took a moment to digest this information. 'Obviously, things have been going on that I didn't know about but, believe me, I have never had any trouble with my daughter, ever. She's always been a good girl. She was top of her class in Brixton.'

Naomi nodded, encouraging her to continue.

'She's had a lot to deal with since we moved here. Her brother is ill, gravely ill. She misses her father and she's, well, going through puberty.'

Ricky looked down at her hands.

'Where is Ricky's father?'

'He's in Brixton.'

'Why didn't Ricky stay with him while your son was in hospital?'

'It's complicated.' Her mother took a deep breath. 'He's looking for work. He has a new partner. They live in a tiny one-bedroom flat. They don't have, ah, the room.'

Naomi nodded.

'They're going to have a baby.'

'I see. You didn't notice anything odd about Ricky's behaviour?'

'No, yes. I thought it was just hormones. My son is so ill. I—' Her mother stuttered. There were tears in her eyes. 'Please believe me. I love my children.'

'I can see that and I will do everything I can to help you. Is there anything else you would like to tell me?'

'Yes, I think there is. Please wait here.' Her mother left the room, returning a few seconds later with something in her hand. 'I brought my daughter up not to lie or steal. She said she found this.'

Ricky's heart sank.

Naomi took the scarab ring from her mother's hand. 'Ricky, can you tell me how you came by this?'

'I found it.'

'Where exactly?'

Ricky had a choice. She could repeat the story she'd told her mother or she could tell the truth. What did she have to lose? 'I found it on the heath.'

'What?' Her mother's voice was a shriek. 'When were you on the heath?'

'I went up there with my friend.'

Naomi wrote something down. 'Is this the same friend who set the fire?'

Ricky nodded and immediately regretted it.

'But I've been up there before. You can ask Caitlin and Abbie. We visited the funfair, together.' Ricky purposefully left Samia out of it. 'There was a fortune teller with a gypsy wagon. Her name was Tina. It's her ring. I found it when I went up there again. It was on the ground where the wagon had been.'

'Why didn't you say this before?' Her mother sounded incredulous, as if she would never believe anything Ricky said ever again.

'I knew you'd be angry that I'd gone there.'

'You're damn right I would have been angry. I'm angry now. I can't believe you've been so dishonest with me. All this time I thought you were going to the community centre. I signed the permission slip and everything.'

'But I was going in the mornings. You can ask Katie.'

'And then spending your afternoons wandering around the estate. You've been lying to me. How could—'

'I never actually lied, Mum. I just didn't tell you everything. You didn't ask so I didn't say.' She took a deep breath. If she was going down, she may as well take someone with her. 'Dan knew I wasn't going to the centre in the afternoons.'

'What?' Her mother's eyes widened.

'Ask him.'

'I'm running out of time, I'm afraid.' Naomi held up a hand. 'There's something very important I'd like to ask you, Ricky.'

She knew what was coming.

'What is the name of your friend?'

'I can't.' Ricky shook her head. 'I don't want to get him into trouble.'

'So, it's a he?'

Ricky clenched her jaw. She'd already said too much.

'Please think about it. The more you tell me, the more I can help. I won't sugarcoat this. You could be in serious trouble.'

Naomi took a small pouch from her tote bag. She removed a business card and slid it across the table to Ricky's mother. 'Thank you for your honesty. I'll be liaising with the police and will be in touch again soon. If you think of anything else or if you want to talk, give me a call.'

Naomi slid another card over to Ricky.

'You are a person of interest in a police investigation. My official job is to assess and report. My real job is to keep you out of trouble. Call me if there is anything you'd like to tell me.'

Ricky's mother walked Naomi out to the balcony where they chatted for several minutes. When she came back inside, she didn't shout or make accusations. In a calm voice, she explained that she needed to call the estate manager. Ricky was allowed to go outside but no further than the front steps.

When Tim arrived, he greeted her warmly before leaping up the steps to knock on their door. She was still sitting on the steps when Samia and her mother returned from shopping. Mrs Mitra stopped on the path below. Her eyes narrowed.

'What are you doing?' she demanded.

'Nothing,' Ricky replied.

Samia was looking at her mother, avoiding Ricky's eyes.

'What is wrong with you?' Mrs Mitra leaned on her trolley handle.

Ricky shrugged. Everything was wrong with her.

'I asked what's wrong with you?'

'Nothing.'

'Do you have a stomach problem?'

'No.'

'But you are sick.'

'No, I'm not.'

'Why are you not eating?'

Ricky hugged her knees to her chest. She was wearing two sweatshirts and a pair of sweat pants under her jeans. No one apart from Jack and Ollie had noticed her weight loss. Why Mrs Mitra, of all people?

'Well?'

'I don't have much of an appetite.'

'There's something wrong with you.' It was a statement.

'I'm okay.'

'No, you are not. You're in trouble.'

'I'm sorry about hypnotising Samia.' She was sorry, too. 'I didn't think it would work.'

'It wasn't your fault,' said Samia.

'My daughter told me what happened.' Mrs Mitra's voice was kinder or at least less severe. 'That nonsense wasn't your doing.'

'I remember everything. Caitlin made you do it.' Samia looked flustered and embarrassed. 'She ripped my blouse.'

Ricky released her knees and dared to relax a little. Something unexpected was happening.

'We heard about the trouble this morning.' Samia announced this not unkindly. 'The police came to our flat.'

Mrs Mitra shushed her daughter and gestured that it was time to go. When she'd hoisted her trolley level with Ricky, she paused.

'If you have trouble, come and see us. We are only next door.' She sucked air between her teeth noisily. 'It's not good for a girl to be always alone.'

Ricky remained on the steps, waiting for Tim to leave. When he finally emerged, it was with her mother.

'Get up,' she said. 'We're going for a walk. Tim's coming with us.'

'Don't look so worried,' he said. 'It's not the firing squad.'

Ricky was relieved the playground was empty. She stayed close to her mother as they followed the path to the tower blocks.

The fire had been a lot worse than she remembered. The garden was charred chaos. All the lattices and the wigwam had been pulled down and burned. All the planting beds had been trashed, either by Jack or the blaze. There was a large dark outline on the side of the building overlooking the garden. But it was the shed that had taken the worst hit. The roof had collapsed and the walls had been incinerated. Only some of the framework remained upright. The rest was a charred heap. Mr Snow was sitting on an upturned bucket, his large hands dangling between his knees. There was a dressing over his forehead. He stood up as they arrived.

'Hello, Snowy,' said Tim. 'Thank you for agreeing to this.'

Mr Snow nodded.

'I've brought young Ricky over to see the damage. I'm hoping she might apologise to you.'

She felt her mother's hand on her back, gently guiding her forward. She didn't want to apologise. Snowy had given the cats away.

'What do you have to say for yourself?' asked her mother.

She shrugged.

'Come on, honey. Please, let's try to sort this out.' Her mother's voice was soft, pleading. *She* needed her to apologise.

Ricky couldn't say anything.

Her mother put her lips next to her ear. 'Ollie's coming home today. Please, do it for him.'

Ricky glanced at Snowy. His eyes were downcast. They were puffy as if he'd been crying. He looked pathetic and lost.

'I'm sorry,' she said.

He didn't look up but she could tell he'd heard.

Tim smiled encouragingly. 'Good girl.'

Ricky felt weak and lightheaded as she walked home with her mother. The destruction of the garden had affected her. So had seeing Snowy.

'Poor old Mr Snow,' said her mother. 'He hasn't had an easy life.'

Ricky didn't say anything.

'Life is difficult for people like him.'

'Why?'

'He's got mental health issues. He's spent a lot of his life in care.'

'Did Tim tell you that?'

'Yes, he's been helping Mr Snow adjust to life on the estate. The poor man has had a difficult time. Tim's worried about him.'

# 26

RICKY SHOULD HAVE said something when she'd had the chance. She should have defended Snowy to Caitlin. Why hadn't she stood up for him? It was all her fault. She'd pushed her way into his garden. He'd never wanted her there. Now she understood why.

At least Ollie was home but he'd been asleep since arriving in an ambulance the previous afternoon. He didn't wake up when the nurse visited. He didn't respond when Ricky kissed or tickled him.

He was sedated, her mother explained. It was for his own good. But what was good about being a zombie? Ollie's face had changed shape. It was bigger, inflated. He looked like a squirrel with acorns stuffed inside his cheeks. It was the medication, her mother said, steroids.

'They need to stop giving them to him,' said Ricky. 'Ollie will have a heart attack when he wakes up and looks in the mirror. He'll never fit a hat the way he's going.'

'They're necessary. They reduce inflammation.'

'Why don't the nurses let him wake up?'

'They don't want to risk another seizure.'

'But I need to talk to him.'

Her mother exhaled slowly and gave her a lingering look. 'I'm sorry but, right now, his needs are more important than yours.'

'But—'

'If it makes you feel better, Ollie's needs are also more important than mine.'

It didn't make her feel better but she didn't blame her brother. She missed Ollie desperately and wanted him to wake up so she could tell him about the huge fight she'd witnessed. It had been a spectacular thing, a nine on the Richter scale argument that had culminated in her mother throwing a loaf of bread at Dan's head. It had been a loaf of sliced white so it didn't do any damage but it did give Dan a fright. Ricky had seen the shock in his eyes and quickly turned away from him. She'd taken refuge on the couch in the other room where she'd listened while their argument raged.

'You knew she wasn't going to the centre in the afternoon and you hid it from me!' her mother shouted. 'She's only a child. Anything could have happened to her.'

'It wasn't like that,' he protested.

'You knew about the shoplifting.'

'It wasn't serious.'

'Wasn't serious? She was banned from Costcutters!'

'They were just being kids.'

'But my daughter was caught shoplifting.'

'She said she didn't steal anything. I believe her.'

Ricky stiffened. Why was Dan lying?

'It was not your place to make decisions about what I should or shouldn't know. You are not her parent.'

'Hang on a minute!' Dan's tone changed. 'You left *me* in charge of your daughter. I didn't ask for the job. I was doing it to help you. And if you want to know why, take a look at yourself. You're a bloody mess. What was I supposed to do? Make life more difficult for you?'

'You should have told me.' There was a note of defeat in her mother's reply.

'You dumped her on me. You didn't have time to look after your own kid. I had to make decisions. And this is the thanks I get.' Dan sniffed. 'I knew she was going to the garden but I had no idea about that filthy old bastard.'

'What do you mean?'

Ricky didn't have to see her mother to know she was now in a highly agitated state. She had a habit of shuffling her feet whenever she was upset. They were moving about on the kitchen floor.

'Cath told me all about him. He's a known pervert.'

'Cath? Who's Cath?'

'Cath Cloney.'

'Why the hell did you talk to that woman?'

'She came here yesterday.'

'Yesterday? But I was here, all day.'

'You'd passed out in the bedroom. I didn't dare wake you. Not in the state you were in. Cath started going on about sex offenders living on the estate. At first, I thought it was a load of rubbish.'

'For god's sake! Why didn't you tell me?'

'You made it clear you didn't like the woman. I knew you'd have a go at me if you found out I'd talked to her. You're having a go at me now, for god's sake. You should be thankful I looked into it all.'

'Thankful for hiding things from me about my own daughter?'

'You weren't around, remember? I was trying to look after you and your family, believe it or not.' Dan sniffed again. 'Not that you care, but I found out it wasn't rubbish. That old man is a degenerate.'

'Get out!'

'What?'

'I said, get out! Give me the keys now. Get your stuff and get out!'

'Come on, love. Don't be like that. I can't just leave.'

'Keys! Now!'

Dan kept talking but her mother didn't answer. After a minute or so, his protests petered out.

Ricky pulled her knees up to her chest and sat very still, hardly breathing, as he walked down the hall behind her. A few minutes later, she heard him coming back. His footsteps stopped outside the hall door. It opened.

'I might not be seeing you for a while, Princess,' he said.

'Uh-huh,' she replied.

'You know I was doing my best, don't you?'

She nodded, eager to be rid of him.

'We had a nice thing going, you and me.'

She waited for him to elaborate.

'We're pals and pals look after each other, don't they?' He attempted one of his charm smiles. 'You probably heard me in there. Remember, I've got your back. Pals and all that.'

He waited for Ricky to nod before picking up his bag.

The front door opened and closed. There was silence.

Ricky counted to ten and released her knees.

Her mother was in the kitchen, leaning over the sink. She was crying silently, great big sobs that made her shoulders and spine shudder.

'Are you okay, Mum?' Ricky asked.

She turned. Her face flushed and wet. 'What were you doing with Mr Snow in the afternoons?'

'I was gardening.'

A sob escaped from deep inside her mother's chest. 'Did he ever do anything to you?'

'No.'

'Are you telling me the truth?'

'Yes.'

'And that's the truth?'

She nodded. 'I wouldn't lie about that.'

Her mother was examining her, looking for a chink, a way in.

It was too much, the tear-filled stare. It made Ricky feel weak and dizzy. She turned away and opened the fridge.

'We don't have any milk, Mum. Can I go get some?'

Her mother sighed. 'You obviously can't go to Costcutters.'

'I didn't steal anything from Costcutters. It was Caitlin Cloney who took the vodka.'

'Ugh, that bloody family.'

'She told lies to get herself out of trouble.'

'How do I know you're not telling lies to get yourself out of trouble?'

'I'm telling the truth.'

Her mother pushed her aside to look inside the fridge. 'God, there's nothing in here except for a bit of old cheese.'

Ricky knew exactly what wasn't in there. For the past two days, she'd been fobbing her mother off, saying she'd eaten when in reality she'd eaten nothing. It had been a surprisingly easy deception to pull off with so much happening: the police and social worker visits, and then the bustle of Ollie's homecoming.

'Get some yoghurt and milk. Oh, and some eggs and spinach.' She shut the fridge door. 'Some fruit, too.'

'What about bread?'

Her mother snorted. She picked up the loaf from the floor and threw it in the bin. 'Get wholegrain. I never want to see this rubbish in here again.'

Apart from the visit to the garden, Ricky had not been outside for two days. She imagined herself as a prisoner of war being released from an underground bamboo cage. The outside world was dazzling and colourful. She lifted her face to the sun and noticed its heat had lost intensity. The leaves on the plane trees were beginning to curl and brown. The long, burdensome summer was finally coming to an end.

Turning in a circle, she took in the small changes that had occurred over the previous two days, marvelling at the relentless cycle of the seasons. Despite all that had happened since moving to Camden, despite her life being flipped upside down and the loss of virtually everything she cherished, summer was giving way to autumn. In her mind's eye, she zoomed high above herself like a drone. She was ant-like, a tiny collection of molecules in a vast universe of black holes and dying stars. She closed her eyes and could feel herself spinning with the earth through space. She searched in this immenseness for something, anything, that made sense, an anchor to hold her steady and give meaning to the chaos of her life.

It was the melancholy call of a blackbird, the summer departing from its song, that brought her back into herself. Shading her eyes, she searched high for the bird she'd been hearing all summer. She found him sitting on the corner of a roof, tiny and powerful, silhouetted against the pale blue of the sky. He looked at her looking up at him and fell silent.

Avoiding the community centre, Ricky took a circuitous route that led her past the flats where the Cloneys lived. She kept to the other side of the street, slowing her pace as she neared their garage. Someone had made an attempt to clean the roller door but Jack's words were still clearly visible: 'EVIL LYING FILTH'.

Mr Snow lived in the next block along in one of the smaller units with a patio. As Ricky took in the full horror of what had happened, her eyes filled with tears. Someone had sprayed 'Peddo' over and over on the side of the flat. Every window had been smashed. Four jagged holes. Pot plants lay uprooted and torn apart. Clothes and other belongings were scattered over the patio.

Ricky had to prop herself against a neighbour's wall. Her legs were shaky. She was fighting with herself, acutely aware of her role in this tragedy, when a familiar figure mounted the steps to Snowy's flat. She tensed, ready to make a run for it but Pauly Cloney didn't glance her way before pushing open the broken door and disappearing inside. Ricky should have taken flight then but found herself unable to move as the sound of breaking glass and crockery became audible. Less than a minute later, Pauly re-emerged, smiling to himself. In his hands was a child's soft toy. As he leaped down the steps, he was examining the large, fluffy teddy and laughing.

Her mother was in her bedroom cleaning when Ricky got home. The double bed had been stripped and the pillows were on the windowsill, airing in the sunlight. She was working in a manic way, stuffing clothes and belongings into a black rubbish bag. Ricky saw one of Dan's t-shirts disappear into the bag followed by a pair of trainers. Her mother dropped the bag and began vacuuming. She was vigorously rubbing the foot of the cleaner over the carpet when Ricky went into Ollie's room.

The Macmillan nurse had been while Ricky was at the shops. Ollie's bedding had been straightened and his little arms had been arranged, perfectly symmetrical over the duvet. His eyes were closed but when she took hold of his hand his face twitched. His palm was very hot, like the core of a nuclear power plant.

The vacuum cleaner died and her mother walked past with the rubbish bag. She took a step back and gave Ricky a nod. Her eyes moved to Ollie. She looked down and kept walking.

Ricky squeezed her brother's tiny hot hand. After a moment, Ollie squeezed back.

'Hello, Big Fry,' he whispered. He smiled in a painful way as if the weight of his inflated cheeks made any facial movement difficult.

'Hello, Small Fry.' Ricky had to swallow twice before she could continue. 'It's about time you woke up. I've got so many things to tell you.'

'What things?'

'Mum kicked Dan out. Hear that noise in the kitchen? That's Mum clearing out his stuff.'

They listened to cupboards being opened and shut, bags rustling. Ricky knew her mother would be hunting out anything that vaguely belonged to Dan – packets of instant noodles and other food they didn't eat. She'd done the same thing when their father had moved out. Anything he hadn't taken or Ricky hadn't grabbed had been thrown away.

'How's your friend?' Ollie asked.

It was impossible to explain why she hadn't seen Jack without telling Ollie what had happened. He listened quietly as she described the bruising on her friend's face and how he'd gone on a rampage, tagging the Cloneys' garage before destroying Snowy's garden.

'He could have killed someone with that fire.' Ollie looked sad.

'I think it was also Jack who set fire to the wheelie bins.'

'Did he paint the duck?'

Ricky was surprised Ollie knew about this. 'Yes, and he smashed the glass.'

'People will think you caused the fire.'

'But I can't tell them about Jack. He'll get into trouble.'

'Hmm.' Ollie closed his eyes and seemed to consider her options. They stayed closed for at least a minute. 'I'm not sleeping.'

'I know.'

'Maybe you should tell them.'

'I need to protect him.'

'Who's protecting you?'

'I'm okay.'

'Hmm.' He opened his eyes. 'Well, I need to tell you something.'

'What?'

'I know I don't have a parasite.'

Ricky's heart started racing. She wanted to contradict him, to shout at him to shut right up, but Ollie was looking at her in that determined, knowing way of his.

'I always knew.'

She thought of all the stories she'd told him, how they had cheered him up. He'd seemed genuinely excited about Amanda Holden.

'I know what's really wrong with me.'

Ricky wanted to put her fingers in her ears and scream. *Don't say it. Don't say it.*

'I've got a tumour inside my head.'

She gasped, unable to contain her fear and sadness. 'No, you don't.'

'Yes, I do.'

She could hardly hear him over the roaring in her ears. The cancer was terminal, he told her, like a train station at the end of a railway line. The tumour was growing too fast and would not respond to any treatment to shrink it. They had given him medication but the lump in his head was like the bread dough their mother made. It was swelling and putting pressure on his brain. One day, the pressure would be too much and something would pop.

'I will probably pee myself when it happens so I apologise in advance.' Ollie chuckled softly. 'Everything will stop. My body will stop breathing and growing.'

Ricky waited for it.

'Then I will, you know.' He took a deep breath. 'Die.'

But death wasn't bad once you understood how it worked, he explained. While in hospital, he'd stopped breathing and in the minutes it took to get his lungs and heart working again, he'd visited the most marvellous place with a big river.

'On the other side was a forest. There was a boat but it was tied up and I couldn't get the knot undone. I wanted to go to the forest but people were calling me, telling me not to cross the river.'

Ricky could see it, the river and the boat, Ollie struggling with the knotted rope. 'You don't have to cross the river.'

'I do. I can feel it pulling me. It's like I have part of the river in my body.'

'I don't want you to leave me.'

'You'll cross the river, too, one day. I'll meet you on the other side.'

The thought of crossing a river to be with Ollie should have upset Ricky but a warm feeling crept over her. They could be together in the forest away from all the trouble in Camden. 'I want to come with you now. I don't want to wait.'

'You've got to stay here with Mum.'

'I'd rather stay in Brixton with Dad.'

'It wouldn't work with him.'

'Why are you always so mean about Dad?'

He smiled. 'Don't you know yet?'

'No.'

'It's because he always lets you down.'

'No, he—'

'He does.'

Ricky had to force herself not to cry.

'You're the best sister ever and I love you more than anything.'

'I love you more.'

'I doubt it.' Ollie closed his eyes again. 'I need to sleep now.'

Ricky felt weightless as she walked up the hall. Her feet seemed to float as if there was a layer of air between her sandals and the carpet. She was feeling light. All she had to do was kick herself off the ground and she would begin to rise in the air.

Tim must have arrived while she was talking to Ollie. He was sitting at the table with her mother, his hands cupped around a mug of tea. There were biscuits on a plate.

Her mother frowned. 'Are you all right?' she asked.

'I've been talking to Ollie,' Ricky replied. On the edge of her field of vision, there were small, twinkling points of light. 'We're going to meet on the other side of the river.'

'What river?' The furrow between her mother's eyebrows deepened. 'Ollie is unconscious. The nurse just topped up his medication.'

Ricky shrugged.

Her mother glanced at Tim. 'We want to talk to you about something serious. It's about Mr Snow.'

Ricky thought of the smashed windows and felt sick. Her legs felt rubbery. Her jaw stiffened as acid gushed into her mouth.

'Tim had to take him to a safe place. People have broken into his flat. They're saying he's a—'

'I know what they're saying.' Ricky was feeling peculiar, unsteady and nauseous. 'That he's a paedophile.'

A sound escaped from her mother. She and Tim exchanged looks. 'You spent a lot of time with him.'

'I did until he decided to kill the cats.'

'What cats? What are you talking about?'

Ricky wanted to explain about the RSPCA but her mouth was full of acid and had stopped working. Her legs were wobbling. She saw Tim leap out of his chair and knew she was falling. Falling or floating.

# 27

WHEN SHE OPENED her eyes, she found her father sitting next to her bed. He was reading *The Complete Gardener*, the book she'd been given for Christmas the previous year. Ricky hadn't moved or made a sound but he was aware she'd woken up because he smiled.

'Hello,' he said.

She realised her bedside lamp was on. It was night-time but her last memory was of morning. She closed her eyes and saw a strange jumble of images: movement, bright lights, people in white and blue clothes. Doctors and nurses. Her mother and Tim had been there. She remembered a journey in a car, the smell of vomit. Tim was driving. She was in the back on her mother's lap. Returning to the flat. Then there was confusion. Fear. A struggle. She remembered the feeling of relief as she was put in her own bed.

'Why are you here?' she finally asked. Her throat was dry. She coughed and noticed her chest felt freer, unrestricted. She realised she wasn't wearing her tight old tank top. She felt exposed, embarrassed that someone had removed it and seen what was underneath.

Her father reached for a glass of water and told her to sit up. She did as she was told but found she had little power in her limbs. Sitting up was a business. He had to help her, lifting her like he'd done when she was little. He gave her a small hug in the process.

'Why haven't you been eating, love?' His voice was soft.

'I wasn't hungry.'

'But a growing girl like you should always be hungry.' He was being too gentle and kind. It made her feel weak.

'I've been taking the vitamins.'

'Vitamins are not food. You've been starving yourself. The doctors say you're emaciated. How could that have happened?'

Ricky didn't say anything.

'They also said you haven't been washing. They found bruises on you, and other injuries. Do you know what I am talking about?'

She gave him a blank look.

'What's been going on, love? Are you in some kind of trouble?'

She shook her head.

'Your mother said you went crazy when they brought you back from the hospital.'

'I can't remember.' But she did remember.

'You smashed the bedside lamp in her bedroom.'

There was a crash of glass, her mother rushing in. 'I didn't want to be in there.'

He frowned. 'But you always loved sleeping in our bed.'

She considered what she should tell him. 'I'm too big to sleep in Mum's bed. You've said so yourself.'

'So I have.' He smiled, satisfied. 'Look, we know something's been going on. You can tell me. I'm your dad. I'm on your side.'

Ricky thought about what Ollie had said, how her father always let her down. There was a time when he'd been on her side but now she wasn't sure. The father she'd known in Brixton was not the man of this summer. Ricky had hardly seen him since they moved. When he had turned up, he'd been distant and harsh.

'Do you remember fainting?'

'I think so.'

'The docs said you had no food in your system. Nothing. Not a green pea. You've got virtually no body fat. It's so severe, apparently, that you might have arrested your development.'

'But I've got a lot of muscle.' She couldn't help herself. There was still a part of her that craved his approval.

He shook his head dismissively. 'Your mother says that you imagine Ollie talks to you.'

'I don't imagine it.'

'Come on, love.'

'He does.'

'What does he say?'

'He told me he's got a tumour inside his head that's going to make his brain pop.' It hurt her to say this out loud. 'He also said he died once while he was in hospital.'

Her father looked shocked. 'Who told you this?'

'Ollie.'

'That's impossible. Ollie can't have told you anything. He hasn't been conscious for over a week. Actually, it's more like two or three weeks.'

'But he did tell me. He also said he's not scared of dying again.'

'Ollie can't have told you any of that.' Her father seemed caught between panic and disbelief. 'Someone must have spoken to you. Was it Dan?'

She shook her head. 'It was Ollie.'

She began to explain about the river and the boat, how Ollie had already visited the place when he stopped breathing in hospital. 'He said it has a really nice forest.'

Her father was shaking his head. 'Who's been saying these silly things to you?'

'It was Ollie.'

'It can't have been. Ollie has been heavily sedated since he was resuscitated. He's been unconscious.'

'But he woke up. He spoke to me. He's been speaking to me all along.'

'Come on. I want to show you something.'

Her father helped her out of bed and, after arranging her dressing gown around her shoulders, led her to Ollie's room.

Her brother was sleeping, his face angelic in the glow of the lamp. Her father knelt beside the bed and picked up Ollie's hand. When he let it go, it flopped on the covers, lifeless. He put his lips to Ollie's ear and told him he loved him. Ollie's face didn't change, not a flicker.

'Notice how he's in a very deep sleep? He might be able to hear what we say but he has no power of speech. Ollie lost that in hospital weeks ago.'

Ricky couldn't prove what she'd seen or heard but it didn't matter. She no longer cared about convincing her father.

He stayed to eat the soft-boiled eggs and toast soldiers her mother had prepared for dinner. They talked quietly while they ate but Ricky could tell they were just pretending to have a proper conversation. Both of them kept glancing at her to make sure she was eating. She couldn't get much down but having them both there seemed to make a difference. She could taste the butter on the toast and the salt on the egg.

Ricky woke up the following day without any memory of being asleep. One minute her mother was kissing her goodnight and the next she was awake and it was morning. She'd almost forgotten what it felt like to have an unbroken sleep. For weeks she'd been waking every few hours, confused as to whether she'd been dreaming or awake. It was like swimming across the surface of sleep without descending deep enough to rest. Exhaustion had made her foggy headed. She'd lost fragments of time and couldn't remember things.

It took Ricky a long time to get dressed. The clothes she'd been wearing all summer had disappeared and she needed something to wear under her t-shirt. It was the tightness she craved. Without the feeling of compression around her chest she felt naked.

In the end, she took one of Ollie's cotton tank tops and, after cutting off the straps, pulled it over her head and worked it down over her chest, folding it over to create another bandeau.

Her mother was in the kitchen stirring porridge.

'Good morning, darling. I'm just making breakfast,' she said. 'Naomi will be here in half an hour. She'd like to have a chat with you.'

'I'm not hungry, Mum,' Ricky said. 'Can I eat after Naomi's been?'

'No, we have to get you back to eating regular meals. I don't know what the hell Dan was doing while I was at the hospital but he certainly wasn't feeding you.'

'I think he was doing his best.' Ricky didn't understand why she said this. Everything was jumbled up, all the rights and wrongs.

'Well, his best didn't cut the mustard.' Her mother poured porridge into a bowl before adding milk and brown sugar. She sprinkled seeds on top like the old days. 'You don't have to eat a lot but I want you to eat three times a day.'

Once again Ricky could taste the food on her tongue. The small stubborn flecks of oats were oaty and the brown sugar tasted vaguely like toffee. The seeds exploded between her teeth, filling her mouth with a pleasant fattiness. She ate half a bowl before the feeling of fullness made her stop.

Naomi was ten minutes late and bustled in apologising for the delay. Her bag was hanging open and she was rummaging inside, looking for something. Her curly hair looked as if it hadn't been brushed. It was flattened at the back where her head must have rested against a pillow. The grey of her natural colour was showing at the roots. She smiled, grateful for the mug of tea Ricky's mother put in front of her. She turned to Ricky.

'How are you feeling today?'

Her manner was friendly but Ricky detected another question within the question, like a hook hidden within the colourful cluster of feathers of a fishing lure.

'I'm fine, thank you,' she replied.

'Glad to hear it.' Naomi pulled a folder out of her bag and opened it on the table. 'Now, I'm going to ask you some questions. First, I want to be clear about something. You are not in trouble and you will not be in trouble about anything.'

Ricky nodded. She doubted very much that she wasn't in trouble.

'You are not on trial here.' Naomi was like a friendly detective, putting the suspect at ease before extracting confessions and information. 'I'm going to be very honest with you and want you to be just as honest with me. Okay?

'Okay.'

Naomi glanced at Ricky's mother before giving Ricky her full attention. 'Would it be easier if your mum wasn't here?'

Ricky looked down and counted to five before nodding.

Her mother's chair scraped.

Ricky waited for the door to close before looking up. Naomi winked in a conspiratorial way and took out her notebook.

'Tell me about Mr Snow.'

Her pen was poised above the notebook. There was a smile on her face. It was almost impossible to detect the hook hidden within her lure. Ricky needed to think like a barracuda.

'He looks after the garden.'

'You worked there with him.'

Ricky described the planting beds, going into detail about the vegetables she had helped cultivate.

'How often did you visit the garden?'

'Most afternoons except on the weekend. Some days I went to the hospital.'

'And Mr Snow was always there with you?'

'He has the key to the gate. I could only work in the garden when he was there.'

'But didn't you climb over the fence the other night?'

'No.'

'Someone did.'

She nodded.

'Was it your friend?'

Ricky didn't say anything.

'You don't want to tell me the name of your friend?'

She shook her head.

'Is he from the estate?'

She nodded and immediately realised she'd given away another piece of information.

'The thing is, Ricky, we can't find any trace of your friend, anywhere. There were no fingerprints on any garden tools apart from yours and Mr Snow's. There's no sign of him on the security cameras either. There's lots of you, though. What were you doing out wandering at night?'

She shrugged.

'As I said before, the cameras don't cover the actual garden but there is surveillance around the paths.' Naomi clicked her pen. 'What the footage did show was a lot of coming and going to that blind spot near the garden. Do you know Pauly Cloney?'

'I broke his teeth.'

'So I heard.'

'He deserved it.'

'You're probably right.' Naomi allowed herself a smile. 'Did he ever threaten you?'

'He threatens everyone.' Ricky described how he'd threatened Snowy. 'He said something to Mr Snow.'

Naomi nodded. 'Go on.'

'He said he could have Snowy done.'

'Those were his words?'

'Yes.' She hesitated, unsure of whether to say more. 'I saw him go inside Mr Snow's flat.'

'Pauly Cloney?'

'Yes, the place was all smashed up and the door wasn't locked. I saw him go inside. I could hear him smashing things. He came out with a toy, a teddy.'

'The police believe Pauly Cloney has been dealing drugs. What about Mr Geddes? Do you see much of him?'

'Mr Geddes?'

'Tim, the estate manager.'

'Sometimes. He's nice to Mum.'

Naomi stopped writing. 'What do you mean?'

Ricky explained how he'd helped them when they first moved to the estate.

'He's very friendly with Mr Snow, isn't he?'

She was circling Snowy like a great white shark. Something was coming but Ricky wasn't sure what. Naomi had a trick up her sleeve. She was sure of it.

'I've talked to the lady who runs the summer workshop.'

'Katie.'

'Yes, Katie. She said you keep notebooks, diaries. I don't suppose you could let me see them?'

Ricky shook her head.

'It would be very helpful. I wouldn't have to ask you so many questions.'

She shook her head again.

'Okay. Then tell me, why did you say that Mr Snow killed cats?'

'It didn't come out right.' Ricky explained about the cat and kittens, how he'd taken them to the RSPCA, how she feared Lola would be euthanised.

Naomi nodded. 'Has Mr Snow ever given you anything to drink or eat?'

She shook her head.

'Has Pauly Cloney or Mr Geddes?'

'Why are you asking me this?'

'The hospital found something in your blood, something that shouldn't have been there.' Naomi put her pen down and, before Ricky could react, she reached across the table and placed a hand on top of hers. 'Please, Ricky. Has anyone been giving you drugs?'

Ricky felt fluttery and panicky inside. They had been peppermints. She was sure of it. They'd come in a bag and everything.

# 28

FRAGMENTS OF GLASS crunched beneath her trainers as she climbed inside the igloo. Crouching low, she waddled to the centre of the structure where no one could see her. The setting sun was making everything glow. Ricky held up her hand to the light streaming in under the arched entrance. It shone through her fingers, outlining her hand as if her fingers were on fire.

She took off her backpack and relaxed against the wall. After all the noise and confusion of the day, the igloo was quiet. Inside the white plastic bubble, she felt safe and strangely elated. Apart from Jack, no one knew where she was and no one would be looking for her, at least not yet. She was stretching out her legs when she heard the clang of the gate.

Pink Nike trainers walked past.

Something wet touched her leg. Baby had entered the igloo and was looking at her expectantly. There was sadness and yearning in the old dog's eyes.

Ricky lowered her head and peered outside, recognising Abbie's lean brown shins and the plump, freckled legs of Caitlin. The girls were sitting on the swings.

'Stop blubbing,' said Caitlin, kicking herself into a gentle swing. 'It's not going to do any good.'

'But I need him,' said Abbie. She sniffed dramatically. 'I need to find him. He's not answering his phone.'

'You don't know a bloody thing, do you?'

'But I *really* need him.'

'He's gone away. You can't see him.'

Abbie let out a small cry.

'Don't give me that look. It's not my fault.' Caitlin angrily pounded her heel on the rubberised surface of the playground. 'It's that stupid bitch's fault for setting fire to the garden.'

'But Pauly had nothing to do with that.'

'You're so fucking thick.'

'No, I'm not.'

'The cops checked all the security cameras.' Caitlin kicked the ground with her heel again. 'They've got Pauly on video, selling. They came to the house and searched everything. They took all the stuff out of our garage. They're going to do Mum for receiving.'

Baby snorted.

Ricky pulled the dog close. As she breathed in the dirty sock smell of the old dog, she thought of Ollie and felt a sharp pain in the centre of her chest as if she'd been stabbed.

'But Pauly will be okay.' Abbie's voice was a whine. 'They can't do anything to him.'

'What are you talking about?'

'He's a minor.'

'You're so stupid. Pauly was held back a year. He's sixteen. He'll do time.'

Abbie burst into tears, loud and uncontrolled.

'Shut up, shut up!'

Abbie kept crying.

'You need to shut up. You're not even in trouble.'

'But I *am* in trouble.' Abbie let out a small howl.

Caitlin stopped kicking the ground. 'What?'

'I've missed my . . .'

A shudder ran along Baby's spine.

Glass bit into Ricky's forearms as she flattened herself on the floor of the igloo. She looked out and saw that Caitlin had stopped moving. She was sitting rigidly on her swing, looking at Abbie. It was a vicious look, one of hatred. Abbie's head was down. Her shoulders were heaving with silent sobs. She seemed unaware of Caitlin getting off her swing and didn't see her raise her arm. By the time Abbie looked up it was too late to raise her own arm in defence. The force of Caitlin's slap sent her flying off the swing. She landed on her back with a thud.

'You slut!' Caitlin's face was red. 'You've ruined everything. Everything!'

The gate opened and clanged shut.

Ricky crawled out of the igloo and, after checking to make sure Caitlin was gone, went over to where Abbie was lying. The girl's eyes were closed but her chest was rising and falling. Baby appeared from inside the igloo. The dog sniffed Abbie's hair and gave her cheek a lick. The girl opened her eyes.

'Are you all right?' Ricky asked, crouching beside her.

Abbie blinked. She raised her hand and began stroking Baby, who was licking her ear. 'I think so.'

Ricky took hold of the girl's forearm and pulled her to a sitting position.

Abbie looked dazed. She felt the back of her head and then seemed to collect herself, rearranging her hair and straightening the front of her dress.

'You need help, Abbie.'

'Caitlin wants to kill me.'

'Don't worry about Caitlin. She can't do anything to you. Her family is in too much trouble.'

'I need to find Pauly. I can't have a baby.'

'Pauly can't help you, Abbie. You've got to sort this out without him.'

'I can't.' She started crying again.

'Yes, you can. I know someone who will help.'

'Who?' Abbie looked doubtful. 'Who would want to help me?'

'Katie.'

'The lady from the workshop?'

'Yes.'

'I don't believe you.'

'She helped me once.'

'How?'

Ricky swallowed. It made her sick to remember what had happened at the museum. 'When I was bleeding. You know, down there. She sorted me out.'

'You really think she would help me?' There was a spark of hope in Abbie's eyes.

'Yes, I do.'

Abbie let out a moan. 'It's so horrible.'

'It will be okay.'

She was crying again. 'I mean I've been so horrible. I'm sorry.'

'It doesn't matter now.'

'You were nice to my granny.' Abbie closed her eyes. 'I should have been nicer but Caitlin wouldn't let me. I needed her. I needed Pauly.'

'It's okay.'

'No, it's not.'

'Yes, it is.'

'There's something I should tell you.' Abbie took a deep breath. 'Remember that night we broke into the flat?'

'Yes.'

'That boy who died, he wasn't killed by a pervert. And he didn't even live in that flat. He got hit by a car or something.'

Ricky shrugged. It didn't matter. Nothing mattered anymore.

Abbie gave Ricky a sly look. 'You know who really is one?'

'One what?'

'A paedo.'

Ricky felt her gut tighten.

'Caitlin's uncle. He isn't even her proper uncle. He's her mother's cousin or something.' Abbie laughed in a small, nasty way. 'It's the big family secret.'

'I thought he was dead?'

'Caitlin made up that murder story after he got her sister in trouble. It was wishful thinking.'

'Was he even stabbed?'

'Not yet. Caitlin's mother is going to kill him if she ever tracks him down.'

Baby had wandered over to the gate and was scratching the ground impatiently.

Abbie stood up and tidied her dress. She picked up the dog's lead and opened the gate. 'Why were you hiding inside the igloo?'

'I'm not hiding. I'm waiting for someone.'

Abbie's face brightened. 'I always think of you being alone. Well, you know, lonely.'

'I've got a friend.'

'Samia?'

'It's someone you don't know.'

Ricky noticed the air had cooled when she crawled back inside the igloo. The sun had disappeared behind the buildings, taking its warmth with it. She opened her backpack and took out Ollie's toy dog. Closing her eyes, she buried her face in Scotty's fur and inhaled deeply, searching for fragments of her little brother.

What a strange, sad day. Since morning, there had been a constant flow of people through the flat: nurses, police and Naomi. It was Naomi who told Ricky about Mr Snow. He'd been kept overnight at the police station and was being questioned. Ricky thought of his big bulk folded up on a cot in a police cell, a long way from his ruined garden. It was her fault he was in trouble. She was the one who deserved to be in jail. She was the criminal.

Her mother had made tea for Naomi and put biscuits on the table before leaving them alone. Ricky had felt bad but it was impossible to talk to the case worker with her mother in the same room. Everything and everyone were making her feel bad these days, especially now that people were being nice. Kindness was a burden. It forced her to think of the feelings of others and gave her no relief from the trouble she'd caused.

Naomi's kindness seemed genuine but Ricky could tell there was purpose and direction to her chitchat. How was Ricky feeling? Was she sleeping better? What were her dreams like? She had removed something from a folder, a sheet of paper. Ricky recognised her own handwriting.

'I got one of your stories from Katie.' Naomi held it up for her to see. A paragraph had been highlighted in green. 'Katie didn't want to give me this. I had to make her. I can do that because this is a criminal case. Katie is a big fan of your work. She says you're very talented. She told me she's been concerned about you.'

Naomi put on her reading glasses. 'I'd like to read you something from the story.'

Ricky could already feel her face starting to burn.

'The starfish didn't tell anyone about the eel because he'd made her promise not to tell. If she said anything, she would be banned from seeing the sea anemone with the beautiful tentacles. The starfish had already caused too much trouble, he said. The other sea creatures were fed up with her, especially the barnacles who lived on the same rock. The barnacles didn't like her anymore. She'd told too many lies. One more problem and she would have to leave the rock. The eel said he was her only friend.'

Naomi stopped reading. 'It's a bit of a sad story.'

'The ending is not sad. The anemone and starfish swim away together.'

'But what happens to the eel?'

Ricky shrugged.

Naomi took a biscuit from the plate and leaned back in her chair. Her movements were slow and relaxed but her eyes never left Ricky's face. 'The eel should have been taken somewhere where he couldn't hurt anyone again.'

'It's only a story.'

'Is it?'

Ricky tried to swallow. She took a sip of water.

'I'm going to be very honest with you and I want you to be very honest with me.'

She nodded.

'The doctors did a lot of tests on you when you were in hospital. You won't remember any of it because they gave you something to make you sleep. The thing is, they found evidence of trauma on your body. Do you know what I mean by trauma?'

'Like from a car accident?'

'Yes, but you haven't been in any accidents, which leaves only one explanation.' Naomi sat up straight. 'Someone has been hurting you. There was recent bruising but also evidence of other trauma. It's been going on for a while, hasn't it?'

She didn't say anything.

'Has a man been hurting you?'

Ricky held her breath.

'The doctors said someone has hurt you *sexually*.'

Ricky made a strange noise. It had flown out of her mouth as if desperate to escape.

'Who's been hurting you, Ricky?'

She wanted to scream and run out of the room. It felt like she was inside a pressure chamber. It was too hot. The air was too dense. She was finding it difficult to breathe.

'It's okay, Ricky. No one is angry with you. No one is going to hurt you anymore. We just need to know who's been doing this to you so he or *she* can be stopped.' Naomi leaned over the table. 'Who is it?'

Ricky shook her head. It was filled with noise, the roar of an angry ocean.

Naomi put her hand on top of Ricky's. It was soft and cool, like one of the damp flannels her mother put on her forehead when she was feverish. 'Are you sure you can't remember or are you just scared?'

Ricky took a breath and tried to speak but nothing came out. She focused and put all her energy into making her voice work. What came out was a whisper. 'Both.'

If Naomi was disappointed, she didn't show it. She remained warm and friendly as she scooped up her papers, assuring Ricky that she was safe and that no one could hurt her anymore. If she remembered anything, she was to tell her mother or call. Naomi gave her another card.

'You are not in trouble,' she said. 'You are safe. You are loved.'

While Naomi was talking to her mother, Ricky went into Ollie's room. The bedcovers were fresh and there was a new bag of saline suspended from the drip stand. Ollie's face had been washed. Someone had tried to tidy his hair but it was too fine and full of static to be combed into any style.

As she sat on the chair next to his bed, she realised the room felt different. It was cooler, emptier. A spiky panic ran through her limbs. She leaned over her brother to make sure he was still alive, feeling under the covers until she found his hand. It was dry but warm.

'Are you awake?' she whispered.

His face was impassive.

'Come on, Small Fry.'

He didn't respond.

She let go of his hand and moved her fingers to his armpit. She wiggled her fingertips.

His lips slowly formed a smile.

'It's you,' he said finally, his voice barely audible.

'It's me.' She tickled him again.

'I've been waiting.'

'What for?'

'You.'

Ricky felt pain in the centre of her chest.

'I have to leave now.'

'Please don't go.'

He opened his eyes and looked directly into hers.

'Don't go. I need you here.'

His mouth opened but, instead of words, he exhaled, long and deep. It was like a gasp but in reverse.

Ricky must have screamed because her mother was suddenly there, her arms wrapped around her. From over her shoulder, Ricky saw Naomi take a mobile phone from her pocket.

After that, everything seemed to happen very fast. Her father was there. So were the paramedics. From the window, she watched them carry Ollie to the ambulance. His room became even colder without him, empty and unfriendly.

She moved like a robot, taking the things she needed, stuffing them in her backpack. No one saw her leave or go to the playground.

It was almost dark when Jack finally crawled into the igloo. He was smiling, pleased to see Ricky.

'I've been waiting for you,' she said.

'I had some things to finish up,' he said, settling himself beside her.

'How is your mother?'

'She's gone.'

'I'm sorry.'

'I'm sorry about Ollie. I saw the ambulance.'

'Are you ready?'

He nodded.

Together, they removed their shoes and placed them neatly at the entrance to the igloo.

'Ready.' Jack held out his hand.

Ricky reached into the backpack and took out the blister pack she'd taken from Ollie's room. She divided the pills and gave half to Jack.

'Down the hatch!' He put the handful of tablets in his mouth and washed them down with her bottle of water.

He looked at her and nodded. 'Your turn.'

# 29

SHE WAS SUSPENDED in a vast white place. It was like the sky, wide and endless. The white wasn't a colour, exactly. It was more like a sound or a feeling. The light was all around her and within her. She was filled with it. The light was her. It was silence and harmony. It was happiness. Ricky had never felt such effortless joy.

To get to the white place, she'd experienced a rushing forward and upward as if she was being pulled by a vacuum. It had yanked her up and away from inside the igloo. All the noise and confusion, all the prickly feelings and troubles were left behind, like stepping out of clothes before a bath. She was weightless and free. Nothing could touch or harm her. She was wrapped in feelings of great comfort yet also exaltation. All that she'd left behind was fading in her wake, all the connections, the memories, the feelings. The light around her was bleaching the physical world of colour and meaning.

And yet.

There was something. A noise. It was persistent, like constant knocking at a door. It was coming inside the white place, disrupting the light, disturbing her. With great reluctance, she strained to listen.

'Ricky!'

A man's voice, loud and very close.

'Ricky!'

She felt a blow. Hard and shocking.

'Wake up!'

She was being ripped away from the white happiness, hauled out and pulled downward. She felt terrible sadness and loss.

She tried to protest, to fight.

With a painful jolt, she poured back into her body. Toes, legs, torso. Life flowed through her like quick-running mercury. Fingers, arms. Neck, head. Her sluggish senses awakened.

She could feel fingers tighten painfully around her arm. She was being dragged along the ground. There was sharpness like needles digging into her back, shards of glass. She was being pulled out of the igloo. She tried to protest again but her brain couldn't find the route to her vocal cords.

Then she was outside on her back, looking up at the great inkiness of the sky.

A face appeared, blocking her view of the night sky. It was a man, someone she knew. He was shaking her by the shoulder and shouting. Her brain, still attuned to the immense, wordless understanding of the white place, heard many things in what he was saying. There was panic and urgency. His voice was like a song with discordant melodic layers. Fear was the loudest note but the constant base melody was one of care or tenderness, like the purr of a cat. It was this that was disconnecting her from the white place.

The man shook her again.

She didn't respond.

Tim was looking into her eyes, shouting at her.

There were others behind him now. Samia and Abbie. Mrs Mitra was there, too. She was on the phone, talking frantically.

Hands snaked under her body. Tim scooped her up.

Samia ran ahead to open the gate.

Tim was running with her in his arms when a sound, high-pitched like a siren, cut through everything. It pierced Ricky like a sliver of glass, cutting through the dullness of her thoughts and the numbness of her body. It was the sound of love and terror and it was coming from her mother who was running toward them, her mouth wide open, arms outstretched. She tripped but kept stumbling forward, closer and closer until she was on her.

With the touch of her mother's hand came the awareness of other sounds: Tim's ragged breathing, Abbie's sobs, the worried murmurs of the gathering crowd, windows opening, doors closing, the crunch of shoes on the path. The sounds were hushed as if she was hearing them from a distance.

'My baby!' Her mother was on her and all around her.

Ricky's senses burst to life as she was wrenched from Tim's arms. All at once, she could see and hear everything in exquisite detail. The blue-black sky. Dim streetlights. The jumble of voices, distant traffic, crickets and a lone blackbird, her blackbird, high above them, singing into the night. Her mind, blasted into the here and now, was awake to it all with painful intensity. She could feel her mother's fear as if it were her own. There was worry and confusion pulsating from everyone around her.

Her mother sank to the ground, cradling her in her arms.

'Can you hear me?' she asked.

Ricky could hear her but she couldn't move or signal. There was bright white at the outer edges of her field of vision.

'Please, wake up. Wake up.'

Ricky's heart seemed to hiccup and stutter. She struggled to blink.

'Please don't leave me. Please don't, baby.'

She could feel the whumping of her mother's heart and hear the high-pitched sound of pain, a keening. It was louder than the squeal of the approaching ambulance.

'Stay with me. Stay with me. I love you so much. So much.'

Her heart hiccupped again. Her fingers tingled. She blinked.

'Thank god. Thank god. Thank god.'

Her mother remained at Ricky's side as the paramedics worked on her. She kept her hand on her, refusing to break the connection, as Ricky vomited before being lifted onto a stretcher. They were wheeling her toward the bright mouth of the ambulance when her father arrived. He was out of breath, shouting for them to wait. He leaned over to kiss her and a tear fell and hit her cheek. It was cool and heavy, and despite the noise and confusion, Ricky found herself wondering why the tears of her father were heavier than those of her mother. His tears weighed on her. They demanded something of her.

She closed her eyes against the brightness of the ambulance. Her mother's hand was a soft presence over her heart. She could still hear the swirl of her feelings but they were becoming fainter, blending with the serious, controlled thoughts emanating from the paramedic.

Then there were doors and noise and her father again, looking red-faced and worried as he followed them down a corridor to a room with metal and lights.

Shouts, whispers, clinking, tapping.

*

As Ricky rose to consciousness, she saw white flecks like snow on the periphery of her vision. Her body felt empty yet heavy, like the hollowed-out iron chassis of a car.

'About time you woke up.'

Her father was sitting beside her with his back to the window. Ricky couldn't turn her head but she could tell by the blue curtain that she was in hospital.

She tried to smile but wasn't sure if her face obeyed. It felt stiff and new, unfamiliar.

'Where's Mum?'

Her father leaned closer, confused by what had come out of her mouth.

She tried again, slower this time. 'I want Mum.'

His smile faded.

Ricky saw hurt in his eyes but she didn't have the strength to spare his feelings. She wanted the comfort of her mother.

'She's talking to the doctor. She'll be pleased you've woken up.' He nodded, eager. 'I've been sitting here all night with her.'

Ricky could see he wanted something, recognition or connection, but she could give him neither. It was too complicated and she was too empty and weak.

'Here she is now.'

He stood up and moved away as her mother draped herself over the bed, kissing Ricky's cheeks and forehead. She pressed her lips to her daughter's hairline, breathing her in.

'I am so happy you're alive,' she whispered. 'So happy.'

Ricky had to close her eyes for a moment to stop herself crying.

'How are you feeling?'

She felt strange. 'When can I go home?'

'Not yet.' Her mother explained that the doctors had got to her before the drugs could do any lasting damage but they wanted to keep her for a day or two.

'What happened to Jack?'

Her mother glanced at her father, who was hovering at the foot of the bed. 'What do you mean?'

'He was with me. In the igloo.'

'Honey, you were by yourself.'

Samia must have been watching out for her because Ricky had been home for less than an hour when the girl turned up. She lingered shyly in the doorway, taking in the books on the pine bookshelf and her desk with its cup of pens and electric pencil sharpener.

'Thank you for getting my backpack,' Ricky said.

Samia had crawled inside the igloo to retrieve her things but it was Abbie who had told Tim where she was. It was strange to think that Abbie had saved her life. A day earlier, the same girl might have punched her in the face if Caitlin had demanded it.

'You're welcome,' said Samia, edging her way into the room.

Ricky pointed to the chair next to her desk. 'Take a pew.'

Samia's big eyes were burning with curiosity.

'What do you want to know?'

She jumped, nervous at being caught out. 'People are saying you tried to kill yourself.'

Ricky shrugged.

'Why did you do that?'

How could she explain? It wasn't a sudden decision. It was more like the natural end to a process, a wearing away of everything that had defined her until there was so little left, she could no longer resist or even care. She had stopped mattering.

'Sorry.' Samia's face coloured. 'You don't have to answer that.'

'I'll try.' Ricky closed her eyes. 'I wasn't feeling solid anymore. It was as if I was being rubbed out and my body was being replaced by air. You can't see air so I was feeling invisible and weightless. It didn't seem to matter if I drifted away. I didn't think people would notice or care.'

'I would care.'

Ricky opened her eyes. 'I didn't know that.'

'I should have told you.'

She wanted to make Samia feel better but she didn't know what to say.

'I should have been nicer to you.'

'That's what Abbie said to me, too.'

'Abbie's gone away somewhere. Her grandmother says she'll be back in time for school.'

Ricky nodded.

'The police came to our place yesterday. They talked to Mum.'

'What did they want?'

'They asked about you. They wanted to know if Mum had noticed anything, any trouble.'

'What did she tell them?'

'I'm not supposed to say.'

'I'd tell you.'

Samia looked at her feet.

'Please.'

'You have to promise not to say I told you.'

'Cross my heart and hope to—'

'Don't!' Samia held up her hand. 'I'll tell you.'

Mrs Mitra told the police she'd been concerned about Ricky for some time. She'd often observed the girl wandering around the estate on her own. It was not safe. There were gangs of boys, drugs and alcohol. Ricky appeared to have been left in the care of a strange man. Mrs Mitra had seen him drinking around the girl and didn't like it. On the night of the fire, she'd witnessed something that had made her worry. An hour or so after the hypnosis incident, she'd come to the flat to return the cape. The man appeared drunk when he answered the door, but it wasn't this that alarmed Mrs Mitra. It was Ricky, who came stumbling out of the living room in a state of confusion. She was wearing nothing but a filthy tank top and underpants, and seemed disoriented. When she'd asked the man what was going on, he'd said the girl had a fever. Ricky had caught a bug and been vomiting. He assured her the girl would be fine but Mrs Mitra did not like what she'd seen. Not one bit.

'I don't remember any of this.' Ricky recalled finding the cape on the end of her bed but had no recollection of Mrs Mitra's visit.

'I shouldn't have told you.'

'Did they ask you anything?'

Samia nodded. 'They wanted to know about the workshop and the funfair. I told them what happened to us inside Cloney's garage. I'm sorry. I had to.'

Ricky smiled to reassure Samia. 'Have they found Pauly?'

'He was at his cousin's place in Finsbury Park. He's in lots of trouble.'

No one had seen Caitlin or her mother for days but all the flyers had been taken down.

'Pauly wrecked Mr Snow's flat.'

Ricky nodded.

'He even made a mess on the floor.'

'What kind of mess?'

'A stinky one.' Samia wrinkled her nose.

Ricky recalled the mess she'd found in the haunted flat. Of course, that had been Pauly, too. She raised her eyebrows. 'The Cloneys are full of shit.'

Samia's eyes widened. She burst out laughing.

Ricky started laughing, too.

Her mother's head appeared in the doorway.

'I'm not going to ask why you're laughing,' she said. 'I'm just going to enjoy it.'

Ricky was tingling after Samia left. It was how she always felt after laughing with Ollie. Not that she could bear to think about her brother. It was too much. The feelings were too big and powerful. She had to push him to the outer edge of her thoughts until he was like an outline in a colouring book. One day she would fill him in but not yet.

Her mother reappeared. 'Are you ready for another visitor?'

'Hello there!'

The dark-haired woman looked familiar but it wasn't until she sat down that Ricky realised who she was. She looked completely different without her heavy makeup and headscarf. She was wearing a pale blue fleece and navy stretch pants. She looked normal, like someone's grandmother.

'I've come to thank you for finding my ring,' said Tina. She held out her hand. The scarab ring was on her wedding finger. 'If it wasn't for you, I would never have seen it again.'

'How did you find me?' Ricky asked.

'It was the other way around. The police found me. There was only one gypsy wagon registered at the fair.' She smiled at Ricky's mother before turning back to her. 'So, you've been in the wars, love.'

'You already know that from reading my palm.'

'I'm not that good.' Tina chuckled. 'Your mum filled me in.'

'But you were right about everything you told me.'

'Well, that's good then.' Tina patted her hand.

'You told me I was a warrior like Joan of Arc.'

'Did I? I don't remember that.'

'Yes, and you warned me that someone would try to hurt me.'

Tina frowned.

'And you said I would find a special friend with the same birthday.'

Tina exchanged looks with Ricky's mother. 'I didn't say those things to you.'

'You did. I remember.'

'I would never tell a child that someone was going to hurt her.'

Ricky felt hot and confused. 'But I remember.'

'I probably told you what I tell a lot of young girls, that you will fall in love one day with a handsome young man. You will marry and have two beautiful children.' She squeezed Ricky's hand. 'I do remember warning you not to wander around the funfair on your own. It's no place for a young girl.'

'But I remember the other things.'

'I think you've had a very confusing time.' Gently, Tina turned Ricky's hand over. 'Let's have another look.'

How could she have got it all wrong? She remembered Tina's words.

'I see some good news in your palm.' Tina smiled. 'Do you want to hear it?'

Ricky nodded.

'Everything is going to be all right. I can see only happiness in this hand.'

# 30

THEY OWED MRS Mitra, said her mother. The small, fierce woman had been a constant and watchful presence throughout the summer. She alone had been paying attention while everyone else was looking the other way.

Mrs Mitra didn't go to Ollie's funeral but Samia was there. So was Naomi. It was supposed to be a small gathering, a family funeral for a small boy. Ollie had been too young to have friends and few people in Camden had met him before he became ill. But word had got out and half the estate turned up at the crematorium. There weren't enough seats for them all in the small chapel. People had to stand along the walls and at the back by the door.

Ricky recognised many faces from the neighbourhood, people from the flats and local shops. Katie was seated a couple of rows back and gave her a friendly smile. Tina waved. Ricky tried to catch Snowy's attention but, although she knew he'd seen her, he didn't look her way. His eyes were on the small white coffin that had been placed on the dais. They remained fixed on it throughout the service. Mr Snow cried more than anyone else, even more than her mother.

The only time he looked away from the coffin was when his name was mentioned during the eulogy.

'This has been a very difficult time for my family,' her mother began. 'To lose a child is a terrible thing. It takes you to a very painful place. You feel angry and confused. Surely, this can't be right, you think. You want fairness or justice but there isn't any because a child's death does not make sense. Ollie's illness reduced us all. It made us feel small and hopeless and ineffective. There was nothing any of us could do. Nothing. It was a mountain of pain.'

Ricky glanced at her father, who was sitting along from her in the front row. He was shaking his head, sobbing quietly. Sophie had her hand on his back. She was whispering something to him. Ricky remembered the thought she'd had about the weight of his tears. It was guilt that made them feel heavy, she realised. Her father was funny and charming but his capacity to care for others, to truly love and give of himself was limited. He would always put himself first. This flaw in his nature was what made Ricky feel guilty. It made her want to make up for his shortcomings. She wanted others to like him for what he could be rather than for what he was.

Her mother paused to wipe her eyes.

'Ollie was a golden child. He was a marvellous little human being, old and very wise for his years. Anyone who had anything to do with my small son soon fell in love with him. We all loved him dearly. To watch the illness crush him so quickly and so spectacularly was unbearable. They say that death brings peace but I know I'll never find peace about losing such a beautiful boy.'

She stopped, her face creased as she tried to stop crying.

'To lose one child is hell but to almost lose another is beyond unbearable. Many of you know that we nearly lost our darling Ricky. And it is thanks to some of you that we still have her with us. Thank you.'

Ricky could feel people looking. She counted to ten and kept her eyes on her brother's coffin. Her shirt felt stiff and prickly against her skin. It was a new white shirt, a proper boy's shirt with a collar. Her mother had bought it, along with a pair of boy's black trousers and a tie from Marks & Spencer. She'd also got Ricky a compression vest from a special shop. At first glance, it looked like an ordinary tank top but it was much thicker and had a zip up the front. Her mother had done all this without argument and then taken Ricky to a hairdresser to tidy up her short hair. These days, no one was trying to force her to be or do anything. They were all making an effort to be kind to her and to each other, even her father who was on the phone at least once a day.

Her mother wiped her eyes and dabbed her nose before continuing. 'I would like to finish with a few words about someone many of you know. His name is Mr Snow.'

A ripple of energy passed through the chapel. People moved in their seats.

'I am going to ask you all to be kind to this man. He is innocent of the crimes for which he was accused. He did not deserve the cruel treatment he received. He deserves only respect and kindness.'

Tim was helping Mrs Mitra in the kitchen when they got back from the funeral. There were plates of sandwiches on the table and pots of food on the hob. The place smelled like curry and fragrant rice. Mrs Mitra took hold of Ricky's elbow as she came through the door and led her over to the hob where she filled a bowl with steaming hot food. She wouldn't let Ricky go until she'd eaten half the bowl.

The spicy food made Ricky's eyes water but she did as she was told because she wanted to please Mrs Mitra. If it wasn't for her vigilance and persistence, no one would have discovered what had really been going on. Ricky's memory was shadowy, a blur of images and feelings without structure or logic. She'd thought they were dreams until Naomi explained that it was her subconscious trying to deal with what was happening.

'The mind sometimes does that when it experiences trauma but the drugs you were being given would have also caused confusion and memory loss,' she said. 'You were the victim of a cunning predator. He's a ruthless man who took advantage of your family crisis to isolate you from your parents, the very people who could have protected you. He might have got away with it if not for your neighbour.'

Mrs Mitra's statement had prompted the police to investigate but it was Ricky's notebooks that gave them what they needed for an arrest. The police had turned the place upside down while she was in hospital and found her notebooks hidden under Ollie's mattress. Her diary was a record of what she'd been doing and how she felt but when referenced against her dreams, the police were able to chronicle the drugging and abuse that had taken place. This led them to Ricky's vitamins in the kitchen. The bottle was empty but a residue showed traces of two powerful tranquilising agents, GHB and Rohypnol.

'Your parents were grieving and distracted,' said Naomi. 'That's very different from being uncaring. You are not responsible for the things that happened even though Dan did his utmost to make you feel that way.'

Ricky understood that Naomi was trying to help her but she couldn't believe she was not responsible for at least some of the damage she'd caused. When she thought about Ollie, the pain felt like a brick wedged behind her sternum.

Her brother still visited her in her dreams but he was becoming less substantial with each visit. He was always just out of reach, always in a hurry to leave. Ollie was becoming paler and translucent with each passing day. The last time he'd visited her dreams, they had been at Brockwell Park. It was early summer again and they were sitting under the old oak, eating sandwiches their mother had made with fresh cucumber from the allotment. The family was reunited. Ricky was lying with her head resting on her father's leg while he told one of his stories. Ollie was flopped against her mother. The smell of freshly mown grass was making her feel joyous and free. Her body felt weightless and bright. Everyone was beautiful. Gold and light. But when she glanced at Ollie, she realised he was fading. The golden light was shining through him as if he was made of chiffon. Her parents seemed oblivious to his imminent departure. It was as if they were asleep.

'Please don't go, Ollie,' she pleaded.

'Everything is going to be all right,' he replied. He smiled and became paler, fading into translucence.

Ricky tried to move from where she was lying but the pull of gravity had become too powerful. She was stuck. Her body was heavy and immobile.

Ollie was dissolving rapidly, now a blurry, golden outline.

She tried to say 'Don't go' again but her voice wouldn't work.

He was glitter, points of light suspended in the air.

The leaden feeling of the dream had persisted after she woke up. As she dressed, there was resistance in her joints and muscles. Everything felt heavy and difficult. It took effort to clean her teeth and wash her face. She had to drag herself to the kitchen. Every thought and movement required too much effort. It felt as if she was wearing a cloak of chainmail over her shoulders, compressing her upper spine, making her small.

She described the feeling to Naomi.

'How heavy is it?' she asked.

'Heavy enough to make me feel slow and weak,' she replied.

'Like a car?'

No, lighter than a car.

'A person?'

Again she shook her head.

'Is it the weight of a child, perhaps?' Naomi nodded meaningfully.

Ricky imagined Ollie draped across her shoulders like a cloak, heavy yet strangely comforting.

'I don't want to let him go.'

'You don't have to forget him. You just don't have to carry him. Ollie should not be a burden. You've done nothing wrong, Ricky. His death had nothing to do with you. Neither did his death have anything to do with all that went on here in the flat. None of what happened was any of your doing. You're a child. You cannot be responsible for the actions of adults. It was not your fault. None of it was.'

Ricky had heard different versions of the same speech from her mother and father. She understood they meant well but she didn't know how to remove the heavy cloak from her shoulders without feeling that she was betraying Ollie.

It wasn't until Katie visited that a shift occurred. Katie arrived unannounced with a bunch of flowers for her mother and a brand-new notebook for Ricky. It was a Moleskin, the

Rolls-Royce of notebooks, and it was red because, as Katie said, red was the colour of love.

Apart from Ollie, no one had ever understood her as well as Katie did. From the very first moment, Ricky had felt a connection. It was a feeling of being understood and appreciated without judgement. Katie called this a 'psychic high five' and said it was rare and precious. In the weeks that Ricky had worked with her, Katie had never tried to change her or shut her down. Instead she'd seen a potential for storytelling in her and had worked to bring it out. Katie had sensed something wasn't right and had kept encouraging Ricky to write down her dreams to help her work it out.

'The unconscious mind never lies,' she said. 'It will mix things up, take all the bits and pieces of your life and put them through a blender, but it never lies.'

It was Katie who helped Ricky understand about Jack. He was a projection, she explained, something that her brain created to cope with trauma, alienation and loneliness. As an exercise, she made Ricky write down all the times she'd met him and what he'd done each time they met. Katie had then created a timeline and marked his appearances and behaviour against what was going on in Ricky's life. As Katie predicted, Jack appeared during times of crises, when things were going badly for Ricky.

'You needed a friend so badly that your beautiful mind created one,' said Katie. 'His mother was ill. Your brother was ill. He was being hurt. You were being hurt. He had no one he could trust. You believed you had no one you could trust.'

'Does that mean I'm crazy?' Ricky asked.

'It means you have a special brain. You've got such a powerful imagination that, when you're under stress, it creates things that are so clever and detailed, they appear real. It's just trying to make sense of all the stimuli.'

'But I know I talked to Ollie. I know that's real.'

Katie shrugged. 'Perhaps it was.'

'What if my brain starts inventing things again? How will I know what's real?'

'Your mum will make sure nothing horrible ever happens again. I will be here whenever you need me and Naomi is going to help you and your mother get your lives back on track. Your mum loves you and only wants the best for you.'

It was true about her mother. Since all the trouble she'd almost become too nice and had even asked if Ricky wanted to move back to Brixton. The offer had been tempting. It would have meant being closer to her father and ultimately her new sister. She would have her old friends and the allotment.

But when Ricky thought of Brixton, she thought of Ollie. Going back without him would have been too sad.

Her brother was the reason she didn't want to return to Brixton but Samia was her biggest reason for wanting to stay in Camden. Ricky didn't know if it was the hypnosis that had opened the girl's eyes but Samia was now officially her best friend.

School was soon going to start, a new big school for both of them. Their mothers had already taken them shopping for their uniforms. Samia had got a skirt, a long green one that ended below her knees. Ricky had chosen pants, boys' trousers with a button pocket at the back for her new mobile phone. The pants were the same green as Samia's skirt and had deep front pockets, perfect for a notebook.

# Acknowledgements

I would like to thank the following friends for reading this book and cheering me on: Susan Allan, Terry Baxter, Ros Bayley, Frank Chalmers, Linda Innes, Jonathan Sale and Trace Taylor.

Kind thanks to my brilliant agent, Jane Novak of Jane Novak Literary Agency.

Kind thanks to my wonderful publisher, Fiona Henderson, and her remarkably supportive team at Simon & Schuster Australia. Special thanks to Anthea Bariamis and Deonie Fiford.

# About the author

DIANE CONNELL was born in New Zealand and has lived and worked in Japan, France and the UK. She began her writing career in a newspaper office in Tokyo before becoming an advertising copywriter and writing for the international non-profit sector. For many years, she lived in Paris where she began writing as a novelist. She later moved to London, where her first two books, *Julian Corkle is a Filthy Liar* and *Sherry Cracker Gets Normal*, were published under the name of D.J. Connell. She now lives in Sydney.

# Reading Group Guide

1. Ricky's storytelling is central to the novel. Is Ricky a storyteller or a liar? Why?

2. The garden holds a special place in Ricky's and Ollie's life. What is its significance?

3. On page 24, Ricky describes the feeling of blending with nature: 'She only had to still her mind and focus to connect with the wordless purpose of nature. It was like slipping, sinking and blending.' Why is this, and why does she feel she is losing this ability?

4. Why does Ricky keep spending time with Caitlin when it's clear she is not a friend?

5. There are several opportunities for Ricky to open up to her parents. What is stopping her?

6. Ricky has a lot of love and sympathy for her father, but Ollie sees him quite differently. Why is this? What do you think of their father's role in their lives?

7. Why does Ricky feel guilty and ashamed about many things that happen over the summer?

8. Ricky has several conversations with Ollie while he is ill, but she later learns he was sedated the entire time. Why do you think she imagined these conversations?

9. In some of Ricky's toughest times she finds support from Katie, her workshop facilitator. Have you had a similar experience with a person, perhaps a teacher or colleague, outside your family and friends?

10. The Camden estate is central to the novel and Ricky's story. Do you think Ricky's experiences would have been different had her family remained in their old home? How?